A Brewed Awakening

A Novel

PEPPER BASHAM

THOMAS NELSON
Since 1798

A Brewed Awakening

Published in Nashville, Tennessee, by Thomas Nelson. Thomas Nelson is a registered trademark of HarperCollins Christian Publishing, Inc.

Thomas Nelson titles may be purchased in bulk for educational, business, fundraising, or sales promotional use. For information, please e-mail SpecialMarkets@ThomasNelson.com.

ISBN 978-1-4003-5139-8 (epub)
ISBN 978-1-4003-5138-1 (TP)
ISBN 978-1-4003-5140-4 (audio download)

Library of Congress Cataloging-in-Publication Data

Printed in the United States of America

26 27 28 29 30 LBC 5 4 3 2 1

Praise for Pepper Basham

A BREWED AWAKENING

"Steeped in resilient hope, *A Brewed Awakening* blends small town charm, cleft lip and palate representation, and a rivals-to-more romance into a sweet novel readers will savor from cover to cover. Fans of *The Great British Baking Show* and southern fiction will adore Pepper Basham's literary love letter to North Carolina with its great food, good people, and galvanizing spirit of community. If you fancy a bookish flavor combination of flirtation and found family, *A Brewed Awakening* is sure to be your cup of tea!"

—Angela Bell, author of *A Lady's Guide to Marvels and Misadventure*

"*A Brewed Awakening* is #anadorablesweetromance full of heart and humor. If you love Southern charm with a dash of British magic don't miss this one!"

—Jennifer Peel, *USA TODAY* bestselling author

"Pepper Basham turns up the heat in the kitchen and on the page in her newest book, *A Brewed Awakening*, a sweet, wholesome romance that's an absolute treat for the heart. This story had me cheering for the sassy Southern, tea-loving heroine as she faces off with a savory Brit who's equal parts tease and charm—pushing all the right buttons in this enemies-to-lovers romance that had me swooning. And yes, I fell for him too, luv. These two whip up a wonderfully balanced story filled with humor, banter, and a cast of characters I didn't want to leave behind. Pepper infuses joy, heart, and faith into this romcom, creating a story I absolutely devoured—and one that left me eagerly awaiting whatever she serves up next."

—Natalie Walters, author of *Spies, Lies, and Alibis*

"Pepper Basham has become THE voice in romantic comedy with heart and sass. In *A Brewed Awakening*, readers will find the perfect blend of British wit, Southern charm, and enemies-to-lovers banter. They'll also find a community that comes together when everything falls apart and a love story that you wish was your own. It is a pitch-perfect page turner of romantic sweetness filled with zany joy."

—Cara Putman, award-winning author of *The Accused* and *Flight Risk*

SENSE AND SUITABILITY

"*Sense and Suitability* is a sweet, second-chance Regency romance with an Austenesque flair. Pepper Basham brings a modern voice to classic themes, offering keen insights into family and community, while never losing her signature humor. An absolutely lovely read!"

—Mimi Matthews, *USA TODAY* bestselling author

"An utter delight! Pepper Basham's debut into the Regency genre sparkles with deft wordplay and a joyous wit. Simon and Emmeline's story charms on every page, while endearing side characters try their best to steal the show. With clever nods to Jane Austen's classic, *Sense and Suitability* is everything romance readers adore: sweet, swoony, and perfectly bingeable."

—Joanna Barker, author of *A Heart Worth Stealing*

"Wow. *Sense and Suitability* is one of the *best* Regency romances that I've read in YEARS. With her signature humor, Pepper Basham has penned an engaging, dreamy tale with a cast of delightful characters and witty dialogue that absolutely sings! I found myself thinking about the hero and heroine while away from the novel, eager to find out how it all ended. This is a must-read for Jane Austen fans!"

—Grace Hitchcock, award-winning author of *To Catch a Coronet*, *My Dear Miss Dupré*, *The White City*, and *The Finding of Miss Fairfield*

SOME LIKE IT SCOT

"In *Some Like It Scot*, a travel writer explores her ancestral roots on a Scotland isle through the misadventures of an Edwardian experience. There, she finds a grumpy Scotsman, a charming bookshop, and the courage to write her own life story. Don't miss this lighthearted romp to Scotland, featuring a swoonworthy tale that's rich in legends and folklore!"

—Denise Hunter, bestselling author of *The Summer of You and Me*

"An utterly delightful read! Basham weaves the perfect blend of charm, humor, and heartfelt moments as a spirited woman and a hot Scot navigate life, love, and the power of faith. Their journey is inspiring and entertaining, offering readers a story filled with laughter and hope. A must-read for anyone who loves characters that leap off the page and into your heart!"

—Kasey Stockton, author of *I'm Not Charlotte Luca*

LOYALLY, LUKE

"Readers, you are in for a pure delight! Luke Edgewood is, in a word, dreamy. At once tough and tender, guarded and vulnerable, he is a book boyfriend to rival all book boyfriends. And despite being a princess, readers will absolutely relate to Ellie's struggle to overcome her past, prove herself to her family, and make the noble choice—even if it means breaking her own heart in the process. Luke and Ellie's love story has the perfect amount of tension, chemistry, and tugging-at-your-heartstrings moments. Simply unputdownable! Even if this is your first trip to Skymar, you'll feel right at home in this funny, cozy, absolute gem of a royal romance! To quote Luke Edgewood, 'I reckon the best kind of love is simple in one way . . . Choosing each other over and over and over again.' When it comes to this book (and the series), these will be stories readers choose to read over and over and over again."

—Emma St. Clair, *USA TODAY* bestselling author

"With a hero who's better at texting and a princess who can wield a hammer, *Loyally, Luke* is 'peppered' with Ms. Basham's signature style of swoony romance and charming characters. She's also added a message we all need to hear and believe for ourselves as two unlikely people wonder if worlds can really merge and not merely collide. This will definitely be another fan favorite."

—Toni Shiloh, Christy Award–winning author

"Fans of Pepper Basham's Skymar series will be thrilled and delighted with this much-anticipated third and final installment to the series. In pure Basham fashion, every page oozes with the magic of romance and characters you won't easily forget. *Loyally, Luke* is an escape many readers look for."

—Sarah Monzon, bestselling author of *All's Fair in Love and Christmas*

"Pepper Basham has done it again! The author's sly wit and enduring tenderness make Luke and Ellie's story a (literal) love letter to the power of authenticity, hope, and redemption. *Loyally, Luke* is sure to hook new readers and delight those who already adore the one-of-a-kind Edgewood family. Prepare to fall head over heels for flannel and fishing!"

—Julie Christianson, author of the Apple Valley Love Stories series

POSITIVELY, PENELOPE

"Basham is a rising star. *Positively, Penelope* is humorous and touching, and everything you want in the perfect summer read. Don't miss this one."

—Rachel Hauck, *New York Times* bestselling author of *The Wedding Dress*

"What do you get when you combine a lovable heroine with characters who have mastered the art of witty banter? A charming read. And that is what *Positively, Penelope* is."

—Sheila Roberts, *USA TODAY* bestselling author

"This book is a positive delight from the first line to the last. I adored Penelope in Izzy's book, and she screamed for her own book, so I couldn't wait to dive into the pages of this novel. Oh my goodness, it was a true, laugh-out-loud joy to read this book. The story was filled with twists and hiccups, but there was also such delight and fun. And fairy tales. And princesses. And Julie Andrews. And Gene Kelly. All the things I adore. In one place. And the kissing. Pepper does enjoy writing kissing books. I highly recommend this sweet, fun, romantic romp of a book. It was wonderful!"

—Cara Putman, award-winning author of more than 35 novels, including *Flight Risk*

"Like the character Penelope herself, this entire book radiates sunshine and magic. The banter between Penelope and her siblings kept me smiling. The theatrical references kept me humming and tapping my toes. And the overall joy that Pepper Basham exudes with her unique writing style and voice kept me engaged in a story I never wanted to leave. Simply put, this book is supercalifragilisticexpialidocious."

—Becca Kinzer, author of *Dear Henry, Love Edith*

"You won't want to put this book down! Pepper has a way of creating characters who are disarming and charismatic in all the best ways, while still reflecting our inner selves. Her stories are charming and witty, and I've never laughed so much while reading! You'll walk away with more joy than you came with and a heart full of assurance and encouragement about the power of our heavenly Father's heart for your love story."

—Victoria Lynn, author of *The Chronicles of Elira*, *Bound*, and *London in the Dark*

AUTHENTICALLY, IZZY

"A long-distance romance anchors this cute contemporary from Basham (*The Heart of the Mountains*) . . . Basham primarily tells her story through emails, texts, and dating app messages, a quirky approach that complements the adorable leads. Filled with humor and grace, this is perfect for fans of Denise Hunter."

—*Publishers Weekly*

"*Authentically, Izzy* is an absolutely adorable, charming, sweet romance that genuinely made me laugh out loud. A wonderful escape you're sure to fall in love with!"

—Courtney Walsh, *New York Times* bestselling author

"*Authentically, Izzy* is witty, endearing, and full of literary charm. Grab your favorite blanket and get ready to snuggle into this sweet book that will make you believe your dreams will find you."

—Jennifer Peel, *USA TODAY* bestselling author

"I can't remember the last time I've read such a truly wonderful romance. Basham's *Authentically, Izzy* was smart, funny, and adorably bookish. I smiled all the way through and finished it with my cheeks hurting. All the *Lord of the Rings* references were the cherry on top for me. Izzy and Brodie have officially overtaken Jane Eyre and Mr. Rochester as my favorite literary couple. You have to read this book!"

—Colleen Coble, *USA TODAY* bestselling author

"Pepper Basham is at her witty and charming best throughout the pages of this bookish delight! Fans of Katherine Reay will feel right at home between the covers of this epistolary treasure. Featuring a perfectly sprinkled smattering of Tolkien, *Authentically, Izzy* proves that the best reality sometimes begins with a little bit of fantasy. I hope you have as much fun with this one as I did!"

—Bethany Turner, bestselling author of *The Do-Over*

"In *Authentically, Izzy* author Pepper Basham has created a delightful cast of characters who quickly become your friends. Izzy beautifully captures the nerd in all of us who adores books and stories—sometimes more than real life. When a family member decides Izzy needs to live her own story, it sends Izzy on a fun romp that leads to a sweet, sigh-worthy romance. Grab this one today!"

—Jenny B. Jones, bestselling author of *There You'll Find Me* and *Sweet Right Here*

"This book was so much fun! I was drawn into the story from the beginning and loved the emails and text messages between Izzy and her cousins. What was even more fun was seeing how Izzy and Brodie's relationship grew from a few funny messages to a sweet relationship. I loved how Izzy grew throughout the story and learned to love herself and find her own strength and love. And her cousins were a hoot! Luke was my favorite cousin. His emails and text messages kept me in stitches. I highly recommend this fun and romantic book!"

—Amy Clipston, bestselling author
of *The View from Coral Cove*

"You don't see enough epistolary novels these days, so the format of this being told almost entirely through emails appealed to me straightaway, and I wasn't disappointed! We follow librarian Izzy as she meets perfect-sounding bookshop owner Brodie online and wonders if he's too good to be true. Filled with the wonderfully warm cast of Izzy's family, and the swoon-worthy email exchanges with Brodie, I absolutely loved reading this book and felt like Izzy was a real friend rather than a book character! A book written by a book lover, about a book lover, for book lovers everywhere! I loved it! In fact, the only issue with this book is that my to-read list has grown exponentially from Izzy and Brodie's recommendations! It's a book lover's dream read!"

—Jaimie Admans, author of romantic comedies

A BREWED AWAKENING
A NOVEL

Other Books by Pepper Basham

CONTEMPORARY ROMANCE

Stand-Alone Novels

Authentically, Izzy

Positively, Penelope

Loyally, Luke

Some Like It Scot

Sense and Suitability

Mitchell's Crossroads Series

A Twist of Faith

Charming the Troublemaker

A Match for Emma

A Pleasant Gap Romance Series

Just the Way You Are

When You Look at Me

Novellas

Second Impressions

Jane by the Book

Christmas in Mistletoe Square

HISTORICAL ROMANCE

Stand-Alone Novels

Hope Between the Pages

The Red Ribbon

Blue Ridge Romances

Laurel's Dream

The Heart of the Mountains

Penned in Time Series

The Thorn Bearer

The Thorn Keeper

The Thorn Healer

Freddie and Grace Mysteries

The Mistletoe Countess

The Cairo Curse

The Juliet Code

Novellas

Facade

Between Stairs and Stardust

To the people of the Blue Ridge Mountains who were affected by Hurricane Helene and who continue to work together to help our community heal. You are amazing!

CHAPTER 1

@WisteriaWeekly: Summer beans are in, y'all. Stop by Bea's for your side dish starters and gossip updates. #ShopLocal #SnapBeansAndSnaps

@OldManRutherforton: If your potatoes don't fight back when you mash 'em, they ain't fresh. Get to Bea's. #RutherfortonReviews

@WisteriaGeneralStore: Picked up my beans and potatoes. Forgot milk. Again. See y'all tomorrow. #SecondTripClub

@PastorNateNHC: Saw Bea singing hymns to her beans again. Not saying it's why they taste better, but I'm not saying it's not. #BlessTheBeans #SmallTownJoy

@RosemaryatThyme: Don't forget to pop by Tea Thyme for the benefit! Daphne's promised free samples of a brand-new scone creation.

> **@JackAustenPhotography:** Don't hold your breath @RosemaryatThyme. I've been trying to convince her of some creative baking for months and she's been stubborn.
>
> **@RosemaryatThyme:** Don't worry. I've used the children as emotional leverage. New tastes bring new people.

@JackAustenPhotography: I think brothers should bring emotional leverage too.
@RosemaryatThyme: They usually bring the wrong kind of leverage.

LADIES DID NOT DROOL over cars.

A freshly baked chocolate croissant with vanilla cream? Yes. A semolina and rosemary loaf with fresh creamery butter? Most certainly. But an electric-blue Volkswagen convertible Beetle Cabriolet with—Daphne Austen gasped—a British flag front plate?

How could she help the unbridled fascination?

Especially since her dearly departed grandmother used to own something so quintessentially British. In fact, Daphne could almost hear her granny's voice nudging her to indulge in the visual appreciation for just a smidge longer.

Sure, Daphne was only one-quarter English, but it was a very loud fraction. Practically *opera-singing* loud.

She sighed and glanced back through the doorway of her tea shop, breathing in the comforting aroma of freshly steeped Earl Grey.

Today was no day for dillydallying—also mentally stated in her granny's voice. Daphne had a job to do. Getting carried away with some automotive miracle on Main Street didn't fit into the schedule.

She forced her body back inside the shop, drinking in the pastel and floral loveliness all around. She'd spent the last two hours making certain every cup, saucer, serviette, and centerpiece in her Austen-inspired tea shop displayed a sense of elegance her upcoming guests deserved and adored. Hues of lavender and pink waved over café-style tables displaying girlish refinement. Dark wooden beams framed the rosebud-print wallpaper, and the shelves—lined with her glorious collection of vintage teapots—offered exactly the right amount of old-fashioned whimsy.

Tea Thyme hosted one of its largest events of the year—the late-summer benefit for the Wisteria Children's Home. It had been Daphne's idea and, for three years, had grown into one of the town's most celebrated opportunities.

And this was the first year she'd hosted it without Granny.

The idea nestled deep in Daphne's chest, tightening with the familiar sting of grief. But not only grief. A little bit of pride and . . . gratitude. That she'd made it almost an entire year on her own with this little shop.

Granny's pride and joy.

She sighed.

Speaking of pride and joy?

Daphne's gaze flew back to the Cabriolet.

Whose car could that be? Nobody in the whole of Wisteria loved England like she did! Was it some sort of practical joke set up by her friends—she narrowed her eyes—or her brother?

Main Street offered no answers. A few people strolled along the sidewalks lined with a quirky collection of rectangular buildings, but nothing seemed out of place.

Except the car. It beckoned to her like antiques in Bryson's Treasures down the street.

Her breaths pulsed in conflict with her plans. In half an hour fifty people (or more) would descend upon Tea Thyme and spiral business from the red to the black for this month. A necessary boost for her fledgling little anomaly-of-a-shop among the small businesses in Wisteria, North Carolina.

She really didn't have time for distractions, but her gaze shifted back to the car. Despite her best efforts at biting her smile into submission, it slipped wide beneath her teeth.

But she *did* have thirty minutes.

"Hey, Daph, do you want me to set the scones out on the counter or the serving tab—"

Daphne turned to find her friend and employee, Rosemary Knight, paused in the kitchen doorway, wearing a somewhat confused expression as Daphne was poised with one foot out the front door and one in. Very ladylike.

"Oh no you don't!" Rosemary raised a finger from beneath the tray of scones, one dark brown eyebrow lifting to add extra warning. "There's no way you're leaving me to work this fundraiser alone."

"I . . . I wasn't planning to *leave*!" Daphne pushed up a bright smile, scrambling for an excuse that didn't sound completely ridiculous. "I was just admiring . . . the weather. It looks like a beautiful day for the event, don't you think?"

Rosemary's golden, marble-hued eyes narrowed to slits. Without breaking eye contact, she set the scones on the nearest table and crossed the room, her brows knitting tighter with every step. "What's going on?"

Daphne's shoulders collapsed and she looked back out the door. "Do you see that?"

Rosemary followed Daphne's gaze, scanning the quaint and quiet Main Street, before turning back to Daphne. "The fine day?"

"No, the Cabriolet."

Rosemary blinked, ending another visual sweep of Main Street with a slow shake of her head, causing her tight curls to bounce a little. "Is that a new restaurant in town?"

"No!" Daphne took Rosemary by the shoulders and steered her in the direction of the car. How could she not know what a Cabriolet was? "It's . . . that car. A Cabriolet."

Rosemary turned in the direction, finally landing her focus on the coveted prize. And then it was Rosemary's turn to release a sigh the size of Texas. "Oh, *the car*."

"Yes, *the car*," Daphne said, practically bouncing on her toes. Everyone close to her knew of her fascination. Daphne lovingly blamed it on her mother. God rest her soul.

And Granny.

God rest her soul too.

"It's perfect, Rose. Exactly as Granny described. And it looks like the one Mom pointed out when I was a little girl. Same color." Daphne teetered back toward the threshold, gesturing with her index fingers toward the doorway as her shoulders rose in a silent plea. "It would be a shame for me not to get a selfie with it while I can."

With another glance from the car to Daphne, Rosemary's demeanor broke and she released a soft chuckle. "You're ridiculous." Then she shrugged, rolled her eyes with enough exaggeration to ensure Daphne didn't miss it, and turned back toward the kitchen. "But you'd better get that selfie before your car disappears in a cloud of English mist."

As if Daphne needed more encouragement.

But it proved the perfect catalyst against her weakness.

With a slight shift in the direction of her pink stilettos, she stepped away from her shop and into the midmorning sunlight, moving forward in a vintage-English-induced trance. She'd daydreamed about this particular car since she was a thirteen-year-old girl sitting at her mother's sickbed listening to a nostalgic conversation between her mom and Granny about Granny's romantic history.

"Your grandfather bought me one a long time ago. Couldn't bring it to America with me, but oh . . ." She pressed her palm to her chest. *"You'd have loved it, Daphne dear. It was cute and stylish, like you."*

Cute and stylish. Even at thirteen Daphne had taken those words as gospel. Her grandmother, who breathed elegance like the fictional Lady Cora Crawley, Countess of Grantham, had already sealed her fate as a hopeless Anglophile.

Maybe the Cabriolet-craze had been the combination of her granny's sentiment and the memory of her mama along with Daphne's near obsession with England, but a deep and abiding fascination with the tiny car had stuck with Daphne ever since.

Electric blue came as a bonus.

She neared the street, expecting the car to disappear as Rosemary had predicted, but its glossy exterior only glinted in the sunshine like a beacon. Thank goodness her brother wasn't around to witness this moment. He'd ruin it by laughing . . . at her.

But he wasn't a Cabriolet kind of guy, so there was that.

Sidestepping a passing bicycle, she smoothed her palm over the sleek hood, her pink nails the perfect shade to complement the car's hue. A giggle bubbled out as she examined every inch of the adorable automobile. It was real! Perfect, all the way down to the leather interior.

How many times had she fantasized about driving through the English countryside in a little beauty like this? Exploring her grandmother's hometown and meeting family members over tea and scones. Her entire body sighed against the car.

"May I help you?"

Heat vaulted up Daphne's neck into her face, and her eyes went wide at the sound of the deep, masculine voice, right before . . . She pulled her cheek from the car's beautiful window.

She stifled a whimper, drew in a deep breath, and turned right into the stare of . . . another daydream.

Holy moly!

His thick dark hair stood in fashionable disarray, one rogue strand falling across his Romanesque brow. His jawline looked sharp enough to cut glass beneath the dark hue of a five o'clock shadow. But it was his eyes that caught her attention—an alarming shade of gold. No, caramel.

Her breath caught. Or maybe the perfect color of tea with just a splash of milk.

Lord, have mercy! She blinked.

But, why not? If God hand-delivered a Cabriolet out of nowhere, why not a perfectly delicious-looking stranger too?

She inwardly grimaced. Okay, God probably didn't refer to men as delicious, but surely He understood the sentiment of this very single, unabashed romantic.

Besides, He of all people knew her unsavory history with a dastardly dad and a Wickham-like best friend. So it would be just like Him to create some wonderful compensation of cosmic proportions, right?

The man crossed his arms, muscles flexing under the thin fabric of his navy T-shirt. His amused expression grew downright wicked as the seconds ticked by. He was fully aware of the effect he was having on her.

Heat blazed a fresh trail into her face.

Well, she could pull herself together like the twenty-five-year-old woman she was. Daphne snapped her lips into a tight smile. "Um . . . I was only admiring."

One of his brows slanted upward, along with a corner of his burgeoning grin. "Clearly."

"The car," she added, stabbing a finger at the Cabriolet. Although, let's be honest—he was just as distracting as the car. And his voice? Pure mocha . . . with a drizzle of something sinful.

He smiled—no, smirked—and the deep dimple in one of his cheeks should have come with a warning label.

Maybe God had sent her more than she could bear, because now her cheeks were dangerously close to sizzling.

"*My* car," he corrected.

Her throat released a sound that she really hoped wasn't a squeak. "Y-your car?" This was officially the most elaborate prank in small-town history.

And then it hit her—that accent.

English.

"Are you certain that's the only thing you were admiring?" His eyes glimmered, his accent like velvet, and Daphne's brain flatlined.

Clearly, the starstruck look on her face answered his question more than her fumbling tongue ever could.

Oh, whoever set this up was going to pay dearly.

No more free scones for them!

Then again, if this man proposed in the next five minutes and handed her the keys to his car, she'd name her firstborn after the prankster in thanks.

"I . . . I was admiring your car and your . . ." Her traitorous gaze flicked down his body and back up, getting caught in those dangerously interesting eyes again. Warmth scorched her cheeks, but she powered through the kettle-steam embarrassment. "Accent," she blurted.

His smile deepened. So did the dimple.

Unfair. All of it!

"My accent."

It wasn't a question. It was a challenge.

And proved he'd witnessed every inch of her not-so-subtle inspection.

There would come a day when she'd respond like a grown-up around handsome men. *This* was not that day.

"It's very English," she said, her mind offering a slow clap for that brilliant deduction. "Otherwise, I would've given you a proper small-town welcome."

"Slack-jawed and pawing my car is not the usual greeting here, then?" His lips twitched.

Her eyes watered from the swelter in her face. She smoothed her blazer with her palms and stood straighter, determined to salvage a shred of dignity. She was Southern and somewhat intelligent. She could handle this. Just don't stare too deeply into his eyes. "How are you enjoying your visit?" Good. Progress. Sensical question.

"Visit?" He chuckled softly. Of course his laugh was sexy. "I'm moving here."

Her heart stopped for the second time in three minutes. "M-moving?"

He gestured toward the vacant building beside hers, the For Sale sign still crooked in the window. "Actually, I've purchased the entire building. Plan to open a restaurant."

The lump in Daphne's throat lodged a little tighter. Harry Coleman had been in and out of the building for weeks, so she'd just supposed he'd purchased it as an additional business for the Wisteria Manor.

But this guy was certainly not Harry.

Her gaze shot to the windows of her little apartment above Tea Thyme and her brain flatlined yet again, this time for a full five seconds. This had to be a prank. "Purchased it?" Or an out-of-body experience. "As in . . . forever?"

For a former English major, she was having surprising difficulty finding coherent words to respond. This magnificent specimen of English masculinity was going to live *and* work next door to her?

"Well, I'll give it a trial run of six months before I answer that question." His voice dipped lower, almost a purr. "You know, see how the neighbors turn out."

Oh for the love of biscuits. Was he flirting? No, surely not. This kind of man didn't flirt with the likes of her.

Argh. She was a mess. And she tried so hard never to be a mess.

But, in her defense, her recent experience with romance consisted of two-dimensional costume dramas, a romantic movie collection large enough to start up her own Netflix channel, and a well-worn edition of Jane Austen's works, which left her poorly equipped for three-dimensional swooniness with a heart-melting grin to boot. Not to mention whatever leathery citrus scent wafted off the man.

Her knees gave a little quake in homage.

She desperately needed more practice with real-life attraction, because practicing in her head was nothing like this.

Harry had mentioned in passing someone opening up a new restaurant in town, but he'd left out dazzling details like handsome, British, Cabriolet owner, *next-door neighbor*, and—her attention dropped to his left hand—possibly single?

The glint in his golden eyes lit her face with another flicker of responsive fire. He oozed charm from the top of his dark head to the soles of his . . . Well, her somewhat dazed perusal of his glorious person hadn't made it to his feet yet, but his shoes were probably adorable too.

She forced a steady breath. "What kind of restaurant?"

"English cuisine." His gaze held hers again and she looked away for sanity's sake. "Do you fancy fish and chips?"

"Fancy?" Her attention shot back to his face. Did Queen Elizabeth II have excellent posture? "Of course. Is that what you do? Make fish and chips?"

Ah yes. Eloquence, thy name is Daphne.

"Hopefully more than that." He chuckled again, the sound sending a residual tingle trembling through her at Richter-scale proportions.

Seizure by accent . . . or English chuckle. Was that even possible?

"Though I'm not sure how it'll do next to a princess tea shop." He hitched a thumb over his shoulder toward Tea Thyme. "Might be a little too much potpourri in the air for the crowd I'm hoping to draw in."

Every hyperventilating scene from her romantic future came to a screeching halt in her head. She examined her adorable storefront with its pink door and picturesque awning, along with a window display featuring her grandmother's favorite tea set. Her brilliant daydream turned monochrome and her stomach collapsed as if someone had just questioned the romantic validity of *Pride and Prejudice*. "Tea Thyme?"

"Clearly there's a great deal of sentimentality in that one." He shook his head. "I suppose the gray-haired ladies who come for tea will be put off by the crowd I draw. Not exactly your mum's sort of company, if you know what I mean?"

All heat drained from her face and rushed back with enough force to boil water. "That's . . . that's *my princess* tea shop." She jabbed a manicured finger at him. "And I'll have you know it's very popular with people of all ages. Not just gray-haired ladies." She raised her chin, though the mental tally of customers under sixty wasn't encouraging.

His eyes widened. *"Yours?"*

"That's right. It was my grandmother's." Her chin lifted a notch. "She was a wonderful English lady who knew how to offer class and charm to all her guests—regardless of their sentimentality."

She focused her attention on his raised brows. Looking him in the eyes wasn't safe for her brain cell health.

"And perhaps"—she glared with every ounce of defense she could muster, her pink nail a fashionable weapon—"Mister Fish and Chips, you could do with a bit of class and charm yourself." She gestured at the car. "Cabriolet notwithstanding."

Notwithstanding? Good grief! So that's when the English major decided to show up.

His grin gave way to another breath-altering chuckle—a deep, rolling sound that did *very bad things* to her pulse.

"Well," he said, leaning in just a fraction closer, "I guess I'll have to drop by for a cup of tea sometime and see what all the fuss is about . . . neighbor."

Before she could respond—before she could even think—he winked, spun on his heel, and strolled toward the building next door, leaving her rooted in place.

Her pulse pounded in her ears. *Did he just dismiss her?*

Dismiss her? After the way he'd acted?

With another glare toward his retreating—and sauntering—form, she marched back toward her precious tea shop, determined to protect it from the likes of a neighboring Wickham. Clearly, dashing men were not to be trusted.

And she'd better remember that fast.

• • • • • • • • • • •

Finn Dashwood leaned one shoulder against the doorframe of his new building, arms crossed, eyes narrowing on the blonde in the pink suit storming into the tea shop next door. Her slim legs carried her with determined efficiency—right up until she shot him a glare sharp enough to peel paint.

The door slammed behind her.

He winced.

Not the most promising start to his transition from successful English businessman to small-town American restaurant owner. But little Miss Tea Barbie was much too easy to fluster to let the opportunity pass. A slow chuckle rumbled in his chest at the memory of catching her pressed up against his car, fumbling over her words and pink-faced.

And those legs.

Her long, blonde hair practically begged for a man's fingers to tangle in it. A petite frame rounded in all the right places—even if she hid it beneath clothes that looked like they were stolen from an uptight librarian. A very brightly colored uptight librarian.

Not to mention that accent.

His chest gave a slight twinge.

If all the women in this town spoke in that easy drawl, he might have to fight a grin on a daily basis.

Attraction always made life interesting—a welcome flirtation—but he had zero plans to act on it. Not with *anyone*, and certainly not with some pink-clad tea shop owner who used words like "notwithstanding" and probably named all of her teapots after Disney characters. He considered her for a moment and then shook his head. No, that one likely named hers after Jane Austen characters.

From the decor on the outside of her shop, there was no knowing what sort of floral explosion the inside re-created. He'd never seen so much pink in his life—which was quite the statement, considering his six-year-old daughter refused to leave her room without wearing at least three shades of it.

Besides, he'd known Miss Tea Shop's type before—romantic, wide-eyed, convinced the universe sent her signs. The kind who'd hand him a carefully curated playlist of "songs that remind me of us" by date two and expect a proposal by date six. Then, when life got hard or the knight fell off the horse or something better came along . . . he'd be the one to suffer.

Him and his sweet girl.

However—he stifled a groan—he could at least remain polite.

He sighed, already planning his apology. He'd smooth things over later with an easy smile and a box of chocolates. Maybe flowers. Unless she was the grudge-holding type.

He frowned. Judging by the door slam, though . . .

Finn shook his head and stepped into the restaurant, surveying his new kingdom. It was still rather empty, except for what Harry had set up for him over the last few weeks—a few tables and chairs, a kitchen in decent shape, and a wall of dark wood trim that suited his plans well. The ghastly blue paint and floral wallpaper, however, had to go. This was meant to be a pub, not a nursery.

At least part of the paper had already been removed, so it was left to Finn to finish before opening in a week. A feat that never would have happened without some long phone calls and careful intervention by Harry, who could get everything in order while Finn moved himself and Lucy across the ocean.

For a fresh start.

No more partners with sticky fingers and roving eyes. No more covering other people's shifts while Lucy went to bed with a babysitter tucking her in.

"Daddy!"

Lucy's voice pulled him from his thoughts. She sat at one of the empty tables with a rainbow of markers spread around her like treasure, her dark braids bouncing as she waved a piece of paper in the air. He'd left her there, drawing to her heart's content, when he'd gone out to check the car for their overnight bags.

Which he'd forgotten in his conversation with . . . their neighbor.

"Daddy, I made you a special picture!" She greeted him with that toothless, barely crooked grin on full display.

His heart gave the familiar twist it always did at the sound of her voice. Her *s* sounds slurred slightly thanks to her repaired cleft lip and palate, but after two years of speech therapy, they'd improved dramatically, along with several of her other sounds. One more surgery—a quick one this time—would help close the tiny fistula in the roof of her mouth and improve her clarity even more.

His little warrior.

The slight scars, barely noticeable above her lip and tracing to the bottom of her button nose, made her upper lip a little crooked—and all the more adorable.

"Daddy!" She held up the paper proudly. "It's for your new restaurant!"

"Is it?" He swooped her up, settling her on his lap as he examined the colorful artwork. For a six-year-old, it wasn't bad at all. He tilted his head. "Is that you?"

The plaits were his only clue. That and the pink dress. She always insisted on pink. Finn inwardly winced at the memory of Miss Tea Shop.

"Mm-hmm." She tapped the taller stick figure. "Dat's you wif your fish slice turning burgers." Her little finger traced the drawing until it stopped near the door of a building on the page where a tiny creature—perhaps a dog?—waited. "And right der, dat's our puppy!"

His lips twitched, trying not to smile. Clever. Very clever. "I didn't know we had a puppy."

Her wide green eyes—a perfect match to her mother's—sparkled. "Oh, but we will have a puppy, Daddy."

The way she said "Daddy" always warmed his heart and often got him agreeing to things he shouldn't. "Will we?"

"You said so! Since I had to leave all my friends." Her bottom lip quivered, the most dangerous weapon in her six-year-old arsenal.

Finn exhaled. He'd always liked dogs.

"We'll see, lamb. Let's settle into our new apartment first." He kissed her forehead. "Then we'll talk about a puppy."

"Oh yes!" She grabbed his face in her tiny hands and planted a kiss on his nose—her favorite form of affection. "And I will name her Princess."

"Her?" He chuckled, setting her back on the floor. "So you think we need another girl around the house?"

"I should like dat very much, Daddy." Her eyes turned impish—a gleam that should have warned him. "A puppy and a mummy and a sister."

All warmth fled him. A mummy? *Absolutely not.* "Let's start with the puppy."

Adding the drama of another woman into his or his daughter's life? Not on his list.

Especially if all they ended up doing was hurting his little family or leaving them.

Or both.

A blessed knock on the door cut off any further planning, and Finn silently thanked his rescuer. Through the frosted glass of the front door, he made out an unfamiliar silhouette.

Harry Coleman, long-time friend of Finn's late father and current owner of the Wisteria Manor, a historical estate-house-turned-event-center, had warned Finn about the Southern culture when he'd encouraged Finn to start his business in this small North Carolina town.

Unexpected visitors being one.

Busybodies being another.

"Southern towns don't do privacy. They do pies, unsolicited advice, and neighbors who invite themselves in for tea."

And yet, Harry had still recommended Wisteria as the best place for this Englishman to start afresh?

Finn drew a breath and pulled open the door. A man, not much younger than himself, stood on the stoop with his hands in his jeans pockets, a relaxed smile on his face. Blue eyes, wavy hair, and the kind of easy confidence that made Finn instantly suspicious.

"You Finn Dashwood?" The man's voice had that Southern lilt—friendly.

"Yes?" Finn narrowed his eyes, waiting for the sales pitch. He half expected the man to whip out a catalog for scented candles or a time-share for some coastal paradise.

"Jack Austen." The man offered his hand. "Harry sent me down from the manor to make sure you hadn't gotten lost."

Jack Austen?

Where would Finn have heard that name?

Ah, the photographer?

"A helping hand," hadn't Harry said? Finn relaxed.

"Or been kidnapped by the local ladies' club."

Finn tensed all over again.

Mr. Austen shot him a grin and tipped his head back toward the way he'd come. "Because once they know you've arrived, well, I can't vouch for your safety or sanity."

Finn allowed the good-natured teasing to uncoil the anxiety he'd acquired during the flight and drive to a town he'd only seen online. He'd put a great deal of faith in Harry Coleman's words. But how could he turn down the opportunity? Harry had already gotten the restaurant nearly ready for opening, spread the word, and used his position at the manor to garner local interest. It was the easiest step into ownership he'd ever had.

And after the disaster of his last business, a welcome redirection. He'd make do with some local tittle-tattle.

"Sanity's overrated from what I hear," Finn shot back, and gestured for Jack to step inside. "Welcome."

Jack strolled in, giving the space a slow once-over. "I've always thought this place deserved a more robust life than it had as a sandwich shop."

"One of the most well-stocked sandwich shops I've ever seen from the high-quality appliances in the back." And a primary selling feature for Finn to save money up front.

"Well, Mr. Morgan—or should I say Mrs. Morgan"—Jack waggled his brows—"had a great deal more interest in what things looked like, not necessarily whether they were needed or not."

"The better for me then." Finn walked deeper into the restaurant, the front windows lined with tables, with booths in the back and along the parallel wall. Tidy. Perfect for a small, consistent career.

"So does this place look like an English pub?"

Finn shot his gaze back to Jack Austen. Had the man never traveled to England? He shrugged. Finn supposed since the US was such a massive landmass, natives likely didn't need to put in the coin to travel across the pond to feel as if they were visiting new places.

"If I can remove the rest of that bright pink rosebud wallpaper." He gestured with his head toward the space that would become the bar, one of the few parts of the shop still needing some renovation.

Jack shrugged a shoulder and sent Finn a knowing look. "*Mrs.* Morgan."

Ah. Well, there was no telling what the apartment upstairs would look like then.

Finn studied Mr. Austen again. "I think Harry mentioned that you're a photographer?"

"I try." Jack shrugged. "I cover most of the weddings up at the manor but pick up a few other jobs here and there. Having grown up in this town, I'm always running into someone who needs help with something."

"So you're a *Jack*-of-all-trades, then?" Finn arched a brow.

Jack released a heavy sigh.

"Ah," Finn said, doing nothing to hide his grin. "You've heard that one before."

Jack's mock glare came in answer. *Right.* He could get along with this chap.

"Are you looking for something more consistent?" Finn asked, already weighing the idea. If Harry trusted him, that was enough. And it wouldn't hurt to have a local on hand while he got his bearings.

Jack tilted his head. "Depends on what you're offering."

"Flexible schedule, steady hours, and the occasional interruption from a six-year-old art critic," Finn said. "Ever worked in a restaurant?"

"As a jack-of-all-trades"—Jack's eyes lit—"how can you doubt it? I've worked in several restaurants and held a few management positions." Jack's response came with an easy drawl. "But I'd need something with enough flexibility to work with my photography."

Before Finn could respond, there was a soft shuffle behind him. He turned to find Lucy peeking around the corner, her wide eyes locked on the stranger. She took a few steps closer, plaits bouncing as she moved to hug Finn's leg.

"Well, here's my little artist now." Finn rested a hand on Lucy's shoulder. "Lucy, this is Mr. Austen."

"Jack," the man corrected with a grin, slowly crouching to her level, the movement hitched a little. "Or Mr. Jack, if your dad insists."

"Lucy, this is *Mr.* Jack." Finn always watched people's faces when they first met Lucy, wondering if they noticed the small scars or tiny remnants of her healed surgeries. He supposed he shouldn't put so much stock in that initial observation, but, as a dad, he felt as though he knew how to move forward with a person based on their reaction.

Lucy stared at him for a beat before tipping her head to one side and offering her hand. "Hi."

Jack shook her tiny hand like she was a CEO. "Pleasure to meet you, Miss Lucy."

Lucy giggled. *All right, Austen. You'll do.*

"Harry said your movers are arriving Wednesday." Jack rose back to his height and thumbed over his shoulder toward the door. "I've asked some guys from church if they'd be on call to help, if you need some."

"Help?" Finn blinked. "You have friends who would help me with my furniture?"

"Sure." Jack shrugged, giving the room another glance, as if taking inventory of what they'd need to bring inside. "Unless you've got some other folks already lined up."

Finn gave his head a shake. "But you and, certainly your friends, don't even know me."

"You're in Wisteria now, Dashwood." Jack's grin shifted with a teasing twist. "Everybody helps everybody else, whether they want it or not." He raised his brows. "In *all* sorts of small-town, country-folk kinds of ways to be . . . neighborly."

The sentence held its weight with unvoiced meaning. Good and bad, Finn supposed, as most small towns went. His thoughts strayed back to his "neighbor," the tea shop woman. Neighborly didn't quite fit his initial interaction with her. A twinge pricked at his conscience again. Yes, he should attempt to make amends.

After all, his plans were long term. No use starting things off with a neighbor on the wrong foot, was there?

"I really don't know how to respond to such kindness." Finn glanced about the room to rein in his surprise. "The movers are paid to move furniture into the apartment next week, but I do have supplies for the restaurant arriving Wednesday morning."

"You got it." Jack gave an easy salute and backed toward the door. "Let's say nine? Unless we hear directly from you."

"Y-yes." Finn's brain continued to digest the information. "Thank you."

"Wisteria is a good place to call home, Dashwood. You'll find most of the people friendly and ready to help." He tipped his head toward Lucy. "See you Wednesday, Lucy."

"Goodbye, Mr. Jack." She tightened her grip on Finn's leg with one arm but waved with the other. Good progress.

"And, Dashwood"—Jack opened the door, stopping on the breezy threshold—"you know another thing about small towns?"

Finn pulled his mind from the memory of the pink lady. "Lower prices? Easy access?"

"Curiosity." Jack tipped his chin toward the front window, where two older women were blatantly peering through the glass. When they realized they'd been caught, they scurried off like guilty schoolgirls.

Finn groaned. "Fantastic."

"You're gonna cause quite a stir. New guy in town. British. Dad." Jack's grin turned devilish. "And from what Harry says . . . single?" His blue eyes took on an added gleam. "Just wait till they start planning the welcome committee."

Jack slid out the door before Finn had time to clarify, but the intention resounded loud and clear. Single man with adorable daughter? In a small town? He looked over at Lucy, who hummed the *Sleeping Beauty* song as she happily moved back to her picture where she'd added a "mummy and baby sister."

Finn groaned. He was in so much trouble.

CHAPTER 2

@WisteriaWeekly: This just in! Former Wisteria native turned international influencer and podcaster was spotted up at @WisteriaManor with her business tycoon fiancé, Travis Langford. What's the scoop? #InquiringMinds #SmallTownGossip

@GrannyDOfficial: Was he that fella with the real purdy eyelashes? Saw 'em from clean across the restaurant. #NotThatIWasLooking #AppreciationIsAgeless

@TheRidgesFineDining: They ate here last night and Maude overheard wedding talk. #SupportSmallBusinesses #LocalFlavorOverCatered

@PastorNateNHC: Let's extend a warm Wisteria welcome, friends—because Hebrews 13:2 says we might be entertaining angels (or influencers) unawares. 😇 Also, the fiancé's car nearly inspired next Sunday's sermon: "Where Your Treasure Is . . . Please Park It in Front of the Church." Btw, Daphne @TeaThymeNC, I nearly laid hands on that car. Something you'd completely understand. #LoveThyNeighbor #AndTheirHorsepower #WisteriaHospitality

> **@TeaThymeNC:** I refuse to acknowledge anything related to what you're talking about. #HowDidYouKnowAnyway? #Busybody

> **@WisteriaGeneralStore:** Should we start printing "Lindsay + Travis 4ever" mugs or is it too soon? Asking for a friend. #WisteriaWeddings #TeamTrindsay #TooSoon
>
> **@SheriffGrady:** As long as they don't double park outside the courthouse, I don't care if Beyoncé shows up.

THE FUNDRAISER HAD BEEN a relative success. Four thousand dollars raised in only two hours of afternoon tea. Young ladies donned their best dresses, and a few dapper gentlemen brought their smiles and generosity.

And she desperately needed all the generosity she could muster, especially after plumber extraordinaire Jacob Lawson's last visit. Old piping. A long-standing leak with water damage behind the kitchen wall.

All much more costly than she'd make in three fundraisers, let alone one.

She needed more events. Try to get another wedding or graduation party or bridal shower? Or all three.

She sighed and swept beneath the chairs, the bristles catching on the worn spots in the hardwood that told stories of thousands of tea sippers who'd come before. She straightened a picture on one wall—an oil painting of a forget-me-not that Granny had haggled for at an estate sale—before moving to the other wall to ensure all the teapots were aligned in perfect formation, like ceramic soldiers guarding the legacy of Tea Thyme.

Daphne had kept everything the same as Granny left it before she died . . . almost a year ago now. The floral wallpaper on one accent wall. The faded tablecloths. The recipes.

All the same.

A year ago, Daphne had done a lot of things differently. Made occasional baking videos for social media. Created adorable graphics pairing certain types of tea with beloved books or movies. Even invented recipes and her own tea blends to match moods or personalities of the dearly loved (or less loved) folks in town.

And her creativity had always made Granny smile.

But change felt different now—like betrayal, like erasing fingerprints from a treasured keepsake.

Like . . . losing something else she couldn't get back.

Her gaze trailed over the tea shop space. Golden afternoon light streamed through the large front windows, casting honeyed shadows across the room and highlighting some of the dents in the wide-planked floor.

She released a long breath, stirring a wisp of hair that had escaped her practical bun hours ago. It seemed that she lived from month to month and really needed a way to move forward enough financially to breathe a little easier.

Her heart squeezed in her chest.

And perhaps change was the one thing she needed to save this shop.

New ideas? Brave chances into bigger, bolder things?

With a drop of her shoulders, she propped the broom against the wall and moved to the nearest kettle, warming up some water for a last cup of the day.

Even a year ago, the shop hadn't brought in massive amounts of revenue—unless you counted the amounts of elderly gossip exchanged over Earl Grey, which sadly couldn't be deposited into a bank account. But with increased repairs for the aging building and the rising costs of supplies, Daphne was feeling the crunch of growing Tea Thyme on her own.

She swore she could hear Granny muttering about "highway robbery" every time she placed an order for loose tea that cost twice what it had just three years ago.

Daphne's lips tipped. Granny's memory breathed in every corner of this place, all the way down to the scuff marks on the hardwoods from her size 6 Mary Janes. And, perhaps, as the one-year anniversary of her death neared, the buffer of time dug the reality deeper:

Tea Thyme was Daphne's alone.

And it was up to her to save it.

Maintaining the fundraiser this first year on her own had boosted Daphne's confidence a little.

Catering a few parties and bridal showers, even two small weddings, had given additional funds and helped Daphne build up a little of the courage grief snatched away . . . *again*.

Being brave was always easier with a sidekick. Or a friend. And maybe a mentor.

And Granny had been all three at some point or other, especially after Mom's death.

But tiptoeing back into being brave had paid off a little.

She just needed to figure out more ways to increase revenue and expand income.

And be braver.

Maybe . . . get back into creative baking . . . even without Granny along to brainstorm? Advertise more? After all, Daphne had started experimenting with new tea blends last month, even selling a few bags of them. *That* was something.

"Finished cleaning up for the night already?"

She looked up to find her brother, Jack, sauntering in through the front door, looking, per usual, as if he didn't have a care in the world.

He faked it well.

The open button-down over a T-shirt and khaki shorts probably helped. No one could look stressed in khaki shorts. It was scientifically impossible. Jack had tried to explain this to her once, complete with diagrams drawn on Tea Thyme napkins, until she'd threatened him with decaf.

And he'd finally grown comfortable enough showing off his prosthetics by wearing shorts. Of course once he'd moved from mechanical to bionic prosthetic legs, he started bragging about being a "bionic man," so maybe that helped.

Daphne stood and took two cups from the holder nearby. Jack's afternoon visits had become a pattern since Granny's death . . . maybe even before. He said he just wanted free tea and snacks, but Daphne knew he stopped in to make sure she was safe. To make sure she was still standing, still putting one foot in front of the other when grief tried to anchor her in place.

Moving forward was a little easier on some days than others.

And, although her faithful retriever, Winston, offered good company, Jack understood.

In ways no one else could.

Wearing his big-brother concern with a smile. He'd been doing that for much longer than since Granny's passing. He'd had to grow up even faster than Daphne when, first, their dad left . . . and then Mom.

But for very different reasons. One had wanted to leave.

The other hadn't.

"Rosemary stayed behind to help before rushing off to her night class."

He walked over to the counter and took a seat on the stool, sliding his hand into the ever-full cookie jar and pulling out a gingersnap with the practiced ease of someone who'd been pilfering cookies since he was tall enough to reach the counter.

Daphne eyed the jar. What would people think if she sneaked in a few of her ginger-pecan snaps? Typical gingersnaps with a bit . . . more. Or some other creation she devised in the secrecy of her kitchen?

She'd started dabbling with Granny's gingersnap recipe last week and her scones last night. Just a little. For some reason, even if only for herself, she needed to prove she'd captured some of that creativity Granny always seemed to have.

She used to have it too.

Death had a strange way of redirecting lots of "used tos."

But what would her patrons think if she started serving some of her own creations?

That she was a culinary rebel? A biscuit bandit? A cookie criminal conspiring to overthrow the monarchy of Granny's recipes one subversive pastry at a time?

She almost grinned. Maybe Granny would actually *like* it.

"How'd the fundraiser go?" He nodded his thanks as she slid a cup of Irish Breakfast to him. His evening routine.

"Good." She nodded, allowing the feeling of success to return her smile as she removed her apron. "Of course Mrs. Jennings and Mr. Thompson were incredibly grateful and the girls were great. One of them—Lily, I think—asked for Granny's cinnamon shortbread recipe. Called it 'revolutionary.' It was one of those rare moments where I actually felt cool."

He chuckled as he took a bite of the cookie. "So it helped?" His blond brow rose, crinkling the scar above his left eyebrow—souvenir from the time he'd tried to teach seven-year-old Daphne to ride a bike and ended up being the one needing stitches.

It had been the week before Mom's cancer diagnosis.

"Enough to put some money back after the repairs last month." She took a sip of her own tea and looked out over her beloved tea shop. "But I've got to think of some more things to increase revenue. Mr. Lawson's news about the plumbing was depressing."

He looked up from his tea. "How depressing?"

"To the tune of more-money-than-I'll-have-in-six-months depressing."

He winced, and then with a deep sigh he set his half-eaten cookie on the little doily she'd provided for him and held her gaze. "I have a few ideas about that, if you want."

"Find a pot of gold? Rob a bank?" She waved a hand in the air. "Marry rich?"

His grin crooked. "You can aim for those, but in the meantime, there are less life-altering, criminal, or leprechaun-finding opportunities for building visibility and revenue, Daph. And you know it."

He'd made statements like that before. Tried to bait her to ask for his suggestions or pick up where she'd left off when Granny died. But putting herself out there had been too hard, too raw. Faking happy when her heart thrummed an aching rhythm didn't fit her.

Some days she'd even had a hard time posting an inspirational quote on her restaurant's chalkboard, or turning the shop sign to "Open."

Granny's absence had come out of nowhere.

Gutted Daphne. Left her unanchored. And it had taken almost a year to start finding her feet again.

She channeled some of her courage from her earlier mental coaching, took another swallow of tea, and slid around the counter to sit next to him. His familiar scent of bergamot and citrus settled over her—he'd started stealing her Earl Grey soap last Christmas and never stopped. She'd pretended to be annoyed, but secretly it comforted her, this small thing they shared.

And it smelled good on him. A definite perk for his romantic future, if he ever actually decided to ask someone out.

Of course she could also use the bit of knowledge as blackmail. Just imagine what the guys on his basketball team would think of their favorite guard using tea soap!

"Start out easy on me." She turned to face him. "How about just two ideas first? Baby steps before marathon running and all that."

Jack's brows rose, and he stared at her for a minute, as if measuring her sincerity. No wonder. She'd pushed away his ideas before. Wasn't ready. Needed more time.

Wanted everything to remain just as Granny had left it.

Heaven knew she and Jack had experienced enough change in their lives.

He leaned back on the stool and stretched out his legs like he was settling in for a show. His grin grew slow and victorious—the exact look he'd worn when he convinced her to bake a cake from instinct instead of blind obedience to the recipe. It had been her first attempt at baking recklessly. She'd nearly broken out in hives.

Jack always seemed to know what she needed to do before she did.

Kind of like Granny.

"Well, first things first—you need to get on social media again." He waved a hand toward the shop. "Let folks who are driving through western North Carolina know there's this charming, little, history-steeped tearoom just waiting to give them a sugar coma doused in Englishness."

Daphne snorted. "Very funny and . . . eloquent." She lobbed a dishcloth at him, but he caught it one-handed and twirled it like some kind of victorious battle flag.

"I'm serious. You used to have an excellent online presence and a faithful following."

"Did I?" But even as she asked, she remembered the fun culinary conversations and beautiful aesthetics. The cooking recs and ambience creators.

The community.

"Of course you did." He waved a hand toward her. "English lovers, tea drinkers, history buffs, classy vacationers looking for a slice of Austen in the Blue Ridge." His gaze flicked back to her, warming. "And you need to show off that humor of yours instead of keeping it locked away like a family secret recipe."

"I do not!"

"You do!" He chuckled, but then his expression softened. "Or, at least, you have been for a while."

Her stomach clenched. She focused on adding sugar and milk to her cup . . . and clearly avoiding her brother's knowing look.

"Daph, you can be really funny when you're not worrying about everything."

"What do you mean 'when I'm not worrying about everything'? I have a lot to worry about." Like paying the bills, keeping up with repairs, holding on to memories so they don't disappear—the usual.

"Exactly my point." Jack shrugged, all nonchalance and infuriating wisdom. "You overthink too much. People love personality, and yours is golden when you let it shine instead of hiding it under a mountain of unnecessary anxiety." He tapped a finger against the counter. "Remember when you narrated that entire tea party in the voice of David Attenborough, and Mrs. Belton laughed so hard she snorted Earl Grey out her nose?"

Daphne's cheeks heated. "That was a onetime performance."

"It doesn't have to be." Jack grinned. "Think about it: 'Tea shop owner provides wildlife commentary on customers in their natural habitat.'" He gestured expansively, as if he could already see the headline. "You could go viral. Old-fashioned has its place, but changing a few things isn't bad either."

She narrowed her eyes at him, stirring her tea with perhaps more force than necessary. "I prefer the term *classic*."

"Right." His tone was far too agreeable. "Classic, like the Pony Express. But even they had to modernize."

She bit into a gingersnap and chewed with renewed vigor, begrudgingly acknowledging his annoying rightness. In all her research, this theme kept resounding in the "grow your business" category. Social media. Visibility.

Sure. She was an old soul. Loved vintage and timeless. But maybe she'd dug her heels a little too deeply into her grief, and those habits kept her afraid.

"And what about the weeklong social media conversation you had with a group of Austen lovers who, by the end of the nauseatingly flowery commenting section, basically invited you to come spend the summer with them in their cottage by the sea?"

"They were just being nice." But, oh, what a lovely exchange it had been about scones, Mr. Knightley, and words that should be restored to the English language.

"Maybe, but you were also being charming." Jack shrugged. "You had a way of making people want to engage with you. It's a gift." His smile softened. "I just end up being awkward."

She snorted and then leaned back on the stool, drawing in a breath before returning her gaze to him. "And the second idea?" She raised a finger in warning. "And it'd better not involve me dancing."

"Well, this one will probably help with the whole humor thing too." His expression gentled. "Start dreaming again."

She stiffened.

"You've been so stuck on keeping things the same for Granny because it was her shop, but you're not growing it. And all those drink and food ideas you've been 'waiting' to try? I think you should give them a go."

Daphne's stomach twisted. It was like he'd peeked into her brain ten minutes ago and decided to narrate the contents out loud. "But Granny's menu has been the same since—"

"It's not Granny's tea shop anymore, Daph," Jack said, cutting her off gently and reaching for her fidgeting hand. His fingers curled around hers. "It's yours."

Him saying it out loud stole her breath.

"And she'd love for you to *make it* yours. You can keep what you love best about her in it—because she'll always be part of it—but you'll love this place more if you bring it to life with your special brand of . . . you."

Daphne swallowed hard, unable to break his gaze. She opened her mouth to argue—to ask what exactly made her *her*—when his attention suddenly shifted. His eyes narrowed, landing on something on the counter.

"What's that?"

Her pulse skittered.

He was pointing at the unlabeled tin she'd absently set down while making his Irish Breakfast.

Every tin in the shop was labeled. Except that one. And it *was* new. Last night kind of new.

She scrambled for a distraction.

Jack leaned in, eyeing her with a slow, knowing smirk. "Don't tell me Daphne Austen is breaking tradition and trying something new again in this shop!"

Heat rushed to Daphne's cheeks as she rounded the counter and casually slid the tin out of sight. "Just . . . just experimenting."

"Experimenting?" Jack's eyebrows shot up with exaggerated surprise. "The same person who refused to change the Christmas decorations last year because 'Granny always put the garland exactly three inches from the ceiling'?"

"Very funny." She rolled her eyes. "It's just a tea blend. Something I've been . . . working on. At night. When I can't sleep." When the shop was quiet and memories of Granny hit particularly hard.

"Like some of those recipes you concocted in the wee hours after Granny died?"

The tenderness in his teasing, the way he understood those moments—and had, in fact, joined her in a few—stung her eyes a little. "Yeah, kind of. I mean . . ." She shrugged, even as her throat tightened around the words. "Like you said . . . Don't you think it's about time?"

Jack shifted closer, resting his elbows on the counter. "Can I try it?"

It was one thing to allow a few of the regulars a taste. Most of them were the sweetest ladies on the planet and never found fault with Daphne (or Granny) in any way. But Jack? Jack knew her better than anyone.

And he'd speak the truth.

She hesitated, her fingers curling around the tin protectively.

Maybe she'd lost her creative touch after so long. "I'm not sure I'm ready for *you* to try it. I mean . . . I think it needs . . . something." Like courage.

"Let me be the judge of that." His gentle urging nudged her bravery up a few notches.

And she *wanted* the truth.

Wanted to be brave.

The old Daphne was practically wrestling to get out.

She loosened her grip on the tin.

"What's the worst that could happen?" Jack waggled his brows. "I hate it, and you never make me tea again? Actually, that might save me from your experimental phase where you nearly poisoned me with that seaweed concoction."

"That was matcha, and it's very healthy," she shot back, laughing. The tension in her chest eased just a fraction. Giving herself permission to . . . dream, like Jack said? Maybe that wasn't so scary.

"Okay, but don't just gulp it down. Actually taste it."

She prepared the tea with careful precision, measuring the loose leaves, monitoring the water temperature, and timing the steep with the ancient kitchen timer Granny had used for decades. The familiar ritual calmed her nerves as Jack watched—and pilfered two more gingersnaps from the jar.

"What do you call it?" he asked as she poured the amber liquid into his cup. The aroma bloomed in the space between them—bergamot and black tea, yes, but with notes of lavender, warm spice, and a hint of citrus brightness that made it distinctly . . . hers.

"Not quite sure yet," she admitted, unwilling to share the whimsical midnight thought that had sparked the blend's creation.

Jack lifted the cup to his lips, eyes twinkling. "Smells great."

Daphne held her breath, watching every minuscule movement of his face.

He tilted his head, swallowing, and then took another sip, longer this time. His smile emerged slowly, brightening his entire expression so much that she actually felt his pride.

"This is really good, Daph. Like, *really* good. It's familiar but . . . different. In a good way." He took another appreciative sip. "It tastes like . . ." He searched for words. "Like tradition with a twist."

"Tradition with a twist?" She arched a brow, unable to suppress a grin. "Is that another hint to encourage me to branch out?"

He chuckled. "I didn't plan it that way, but sometimes I'm brilliant without trying."

She shook her head, pouring herself a cup.

"Somehow it fits you." He moved his palm across the air as if displaying a headline. "'Classic with Spice.'"

"You're ridiculous." She shook her head and drew her cup close, breathing in the tiny hint of orange she'd slipped in among the other ingredients. Something in her chest loosened at his words. "By the way, Mrs. Abernathy liked it too."

"You served this to the Dragon Lady of Rosewood Street? And survived?" Jack nearly choked on his tea. "Wait—she liked it?"

Daphne bit her lip, fighting a smile. "Asked for seconds, even."

Jack let out a whoop. "Then it's official. You've created magic in a cup." He raised his mug in a toast. "To Daphne's . . . wait, it still needs a name."

She hesitated. Then, on a breath, "What about Midnight Muse?"

His smile softened. "Perfect." He clinked his mug against hers. "To Midnight Muse—Daphne Austen's first official"—he raised a brow—"and solely original contribution to Tea Thyme's legacy." He took another sip and pointed at her with his cup. "And this only proves my point."

She narrowed her eyes. "Oh?"

"You've got the talent, Daph. You've always had it. This tea is both a tribute to Granny and completely your own. That's exactly what this shop should be." His voice dipped into something quieter, something that brushed against the most vulnerable part of her heart. "And before you argue"—he lifted his brows—"I just want to add that Granny would approve."

Warmth swelled into her vision. Having Granny's approval had always meant something special. She'd been their anchor when Mom got sick, taking them in, making ends meet, all while watching her only daughter succumb to the relentless grip of aggressive cancer.

Daphne turned away, walking to the tea tins, giving herself time to gather her emotions as she nestled Midnight Muse among the others.

Change had always felt hard.

Life-alteringly hard.

Goodbye hard.

But with Granny encouraging her, she'd navigated and even grown through it.

Yet maybe, just maybe, some changes could still be . . . good?

And maybe all those times Granny had been helping her made her brave enough to make changes on her own. Maybe?

"So, have you had a chance to meet your new neighbor yet?"

And just like that, all the warm, budding feelings of growth and optimism fizzled into the ether.

She snatched a pair of tongs and turned toward the pastry case. "Briefly." With swift, possibly aggressive movements, she began relocating the leftover scones to their overnight container.

"And I take it that 'briefly' wasn't a good experience, judging by the way you're attacking those pastries."

"He made fun of Tea Thyme, Jack." She whirled toward him, raspberry scone gripped tightly in the tongs. "Called it a princess tea shop. Had the audacity to assume my clientele consists solely of gray-haired ladies and my shop smells like potpourri."

Jack's lips tightened before he shoved a cookie into his mouth. Whole.

He'd better not even slightly agree with Mr. Fish and Chips. Not a bit.

Daphne pointed the scone—tongs and all—directly at him. "You know I have more variety than that. Today I had a whole host of ages."

Jack took an exaggerated sip of tea, expression bursting with the effort to contain laughter. And that boorish British bad boy wasn't right. Her precious tea shop was relevant. Special.

She'd prove it!

"And just like we discussed," she continued, tossing the scone into the container, "I'm planning some changes. Create a"—she shrugged—"cool online presence. Social media, promotions, the works."

Jack only nodded, humor dancing in his eyes.

She pointed the tongs again, warning him to contain that laughter. "Just because I have a vintage shop, enjoy classic fashion, and may have a slight obsession with England—"

"Slight?" Jack coughed. "Your goldfish were named after the Brontë sisters."

Her jaw dropped. *Traitor.* "There were three. It made perfect sense."

"You dress in costume on Jane Austen's birthday." Jack nodded, stealing another cookie. Where the man put those calories, she had no idea.

She scoffed. "It's a sign of respect."

"And I know how many classic British literature books you own. I moved them. With my own two hands."

"I'll take that as a compliment. And being well-read does not equal obsession."

Jack gestured broadly to the shelves of tea tins. "Daphne. All of your specialty blends reference English literature, movies, or gardens." He sipped his tea. "You're obsessed."

"I would like to say to you, brother dear"—the tongs returned as a pointer, this time holding a blueberry muffin—"that I inherited this tea shop from Granny. If there is any hint of an obsession, it first began with her. So if you're going to be snippy about it, I just want to remind you"—Daphne looked toward the ceiling—"that Granny can hear you, you know. Probably."

Jack should have looked a bit more intimidated by the idea. After all, she was his granny, too, but he just tilted his head toward the ceiling and said, "Granny, your granddaughter caught your obsession and let it spread like monkey grass."

Daphne huffed, slamming the muffin into a container. "Obsession or not, I can safely say I never want to see my British neighbor again." Daphne sent a glare toward the opposite brick wall as if it held power enough to sting Mr. Rudeness out of sheer force of will. Her whole body tensed. He'd looked at her with those dreamy, arrogant eyes, then laughed at her and her precious tea shop. Perhaps it was time to fill her movie and book quota with a healthy dose of American heroes instead of English ones.

Maybe some obsessions needed to die.

"He's staying, at least for now, and I can assure you, you'll see more of him." Jack stood, dusting off a few crumbs from his shirt before raising those sharp, knowing eyes to meet hers. "He's not that bad, Daph."

Daphne's entire body came to a standstill, except for her neck, which turned, almost owl-like, toward her brother. "You've met him?"

"He's Harry's friend, and you know if Harry likes him, he's got to be all right."

Harry—the epitome of English grace and welcome. Poised. Pleasant. Polite.

"Everyone makes mistakes in their friendships now and again."

Jack exhaled a voiceless laugh. "You know how sometimes you can jump to conclusions?"

Her glare was painfully impotent where her brother was concerned.

"And you're too sweet to hold a grudge."

"Is that a challenge?" She wrapped up the last blueberry muffin along with a cinnamon scone and placed them in a bag before handing it to Jack.

"He's got a lot of adjusting to do. New town. New country." Jack nodded his thanks. "You remember how Harry felt when he first arrived in Wisteria? Poor guy thought everyone was nosy, trying to assault him with Southern hospitality, or attempting to offend him at every turn. We mountain folk can take a minute to get used to."

And there it came. The post-reaction compassion. Jack was right.

Daphne did not want to weaken.

And yet, the tongs began to lower from their attack stance.

But Daphne's tea shop deserved a little more fight before she'd give in to the compassion. "But even Harry liked tea."

"Maybe Finn does too." Jack shrugged.

Finn? That was the guy's name?

She frowned. It even sounded English. Was it short for Finnley?

Argh. She didn't care!

"And not everyone is ready for all the . . ." Jack opened a palm to the room. "Power of this place."

Daphne rolled her gaze heavenward. "Granny is still listening."

Jack backed toward the door, palms raised in innocence. "And Granny would agree. It's always nice to be neighborly."

With that, the door closed on her brother's self-satisfied smirk, and Daphne followed his steps to lock up behind him. Her gaze flicked toward the street, to where the Cabriolet had been parked a few hours ago. It was gone now, and most of the shops on Main Street were winding down for the night. Only Marla and Max's Ice Cream Shop and Joe's Diner still buzzed with late-evening customers.

Finn whatever-his-name was new to town.

And probably lonely.

She sighed and walked back toward the counter, weaving between her cozy café tables and delicate floral centerpieces. As she scanned the space, Jack's encouragement replayed in her mind, and a flutter stirred in her stomach like tea leaves unfurling in hot water.

Tea Thyme wasn't just Granny's legacy anymore. It was hers to grow, to shape, to fill with her own voice and her own creations.

Her gaze landed on the small tin of Midnight Muse, then on her phone, the social media apps she'd used so frequently a year ago now painfully inactive. Maybe tonight she'd open one again. Post a re-introduction. Experiment with sprinkling in a bit of her humor to see how it steeped.

Tiptoe forward.

Maybe bring back a bit of the woman she used to be.

Take new chances.

Her attention shifted to the wall separating her from Mr. Obnoxious and his forthcoming pub.

She rounded the counter and tipped her gaze to the ceiling again. "Fine, Granny. I'll give him another chance. To be more neighborly."

She picked up her dishcloth and backed toward the kitchen doorway. "But it's not because he's handsome."

She exhaled into the empty room and flicked off the lights, the dim glow of the evening casting warm, dusky hues over the shop.

"And it's certainly not because he's English."

CHAPTER 3

@TeaThymeNC: Running a tearoom: 10% tea pouring, 90% wondering where I left my spatula and teaspoon. But at least there're scones. Stop in and try some. They'll go great with a delicious cup of tea. #TeaLife #SendHelpAndSugar #TeaThymeNC #TeaLoversUnite

> **@JackAustenPhotography:** Hold up. Is this my sister? Posting. On the internet. Voluntarily?? Is the Wi-Fi stronger in the tearoom or is this one of the signs of the apocalypse? #ProtectTheScones #ICaughtItOnCamera
>
> **@TeaThymeNC:** You are not as funny as you think you are.
>
> **@PastorNateNHC:** The Lord moves in mysterious ways. But really. Were there threats or bribes involved? #IKnowYourBrother #FaithAndFlour #TeaAndTestimony #HoldingTeacupsHostage
>
> **@WisteriaGeneralStore:** New tote idea: "Where is my spatula?"—A Daphne Austen Original. Comes with pockets for rogue teaspoons. #MerchDrop #TeaRoomEssentials

@RosemaryatThyme: Daphne? Posting? Finally! #HerBrotherMadeHerDoIt

DAPHNE BALANCED THE TRAY carefully on her hip as she stood before the freshly painted door of what would soon be Finn's pub. The simple "COMING SOON" message on the large chalkboard outside the restaurant lacked the charm she would have chosen, but what did she expect from someone who dismissed Tea Thyme as a "princess tea shop"?

Yet, here she was, armed with fresh cranberry-orange scones and a thermos of Midnight Muse—all in the spirit of goodwill. Jack was right. Being neighborly was what Granny would have wanted. And maybe, just maybe, proving Finn What's-His-Name wrong about her and her shop would be satisfying in its own petty way. Plus, if she were being honest with herself (which she tried to avoid before her second cup of tea), she was curious about the man behind the accent and the attitude.

After all, he was new to Wisteria.

And there was no one better at oozing welcome with the same flourish as Southerners. It was practically written into their DNA, right alongside an appreciation for sweet tea and the ability to say "Bless your heart" with seventeen different meanings.

She certainly wouldn't hurt that reputation by being aloof just because Finn proved a tea shop snob.

Drawing in a steadying breath that carried the scent of drying paint and sawdust, Daphne rapped her knuckles against the door. Nothing. Curious. She'd heard movement in there for the past half hour.

She tried again, louder this time, and heard a muffled curse followed by the sound of something—or someone—falling. The crash was impressive enough to suggest either serious property damage or wounded pride. Possibly both.

She cringed. Oh dear heavens, had she just killed him?

Definitely not the best way to prove Southern hospitality.

She took a step back from the door, contemplating whether to run away, when the door swung wide.

There stood Finn, looking decidedly less put together than during their first encounter. His dark hair stuck up at odd angles, and a fine layer of dust covered his plain white T-shirt, which clung just enough to his frame to make Daphne acutely aware that he must work out regularly. A small streak of dark red paint decorated his left cheekbone like he was either preparing to free Scotland or make a touchdown. The overall effect was irritatingly appealing.

Finn blinked, the surprise in his eyes quickly replaced by that infuriating half smile that did absolutely nothing to her heart rate. Nothing at all. The same way she absolutely didn't notice how his forearms looked with his sleeves pushed up or how his eyes were the exact shade of chamomile with just enough cream.

She preferred surprise. At least surprise didn't make her stomach do that annoying little flip.

"Ah, my tea . . . neighbor," he said with a nod, his British accent somehow both crisp and lazy at once. "To what do I owe this unexpected pleasure at"—he glanced down at an imaginary watch on his wrist—"half past too early in the morning?"

Daphne's smile died on her lips. She'd waited until seven thirty! And clearly, he'd been awake already!

Costume dramas failed to prepare her for the sunny side *down* of the English. Mr. Darcy never gave Elizabeth Bennet sass about visiting hours. Then again, Mr. Darcy never had bedhead that managed to look artfully tousled rather than like the victim of a ceiling fan accident, which was Daphne's usual morning look.

Perhaps it was time to call upon the strength of someone much greater than Granny. *God, help her.* "We weren't properly introduced yesterday."

"No, I don't believe we were. I think you were much too distracted by my car to adhere to such whims as introductions." His brow rose at a flirty tilt, somehow increasing the heat in her cheeks to the temperature of freshly baked scones.

She attempted to ignore the fluttering in her chest. Because of the car. Not the man. Or the grin. Or the way his eyes crinkled at the corners when he was trying not to laugh at her. Definitely the car.

"I'm Daphne Austen." She thrust the tray forward before she could change her mind, before her traitorous brain could conjure up any more inappropriate thoughts about accent-wielding pub owners. "And I brought breakfast." She clung to a smile that was threatening to flee the premises along with her dignity. "A neighborly gesture as a welcome to Main Street, Wisteria."

"I thought you gave me a welcome yesterday." His lips crooked a bit higher, topped with a wink, and her face jumped into sauna territory. At this rate, she'd need to market her tea as "Embarrassment Flush: the exfoliating heat treatment you never asked for."

Hmm . . . maybe that would prove a good social media post?

"Can we please move beyond yesterday?" she snipped. "It was a momentary weakness that will *not* happen again." She emphasized *not* for her own benefit.

"Disappointing. It's been much too long since my . . . car has benefited from such open appreciation." He leaned against the doorframe, somehow rocking "disheveled" in a way that defied human logic.

She narrowed her eyes at him, attempting to sort out if he intended the double entendre or not. The gleam in his eyes suggested he absolutely did. "Do you like scones? Muffins?" she blurted, desperate to redirect the conversation to safer territory.

"Scones?" Finn's gaze dropped to the covered tray, and another look of genuine surprise crossed his features, softening the sharp edges of his smirk. "You baked for me?"

"I thought you might appreciate a civilized start to your first morning in Wisteria."

"Civilized?" One brow lifted. "You do realize it's barely eight? In Britain, this would qualify as a dawn raid."

"From the paint on your face, I'd say you're well prepared." The comment just popped right out, and instead of offending him, it only inspired his grin all the more. Ack! She rushed ahead. "I happen to believe that breakfast is the most important meal of the day, and besides, we didn't start off on the best footing. I thought I'd extend this olive branch, or scones, as the case may be, as a second attempt at a first meeting." She smiled, despite the fact that her inner voice was screaming, *Retreat!* with the—to keep with the raid theme—vigor of a general facing an army.

The problem was, retreating would mean admitting defeat. And if there was one thing Daphne Austen wouldn't do, it was admit defeat to a handsome Englishman who mocked her tea shop. Even if he did look unfairly attractive while covered in paint and . . . flour?

Finn exhaled a laugh that shouldn't have sounded so appealing. "So this is an attempt at diplomacy? I'm flattered. Though I should warn you, the English have a rather spotty history with that."

She almost laughed. He shouldn't be funny.

"An opportunity," she corrected sweetly. Too sweetly. Sugar-coated poison apple sweetly.

A glint lit his eyes, something between amusement and . . . was that appreciation? "Miss Austen, I feel we are not acquainted well enough for—"

"For you to apologize, Mr. Gutter Brain." She thrust the tray into his chest with just enough force to make him catch his breath. "You insulted my business, my livelihood, and, frankly, my excellent taste in decor. The least you could do is accept my neighborly gesture without innuendo."

Finn took the tray with a chuckle, stepping back from the impact enough for Daphne to enter. "By all means, come in." He waved toward her with exaggerated gallantry. "Though, I warn you, the amenities are somewhat lacking at present."

Daphne stepped into what used to be the Morgans' sandwich shop. But before that it was—Daphne almost smiled from the memory—Mrs. Duncan's antique shop. She'd bought her first secondhand teapot from Duncan's when she was nine, a chipped little thing with pink roses that Granny had helped her restore. It still sat in her shop window, a reminder that sometimes the most precious things are a little broken.

The Morgans hadn't kept the ornate Victorian display cases that had once stood along one wall of the shop, but for the most part they'd retained other beautiful decor framed by the oak-lined walls and hardwood floors. Except, right now, despite the booths and tables, a few construction materials lay strewn about. Some paint cans nestled in one corner. But otherwise, the place looked ready to receive customers.

How had Finn achieved this miracle?

Had Harry been working on this place for Finn all along? Is that why she'd met him going in and out of the vacant shop so many times over the past two months?

Tricky Harry. *He'd kept it all a secret.*

He'd definitely hear about that when she saw him again.

And then—she almost gasped—on the far wall, someone had started ripping down the vintage rosebud wallpaper that had been Mrs. Duncan's signature touch.

Half the wall stood bare, exposing drywall beneath, while the other half still bloomed with the delicate pattern that had made this shop feel magical to Daphne as a child. It was like watching someone tear down a piece of Wisteria's history.

"You're removing the wallpaper," she said, unable to keep the accusation from her voice. She shifted a few steps nearer the devastating sight and placed a palm to her chest.

"Astute observation." Finn glanced over his shoulder as he cleared a space on a makeshift worktable. "The pink roses don't quite fit the English pub aesthetic I'm going for."

"Some people appreciate tradition and history," Daphne said pointedly, stepping closer to the scarred wall.

"Some people appreciate not having their restaurant look like it was decorated by a twelve-year-old girl's diary," Finn countered, his smile slightly softening the barb. "Though I suspect you were that twelve-year-old girl, which explains the attachment."

Daphne bristled. "That wallpaper survived three businesses, two renovations, and one particularly enthusiastic church youth group's attempt at painting murals. It's practically a Wisteria landmark." Daphne reached out to touch one of the intact roses. "Mrs. Duncan chose it because the very first business in this building in the early 1900s was a florist shop. The roses were a tribute."

Finn studied her for a long moment, something unreadable in his eyes. "And that matters to you? The history of it? It's just worn, peeling wallpaper."

"To you, maybe." Daphne turned to face him. "But to some, it's . . . continuity. Something to hold on to when everything else changes."

A shadow crossed Finn's face, so brief she almost missed it. "Not everything that changes is bad, you know. Sometimes the past needs to stay in the past."

There was something in his tone—a weight to his words that seemed to carry meaning beyond wallpaper. But before Daphne could puzzle it out, he waved toward the room, smile returning to his lips but not his eyes. "After all, I'm hoping this change for me will be a good one."

She studied him for a breath longer. Had something happened to send him running from England to small-town North Carolina? A scandal? A heartbreak?

Perhaps Jack was right all the more. Just like so many others who'd moved to their town from various places around the country, or world, Finn . . . What's-His-Name *needed* Wisteria.

Her ire bent a little beneath this revelation. "Well, you've picked a wonderful place for a change."

He shrugged. "That's what Harry says."

"And Harry's right." Daphne pulled her gaze from his and stepped to the tray, quickly removing the items and laying out a cloth napkin, the scones, and the thermos of tea.

She sighed and raised the thermos like a peace offering. "I brought some of my own special tea blend called Midnight Muse, if you'd like to try some."

Finn glanced at the thermos with a look that could only be described as mild suspicion. "You're own blend, is it?" His expression soured slightly. "I appreciate the gesture, but I'm afraid I don't drink tea."

Daphne froze, the teacup poised midair on its way to the thermos. Did she hear him correctly? No, of course not. Next he'd tell her he enjoyed small talk and had never used the word *cheeky* in his life.

"You own an English pub, but you don't drink tea." She didn't phrase it as a question, because clearly, she had misheard.

"I own a pub that serves beer, ale, fizzy drinks, and hearty food. Tea doesn't factor into the equation." He had the audacity to look amused at her shock, as though he hadn't just committed the equivalent of cultural treason.

She reeled. This was like finding out a chocolatier was allergic to cocoa. Or that a Frenchman refused to eat bread. Or—a shiver of horror—that a Southerner preferred unsweet tea.

And the fact that she'd packed her best china teacups now seemed ridiculously optimistic . . . and absurd. What sort of tragic, tea-related accident had turned a Brit against his own national beverage?

"Isn't that like running a pizzeria and hating cheese?" She clutched the teacup a little tighter, protecting it from such heresy.

"I'd argue tea is optional." Finn's brow quirked. "Cheese is fundamental."

"But . . . you're English," Daphne said, trying to make sense of this rudimentary contradiction.

"Ah, there it is. The assumption that all Brits survive on tea and crumpets."

"Well, yes! And rain, and sarcasm, and *queuing*."

Something almost fascinating lit his eyes, and Daphne might have appreciated it more if she hadn't been so—what would Granny have said?—flummoxed?

"I prefer coffee." His grin broadened for a moment, the dangerous dimple giving a flicker. "Black, bitter, and strong enough to stand a spoon in."

A possible description of his personality, maybe?

His eyes met hers with unexpected intensity that made her stomach do a little flip. "Not everything about me fits your stereotype, Miss Austen. I assure you."

Something about his tone suggested they weren't just talking about beverages anymore.

"But—"

"Look, princess—"

"Daphne."

"Fine, *Daphne*." He ran a hand through his already disheveled hair, and she absolutely did not notice how it made him look even more unfairly attractive. "I know you mean well, but bringing tea to convert the wayward Englishman feels a bit . . . presumptuous, doesn't it? Like me bringing you a jar of concentrated yeast extract and expecting you to worship it because it's 'authentically British.'"

She actually liked the stuff! Not that she'd tell him now.

Heat crept up her neck, and she was certain she was turning the same shade of pink as the half-demolished roses on the wall. "That's not—I wasn't trying to convert you. I was being neighborly." She began gathering up her cups and napkins, the heat that had been in her cheeks now cascading through her entire body like a flash fire.

What an idiot! That's what she got for taking a risk, wasn't it?

Kindness? Unappreciated.

Authenticity? Treated with sarcasm.

Dignity? Bleeding out on the metaphorical battlefield.

Why did her life always involve some sort of Wickham?

Between her own father, an ex-boyfriend (of two years), and her high school best friend, she'd borne the brunt of one-sided relationships and faulty expectations.

Jack was wrong. Some people didn't appreciate kindness.

She stuffed the rosette cloth napkins back into her basket with more force than necessary.

"Wait, Daphne." Finn reached out to stop her frantic packing. He said her name with such gentle . . . Englishness, her feet froze in their retreat.

His hand brushed hers, and she tried to ignore the little spark that jumped between them. Probably just static electricity from all that synthetic wallpaper, or maybe it was her humiliation at the fact that taking such a chance just made her look like an idiot. "I was being a git. Again." He released a sigh and caught her gaze. "It was incredibly kind of you to bring breakfast. I'm just . . . not much of a morning person."

"Or a tea person," Daphne muttered.

"Or a tea person," he agreed with a hint of *that* smile. "But I am a scone person. And these"—he picked up a half of one, examining it with genuine interest, his fingers tracing the golden-brown crust with something approaching reverence—"look amazing."

Why did he have to go and compliment her baking when she had such excellent momentum to dislike him? Unfair!

She attempted a glare, but between the compliment and her desire to see him appreciate something she'd made, she offered, "They're cranberry-orange. With a hint of cardamom."

She was such a weakling.

"Adventurous. I like that." His eyes caught hers, and for a moment, the distance between British pub owner and American tea shop proprietor didn't seem so vast. Or disastrous.

That little annoying flutter she didn't want to feel came alive in her chest again.

Bad. Awful. Nope! She needed space from him ASAP.

Just as soon as he tried her scone.

The crook of his smile deepened—that smirk she was half convinced he practiced in the mirror—as he took a generous bite. His eyes closed, a low sound of appreciation humming in his throat. And just like that, Daphne found herself staring, with truly mortifying focus, at his lips.

The same lips that had, not too long ago, insulted her beloved tea shop with devastating precision. Those very same lips were now wrapped around her scone, experiencing, what appeared to be, unmitigated joy.

Her pulse ratcheted right up into a fevered pitch.

A true battle between liking him and loathing him took up residence in her chest. Which proved even more that she needed to keep her distance.

"These are actually fantastic," he admitted, something warm flickering in his eyes. "You're wasted on tea, Austen. You should open a bakery instead."

She shook her head from the allure of his appreciation and continued packing up her things. "If you took five minutes to actually learn about my 'princess tea shop,' you'd realize I bake *and* serve tea. They go together."

With a tug, she picked up her tray and took a few steps toward the door. Even if he liked her scones, she needed to steer clear of his smoldering glances and mesmerizing accent that made even insults sound like poetry.

He wasn't nice.

And he wasn't safe.

At all.

The flirt vibes practically screamed warning.

And his attitude practically promised heartache.

"So you claim." He picked up the other half of the scone, then hesitated, a sudden vulnerability replacing his ridiculous swagger. He gestured back toward the kitchen. "I could make coffee. As a counter-offering. You bring tea, I subject you to proper coffee?" The invitation hung in the air between them.

"Subject me?"

"Proper coffee is an acquired taste, princess," he said, the nickname softened by the smile playing at the corners of his mouth. "Especially for someone who probably drinks . . ." He peered at her thermos suspiciously, like it might contain some mystical potion. "What did you call it? Midnight Moose?"

"Muse," she corrected and took another step back toward the door.

Something in her heart hurt. A disappointment, maybe? That she'd hoped for something better and had been sadly wrong. That the scenario in her head about offering a welcome had ended in her feeling off-balance and maybe a little ridiculous. Why did chivalry have to be dead? Or relegated to fiction? "It's a specialty blend with notes of bergamot, vanilla, and star anise."

Finn grimaced. "You've just listed three flavors that have no business being in a beverage. Next you'll tell me you put pumpkin spice in your porridge."

Did he have to criticize everything? All right, no more Miss Nice Southern Girl. "Says the man who drinks coffee that could likely double as motor oil," Daphne retorted, a scathing warmth creeping into her voice despite her best efforts.

"Touché." Finn leaned against the worktable, and the motion caused his T-shirt to ride up slightly, revealing a glimpse of toned abdomen that Daphne absolutely did not notice. Not at all.

"Well," she announced, wrenching her focus to the door. "I have a tea shop to run. One that caters to more than just 'gray-haired ladies and smells of potpourri,' despite what *some* people might think."

Finn winced, running a hand through his already disheveled hair. "About that . . . I may have been a bit harsh during our first meeting." The admission seemed to cost him something.

"May have been?" Daphne arched an eyebrow as a very unhumorous burst of air emerged. It wasn't quite a laugh—more the sound of disbelief crystallized into sound.

"Was. Definitely was." He had the grace to look sheepish, his eyes meeting hers with unexpected sincerity. Those warm milky-brown depths a treacherous pairing with a coffee snob.

"You're not really improving upon a second one," she said, smile tight.

"Look, I've been under a lot of pressure with this move, and—"

"And taking it out on me and my tea shop seemed like the logical response? Mature even?" She took a few more steps back toward the door. "What next? Kicking puppies because your contractor is late?"

"I draw the line at puppies." His lips quirked. "Contractors, on the other hand . . ."

"I'm sure they're thrilled to work with you."

"I'm trying to apologize here." The English lilt of frustration in his voice made everything worse. Because why did the English have to sound so good even when they were being difficult? Even when they played villains!

"Are you? Because it sounds more like you're making excuses. Besides, I've imposed enough on your wallpaper demolition." Daphne made it to the door, but it was closed, and her arms were too full to make a quick escape. She fumbled with the knob, dignity crumbling by the second.

"Allow me." Finn reached past her, his arm brushing against her shoulder as he moved to open the door, enveloping her in a scent that was part smoked vanilla, part . . . cedar? But all uniquely him.

She held her breath.

She was never listening to Jack again.

"I can manage," she insisted, stepping back and nearly colliding with his chest. They performed an awkward dance of almost-contact, like magnets simultaneously attracting and repelling.

"Now you're just being dramatic." Finn sighed, reaching for her arm as she turned to leave. His fingers were warm against her skin, sending an unwelcome jolt through her body. Did he feel it too? That current that seemed to jump between them at the slightest touch.

Ridiculous, Daphne. Another utterly ridiculous thought to add to the growing mental quagmire.

"Surprisingly, I'm sure, not everything about me fits your stereotype, Mr. . . ."

"Dashwood." His gaze searched hers, his hand on the doorknob, arm blocking her escape. "Finn Dashwood."

Gee whiz, did he have to have an Austen character-esque last name too? The universe was clearly having a good laugh at her expense. Next thing she knew, he'd mention having a sister named Marianne.

His entire expression softened and he released a deep breath, gesturing toward the bar. "Stay, have coffee. I promise not to insult your tea shop again . . . for at least fifteen minutes." He gestured back toward the shop with his chin. "I'll even time myself."

Daphne pulled away, hating the lingering warmth where his hand had been. "Tempting, but I'll pass."

"Even if I sweeten the deal with tales of the haunted pub I ran in Yorkshire?" His eyes danced with mischief. "Complete with mysterious footsteps, moving objects, and one very disgruntled Victorian barmaid?"

Her lips twitched just a little. "Ghost stories over morning coffee? How charmingly macabre."

She nearly blinked at her own comeback. Clever. Sarcastic. She usually saved such little treasures for her brother or Pastor Nate. Sometimes Rosemary.

One of his dark brows jutted northward, matching the corner of his mouth. "I find it pairs well with scones." He leaned against the doorframe, all casual grace and surprising vulnerability. "Look, I know we got off on the wrong foot—"

"Both feet, really," Daphne interjected. "Yours."

The other corner of his mouth peaked a little, his gaze holding hers. "Fair enough. All appendages. But I'd like to . . . not be enemies." He ran his hand through his hair again, a gesture she was beginning to recognize as a nervous habit. "Neighboring businesses and all that."

Ah, right. Not nice to be nice. Just nice to make his life easier.

Yeah, she got it.

She stepped over the threshold of the door but paused to turn back for one final look. Finn was watching her with an expression she couldn't quite decipher. All the compassion she didn't want to feel started wrestling with her ire, but she gave it a hefty shove.

"A bit of advice, Mr. Dashwood—most people around here want to see you succeed. They're usually nice, maybe too nice, but you'd find a lot more friends and future patrons if you showed a little . . . welcome too." She glanced at the half-demolished wallpaper, pink roses fading into oblivion. "And maybe consider that sometimes a little pink isn't the worst thing in the world."

"Is that an invitation to visit your princess tea shop, Austen?" The corner of his mouth lifted in that infuriatingly attractive half smile, the one that suggested he knew exactly how it affected women. Including, irritatingly, her.

But at the moment, her disappointment dimmed the attraction.

"It's a suggestion to be less of a judgmental jerk," she shot back, but there was less heat in her words than she'd intended. Like a cup of tea left too long, her anger had cooled, leaving something more complex behind.

"Noted." He raised the half-eaten scone in a mock toast. "And for what it's worth, these really are exceptional. You've set a high bar for my counteroffering."

"Your counteroffering?"

"Mm-hmm. For every specialty tea blend you subject me to, I'll introduce you to a proper coffee." His eyes held a challenge. "Cultural exchange. Very diplomatic."

Daphne found herself almost smiling despite everything. "I look forward to being thoroughly disappointed by your motor oil."

"Challenge accepted." His eyes lit with something dangerous—something that felt like the beginning of a game she hadn't agreed to or had any interest in playing. Yet something in her rose to meet that challenge.

Daphne closed the door behind her and slipped into Tea Thyme, its familiar facade extra comforting. Inside, she set the tray on the counter and drew in a deep breath as she dropped to the stool. The shop was still empty, not yet open for the day's customers, and the silence broken only by the gentle tick of the antique clock Granny had insisted created "proper tea ambience."

"Well, Granny," she said to the empty room. "I tried being neighborly."

But some people weren't the sort to win over.

Selfish, shallow, and probably unreliable.

Just like her dad.

And as much as she loved history, she had no intention of repeating that pattern.

CHAPTER 4

New Tea Alert! Introducing Embarrassment Flush—the exfoliating heat treatment you never asked for!

Perfect for those moments when your face jumps into sauna territory after an unexpected wink (or, you know, when you spill your tea literally and figuratively). Made with the finest hibiscus, ginger, and a touch of mortification. 😉

Stop by Tea Thyme and try it—because blushing should at least come with good flavor! #ChooseWisely #TeaThyme #EmbarrassmentFlush #WisteriaLife #BlushingAndBrewing

OPENING SOON: The Green Dragon Pub!

Wisteria, you've been far too long without a proper English pub, and I'm here to fix that. The Green Dragon opens one week from today. Classic British comfort food, a stellar pint selection, and just enough charm to make you feel like you've stepped into a cozy pub across the pond.

And because I'm trying to be a good sport about this whole living in the South thing . . . sigh . . . I suppose I'll be serving sweet tea. But only because I hear it helps make friends.

So come grab a drink, a bite, or even a ridiculously sugary tea, and let's make The Green Dragon your new favorite spot.

Opening in 1 week! Cheers! #TheGreenDragonWisteria #British-PubMeetsSouthernCharm #PubGrub

FINN COULDN'T SHAKE THE gnawing discomfort from his morning meeting with Daphne Austen.

He'd expected some hurdles in getting his restaurant up and running—permits, inspections, the occasional misplaced shipment. Most things Harry had already put into motion so Finn could open the restaurant with all due speed and lose as little money as possible.

What Finn hadn't expected was *her*.

The woman had shown up at the break of dawn like some kind of benevolent breakfast fairy, all sunshine and scones, wielding a tray like it was her personal mission to ensure he didn't starve.

And Finn wasn't prepared for her charm.

First impressions truly didn't give a full picture.

Of course the first time he'd seen her, she'd been wearing a bright pink suit with her face pressed against his car window, which had been more alarming than endearing. This morning she'd swapped that for a crisp white blouse and pale blue slacks that hugged more than hung. And it turned out that when she wasn't glaring at him, she was actually quite . . . pretty.

Not the sort of woman who turned every head in the room, but definitely the sort that could hold a man's attention longer than was good for him.

But the real problem wasn't the way she looked.

It was something else—something intangible but potent enough to tighten his chest with a warning.

Dangerous didn't always come in dark alleys or in the form of scarred villains. Sometimes it came wrapped in warmth and good intentions, in the sort of temptation that could make a man think about things he'd sworn off.

He had a sneaky suspicion that Daphne Austen was the sort to tempt thoughts of "till death do us part." She had that small-town, inviting spark about her.

He shook his head. But he knew her type. He scoffed. In fact, he'd married her type. Positive, funny, willing to take on the adventures life posed for a couple, but when life grew harder than what she signed up for, she'd leave. When hardship forced a choice between herself and her family, she'd choose herself.

The old ache squeezed to a painful point in his chest, but he shoved away the thought.

It was so much easier to play the short game. Flirt, compliment, go on an occasional date here and there.

But forever?

Finn had already tried that story. And failed.

He wasn't signing up for a sequel.

He sighed, remembering the disappointment on Daphne's face at some of his less-than amiable responses. He'd been critical, dismissive—no doubt the opposite of what a woman like Daphne expected from a neighbor.

In fact, he'd even disappointed himself.

But something about her seemed to inspire his . . . defenses.

He tried to shake off the unexpected feeling.

It wasn't her fault he hid a gaping wound in his heart and carried a chip on his shoulder. But he'd let her feel the brunt of both this morning, hadn't he? Like a real clod.

Maybe he could at least try to be civil. No need to be best friends, but a little good-natured diplomacy between fellow business owners wouldn't kill him.

His gaze landed on the single square of floral wallpaper he'd left up behind the bar—one last remnant of the antique shop that had existed before he had come along to gut the place and turn it into The Green Dragon. He'd framed the piece with wood, telling himself it was a nod to history, but now . . .

He nearly groaned.

It was a good thing Lucy had fallen back asleep in the rear of the shop, because he had the sinking suspicion that if she had met Daphne Austen, the two of them would have been fast friends.

Which would mean more time spent around Daphne.

Which was not in Finn's plans.

But he did owe her a legitimate apology. Maybe he'd pop over later. Smooth things over. He could even try out the oven in the back—make something properly English as a peace offering.

Maybe a treacle tart? She seemed the sort to like something like that.

Before he could dwell on the idea any longer, the bell above the front door jingled with a rather . . . loud entrance.

A trio of older women bustled inside, all wearing expressions that suggested they were here on a mission. And, from the drop in his stomach, he was the target.

"Mr. Dashwood!" The leader of the pack, a woman with a towering gray bouffant, who somehow stretched his name into seven syllables, flashed a bright smile framed in dark red lipstick. "We *had* to come by and welcome you properly!"

This isn't an attack, he repeated to himself. *This is . . . Southern hospitality.*

Keep calm, mate.

He pushed up a smile and was opening his mouth to greet them when the second woman, a plump lady in a floral dress, stepped forward, pressing a very large casserole dish into his arms. "I'm Trudy Wallace. Made you my famous chicken and dumplings. Thought you might be too busy to cook while you set up your business all by yourself, bless your heart."

Finn *very much* did not like being blessed in that tone.

"Mrs. Jenkins." The third woman, a wiry thing with sharp eyes that seemed to miss nothing but were uncomfortably focused on his mouth, held up a tin. "Homemade biscuits. None of that store-bought nonsense. If you're gonna be a real Wisterian, you'll have to learn the importance of a proper biscuit."

Finn wasn't sure if that was a threat or a friendly warning.

And, he hated to tell her, but those fluffy clouds of flour were not "biscuits."

"Thank you?" He set the casserole on the bar, wondering how long a Southern welcome usually lasted, because his expiration date was approaching much more quickly than he had predicted.

The gray-haired woman leaned in, lowering her voice, the glint in her eyes almost terrifying. "Would your wife be somewhere hereabouts that we could welcome her too?"

For some reason, Finn had the strangest notion that this woman knew the answer already. How on earth was Lucy sleeping through all this on her little couch in the back?

"I'm not married." He squeezed out the confession, preparing himself for the response.

And all three gasped . . . in delight.

"Well, what a shame for such a nice-lookin' fella like yourself," Mrs. Chicken and Dumplings offered, without a trace of sorrow on her face. "But don't you worry one bit."

"That's right," the gray-haired lady continued. "We've got some lovely ladies in town who'd just adore an English gentleman."

Of this, he had no doubt.

Daphne Austen's mild revulsion suddenly took on an appeal he hadn't known he'd wanted.

"That's . . . very kind," he managed, though the words felt strange in his mouth. In London, neighbors barely managed eye contact, let alone this coordinated assault of Southern hospitality. "But I'm not actually looking for—" A small voice piped up from behind the bar in interruption.

"Daddy?"

Lucy.

Ah! Apparently, she wasn't sleeping through it! His daughter appeared around the corner of the doorway rubbing sleepy eyes and clutching the stuffed dragon she insisted on bringing everywhere. Her dark curls were still mussed from sleep.

Immediately, the three women let out a collective "aww"—their expressions melting into that particular brand of maternal adoration that only a small child and, possibly, cute animal could summon.

Lucy offered the trio of strangers a wide-eyed look before slipping to Finn's side, fingers clutching the bottom of his shirt, likely feeling the "welcome" with the same potency as he had.

He smoothed a hand over her curls to reassure her.

"Oh my stars! Is this your little girl?" Mrs. Wallace gasped, clutching her ample bosom as if overcome.

"What a precious angel!" the sharp-eyed one declared. "And look at those curls! Just like a little cherub!"

Lucy blinked up at them, her lips pursed as if she wasn't certain which expression to choose. He knew the feeling, but her reticence was much more forgivable.

Finn sighed. "Lucy, meet our very enthusiastic neighbors. Mrs. Wallace?"

He looked at the woman and she nodded as if electricity had just jolted her neck into motion.

"And . . ." He tilted his head, studying the biscuit woman. "Mrs. Jenkins, was it?"

The woman gave a firm nod, her smile broad.

And then he looked over at the ring leader. "I don't recall your name, Mrs. . . . ?"

"Ambrosia Clark." The woman pronounced the name as if every syllable deserved special consideration.

"And how old are you, sweetheart?" Mrs. Wallace cooed.

Lucy looked up at Finn, and after a nod from him, she held up six fingers, which prompted another round of delighted noises from the trio. Then, before Finn could redirect the conversation, the bouffant-haired leader leaned in again.

"You know, my daughter, Emily, is a speech-language pathologist at our local elementary school." Mrs. Clark blinked a few times with her nod. "Very good with children."

Finn exhaled sharply through his nose, wondering if there was a polite way to end this conversation without somehow finding himself engaged by the weekend.

"I'm certain it does you credit, Mrs. Clark, to have raised such a lady."

The woman's palm fluttered to her chest. "Oh, how very good of you to say . . . in that particular way."

"And how's your precious little girl settling in?" Mrs. Wallace asked, attention still fastened on Lucy. "Six is such a wonderful age. You know, Beverly's daughter runs the most darling dance studio—"

"And my Sunday school class always welcomes new faces," Mrs. Jenkins interjected.

"Speaking of new faces . . ." Mrs. Jenkins smiled with disturbing sweetness. "Have you met our dear Daphne next door? Such a lovely young lady . . ."

Finn felt his collar tightening. "Yes, actually—"

"Single," Mrs. Wallace stage-whispered to her friends. "And so good with children."

Good heavens, they were shameless.

Before they could launch into another wave of not-so-subtle matchmaking, Lucy tugged on his sleeve. "Daddy, can I have a biscuit?"

Mrs. Jenkins beamed. "See? Girl knows what's good! Here you go, sugar." She removed the cling film from the food and passed Lucy one of the . . . American biscuits.

To Lucy's credit, she took the item, examined it, and then looked up at Finn with an incredulous expression. His daughter knew a counterfeit biscuit when she saw one.

How did one gracefully relieve themselves of Southern women?

Finn opened his mouth—probably to say something he'd regret—when the door swung open again and a familiar deep voice cut through the air like a lifeline.

"Now, ladies, you best not be overwhelming the poor man. He's not even gotten settled yet."

Harry Coleman strolled inside, an amused glint in his dark eyes. An imposing figure with skin nearly the color of his dark brown hair, the man easily stood two inches above Finn and at least a half foot above all three ladies. The gray at his temples only made him look more refined.

And he always appeared to look as if he'd just stepped out of a fashion magazine, regardless of day, time, or place—or so that was Finn's memory.

This day didn't prove otherwise.

Finn had never been so grateful for an interruption in his life.

"Harry!" the women chorused, but the older man was already moving purposefully toward Finn. His assessing gaze must have seen Finn's . . . discomfort.

"I'm sorry to interrupt this welcome party, but Finn and I have a meeting to discuss his business, and I'm certain none of you ladies would find it the least bit entertaining." Harry's disarming smile worked its magic.

The little gaggle donned their apologies, and with a few lingering glances, comments, and extractions from Finn to "stop by anytime" and "bring that sweet little Lucy around," they slipped from the room, leaving a delightful silence behind.

Finn slumped against the bar. "I owe you a pint."

"Make it two." Harry chuckled. "Welcome to small-town Southern living, son. I thought you might need some cultural translation services."

"Oh, I believe my translation abilities were quite accurate for this meeting. What I needed most was rescue." He waved toward the older man. "Thank you for providing it."

Finn drew Lucy back toward him as she took a tentative bite of the so-called biscuit. "Is it always like that?"

"Worse, usually. They're just warming up." Harry shot Finn a grin before he bent his head toward Lucy. "Nice to see you, Lucy. You've grown much taller since last we met in person."

Which was a fact. His darling girl had added at least an inch or two to her height in the past year. Finn's stomach pinched a little at the thought.

But Lucy only grinned at Harry's compliment. "Where is Mrs. Margaret?"

"You shall see her soon enough." Harry winked. "The two of you are invited to the manor for supper tonight, and Ms. Margaret has already purchased a few little gifts to welcome you to your new home, Lucy."

"Harry . . ." Finn offered a powerless warning.

"Allow her the joy of it, Finn." He waved Finn's comment away. "She's aching to lather someone with all this motherly affection that has no outlet at the moment."

Finn relaxed at Harry's words. This was one of the reasons he'd come to Wisteria. When Father had been alive, Harry had become almost like an uncle to Finn, providing encouragement and support like family. Three years ago, when he'd finally met Margaret, who was attending culinary school in England, she'd only added to the sense of family. Even over a year ago, when the pair had moved to the States to take over Margaret's parents' inn and wedding venue, they'd kept in touch. Video and phone calls. A few visits from the Colemans, especially during Finn's toughest times. And with Finn's mother having died well before he could witness his parents' relationship, the Colemans' happy marriage encouraged Finn that some relationships worked.

Better than worked. *Thrived.*

So when Finn's business partner swindled him and took part of Finn's savings with him, Harry had offered an unexpected option. This. An English pub in the middle of the small town of Wisteria.

Harry surveyed the room and gestured with his head toward a wood carving Finn had hung over the bar. "Ah, you finally decided on a name?"

Finn followed his gaze and nodded. "Lucy and I agreed."

"The Green Dragon, then?" Harry's eyes sparkled as he sent Lucy a wink. "Prancing Pony was taken, was it?"

"We're more inclined toward dragons," Finn answered with a nod down to Lucy. "Besides, Gandalf never got thrown out of The Green Dragon."

"Fair point." Harry chuckled, giving the space another assessing look. "Though I suspect even the Grey Wizard himself might've met his match in our local welcoming committee." Harry brought his attention back to Finn. "Jack said the last bit of the restaurant furniture comes in this afternoon and your apartment furniture tomorrow evening?"

"Aye. The kitchen's in good shape, the prep work's all sorted. No reason to wait." Finn nodded. "With what you've done to prepare the place before our arrival and the final touches I'm making this week, we're in good shape to open as planned."

"The end of next week then?" Harry's lips twitched. "Ambitious."

"Assuming the permits come through without any trouble, but you've helped me navigate all of that fairly successfully."

"I'm happy to have you and Lucy here, Finn." Harry shrugged a shoulder. "And you should have an easier adjustment than I did moving to Wisteria."

Finn raised a brow in question.

"A Black man with an English accent who married one of their darling white lily Southern women?" His eyes squinted a bit as his grin crooked. "They weren't certain what to make of me." His smile softened. "It's been a good fit, though. I like the pace and the people, but it will take some getting used to. Emotions are usually . . . enthusiastic."

That was an understatement. And as far as getting used to? Finn had no doubt, especially after the recent invasion of Southern food, curious neighbors, and potent perfume.

"So you're saying it's always like this?" Finn waved toward the door the ladies had exited.

"If you mean nosy, then yes. But they mean well. They're a good lot once you find your place among them." He nodded toward the casserole. "And I'd eat that if I were you. Trudy's chicken and dumplings are extraordinary."

Finn grunted, glancing at the dish. Why did everyone bring food? He was a chef, for heaven's sake! "I'll take your word for it."

"Had any visits from the tea shop owner next door?" Harry tilted his head in the direction of the shop.

Finn's smirk vanished. "Why?"

"It would be like her to try and make you feel welcome." Harry's grin brimmed. "One of the most generous neighbors to have, I'd say. Much like her grandmother, even though I only knew the latter for a short while before she passed."

Finn exhaled, heat climbing up the back of his neck. "She did pop in this morning with scones."

"Sounds like her."

Finn ran a hand through his hair. "And I was a bit of a prat about it."

Harry hummed. "Also sounds like you."

Finn shot him a look.

"Well, you've not been yourself since the divorce, and then to have Chase betray you?" Harry sighed. "It's a lot to bear. And good to start over, I think." Harry cupped Finn's shoulder, giving it a squeeze Finn felt to his heart.

He'd missed Harry's camaraderie. In fact, Finn hadn't realized how much he'd been isolating himself from others until Harry made that simple gesture. When everything came out about Chase's betrayal, Finn forced his smile, as usual, and cocooned into his father role. He'd spent a year in a legal battle and tending his own wounds.

Charm had always been his defense. It distracted people from peering too close and from caring too much. A skill he'd honed during his father's illness to hide his own pain at watching cancer eat away at the best man he'd ever known. A talent he'd flashed to his customers even as his wife left him to tend to a baby girl on his own. Play the game. Keep the customers happy.

Protect your heart.

Finn pushed up a grin, despite the emotion lodging in his throat. "The start has certainly been . . . interesting."

"You'll get used to Wisteria, lad." Harry laughed, slapping a hand on the bar. "But a bit of advice?"

Finn sighed. "Go on."

"Kindness is a very important commodity around here." Harry tipped his head and backed toward the door. "And being neighborly will get you far."

Another hit to Finn's interaction with Daphne.

"So I'll see you two tonight?" Harry took a few more steps back. "Six?"

Finn nodded.

Harry stopped at the threshold, a strange look on his face. "Oh, and you might want to check your chalkboard out front. Seems someone's added their own review."

Finn followed him with Lucy trailing behind.

Instead of seeing his own handwriting, a new note, in a delicate hand, showed the following message:

English Pub Coming Soon.

What can you expect?

Ambience: ★★★★
Tea Selection: ★
Scowling Proprietor: ★★★★★

Despite himself, his lips twitched. Five stars for scowling indeed. He ought to be irritated, but somehow the clever jab only inspired a broader grin.

He definitely wasn't interested. But he did find himself wondering what other surprises Daphne Austen might have in store. And . . . Finn Dashwood was always up for a playful battle of wits.

CHAPTER 5

@TeaThymeNC: Tea: 1, Coffee: 0
They say coffee gives you energy, but have you ever sipped a perfectly steeped Earl Grey and felt your soul realign? No burnt bitterness, no jittery regrets—just warmth, flavor, and the quiet promise that everything will be okay.
No shade to coffee drinkers . . . okay, maybe a little. 😉
But let's be honest—tea doesn't need sugar to be sweet.
#TeaWins #SipSipHooray #DaphneApproved

> **@PastorNateNHC:** You're going too far, Daph.
> Let's not pit God's beans against God's leaves, okay?
> #GraceForCoffeeToo #BlessedAndHighlyCaffeinated
> **@TGDPub:** Look, not everyone needs a tea séance to feel whole in the morning. Some of us just want strong coffee, loud music, and a biscuit that bites back. #BeanWaterIsLife #CaffeineAndChaos #AustenStartedIt
> **@GrannyDOfficial:** Back in my day, folks drank what was hot and didn't write love letters to their beverages. Still . . . that Earl Grey is mighty nice with shortbread. #GrannyKnowsBest #CoffeeShmoffee

@WisteriaGeneralStore: Why choose? Have both! COMING SOON: "Tea Séance" candles and "Bean Water Is Life" tote bags. We are here to fuel your small-town drama. #MerchWar #ShopWisteria

"OKAY, WHAT'S WRONG?" ROSEMARY'S question bristled Daphne's spine as her friend slid behind the counter to palm the strawberry-banana smoothie Daphne left for her to take to a table of vacationers from New England.

The nearby Blue Ridge Parkway had a wonderful way of introducing folks to their little town. And tourists left the best tips. Some of the locals did too, but there were too many, especially the older men, who'd grin and leave "verbal tips" behind like, "Don't walk in the rain or you'll get wet" or "Watch your step when treadin' through a cow field."

Very helpful.

"What makes you think something's wrong?" Daphne refused to turn from her place by her precious teapot shelves. Her collection stood on the back-corner wall of her shop, carefully positioned in perfect order of when her grandmother had purchased them. Daphne adjusted another handle by a quarter of an inch and then stepped back to examine the results.

"This is the third time in two hours that you've straightened your perfectly straight teapots." Rosemary leaned against the counter, refusing to budge from the topic, so Daphne did what any adult should do.

She shot a grimace over her shoulder and proceeded to ignore Rosemary by moving to the adjoining wall where her most prized teapots stood on a shelf all their own. Her grandmother's very first teapot—a Victorian John Bevington in white, encrusted all over with porcelain flowers, even on the handle. Next to it stood a Victorian sterling silver classic teapot her grandfather bought her grandmother for their tenth wedding anniversary. Beside it stood Daphne's favorite, though of lesser value than the previous two—Johnson Brothers Old Britain Castles series, decorated with ancient castles from around England.

A few empty spots waited to be filled with her future purchases . . . someday.

When she had more money than worry.

"Karen Johnson is coming in to talk to me about catering her daughter's bridal shower, and Lisa Jacobson is stopping by in"—she looked down at her dainty watch—"an hour to discuss hosting a rehearsal dinner in the spring. Both thought of me when they saw some of my new posts on social media." She grinned, then shrugged at Rosemary's raised brows. "Okay, so Jack shared the posts, but still, it's visibility." She lifted a finger as if proving her point. "I love weddings, and if I can make this one shine as well as Morgan Dean's this summer, I know I'll get more requests, and those pay well." She nodded, hands on her hips. "So everything needs to be perfect to showcase the atmosphere and skills I can offer."

"No, it needs to be *nice*." Rosemary's raised brow needled higher. "They already know you're professional. But something else is wrong. You're doing your whole"—Rosemary waved her hand toward the teapots—"nesting thing, where you straighten everything like one of those obsessive people."

"I already told you about Mr. Lawson's estimate for the plumbing repairs," Daphne whispered, sending a glance around the room as if the whole shop could hear. "Isn't that enough to cause me to be a little . . . distracted?"

Rosemary's frown crinkled as she slowly shook her head. "I feel like it's something else."

As if her brain had no control of her body, Daphne's gaze flipped to the wall she shared with Finn, hoping he could feel her annoyance through the brick. He'd done nothing to make up for his grumpiness this morning.

Well, nothing but make a lot of noise next door.

One construction worker or appliance delivery man after another, banging, scraping, and yelling so much she had to turn up the volume of her classical music to drown them out. Thankfully, none of her patrons had seemed to mind, but she really needed to talk to him about it.

Which meant she'd have to see him again.

And *seeing* him was the problem.

God really shouldn't make men that handsome if they weren't going to be nice. It violated some unspoken cosmic rule, like serving lukewarm tea or shelving a Dickens novel in the romance section.

"Ah, I see how it is." Rosemary released a long sigh, her lips quirking into that knowing smile that had annoyed Daphne since third grade. "This guy really must be a piece of work to have rattled you so thoroughly." Her lips tipped farther. "I can't wait to meet him."

Traitor!

"He has not rattled me." Daphne sent Rosemary another glare as she moved to the back counter, lowering her voice so that the few patrons sitting nearest her spot wouldn't be disturbed by her little diatribe on the great disappointment that was Finn Dashwood.

A sudden craving for chocolate pushed her into creative mode. "I just don't want to have much to do with—" She paused and leaned toward the wall. From the other side came a deep, rhythmic rumble of bass notes followed by a sudden scream of an electric guitar. What on earth? She gestured toward Finn's shop. "Do you hear that?"

Rosemary rounded the counter and stood beside her by the brick wall. "Sounds like . . . Is that Def Leppard? No, wait." Her palm came up to still Daphne's gasp. "Nope, it's AC/DC."

And the gasp released. Why did he continue to smash all of her ideals about an English gentleman? It was like he was doing it on purpose.

And he'd be the type who would.

She grimaced at the wall as if he could see her. "He is so . . . so . . ."

"Jack says he's a great guy."

"Jack still blows bubbles in his chocolate milk," Daphne shot back.

Rosemary shrugged. "Who doesn't?"

She was surrounded by children!

Daphne's fingers paused on the ingredients in hand, her shoulders deflating at the way her brother could sneak into conversations without even being present. "Besides, Jack would say that about everybody."

"Ooh, this guy has really gotten under your skin." The laugh in Rosemary's voice forced Daphne to get a larger scoop of dark chocolate ice cream from the freezer. "I've *got* to meet him."

"No, you don't." Daphne turned her attention back to the silver malt cup she was holding and poured a touch of salted caramel flavoring into the blend. Too much, probably, but it was salted caramel. She could live with it.

Then she picked up the ice cream scoop again. "What I mean is that we can't always trust Jack. And from what I saw, Mr. Finn Dashwood is not the good sort of neighbor." She pointed the scoop toward the brick wall. "The music? The . . . attitude? He doesn't even like tea."

Rosemary's eyes widened in mock horror. "Oh dear, the unforgivable sin."

"And he's a flirt."

The glimmer in Rosemary's eyes failed to match the seriousness in Daphne's warning. "An Englishman who is single, handsome, a business owner, and a flirt?" She stepped back with the latte in hand. "How can you resist, Daphne?"

Before Daphne could respond with a very thorough answer, Rosemary snatched up the milkshake and turned toward the tables to deliver the smoothie. Daphne fought the urge to stick out her tongue at the back of Rosemary's retreating form.

Resist Finn Dashwood's charm?

She stiffened her resolve. Quite easily.

Wickhams were Wickhams, and she knew the end result of liking one. She'd experienced it before. Sure, it had been in high school, but those first loves should count double.

Maybe triple.

Daphne eyed the French vanilla on the shelf. With a shrug, she added some of it to the malt cup before placing the cup in the mixing machine.

It was bad enough she'd let herself indulge in that little bit of petty revenge with the chalkboard. But it had felt so satisfying to see her handiwork this morning—especially when she'd spotted him through the window, reading it with that reluctant almost-smile tugging at his lips.

Not that she'd been watching for *him* or anything.

She reached for the whipped cream canister, pausing as AC/DC gave way to "Welcome to the Jungle." Good heavens, the man's musical taste was as subtle as a wrecking ball. And as welcome.

Fit his personality.

"Daphne dear."

The familiar sound of Granny D rose from the woman's regular table by the front window. Every day she came. Every day she talked about how much she'd loved her dearest friend, Daphne's grandmother. And every day Granny D tried to convince Daphne that "romance was very close" for her. She'd been saying it for two years. Evidently, Granny D's definition of *close* was different from Daphne's. Two years of "very close" seemed more like "wildly distant" in Daphne's dictionary. But there was no one like Granny D to fill in the gap of a missing grandmother. She'd been Granny's best friend, after all. As opposite as chalk and cheese, as Granny would say, but a great match. Granny D probably knew Daphne and Jack better than anyone in town. And even though Granny's class clashed with Granny D's . . . uniqueness, no one spread love around, in her own quirky way, like Granny D.

Daphne left the milkshake and picked up a fresh pot of hot water along with a Ceylon and India tea bag, moving to the woman's table. "Here you go."

Wrinkles creased the woman's face, and her pale eyes twinkled. "Thank you." But as Daphne stepped back, Granny D grabbed her wrist, the woman's six beaded bracelets clinking together like tiny wind chimes. "I dreamed about you again last night, sugar. Three times with the same dream. You know what that means."

That Granny D was bound and determined to keep Appalachian wives' tales alive and daunting. "That you love me a whole lot to be thinking so hard about me?"

Her smile stretched full, crinkling her face all the more. "Now, sweet girl, you know good and well I pray for you every night afore bed, but this was a surefire promise that love is comin' your way, Daphne. I've dreamed of your wedding day *three times in a row.*"

She emphasized her final sentence with enough volume to draw a look or two from the neighboring tables. Heat skirted up into Daphne's face, so she bent closer to the woman, lowering her voice in a subtle hint. "You keep praying those prayers for me then, Granny D."

With a kiss to the woman's cheek, Daphne checked on a few guests and then returned to the counter to pour the creamy chocolate mixture into two glasses. Rosemary didn't deserve one after her teasing.

Daphne sighed.

But she'd give the other milkshake to her anyway.

Because she was friend-since-grade-school and knew-all-Daphne's-secrets Rosemary. Also, probably deserved a best employee award just for putting up with Daphne over the past year.

Tossing a straw in each of the glasses, she closed her eyes and sipped up the contents of the nearest one. Flavors and chilly cream poured over her tongue. Rich chocolate inspired by the sweet hints of French vanilla and edged with salty caramel. Salt. Sweetness. Rich and dangerously delicious.

Who said she only had to serve tea, right?

For some reason, that had been another crazy rule Daphne had given herself.

She took another taste, and the flavors deepened.

This was definitely a new treat to add to her summer specials list.

"Rosemary." She rushed from around the counter toward her friend, who stood near the front window, just as the bell over Tea Thyme's door chimed to announce a new guest. "You have to try this! It's going on the menu—"

Someone entered, and the air shifted as if the entire shop had been reset to a different frequency.

Daphne's feet and expression froze.

Finn Dashwood stood in her doorway, looking both out of place and frustratingly at ease, a small container in his hands. His presence alone seemed to dwarf the dainty decor, and the contrast of his dark jeans and fitted gray Henley against the pastel paradise of her tea shop was almost laughable.

He wasn't a Darcy. Or a Knightley. Or a Brandon.

So he shouldn't make it work.

And yet . . . he did.

Her gaze drifted to the container he carried, and her heartbeat skittered. Had he actually brought her something?

Could it be that the jerk had a conscience?

"Good afternoon, Miss Austen."

His voice! That unfair, glorious British accent dipped in baritone.

"Welcome to Tea Thy—" Rosemary's greeting cut off as her pale green eyes locked onto Finn. "Goodness. Sakes. Alive."

"Don't start," Daphne muttered under her breath, shooting Rosemary a look, but it was no use. The woman stared with sheer appreciation and absolutely no self-control of her facial muscles. Nothing like reinforcing Finn's ego with Rosemary's impression of a cartoon character who'd just seen a twelve-foot sandwich.

Finn's grin crooked, clearly missing nothing of the little exchange and Rosemary's near hyperventilation.

"That new creation looks very suspiciously unlike tea." He nodded toward the milkshake in her hand.

The residual chill from the ice cream evaporated beneath the sudden flush in her cheeks. "I happen to serve many things in my shop besides tea, Mr. Dashwood. If you'd taken the time to ask rather than tossing around uninformed critiques, I'd have been happy to enlighten you."

Why did he seem to bring out her snarky side? And why did she suddenly want to go bake three batches of dark chocolate croissants?

And why did he have to possess such expressive eyes? Her fingers tightened around the glass in her hands. Tea should only prove a temptation in liquid form.

Not eye color.

"Now, Daphne honey, that ain't no way to talk to our new neighbor."

Granny D had made remarkable speed from her table to the door, clicking her tongue like a chicken on the hunt. "Lord, have mercy," she exclaimed, fanning herself dramatically with a weathered hand adorned with tarnished silver rings. "If you'd told me handsome was comin' to town, I'd have worn my good teeth."

Finn turned, brows high, then broke into a slow, amused grin. "Good afternoon, ma'am." He offered his hand. "Finn Dashwood."

"You sound as good as you look, don't ya'?" Granny D hummed her appreciation as she circled him, making no attempt to hide her appraisal.

She almost whimpered.

There were wonderful things about small Southern towns.

And then there were . . . these moments.

Daphne's face reached a blistery temperature. If Malcom Dean showed up now with his banjo and his toy poodle wearing a hat, the humiliation might just be complete.

"I'm Granny D to everyone here in Wisteria." She placed her hand in his.

"It's a pleasure, Granny D." And Finn raised Granny D's bedazzled hand to his lips and kissed it like the gentleman he was not!

Daphne scowled. Casanova. Evidently, Finn Dashwood saved his surliness for her alone. How special.

Granny D's grin stretched to Sunday lunch proportions. Beside her, Rosemary sighed. "So you're opening a restaurant next door?"

He turned that devastating smile on Rosemary, clearly enjoying all the attention.

In fact, the previously chipper room had grown incredibly quiet.

Just beyond Finn, Mrs. Brubacher, Mrs. Stevens, and Miss Long had stopped their teatime chatter to take in the view. Mrs. Stevens had even resorted to fanning herself with a tea saucer. Edna Rossi sat frozen with a scone halfway to her lips. This did not help Daphne's cause at all. She wanted to scream, "Pretty is as pretty does, so don't let him fool you."

"An English pub, actually."

"Well, that's fantastic." Rosemary sighed . . . again. It was a miracle she still had any air in her lungs at all. "I've never been to England, so thanks for bringing a little of it here."

Her lingering gaze thanked him for more than just the future food. Good grief! Was there anyone in this town capable of maintaining composure in the presence of a British accent? Coming from her, that was saying something!

"I'm Rosemary." Did she just bat her eyelashes? "I've been friends with Daphne since elementary school, which means I know all of her secrets."

Daphne's bottom lip dropped as she turned to Rosemary. Why on earth did she say that?

"Do you now?" Finn's eyebrows rose with interest, and Daphne didn't miss the slightly wicked edge in his smile. It was the look of a man who collected information like valuable currency.

Daphne twitched. "None of which are relevant," she cut in, shooting Rosemary a lethal look that bounced right off her friend's dazed expression. "So? Did you step inside to try a *real* beverage or merely to charm my patrons?"

His grin deepened. Oh, he liked the challenge.

No matter.

She gave her head a shake. Let him charm the room. Daphne wasn't interested in . . . her gaze skimmed down him. *That.*

"You ever notice how the pricklier the berry the sweeter the jam?" Granny D mused to Rosemary, loud enough for everyone to hear.

Rosemary nodded sagely. "Always."

Then they had the audacity to turn and look directly, and quite pointedly, at Daphne.

She narrowed her eyes at both of them, but her glare failed to impact the moment.

"I'm standing right here," Daphne reminded them, and then she waved toward Mr. Demeaning and Dangerous. "Besides, Mr. Dashwood was very clear that he doesn't like tea or . . . neighbors, so I'm at a loss as to why he'd step foot into my tea shop at all."

"A man who don't drink tea ain't died yet from the lack," Granny D declared. "My daddy never touched nothin' but moonshine and creek water. Lived to be ninety-two." She leaned toward Finn conspiratorially. "Course, he did see the wampus cat three times, but that might've been the moonshine talkin'."

Finn cast a wide-eyed look at Daphne. "Wampus cat?"

Daphne mouthed, *"Don't ask."*

His gaze held hers, and his slow smile sent her pulse skittering like a runaway rabbit. On steroids. She ignored it . . . and thought of icebergs.

"I'm actually here to provide a peace offering." Finn dipped his head and set the container on the empty table nearby, his look searching. Almost . . . penitent? "My gran's sticky toffee pudding."

The icebergs in her mind melted. And then the scent hit her. Butter. Vanilla. Caramel. Oh no.

Do not give in to the temptation. Her attention shifted from the pudding to the man.

"You bake?"

"Among other talents." His gaze locked onto hers. "Stereotypes are tricky things, aren't they?"

"Lord a' mercy." Granny D fanned herself again. "A man with an accent who bakes? That's like finding a four-leaf clover under a full moon. Powerful lucky." She nudged Rosemary. "Ain't that right?"

"*Very* lucky," Rosemary agreed with exaggerated seriousness, the humor in her eyes sending another flush into Daphne's face.

With friends like these . . .

"Well, I hope I'm lucky enough to make up for my earlier behavior to Miss Austen." Finn's confidence never wavered, but was there a hint of genuineness in his tone. He *had* brought dessert, and Granny always said that anyone who used their own hands to make a dish should be worth listening to.

Daphne blinked a few times. The stares of the whole room seemed to be on this embarrassing performance. Heaven help her, she couldn't seem to sort out what to say.

"Why don't we continue this conversation away from the front door?" And out of view of the entire restaurant. She could practically hear the rumors spinning down Main Street about her imminent nuptials with the British bad boy. Ridiculous.

Without waiting for his response, she sent the room a tight smile, gingerly picked up the container of sticky toffee pudding, and wove through the tables and patrons until she slipped through the kitchen door.

Finn—and Granny D—close behind.

"I had no intention of upsetting your afternoon, Daphne," Finn said, his gaze roaming over her kitchen, likely finding fault with it as he seemed to do with everything else. "I only wanted to start over. Fresh, as you'd suggested."

Daphne set the sticky toffee on the counter and turned, milkshake still in hand and growing colder by the second. "It seemed my suggestion didn't work so well this morning."

He rubbed his jaw, his lip arching slightly. "I did mention I wasn't the best morning person."

She opened her mouth to call out his excuse, but he rushed ahead. "Would it help if I told you I spent a large part of the afternoon making that pudding instead of painting the kitchen? Penance for my poor behavior." He searched her face, brow creased. Penance should not look so . . . pleasant. "And . . . there may have been a small fire involved."

"A fire?" The women spoke in unison, though their tones varied from alarm to unholy delight.

"Hardly worth mentioning," he said smoothly. "The point is, I'm trying to make amends. Even if your shop does look like a Victorian valentine exploded in it."

Daphne narrowed her eyes. "And you were doing so well."

Granny D leaned around Daphne, plucking a fork from the drawer. "Fire's a good sign. Shows passion." She nodded, waving the fork. "My third husband, Walter, set fire to our chicken coop tryin' to impress me with fireworks. Knew right then he was the one."

Daphne pressed a palm to her forehead.

Finn, clearly enjoying her discomfort, winked at Granny D. "Baby steps," he said, all easy confidence. "Now, are you going to try the pudding?" And without waiting for consent—because why start now?—he plucked the milkshake from Daphne's hand, replacing it with the pudding container in one smooth motion, even producing a fork from his back pocket like a magician.

Presumptuous.

"I'll taste test this in the meantime." He raised the milkshake to her as if cheering her health.

Her eyes narrowed even more.

"Oh honey, you know another thing they say about men who can bake," Granny D stage-whispered to Daphne, peeking around her shoulder to the container.

Daphne really wondered who "they" were and their impeccable, timely advice.

"They're good with their hands and patient in the kitchen." She waggled her eyebrows.

Finn didn't even try to hide his grin.

"Stop encouraging him," Daphne hissed to them both, her face at four hundred degrees.

"You first." Finn twirled the straw in the milkshake, grin wicked. "I already know of your excellent baking skills."

"Fine." Daphne stabbed her fork into the pudding with a little more force than necessary. "Especially if it will help you return to your side of the wall and stop being such a"—she gestured vaguely at him—"distraction."

"I don't think anyone else minds such a distraction, especially midweek," Granny D offered. "Helps get us through the rest of it, I'd say."

Daphne tried not to wince at the scene they'd just caused out in the restaurant.

Dinner and a show?

Sigh.

Best to get this over with. She lifted the lid, and the rich aroma of warm toffee and dates enveloped her senses. One bite into the warm sponge cake and decadent toffee sauce, she nearly forgot her predicament—until she glanced up to find Finn watching her.

Closely.

With such an intensity, she nearly forgot how rude he was, but then . . . the pudding flavors reignited in her mouth.

Delicious. She'd had sticky toffee pudding before, but this? This had layers.

She swallowed the bite, her tastebuds assessing the flavors still playing across her tongue. "Did you add . . . rum?"

Something flickered in Finn's eyes. Different from the usual smug amusement. A hint of surprise? And something . . . else?

"I did."

"And . . . is that a hint of cinnamon?"

One side of his mouth curved. "Indeed."

The air thickened, her attention unable to shift from his eyes. "It's very good."

Silence hitched the moment between them. Slowing it. Squeezing Daphne's breath a little tighter. And—for only a second—Daphne thought she could name his expression.

Admiration?

Respect?

And the very idea threatened to derail the bad-boy images about him from her mind.

"You know what my granny always said?" Granny D piped up, dipping her fork into the pudding. "When a person makes you somethin' sweet after a quarrel, it means they been thinkin' about you."

Daphne stiffened. She cleared her throat and stepped away from the pull in Finn's eyes. "Probably only thinking of ways to insult my shop."

"Only part of the time," Finn admitted, the dimple making an appearance.

Was he just an entire collection of distracting clichés meant to develop her self-control? She glanced heavenward for clarification.

"And if it tastes this good," Granny D declared, eyes closing in appreciation as she took a generous bite, "then he's been thinkin' mighty hard."

Daphne nearly wrestled the fork away from the woman. Clearly, good food only encouraged her to say embarrassing things. "Or, he needed it to be really good to make up for being insufferable."

Finn lifted the milkshake to his lips with an infuriating lack of concern. Hero-quality lips, Daphne's treacherous brain noted. Pity about the words that came out of them.

She shook away the thoughts of English accents and biceps and tea-colored eyes and that dimple. Even if she were the only person in the entire town, she would not be charmed by Finn Dashwood.

His golden eyes met hers. Heat flared across her face, but she refused to look away.

Daphne needed to make one thing very clear.

Despite the near-hyperventilation his cologne, accent, and presence caused, she was not an idiot.

And she would be certain to reassure him of that fact . . . once he tasted her milkshake.

••••••••••

Daphne Austen's eyes had taken on the most mesmerizing glow, deepening those azure hues to cobalt. Had he held such an expression when he watched her taste his pudding? The anticipation? The unmitigated desire to please another food connoisseur?

Finn placed the straw to his lips.

Daphne leaned forward slightly. "The . . . the second sip is when you get the full effect." Her voice carried a soft, measured quality that somehow made him nearly forget everything else. Not in a seductive way but in true curiosity, kinship. This shared bond of creation and cooking like-minded inventors understood . . . with an added something else he couldn't quite define. A sweetness? Genuineness?

And, God help him, something inside him wanted to keep that glint alive, stoke the teasing, the fire, the challenge.

And that was not a common occurrence in his world among single women.

He held her gaze. "Like a second chance?"

Her smile faltered, and something in his chest squeezed tight. Too much. He'd gone too far, let something slip he hadn't meant to. He drew in another sip of the milkshake. Delicious. Surprising.

Like her?

Clearing his throat, he forced a shrug and raised the glass toward her. "This certainly bests any of your teas, no question."

Her shoulders slumped, and though he'd meant for the deflection, he hated the disappointment in her eyes. Despite himself, he offered, "I suppose you could call it something like . . . The Lizzy Bennet."

Her gaze snapped back to his, blue eyes wide. "Why?"

He shrugged and took another sip, rolling the flavors over his tongue. French vanilla. A great addition to dark chocolate. "Well, the salty part certainly suits her sharp wit."

Daphne tilted her head, studying him. He couldn't resist continuing, removing the disappointment. "And the dark chocolate? That's the depth of her character."

Her lips parted slightly, the pink bottom one looking entirely too soft for his peace of mind.

"But the surprising hint of French vanilla . . . with almonds, is it?" He leaned in just a fraction. "You taste it as an afterthought. Subtle, unexpected. It makes you take a second sip just to be sure. Much like Elizabeth and Darcy, wouldn't you say? The first impression wasn't as clear as the second."

A tiny, strangled sound came from her throat before she abruptly looked away.

"Wowee, sounds like I need a sip of this here milkshake, Daphne dear."

Finn turned just in time to catch Granny D arching a knowing brow at him, humor twinkling in her pale eyes. "She has a tendency to experiment with new drinks when she's bothered about somethin'."

Bothered. His gaze flicked back to Daphne, whose cheeks had taken on a shade that would put the raspberries in her scones to shame. A rather fetching hue on her.

"That's not true, Granny D."

"So frustration inspires your creativity, does it?" He took another slow sip of the milkshake, his gaze never leaving her face. "I'm surprised you haven't invented at least a dozen new recipes since I moved in."

"Actually," she muttered, recovering just enough to give him a defiant tilt of her chin, "I have had more ideas recently."

"I wonder why."

She ignored that. "I haven't modified the food recipes, though. They're exactly as my grandmother made them."

"Are they?"

Her spine straightened, that familiar fight stance kicking in. "Some things are already perfect as they are."

Ah yes, the color-coded kitchen, the meticulously arranged canisters—this woman lived for structure. "I'm certain she wouldn't mind. Experimenting is part of the fun of cooking."

Granny D chuckled and took another bite of the toffee, waving the fork at him. "Now I'm gonna get back to my tea afore the two of ya'll come to blows, but it was a real pleasure to meet you, Finn Dashwood."

He dipped his head to the woman, her colorful clothing and string of varying length necklaces marking her in his memory. "A delight, Granny D."

She reached up and patted his cheek. He nearly flinched at the unexpected . . . affection. His mind wanted to label it as assault, but he was in the South. Not England.

"I'll stop by tomorrow with some of my homemade lemonade."

For some reason, the statement sounded more like a warning than an offering. Daphne's raised brows may have confirmed the former.

As soon as the woman exited the kitchen, Daphne added, "It's adult lemonade. Just to prepare you. Homemade." Her look turned pointed. "From the *mountains*."

"And that's a bad thing?"

"No, the mountains are great. I'm just saying that Granny D's lemonade packs an unexpected punch." She dipped the fork back into the pudding and took another bite before jabbing the fork toward him. "And, for your information, I don't have to experiment to know when a good thing is good."

Ah, he'd hit on her pride. Why not poke a little more? "But not great?"

"Do you just like to argue?"

"Not usually." He lifted the glass again, watching her over the rim. "But you make it so much fun."

Her lips twitched, and for a moment he thought she might actually laugh. Then, as if remembering herself, she abruptly restacked a nearby row of napkins.

He had to admit the game was entertaining. He only needed to be careful to keep it light. Simple. Uncomplicated.

"I know we didn't get off to the best start, but I'm not the villain you think I am, Miss Austen. Most people find me quite friendly. Honest. Charming, even."

A spark lit in her eyes, but before he could enjoy it, she pulled back, doubling the distance between them. Pity. He was developing a fondness for that spark.

"Friendly, huh?" She raised a brow. "Well, then, I think it would be particularly friendly and charming if you'd do me a little favor."

He shrugged. "What is that?"

"Turn down that music you have blaring from the other side of the wall."

He leaned back, feigning offense. "Blaring?" He paused, listening. AC/DC barely hummed through the walls. "You can hardly hear it."

"You might not be able to hear it." Her words dropped to a whisper—a harsh whisper. "But I hear it very well. Would you mind turning it down a little?"

He took another drink of the milkshake. "No, I can't." He even softened it with a small bow of his head. "I do apologize."

"Why not?" Her question curbed into a little squeak. "You can't expect people to enjoy eating to that"—she gestured to the brick wall separating their establishments—"that hideousness."

AC/DC? Hideous? He feigned a look of deep injury. "It keeps me from hearing the classical nonsense you blast in your princess tearoom."

Daphne's mouth dropped open, and Finn immediately regretted his reaction, but she gave him no time for an apology.

"Nonsense? Babies' brains develop better when they hear classical music."

Oh well, why let the moment go without a chance to wind her up a bit. "So that's your excuse for listening to such snobbish drivel then?" He pushed back from the counter, heat crawling through his middle in a mixture of regret and frustration. What was it about this petite, pink-clad woman that inspired his . . . engagement?

Her lips parted, but then, like a true warrior, she regrouped. "First of all," she said, stepping closer, "a man with such a deliciously rich voice and utterly delightful accent should never waste it defending bad taste in music." She pinched the air as if trying to squeeze the words from floating in her memory. "*Ever.*"

His lips twitched. "And yet, here I am. Wasting away, one power chord at a time."

His response clearly derailed her attack list of his music choices because her lips tipped the slightest bit. "Tragic, really."

"Tragic," he agreed. "But you know what they say—every villain is the hero of his own sound system."

Her eyes narrowed for the briefest moment before she continued, "Which leads me to my second reason." She leaned in, just enough for him to catch the faint scent of lavender and sugar. Her sudden smile, all soft and welcoming, shot through him like a warning light, but he fell for the trap. "Do you really think I'm a princess?"

He grinned. "Most certainly."

Her own smile was slow. Dangerous. "Then do as I say and turn down your abominable music."

He chuckled. "This has been fun, but as you said, I must get back to my side of the wall."

He dipped his chin, keeping the milkshake in hand just to irritate her. To his surprise, she followed him all the way to the front door.

"The least you can do is try to be neighborly," she hissed behind him. "Just a little less rock music during afternoon tea?"

Of course he would turn it down. It was a small request, after all.

But why let her know that.

And, neighborly? Oh, he could do even better than neighborly. A deliciously infuriating idea came to mind. Well, infuriating for her.

"I'll consider it, of course." He paused at the threshold. "And I should probably thank you for the sweet message you left me this morning."

Daphne's blush evaporated and her bottom lip dropped. Every head in the room swiveled toward her. Finn nearly lost control of his laugh. Turnabout and fair play . . . and all that?

He dipped his head, stepping back through the door. "So I returned the favor." And with one final wink, just to sweeten the deal, he was gone.

....

Sweet message?

All the heat drained from Daphne's face. What was Finn Dashwood talking about?

Every head in the room swiveled toward her.

His wink landed like an exclamation mark on his ridiculous statement. How dare he turn her chalkboard joke into some kind of romantic gesture? There wasn't a single ounce of romance in that little prank.

And he knew exactly what sort of rumors his implication would spark.

At teatime.

In front of her entire tearoom.

Daphne blinked as the room narrowed into a tunnel of stunned silence, the door swinging shut behind Finn. Her fingers curled into fists at her sides. She nearly did something entirely unladylike—like chase after him and pummel him with . . . her shoe!

Instead, she turned back to the room with what she hoped was a composed smile. "Just so we're all clear, Mr. Dashwood does not like tea." She nodded for emphasis. "That should clear up anything he may have implied about me. And him."

The glimmer in Granny D's eyes only fueled Daphne's humiliation . . . and determination. She was not, nor would she ever be interested in Mr. Finn Dashwood.

With that, she bolted for the door, rounding the front of her shop.

Her carefully curated chalkboard—previously home to an elegant list of tea specials and baked delights—had been defiled. Scrawled across it in atrocious handwriting (honestly, was he six?) was a new message:

Tried coffee again.

Smelled like determination.

Tasted like success.

Gave me the energy to win an argument I
wasn't even having.

Would recommend to all tea drinkers looking to upgrade their lives.

Final Rating: ★★★★★

Daphne inhaled sharply and snapped a glare to the front door of his pub.

Oh. It. Was. On.

CHAPTER 6

@TeaThymeNC: Out of sugar, running low on patience, but still steeping. If it's too hot for tea, cool off with our newest treat: The Lizzy Bennet—a dark chocolate milkshake with a twist. Sweet, bold, and impossible to resist. #TeaLife #CaffeineAndHope #PrideAndDeliciousness

> **@WisteriaGeneralStore:** New merch drop: "Sweet, Bold & Impossible to Resist" T-shirts available in four pastel shades. Now taking preorders for matching mugs. #WisteriaStyle #LizzyBennetEnergy #GrannyApproved
>
> **@TGDPub:** Naming a milkshake after a literary heroine and giving a neighbor chocolate? Flirtation or foreshadowing, Miss Austen? Asking for . . . literary purposes. 😏 #DarkChocolateAndDenial #TeamLizzy #BeanWaterStillWins #IllTakeOneOfThoseTshirts
>
> **@TeaThymeNC:** There was no flirting. There is no flirting. Just a responsible milkshake and an alarming number of unsolicited opinions. Now, if you'll excuse me, I have spoons to polish. #Chocolate4All #NoRomanticSubtextWhatsoever

@GrannyDOfficial: Had one. May marry it. If Mr. Darcy doesn't show up soon, I'll settle for that milkshake. #GrannyKnowsBest #DarkChocolateIsMyLoveLanguage #FlirtingPairsWithChocolate

@PastorNateNHC: Some of you are dangerously close to idol worship. That said . . . I might have baptized mine with espresso. #CaffeinateAndRepent #GraceTastesLikeChocolate

@TheRidgesFineDining: Bold of you to create emotional dependency in one menu item. We approve. And fear you. #CulinarySassQueen #TeaRoomDominance

FINN HALF EXPECTED DAPHNE to appear later that evening with some form of retaliation—a glitter bomb perhaps or her attempt at a "strong" tea. Which, coming from her, likely meant something floral and vaguely offensive. But no sign of her. Not so much as a glare from the shop window.

She was staying well behind her wall.

While setting up The Green Dragon's online accounts, he'd stumbled across a handful from Wisteria, including Daphne's. Clearly, she hadn't been at it long—her follower count barely cleared triple digits—but her humor peeked through, nonetheless.

And she'd actually taken his suggestion about The Lizzy Bennet? Finn tried—really tried—not to grin, but it clawed its way out anyway. No doubt her reference to being "low on patience" had everything to do with him. He wouldn't deny he enjoyed lingering in a woman's mind long after he'd left, even if it was for all the wrong reasons.

Still, he hated to admit he was mildly disappointed she hadn't turned up at the pub before he and Lucy left for dinner at the Wisteria Manor. Surely a woman who'd dared a chalkboard duel wasn't above escalating hostilities.

Then again, maybe his implying their "fake amor" in front of her tearoom had been a bit much.

But honestly, she'd started it. He'd been perfectly content in his antisocial Britishness until she'd shown up with her sunshine and scones far too early in the morning for civilized conversation.

And then left him a note on his own chalkboard.

Her fault. Plain and simple. He was merely finishing what she started.

If flirting and milkshakes followed, then all the better.

Still grinning to himself, Finn crested the hill and spotted the large stone sign that read: Wisteria Manor.

And the sprawling stone house poised on a hill overlooking the town of Wisteria certainly lived up to its reputation with its grand Victorian architecture softened by cascading wisteria vines. As lovely a combination of quaint and elegant as anything Finn had seen back in England.

Lanterns flickered along the drive, drawing them through a tangle of wildflowers and towering trees. Against the evening blush, the gray stone glowed, the mountains rising like silent sentinels behind it. The whole thing looked like the kind of place you'd find in a painting.

Which, annoyingly, made him think of Daphne again.

He frowned and guided the car around back, where Harry and Maggie's portion of the manor branched off like an annex. The rest of the house held guests eager for that blend of small-town charm and old-world grandeur—a tagline Harry had leaned into with unrelenting glee.

In the rearview mirror, Lucy's wide-eyed awe reflected back at him. "It looks like a castle, Daddy."

Right on cue.

"Fits this town, doesn't it?" he said. The place was nothing like the old manors back home, but it belonged here somehow, nestled into the wild tangle of mountains.

Margaret Coleman met them at the door, her golden hair touched with silver, her smile so warm it erased any hesitation Finn thought Lucy might have had in being apart from them for a year.

"There's my sweet girl!"

Lucy darted into Maggie's arms before Finn could so much as blink.

"Look how big you've grown," Maggie said, casting a grin up at Finn. "Whatever you're feeding her, it's working."

Finn grinned and followed Maggie and Lucy through the door into a cozy sitting room complete with rock fireplace to match the exterior of the home.

"I brought the dragon you gave me for my birfday." Lucy brandished her green stuffed toy for Maggie's inspection.

"It rarely leaves her side," Finn added, leaning in for his own hug from Maggie. "Even inspired the pub's name. Bit of Tolkien thrown in."

Maggie's smile softened. "Isn't that the sweetest thing? I thought after not visiting for a year, she'd have forgotten about us."

"Not with the weekly video chats." Finn slipped farther into the entry. The chats had helped ease some of the ache after his father's death. Harry and Margaret had taken on the role of surrogate grandparents for Lucy as if they'd been made for it.

"Well, I'm glad they bridged the span of time until I got to hug her again." Margaret pressed a kiss to Lucy's head, then looked back up at him. "And I have a good notion Wisteria is going to love The Green Dragon as much as the folks who run it."

"Well, maybe not the local tea shop owner next door." Harry's rich laugh preceded him into the room.

Maggie's chuckle blended in with her husband's as Harry came up beside her, his arm resting at her waist. "News travels fast around here, Finn."

"So it seems." He ground out the phrase.

Harry clapped him on the shoulder and led them through French doors into a small dining room bathed in sunset. The mountains smoldered in the distance, bathed in gold and rose like some painter's fever dream.

Finn paused by the window, letting the view settle the tightness in his chest.

"Spectacular, isn't it?" Harry murmured beside him. "People say the mountains grow on you. At first I laughed. But it's true. There's something about them that weaves into your soul."

Finn studied him, one brow listing.

Harry shrugged, grinning. "I know. I responded the same way too." He gestured with a nod toward the table. "Let's join the ladies at the table."

They all settled around the table, and the scene grounded Finn. Something about being near Harry and Maggie again offered a comfort he'd not fully expected. Perhaps it was because Harry reminded Finn so much of Dad in the way they interacted and teased. Or maybe it was the solidness of Harry and Maggie's relationship that afforded a sense of certainty about relationships he'd not felt in a long time.

Their relationship was good for Lucy too.

"Harry says you're hoping to open the pub next week?" Maggie passed him the mashed potatoes.

"It's only because of Harry that I can say that." Finn scooped some onto Lucy's plate, then his own. "Our apartment furniture should arrive tomorrow, and I'm waiting for just a few extra supplies, but otherwise we're ready."

"He's already got the menu sorted." Harry passed his phone to Maggie. "He sent me a snap of it earlier today."

"'Shepherd's pie, fish and chips,' of course," Maggie read off. "The Dashwood Burger? You've gone full British."

"Just the start," Finn said, warming at the thought. "Once I've got a better handle on Southern food, I'll work some of it in as well." He moved his palm across the air as if reading a placard. "Where proper pub fare meets Southern charm."

"Funny," Harry mused. "Sounds like a perfect pairing with the tea shop next door." Harry waggled his brows. "Whether you like it or not."

Finn rolled his eyes and sighed. "Let's not start *that* conversation."

"Oh?" Margaret's eyes lit up. "Daphne is such a dear. She brings me the most wonderful lavender scones when I'm feeling under the weather and is one of the most generous souls you'll ever meet, Finn."

"Can we go to her tea shop?" Lucy bounced in her seat, practically vibrating with excitement. "She had flowers and teapots in her window!"

"Absolutely not," Finn said too quickly, then softened his tone at Lucy's fallen expression. "We're too busy getting the pub ready, lamb. But . . . perhaps later?"

Across the table, Harry leaned back in his chair, eyes twinkling with far too much amusement. "Afraid your daughter might prefer tea parties to pub grub?"

"I'm afraid of nothing of the sort." Finn stabbed at his roasted salmon with unnecessary force. "I simply don't need Lucy getting attached to"—he waved his fork vaguely—"all that frilly business."

"All that frilly business," Margaret repeated slowly, "or the lovely young woman running it?"

"Either," Finn said firmly, but the heat creeping up his neck betrayed him. "She's just so . . . *feminine*."

"Feminine?" Harry barked out a laugh. "I was under the impression you tended toward the feminine sort quite regularly."

Finn glared at Harry as he rubbed at the heat climbing his neck. "I mean all the pink cardigans and vintage teacups and Jane Austen quotes."

"And quick wit," Harry added. "And kindness. And quite capable of giving you a run for your money, I'd say, based on that chalkboard war you've got going."

"Oh, right." Margaret's eyes caught some of Harry's twinkle. "I heard about this. Are you in a sour mood because Daphne's winning?"

"No one is winning, because there is no war," Finn insisted, but he couldn't quite hide his smile. Harry and Margaret were plainly baiting him. And—dash it—he was falling headlong into it. "It's merely a . . . professional disagreement about beverage preferences."

"Of course it is." Harry nodded, his entire expression comprised of mock seriousness.

Margaret, watching with keen observation, took a sip of her wine and casually joined the fray. "I've known Daphne since she was about Lucy's age," she mused. "Watched her grow up in that tea shop with her dear grandmother. Despite all those lace doilies and tasty sweets, she's borne her share of difficulties. There's steel under all that pink. I wouldn't discredit her ability to challenge you, Finn."

Finn scoffed internally. His definition of *difficulties* and Daphne's were likely worlds apart. Life was hard. Messy. It required sacrifice. Princesses rarely came prepared for the cost of a ready-made family.

"Which is exactly why Lucy doesn't need to meet her." Finn pointed his fork at Harry. "The last thing I need is my daughter conspiring with the enemy."

"The enemy?" Margaret's eyebrows rose. "Such strong words for someone who declared there was no war."

Lucy giggled. "Daddy's ears are getting red."

"They are not," Finn muttered, though he could feel the telltale burn. "And this conversation is over."

"Of course," Harry agreed too easily. "Though I should mention that Daphne does host a weekly children's story time. In full princess costume, I believe. Complete with tiaras for all the little guests . . ."

Lucy's gasp of delight was matched only by Finn's groan of despair. "Harry Coleman, you are an evil man."

"Just doing my part to support local businesses." Harry raised his wineglass in a mock toast. "And perhaps encourage some . . . community bonding."

"Don't you even—" Finn started.

"Daddy, can we go to story time? Please?" Lucy clasped her hands together. "I promise I won't become a tea princess. I'll still be your dragon girl!"

Finn looked at his daughter's pleading face, then at Harry's smug expression, and finally at Margaret's knowing smile. He was fighting a losing battle on all fronts.

"We'll see," he conceded.

Lucy squealed with delight. Harry chuckled into his wineglass.

Finn groaned and reached for his own drink. He was going to need it.

To survive this dinner. To survive this town.

And definitely to survive whatever inevitable disaster would come when his impressionable daughter joined forces with Daphne Austen.

Heaven help him.

....

@TeaThymeNC: Public Service Announcement: If your morning tea tastes slightly more dramatic than usual, don't worry—it's just been infused with the stress of waking up to "Under Pressure" blaring through the walls. Some neighbors prefer coffee-fueled chaos. Others appreciate the finer things in life . . . like peace, quiet, and a properly brewed Earl Grey. #PrayForMySanity #TeaOverTurmoil #SoundproofingFund #SomePeopleHaveNoTaste

@TGDPub: Strange. My morning coffee had just the right hint of smug satisfaction. Might be why

"Don't Stop Me Now" has been stuck in my head all day. #PurelyCoincidental #CaffeineAndClassics #SomePeopleAreTooDramatic

@WisteriaWeekly: Breaking: Local café war escalates as Daphne Austen and Finn Dashwood go steep-to-brew over hot beverages. Sources say tension is "positively cozy." #SipsAndSpats #WisteriaWatch #WillTheyWontThey

@JackAustenPhotography: I'm just here for the inevitable slo-mo montage of Daphne angrily steeping tea to "Bohemian Rhapsody." #ComingToCinemas #AustenUnhinged #SteepItReal

@WisteriaBookClub: Pretty sure the neighbors are communicating exclusively in Queen lyrics now. Next up: "Somebody To Love." #LiteraryShenanigans #MusicalMatchmaking #YouHeardItHereFirst

@PastorNateNHC: We are not starting a battle of the brews before morning prayer. Although, hypothetically speaking, if one were to choose a side . . . #TeaByGrace #EspressoForgiveness #HolyGrounds

@WisteriaInn: Just a gentle reminder that all emotional breakdowns (tea or coffee induced) are welcome at the inn. We have robes and lemon shortbread. #FromBeverageWars2Dating #TheresMoreThanMochaInTheAir

@TeaThymeNC: I'll respond when my hearing returns. And once I've finished brewing tranquili-tea. Which, by the way, pairs beautifully with noise-canceling headphones. Btw, the scones are fresh, so we carry on. #BlessedAndSoundproofed #OneOfUsWillBreak #ItWontBeMe #SurvivalByScone

@SheriffGrady: Wisteria's version of gang warfare: Tea drinkers with embroidered aprons vs. coffee folks in vintage band tees. Y'all need to calm down and eat a muffin. #SconePeaceAccords #SmallTownSheriffChronicles

Despite the bridal shower in the books and the possibility of another next month, Daphne's savings account remained much too low to afford Mr. Lawson's repairs yet, which meant her lovely shop was a ticking time bomb. At any moment, those pipes could go.

Plus, Daphne desperately needed to replace her refrigerator. One of her ovens edged near extinction too.

But she needed more income. Bigger or more catering options.

Branching out to add a few more items to the menu had shifted her usual morning routine a half hour, so even the sun wasn't awake when she entered the tea shop's kitchen to prep. Winston, her loyal retriever, hadn't approved.

She drew in a breath.

But sometimes change was good.

Or, in this case, necessary.

At least her social media presence was slowly growing. Jack had assured her that online engagement took time and consistency, and she was starting to see some results—strangers commenting on photos of her pastries, reposts of her aesthetic tea setups. But likes and shares weren't going to pay for her much-needed renovations, a truth she'd only mentioned to Rosemary and Jack.

The former said she'd keep an ear out for more opportunities.

The latter offered her money.

Which he really couldn't spare since he was renovating his own place.

The dimly lit tea shop ushered her forward, and she flipped on the light switch. They flickered before brightening the room. With a little hum to mark her morning routine, Daphne was filling the quiet with welcome percolation of boiling water and working her morning magic on some breakfast pastries when the back door screeched with someone's entry.

"Raspberries!" Rosemary's voice came before she rounded the doorway into the restaurant. "You know how to make my morning spectacular."

"I'm self-medicating." Daphne set the tray of scones on the counter, drizzling a thick swirl of vanilla icing over each one.

"Oooh." Her friend rounded the counter and slid her purse into its usual hiding spot. "Still brooding about yesterday's Finn dilemma?"

Daphne sighed dramatically, pushing the raspberries just out of Rosemary's reach in protest. She'd already endured two unsolicited lectures on dating a "foreigner," one glare from a jealous nineteen-year-old, and a collection of knowing looks from half the town. If she had a dollar for every suggestive smirk she'd encountered while walking downtown, she could upgrade the plumbing tomorrow.

All of which confirmed what she already knew: She absolutely, positively would never date Finn Dashwood.

He wasn't her type. At all.

And apart from being female, she wasn't his.

Men like Finn didn't settle down. They charmed and dazzled and flitted off like very attractive mayflies, leaving a trail of broken hearts and questionable playlists. The whole flirty, devil-may-care attitude reminded her too much of her dad. Finn Dashwood was the poster child for temporary.

And Daphne? She'd had her fill of temporary.

"There is no dilemma. Just an annoyance." She rolled some of her tension off her shoulders. "An annoying distraction." Though, to his credit, he had turned down his music yesterday afternoon, making him a little less annoying.

"You're not kidding." Rosemary whistled low. "That much-too-short glimpse I got of him yesterday? Let's just say, if he's the standard for British masculinity, I'm relocating."

Daphne snorted and busied herself by adding diced peaches to a new scone recipe that had popped into her head this morning. "Maybe focus on helping me drum up some business before you apply for citizenship."

"Oh, right!" Rosemary slid into her apron, tying it in the back as she moved toward the counter. "I've passed the word around a little."

"Thanks." Daphne nodded. "And I'm thinking of running an ad in the *Journal* to promote the tearoom for bridal showers and maybe even small wedding receptions. What do you think?"

"Well, that's daring of you." Rosemary's head came up. "Wait. You've never advertised?"

"Not really. I just hoped for word of mouth, which has worked well with birthday parties and family reunions, but weddings are where the real money is and—"

"Listen, if anyone was created to make a wedding or bridal shower or whatever else beautiful, it's you, Daph." Rosemary dropped on the stool and slid the raspberries close enough to snatch a few. "You make people feel special. It's just what you do! You just need to let more people know."

"Thanks for that." She sent Rosemary a smile and cast the room a glance. "I love this place." Daphne stepped around Rosemary and walked toward the front door, working up the courage to voice an idea. For some reason, ideas kept coming in spurts over the past few days. "And there's something else. You know the large patio I share out back with the building next door?" Her thought immediately escalated in to Mr. Hotface Next Door territory. Her throat burned.

Rosemary perked up. "Sure. Cute spot."

"Well, it's got a great view of the river and the manor's pastureland. I was thinking . . . it might work as a venue for small bridal showers or rehearsal dinners."

"With the gazebo? And the mountains?" Rosemary practically

sprinted to the French doors leading to the terrace. "Daphne, that's brilliant. Why didn't you think of this a year ago?"

Daphne followed, refusing to dampen the mood with the obvious. Granny had been in a hospital bed, fading away after her heart attack. "I didn't have my Pinterest problem a year ago. Pinterest changes you."

The morning crowd trickled in, offering a welcome distraction. Regulars like Mrs. Hayes and her usual party, Mr. Lux and his wife of sixty years, and Mr. Harmon, her grandfather's old friend. A couple of out-of-towners admired her teapot collection and stayed long enough to order breakfast.

Two college girls on their way to the community college ducked in for their usual London Fog lattes and cranberry-orange muffins, waving on their way out with sleepy smiles and lavender-sugar smudges on their sleeves.

A good morning, all things considered.

And not one sound from her next-door neighbor.

Then the door jingled again.

Rosemary sucked in a breath so sharp Daphne thought she might have to perform the Heimlich maneuver. "Heaven have mercy," she whispered in a reverent hush.

Daphne turned from the cash register just in time to nearly drop a roll of quarters.

Finn Dashwood strolled in like the cover model for some magazine called *Effortless British Charm*—pale blue button-down (the top buttons daringly undone), dark jeans that frankly ought to require a warning label, and sunglasses that probably had their own agent.

Thankfully, those sunglasses kept his infamously infuriating eyes under wraps.

Unfortunately, nothing could shield her from his voice.

"Ladies."

Just one word. Rich. Smooth. Laced with so much teasing it should've come with a side of whipped cream. The sound sent an unwelcome tingle from her eardrums straight down to her collarbone. Granny had never prepared her for weaponry of this variety . . . or potency. She had to summon every BBC adaptation of Wickham and Mr. Churchill just to stay upright.

Definitely an unfair advantage to her English-loving heart.

"Mr. Dashwood."

"I came to thank you for my special delivery of . . ." He set a mug on the counter with theatrical disgust, lifting one brow over the rim of his glasses.

Daphne bit the inside of her cheek to keep from grinning. She'd heard his door unlock half an hour ago and seized the opportunity to sneak next door and leave a steaming cup of her *special blend* on the pub's counter.

He gestured to the mug with an exaggerated shudder. "This abomination."

"Abomination?" She feigned offense. "That, I'll have you know, is Earl Grey with oat milk and just a hint of lavender. Specially brewed for those who want to upgrade their lives." She even quoted his own chalkboard slogan while she was at it.

Finn leveled her with a flat stare. "I took one sip and immediately questioned every decision that led me to this moment."

"I hope music choices were involved in those questions." She smiled sweetly, and it was probably a little too satisfying to watch him grimace. "You're welcome."

"How did you even get in?" He leaned closer, lowering his shades. Unfortunately, it was at the exact moment his warm, ridiculously appealing scent hit her like a sneak attack.

She did not sway. (Barely.)

"Do you have a secret passage or something?" His eyes narrowed. "You'd be the sort."

Daphne pushed back from the counter, doing her best to clear the mental fog of Eau de Dashwood. "Like I'd tell you." She slid a raspberry muffin toward him. "Muffin?"

"Hmm . . ." He accepted it, keeping his gaze on her like she was the puzzle he hadn't quite solved. Then he sighed and pushed back from the counter. "I just wanted to be neighborly and let you know a few workmen will be here within the hour to replace some floorboards behind the bar. It might get noisy."

Daphne angled her body slightly, trying to maintain her composure. "Thank you for the warning this time."

"When do you hope to open up the pub?" This from Rosemary, who'd rounded the counter to sit right beside Finn, plopping her chin on her hand and staring up at him in rapt wonder.

"The end of next week."

Wow, that was fast.

Finn glanced back at Daphne. "But I assume my competition isn't worried?"

A very unladylike snort emerged from Daphne's nose as she folded her arms. "Not in the slightest."

"Good." His grin widened. "I'd hate to think I was intimidating."

She arched a brow. "If that's your goal, you might want to reconsider leading with oat milk slander and boy band playlists."

Finn leaned his elbow on the counter, gaze flicking lazily over her like he had all the time in the world. "You say that like you didn't grow up imagining a duet with Mr. Darcy, or are you more of a Rochester fellow? He broods enough for a classical composer."

Daphne's mouth opened. Closed. "I'll have you know, I was partial to Captain Wentworth."

"Ah." He nodded solemnly. "The emotionally repressed sailor. Should've guessed."

Rosemary barked out an unhelpful laugh and immediately tried to disguise it as a cough.

Daphne narrowed her eyes. "You're deflecting."

He leaned in just slightly, lowering his voice. "Am I?"

Too close. Too casual. Too charming.

"Yes." She jabbed a finger toward him. "Because deep down, you're worried your gastropub can't out-charm a proper tearoom."

Finn's grin was maddening. "Tell you what, Miss Austen—I'll save you a front row seat at the opening. That way, when I win, you can say you witnessed history."

"Oh, I'll be there." Her smile turned as sweet as lemon curd over arsenic. "I like comedy."

"And I like confidence," he murmured, eyes dancing. "Even when it's misplaced. But because I'm such a nice chap, I'd be happy to show you some expert baking skills if you want to get inventive with your little . . . pastries." He waved toward her kitchen as if his magnanimous gesture would change her world. "Spice up the place a bit, luv?"

The way he said "luv"—low, warm, like a secret just for her—sent tingles up her arms to land on the back of her neck. Not to mention the nuanced mention of spice, but from the look in his eyes, he had it clearly defined.

She stiffened against the renewed heat shimmying all the way up her body. He was attempting to weaken her defenses. But she refused to break eye contact. "I'm too cautious to misplace confidence, Dashwood." Good, using his last name felt less . . . personal. "And the last thing I need in my kitchen is your coffee and Led Zeppelin."

His expression twisted in mock sadness. "Tragic, really." Repeating her from earlier.

"I'll take baking tips," Rosemary offered, her dazed expression very un-Rosemary-like.

What sort of spell did this guy cast on people?

Finn kept his attention on Daphne for a beat longer, brow raised, before he made a deliberate turn in Rosemary's direction. "It would be a shame if I stole Daphne's favorite employee to work for the dark side."

Dark side was accurate. Daphne rolled her eyes so hard she strained a muscle. Then she leaned in, dropping her voice to a conspiratorial whisper. "Trust me, Dashwood. The only thing you're stealing is my patience."

"Ah," he said, eyes twinkling. "Patience is overrated."

"Not in a shared-wall situation, and certainly not where your music is concerned," she shot back, quickly biting into her muffin to suppress her laughter. Why, oh why, did he draw out the desire to fight! It was like she couldn't help herself. "Last night, I even dreamed about you at a Queen concert listening to 'Under Pressure.'" She grimaced for effect. "I think the song choice was no accident in my psyche."

"I'm flattered." His palm covered his heart. "Usually it takes a few dates to get inside a woman's dreams."

Ugh. Seriously? His tea-colored eyes lost their appeal. Mostly. "Did I say 'dreams'? I meant nightmares of you and your music ruining the peace and quiet of my kitchen."

"Well, with that sweet thought in mind . . ." Finn pushed his sunglasses back into place. "I should get back to the pub. My contractors will be here soon."

"If you need a taste tester, let me know," Rosemary offered, sounding much too energetic. What was she doing? It was almost like . . . Daphne's attention zipped back to Rosemary. Was Rosemary attempting to bait her? No.

But her friend continued without a look in Daphne's direction. "After working here the past few years, I've developed excellent taste discernment."

Daphne blinked a few times. "Taste discernment?"

Rosemary shrugged, a look of faux innocence on her face. She was deliberately lengthening this conversation.

"What would you call it?"

Finn smirked. "A refined palate?"

Daphne stared hard at her friend, who blatantly avoided eye contact. *Coward!*

Well, Daphne would nip Rosemary's misconception in the bud. Daphne did not have any interest in Finn . . . apart from his sticky toffee pudding recipe.

"Despite her love of coffee, Rosemary is really good with dessert testing." Daphne sent Rosemary a grin. "She's my first taste tester apart from Jack, so I think she would give you some great advice." Daphne waved between the two of them. "Maybe the two of you should make a . . . date of it? Besides, her musical tastes are suspect too."

"Hey." Rosemary frowned, but the glint in her eyes proved she caught on to Daphne's subterfuge.

But Finn's reaction was more interesting. Mr. Flirt's expression lost all humor for a split second, attention darting from Rosemary back to Daphne before morphing into nonchalance. What was that about? A chink in the philanderer's armor? Hmm . . .

She ignored the curiosity.

A little.

"Now, let's not berate rhythmic diversity, Miss Austen." He tsked. "Someone would think you're a music snob."

Daphne's smile dissolved into a glare, but before she could rally, Finn continued, "And, I've met Jack. Fine fellow. Not a whit of snobbery. In fact, I hired him."

"Hired him?" Daphne's body stilled. Not to mention the fact he'd implied she was a snob . . . twice. "My brother is working for you?"

"Will be." Finn's grin crooked a little higher as he backed toward the door. "But since you're not afraid of healthy competition, it shouldn't be a problem, right?"

"Of course not." Daphne straightened. "In fact, Jack could very well be my spy."

With another chuckle, Finn doffed an imaginary hat and, thankfully, sheathed those eyes of his with his sunglasses once again, before backing toward the door. "In that case, I'll be sure to feed him plenty of abominable tea."

The door closed behind him, and Rosemary turned on Daphne. "You like him."

Daphne propped both fists on her hips in full nonverbal declaration against such an idea. "The only things I like about him are his hair and his baking. And especially the way he exits a room."

"Mm-hmm." Rosemary picked up a pot of hot water and stepped back toward the far table of guests enjoying morning tea. "You keep telling yourself that."

"What do you mean?"

Rosemary shook her head, her smile almost conciliatory. "Henry Tilney is your favorite Austen hero." Her brows rose. "If I remember correctly, it's because of his . . . charm."

"No. It's because of his good heart and sense of humor," she called after Rosemary, and then dropped down on the stool. "Not charm," she repeated, more to herself, but Mrs. Dawson glanced up from her blueberry banana muffin and nodded.

"A good heart and sense of humor are very charming." She raised a brown brow, which stood in stark contrast to her very fake blonde hair. "An accent helps."

Daphne released a long sigh and then . . . crammed a handful of chocolate chips in her mouth. She did not like Finn Dashwood. And she certainly didn't have time to think about whether he had a good heart or not. She had a tea shop to save.

As if in response to her thoughts, the piping from the back made a little creaking noise.

And time was running out.

CHAPTER 7

@TeaThymeNC: Some occasions call for a touch of grace and refinement. Others . . . well, let's just say "hearty" has its place. But which would you trust for a restful and classically enjoyable event or experience? #TeaOverTaters #SomeOfUsHaveStandards #NoShadeAllStew

> **@JackAustenPhotography:** I dunno, Daph . . . I've seen you throw hands over the last biscuit. That wasn't very refined.
>
> **@PastorNateNHC:** "Man shall not live by bread alone." But if he must, it should at least come with a side of mashed potatoes. Just saying.
>
> **@TGDPub:** Ah yes, because nothing says "restful" or "classic" like a sandwich you have to eat with your pinky up.
>
> **@TeaThymeNC:** @TGDPub It's called presentation. Some of us believe in making meals memorable.
>
> **@TGDPub:** @TeaThymeNC Oh, don't worry, luv. I fully intend to make this very memorable.
>
> **@WisteriaWeekly:** In other news, Lindsay Monroe and Travis Langston were seen at the inn again, and overheard

conversations hint at a catering debacle. Let's hope love still blooms for Wisteria's favorite famous daughter and her beau. Drop your thoughts below.

"I'VE HEARD THERE'S BEEN quite a stir in town about the new pub owner."

Daphne glanced over at Pastor Nate as she sat her green bean casserole on the table beside Granny D's famous corn bread stuffing, schooling her features to keep any annoyance—or interest—concealed.

Which wasn't an easy feat with Rosemary staring a hole in Daphne's profile from the end of the table.

Nate wasn't just the youngest pastor in New Hope Church's history—he also had the highly inconvenient gift of being alarmingly perceptive. Worse still, he'd grown up running wild with her brother, Jack, which meant he had an inside track on all her weaknesses.

Having Pastor Nate in Granny D's hundred-year-old farmhouse for Sunday lunch wasn't a surprise. Granny had given him an open invitation, like with Jack, Daphne, and Rosemary, and many times strongly encouraged acceptance in her Southern matriarch sort of way. (Which meant no refusals or something bad might happen, like being forgotten at Christmas or—heaven help them all—being volunteered to help with the church's annual live nativity, complete with a real donkey and an itchy burlap robe.)

Rosemary's family lived in town, so she didn't come as often. But the trio of Jack, Nate, and Daphne remained fairly consistent Sunday lunchers.

At the current direction of the conversation, however, Daphne wished she'd made other meal plans for today.

She trained her attention on her task and away from the "annoying brother" vibes she had to endure from the preacher. New folks usually stirred up town gossip, but Nate's overt implications in her direction made her hackles rise.

She busied herself aligning the casserole dish with mathematical precision. "There usually is with new folks."

Nate hummed in response, exchanging a look with Jack across the room. A look Daphne hated almost as much as liver pudding.

Jack, the traitor, grinned as he leaned against the counter, arms crossed like he was just settling in for a show. "Yeah, but this one seems to have caught a certain someone's attention."

"You mean Rosemary?" She waved toward the end of the table, but Rosemary only offered a wrinkle-nosed (and fake) grin back at her.

"Nice try, sunshine!"

Daphne exhaled through her nose. "I hope y'all aren't referring to me, because the only thing that's caught my attention lately is how Granny D almost started a riot at Papa Malone's Café when they ran out of Duke's mayo."

Nate laughed, plucking a green bean straight from her dish like the audacious bean thief he was. "Oh, we heard about that too. The mayo mutiny made it into this week's prayer chain."

"Mama Malone may never recover," Jack added, completely deadpan.

"But nope," Nate continued, as if he and Jack shared one brain cell between them. "We're talking about you. More specifically, your habit of accidentally running into one Mr. Finn Dashwood."

"I even heard you were . . . courting." Jack shrugged, the absolute menace.

Daphne nearly lobbed a biscuit at his head. "Who even uses that word anymore, dork?"

"I do," Granny D announced, sweeping into the room with a bowl of mashed potatoes like it was her stage entrance. "But they ain't courtin', boys."

Finally! Sanity.

"They're just in the early phases of playful bickering."

Rosemary snorted into her napkin.

Daphne closed her eyes. Surrounded by traitors. All of them.

"I think that's called 'banter' in modern terms, Granny." Nate raised a brow in Daphne's direction before sliding down in the chair. "Isn't that a sure sign of budding romance, Jack?"

"If you watch those movies Daph made us suffer through growing up—absolutely." Jack did nothing to hide his amusement as he joined Nate at the table. "It's a classic setup."

"Rom-com gold, I believe, is what Daphne called it," Rosemary added from the kitchen doorway as she carried a pitcher of tea to the table, completely unapologetic. "They're basically Meg Ryan and Hugh Grant but with caffeine and unresolved tension."

"There is no setup and there is no courting," Daphne snapped, brandishing a serving spoon like a weapon to point at each of them, except Granny D. Even in her ire, she wouldn't go that far. "Right now, I'm just trying to muster up the ability to tolerate the man."

"That sounds suspiciously like a—" Nate looked over at Rosemary, brow creased in thought. "What's it called when stories have these little—"

"*Trope* is the word I believe you're looking for, Pastor," she finished, a mock serious frown pulling at her lips. "Enemies to lovers?" Rosemary made a dramatic "check" motion in the air. "Check."

"Oh, right." Jack snapped his fingers. "Opposites attract?"

"Definitely fish out of water," Rosemary added.

"I am surrounded by walking, talking Goodreads tags," Daphne muttered. "This is not a rom-com. There are no tropes. And for the record, I am not Meg Ryan."

"You kind of dress like her in *You've Got Mail*," Rosemary offered with a saccharine-sweet smile as she raised her tea in cheers.

Daphne stirred the potatoes with added gusto. What was wrong with the way Meg Ryan dressed in that movie? Adorable. Cute. Effortlessly classy.

"That's exactly how it was betwixt me and my first husband," Granny D interjected as she poured tea into Jack's glass. "First time I met him, I told him he was about as useful as a screen door on a submarine. Three months later, we were married."

Daphne breathed out a sigh. *Thanks, Granny D.*

"Well, that's convenient." Jack checked an imaginary watch. "You've always wanted a Christmas wedding, Daph."

She shot him a death glare. "I hope both sides of your pillow are warm tonight."

Nate's laugh erupted while Jack clutched his chest in mock offense.

"The church is already decorated for Advent, so you'd save a fortune. Good stewardship, really," Nate said.

Daphne rolled her eyes so hard she briefly saw next week.

And there was no wedding. Just the continued emotional sabotage of living with these people.

"Finn Dashwood has barely been here a week," she ground out. "And other than being distressingly popular with the single women in town"—she jabbed the spoon into the potatoes—"and making sinfully good sticky toffee pudding, he is nearly insufferable."

"That was what I said about my second husband," Granny D added, pulling her apron over her head as a sign it was time to eat. "I did my level best to convince myself he was insufferable. Didn't do a lick of good because he was also real good at kissing, so that ruined my plans."

Daphne choked on her sweet tea. Her entire face caught fire. Kissing Finn Dashwood? With that smug grin! And irritating cologne! And intoxicating accent!?

No. Absolutely not. Never.

Nate and Jack howled.

"That's taking the commandment to 'love thy neighbor' to a whole new level, Daph." Nate sent her a wink. "I'm required by profession to appreciate it."

She rolled her gaze to the ceiling and hoped her prayers had more power than the preacher's, especially this preacher. Unlikely, but one could hope.

She slid into her chair like a sinking ship and scooted a very obvious six inches from her brother. "I have a business to run. Not time for flirty nonsense from meddling newcomers with questionable playlists." Her eyes landed on Nate. "And my neighborliness ends at general greetings and rerouting lost Amazon packages."

Daphne scanned the table to make sure everything had its place. Where was the meat dish? Before she could ask, Granny D took the short pause in the conversation to have Nate say grace, which consisted of usual thanksgiving and a jab at Daphne's need to improve her sense of humor. Ugh.

She only lightly kicked him under the table.

God gave her only one brother for a reason. Why did Nate have to keep taking up Jack's slack?

"Speaking of businesses," Jack said once the prayer ended. "I heard some news yesterday that might be of interest to you."

Daphne looked over at him warily, reaching for the mashed potatoes. "Interesting how?"

"Turns out the Wisteria Inn is in a bit of a bind. You remember how I told you that Travis Langford and Lindsay Monroe were going to have their big celebrity wedding next month at the inn?"

"Travis Langford?" Nate paused his glass to his lips, brows high. "As in *the* Travis Langford? Billionaire tech guy?"

Jack nodded. "And Lindsay Monroe, the small-town Wisteria girl turned social media phenom and model."

"I went on a date with her once in high school," Nate offered, passing his plate to Daphne for some bean casserole. "She wasn't a fan of my truck."

"Is that how you remember it?" Jack barked out a laugh. "As I recall, she wasn't a fan of your acne."

"Or the mullet," Rosemary added with a grimace. "Not a good look for you, Nate."

Daphne nearly spat out the tea she'd just sipped. She sent Nate a smirk. At least these people of hers spared no one in the teasing department.

"But look at you now, sugar," Granny D chimed in, waving her fork toward him like a wand. "Sweetly handsome, as my mama used to say. And that clean-cut look does you all sorts of good."

"Sweetly handsome?" Nate asked, visibly offended.

"Mm-hmm . . ." Granny D nodded her thanks for a spoonful of potatoes. "If you'd just put some fuzz on that chin of yours, you'd look like a full-growed man."

Jack's laugh burst out again, nearly tipping his glass. Rosemary snorted so hard she startled the cat off the windowsill.

Trying to salvage Nate's dignity—because apparently, she was *that* kind of friend—Daphne redirected. "I'd die to be a fly on the wall for that wedding, Jack. Can you imagine the food? The decor? That cake is probably going to need its own security detail."

"Actually"—Jack slid his empty plate toward Granny D, who rewarded him with a healthy scoop of corn bread pudding—"that's the problem."

Utensils paused midair. All eyes turned toward him.

"The catering plans fell through."

Daphne blinked. "Wait—what?"

"They'd hired some fancy celebrity chef—friend of Travis's—and last week he ghosted them. No calls, no emails. Gone."

Daphne coughed on her potatoes. "That's a nightmare. For a wedding that high profile? The internet will eat them alive."

"And it's awful for Lindsay," Rosemary added, more serious than usual. "I mean, I'm no expert on wedding stuff—"

"She says, while curating an entire Pinterest board titled 'My Accidental Wedding,'" Daphne muttered.

Rosemary grinned but continued, "Still, the girl's from here. This whole town is watching. She doesn't need public humiliation on top of wedding stress."

"And it's not a great look for Wisteria either," Jack added, his tone shifting just enough to catch Daphne's attention. "Especially heading into autumn tourist season." He gave her a look that should've come with a siren. Daphne slowly lowered her fork. "Which is why Harry and I thought someone local could step in. You know . . . bring a more homespun feel to the big day."

Who would be crazy enough . . . Daphne froze, mashed potatoes midair. "No," she said. "No, no, no. Me? You want *me* to cater a celebrity wedding?"

"Why not?" Jack shrugged like it was just another Tuesday. "They want it small. Local. Detailed. Thoughtful. Travis is pulling every string he can to fix this for Lindsay, and she specifically asked if someone local could step in."

He gestured toward her with his glass. "And you're good at detail. At class. And muffins."

"That much flattery means they're really desperate." Daphne pinched her eyes closed. She'd never done anything as classy or visible as a celebrity wedding! A birthday party for the mayor's daughter, but that wasn't even close.

"Seriously, though," Nate chimed in, tilting his tea, "this could do wonders for Tea Thyme. And Wisteria in general. People are gonna eat this up—literally and figuratively."

"And"—Jack held her gaze—"it might be exactly what you need for the shop."

"Think of how we can spin it for social media," Rosemary said.

Daphne opened her mouth to—well, she wasn't exactly sure what she was going to say—but at that exact moment, a knock echoed from the front door.

Then came the deep, unmistakable purr of a very British voice.

Daphne swung her attention to Granny D, who was pushing back from her seat. "Oh good, they got here in time."

Granny D rose from her place and rushed to the entry hall.

"Oh no," Daphne whispered and pinched her eyes shut before opening them just in time to see Nate and Jack exchange twin grins. Oh, she hated them.

"I do apologize for being late," came the voice—*his* voice—floating down the hallway like it was being piped in from a cologne commercial. "We got a bit turned around leaving the church."

We? What sort of magnified torture was this?

"Don't you worry one bit, sugar," Granny D responded. "We just got started."

"Thank you again for the invitation," the voice continued, drawing closer. "I've heard about your legendary corn bread pudding."

Daphne resisted the urge to launch herself out the window.

She could already see him in her mind's eye—white button-down, top button undone, dark jeans, and that ridiculous ability to make a room tilt slightly in his direction. Her retinas should be ashamed for how quickly they betrayed her carefully cultivated disinterest.

He'd practically caused a silent revolt in church that morning, sauntering down the aisle to take his seat on the fourth row next to a nearly hyperventilating Mrs. Gloria Ross and her two teenage daughters. Not one single female in church heard a word of Mrs. Rogers's lengthy recitation of what types of food items to bring to the next fellowship dinner.

And now he was *here*. In Granny D's kitchen.

"Look who's stopped by for lunch today." Granny D ushered Finn into the room with—what was this?—the cutest little girl at his side.

"Good afternoon." Finn's eyes landed on Daphne, and his mouth curled into that insufferably charming, just-on-the-edge-of-smug smile. "Miss Austen. Fancy meeting you here."

She fully resisted making eye contact with her brother. And the preacher.

"And I'm as pleased as punch to get to meet your little darling daughter, Lucy," Granny D continued, guiding them to chairs. "You're just the prettiest little thing, ain't cha?"

Daughter?

Flirty Finn was a dad?

And Lucy? One of the best names ever!

Daphne's brain glitched for a few seconds, trying to process the updated version of this man.

The little girl blinked wide, green eyes at Granny D, seemingly caught between fascination and fear of Granny's feathered earrings. Eventually, she edged closer to Finn's side. Smart girl. Granny D's hugs were like emotional flypaper—once caught, you were hers for life.

Her unconventional earrings sure provide ample warning.

Finn rested a casual hand on Lucy's head, the protective gesture shooting a warm, confusing pang straight to Daphne's chest.

Handsome. British. And a dad?

Lord, we are going to have a serious conversation later.

She squinted at the little girl. Had she missed her this morning? Maybe Finn had dropped her off at children's church? Because Daphne was pretty sure she wasn't so distracted by Mr. Winks-A-Lot to ignore such a welcome addition to Finn's personality as a daughter!

"What did you bring that smells so good?" Granny D leaned in and then motioned toward the table.

"Shepherd's pie." Finn placed the dish where directed. "I was told it's customary to bring a dish to Granny D's famous Sunday lunch."

His charm worked a laugh and an arm pat from Granny D before she rounded the table back to her seat. "I'm excited to try some of your cookin' before the rest of the town gets a taste."

"Sounds like a Sunday-worthy dish to me," Nate added, without waiting for an invitation to dive into the steaming dish. "Shepherd's pie? Psalm 23 on a plate."

Jack groaned at Nate's appraisal, but it didn't stop him from being next in line for the food. Such gentlemen.

Daphne avoided eye contact with Finn and focused on Lucy. She had the prettiest green eyes and held a little dragon in her arms. A green dragon? "Do you like dragons, Lucy?"

Lucy's eyes flicked up at her, and she gave the tiniest nod.

"Good choice," Daphne said, sliding the corn bread pudding closer to Finn without acknowledging his existence. "They're much more reliable than unicorns and fairies."

"And stronger," came her little voice.

"For sure." Daphne grinned.

"So, Lucy's not much of a princess girl, Daph," Jack teased. "Guess you two won't have much in common."

"I like princesses too," Lucy piped up, her tiny brows furrowing in protest.

Daphne beamed. "Of course you do. Only the best girls like both dragons and crowns."

Lucy giggled, her crooked grin lighting up her whole face. Daphne caught a glimpse of a faint scar above her lip—subtle but unmistakable. Something in her heart squeezed.

Poor little thing.

"This here is mighty good, Finn." Granny D raised her forkful of shepherd's pie. "Can't wait to tell folks 'bout it. You mean to open this upcoming weekend?"

"That's the plan," Finn answered, dishing out some green bean casserole.

Daphne stiffened just a little. It was one thing for her regular group of people to eat her cooking. It was quite another to share her food with a . . . chef . . . unless she'd specifically curated it for him like she had those scones.

"Saturday," he continued, scooping a little for Lucy, whose nose wrinkled. Clearly, her love of green did not extend to beans. "I'm planning a limited supper menu for folks in the community to try, then rolling out the full offerings in stages."

"You should try his bangers and mash." Jack leaned back in his chair and rubbed his stomach. "That's a Monday-through-Sunday kind of meal."

Rosemary murmured something appreciative, probably flirt-adjacent, but Daphne barely heard her. Her gaze had locked onto Finn, who lifted a forkful of her green bean casserole to his lips. He paused, brows drawn in mild concentration, like he was parsing out ingredients and intention all at once.

Which—ugh—meant he might be a flavor-notes kind of person, just like her.

But . . . he was *nothing* like her. At all.

He took another bite, slower this time, and the faintest curve at the corner of his mouth gave him away. He liked it.

Heat bloomed in her chest. Pride? Possibly. Satisfaction? Definitely. Gloating? Not outwardly, but it stirred in ridiculous happy twirls in her stomach. With careful precision, she took a polite bite of his shepherd's pie. The rich broth and warm earthiness of rosemary and thyme practically sang on her tongue. Her eyes fluttered closed, tabulating each new flavor.

"Looks like Daphne's in love," Jack said.

Her eyes snapped open in horror.

"With the food," he clarified, twirling his fork toward her. "The dreamy sigh was a dead giveaway."

She flung a napkin at his face. "You're ridiculous."

"So I've been told." Jack winked.

Her attention snapped to Finn, only to find one raised brow and that disastrous grin.

Daphne attempted to salvage some of her bottomed-out pride. "It's very good, Finn."

"Thank you," he replied, eyes steady on hers. "I hope to add it to the final menu."

"Definitely keep it," Nate chimed in. "It's mountain food. Meat, potatoes, messy . . . the holy trinity of comfort."

"With that response, it's a must, isn't it?" Finn chuckled. "I'm hoping to gain traction quickly, financially speaking. The pub's a big investment. That's why I was grateful for Harry's suggestion—about possibly catering that high-profile wedding next month."

All the heat drained from Daphne's face. Her attention shot to Jack. How did Finn know about the catering opportunity?

Jack caught her look. "Harry and I thought it would be good to give the couple some options."

"You're considering the job?" Finn's gaze locked with Daphne's. "But you run a tea shop. That's not exactly real food."

Rosemary set down her glass. Jack and Nate pushed back from the table at the same time, as if preparing for World War 3. Granny D leaned in. Even Lucy glanced up from her mashed potatoes.

Daphne lowered her fork.

"I'm considering it." Her voice was as smooth as buttercream, despite the flush creeping up her neck. "Real food comes in many forms." She dabbed her lips with her napkin. "And I've catered events before, but since you barely know me, you wouldn't know that."

"Have you now?" Finn leaned forward, eyes sparkling. "Cucumber sandwiches and petit fours don't exactly scream *wedding feast*."

Her jaw clicked shut, then popped open again. "And yet, my tiny 'not real' food keeps locals coming back for more."

"Harry said the couple wanted a blend of upscale and homegrown," Jack offered, attempting to mediate. "Class with local charm."

"Which I can provide," Finn and Daphne said in unison, then glared at each other.

Nate chuckled nervously, clearly sensing the brewing storm. "The Lord made room for both manna and milk and honey."

"What's manna?" Lucy asked, head tilting toward him.

"Something less delicious than this shepherd's pie," Granny D interjected, helping herself to seconds. "Though Daphne's lavender scones could give it a run for its money."

"Lavender scones?" Finn's eyes narrowed slightly. "Bit fussy for a wedding feast, isn't it?"

"Says the man who probably thinks wedding cake should be meat pie with gravy frosting," Daphne retorted, instantly regretting the childish tone.

To her utter horror, Finn laughed—a full, unguarded sound that made her insides tighten like a twisted apron.

"Lord, help us," Nate said, buttering another biscuit like a man preparing for a long siege.

"You might be surprised by what I can do beyond meat and potatoes, Daph." The nickname rolled off his tongue so easily it made her pulse quicken, but she wasn't sure whether it was to fight, flee, or . . . well, she didn't want to consider any other options. "I did train in Paris after all."

Daphne gasped. "Paris?"

"Oui, mademoiselle." His accent was flawless, his smirk incendiary.

"Oh, that was beautiful," Rosemary mumbled.

"Well," Jack said, scooping up the last bit of his shepherd's pie, "sounds like we've got ourselves a proper culinary competition brewing."

"Oh, it's a competition now?" Finn teased, twinkling gaze shooting back to Daphne.

"If it means proving that my business is the best choice for one of the biggest weddings in Wisteria?" Daphne folded her arms to prove her fitness. "Then absolutely."

"Fine by me." Finn raised his glass toward her. "I'm always up for a challenge."

"As am I." Daphne narrowed her eyes, refusing to budge an inch, despite the quavering in her middle. She might've never catered a celebrity wedding before, but she'd sooner serve boxed mac and cheese than let Finn Dashwood win by default. "I'm sure the high-end couple will appreciate someone who understands the nuances of refined palates."

"And someone who can serve substance *and* style," he countered, but this time his voice held a note of respect. "Though I have to admit, this green bean casserole has both."

It was the closest thing to a compliment she'd received from him in days. A pulse of pride hit her before she could bat it away.

She stabbed her fork into her pie and tried not to smile. Or look at him.

Why was arguing with him so much fun?

"Just to be clear," Jack said, grinning from ear to ear, "this is still about a wedding, not the next season of *Top Chef: Passive-Aggressive Edition*. You know, not a declaration of war."

Nate snorted. "With these two? Might be both."

Daphne stabbed a forkful of shepherd's pie, refusing to give Finn the satisfaction of seeing how much she enjoyed it. But when she caught his eye again, she saw something beyond the competitive gleam—appreciation, perhaps. Something . . . else?

"Bless it," Granny D muttered, refilling her iced tea. "If the sparks get any thicker in here, I'll need my fan."

"You know"—Rosemary slid a glance Daphne's way—"there's a fine line between competition and courtship."

"Which trope is that?" Jack scrunched his brow as if he hadn't just sent Daphne's cheeks into a broil.

She wanted to strangle everyone at the table and then hide for a thousand years.

But she wasn't a quitter, so she lifted her glass toward Finn. "May the best chef win."

Finn met her toast for toast. "To good food and worthy opponents."

CHAPTER 8

@TeaThymeNC: Pro tip: When life hands you salt instead of sugar, remember that though some people say revenge is a dish best served cold, I'm thinking warm, with clotted cream, and just the tiniest hint (or a great deal) of cayenne. 😌 #BakerBeware #PlottingInThePantry

> **@TGDPub:** I hear salt is underrated in baked goods. Some might even say . . . essential. Just trying to elevate your flavors, cupcake.
>
> **@JackAustenPhotography:** Bold of you to show your face here, mate. I suggest witness protection.
>
> **@MaggiesFlowerCottage:** I knew those scones tasted like the ocean. Bless your heart, Daphne. 🌼
>
> **@TeaThymeNC:** @TGDPub Oh, you've elevated something, all right.
>
> **@TeaThymeNC:** @JackAustenPhotography Would you mind drafting the obituary? Something tasteful.

....

PM from @TGDPub to @TeaThymeNC: In all sincerity, I'd only meant to exchange salt in your personal sugar bowl so it would only affect you. NOT your customers.

@TeaThymeNC: And that's supposed to make me feel better?

@TGDPub: It was only meant to be a windup, luv. I'm not a villain.

@TeaThymeNC: You know, most villains would say something like that.

@TGDPub: Now you're just trying to make me smile, aren't you?

@TeaThymeNC: Ending the conversation now.

@TGDPub: Were Ms. Maggie and her friend all right after the salty exchange?

@TeaThymeNC: (insert extra-large sigh): Yes. Thank goodness your little "windup" debacle only impacted two of the sweetest people in Wisteria.

@TGDPub: Besides you, of course.

@TeaThymeNC: Nice try, but the competition is still on.

OF ALL THE THINGS to go wrong, it had to be this.

Finn shoved his mobile back into his pocket and scowled at the barren apartment, as if staring it down might magically summon the missing moving truck. After a week in a hotel, waiting for their personal belongings to arrive from the UK, the moving company had promised delivery today.

But with one delay after another, they'd finally moved delivery to first thing the following morning.

So here they were in their apartment above the pub.

No furniture. No extra clothes. No towels.

A small disaster in the grand scheme of things, but still . . . frustrating.

He could've booked another night at the hotel, but the moving company had promised—*promised*—they'd be here at seven a.m., and Lucy had been so excited to sleep in her new home. He could endure one night of discomfort if it meant letting her settle in.

And it was only for one night.

A sweet humming drifted through the empty space, pulling his attention away from the movers' latest apologetic text. Lucy patted her plush unicorn and green dragon into the pink folds of the sleeping bag he'd procured from the local hardware store, as if sleeping in the middle of their empty living room wasn't unexpected at all.

A delayed moving truck failed to tip her happy disposition.

The tension in his face relaxed, and he sighed. Oh, she gave him perspective. She'd spent her whole life doing that without even trying.

A childhood full of surgeries, an absent mother, and a scar that had rewritten her smile—Lucy had faced it all with more grace than most adults. And though another operation loomed in the future, she never let it dim her joy. She'd become one of the best teachers on optimism, gratitude, and perseverance in his life.

Clearing his throat, he stepped toward her. "Are your animals ready for bed, lamb?"

Lucy beamed up at him, loose dark hair tumbling in soft waves from a day wearing plaits. "Dey like to camp on de floor, Daddy. It's an adventure."

An adventure? He scanned the empty room and shrugged a shoulder in acceptance. The past week had certainly been an adventure. "It is." He crouched to her side, his voice dropping to a whisper. "I wonder what will be next? A rescue? A battle?"

And his thoughts immediately shifted to Daphne Austen. *Battle* seemed an appropriate word when in reference to her. A fun sort of sparring, because she not only was easy to irritate but rose to each occasion with a quick wit he couldn't help admire. He couldn't remember the last time he'd enjoyed such easy and fun conversations with a woman. And despite her glares, he had a sneaky suspicion she enjoyed the banter too.

Or, at least, as she'd confessed, found some inspiration in it.

His lips twitched. Then the memory of replacing her sugar bowl with salt, only to have the prank misfire on a customer, nearly wiped off his grin.

As a small business owner himself, he'd never want to damage her reputation or business, so her private messaging with him helped allay a little of his concern. But he'd take a chance to apologize again, in person.

His shoulders almost sank. That's all he seemed to do with Daphne.

Apologize.

And verbally spar.

His grin almost resurrected. Sounded like a fitting relationship.

Well, and flirt a little. Because she was long overdue for some solid flirting.

The squeeze of her pink lips and tension in her brow proved an almost overwhelming temptation to soften her features, if nothing else, to see if he could.

And then he gave his head a shake.

No, Finn! No romance. Especially not with someone who . . . well, with her.

She was the type of woman who slid beneath a man's skin.

Who promised something wholesome and as fairy-tale-ish as one of Lucy's children's books.

Lucy's eyes widened, sparkling in the glow from the lamp he'd purchased from the hardware store as well. "A sleeping princess," she whispered back.

"But we already have a princess in this house, lamb." He kissed her head and gestured toward her plush toys, to keep the conversation safely redirected from any talk of other princesses in their lives. "Posie and Dragon seem at home in these royal quarters, don't they?"

Lucy leaned her ear down to the toys, as if listening for their responses, and then turned her dimpled smile on him. "Dey're very happy wif camping, Daddy, but dey miss my princess bed too."

Finn ruffled her hair. "No doubt." He helped her into the bag.

"Will you tell me a story tonight, Daddy?"

"Not tonight." He knelt and smoothed back her hair from her face. "All of your books are packed away and it's far past your bedtime."

"You can make one up from your brain." Her eyes shone. "I like de ones you make from your brain."

He tapped her nose. "Tomorrow night when you are snug in your princess bed at a reasonable hour, but tonight our brains need to rest."

Lucy sighed back into the pillow, a pout pulling at her crooked mouth. "Do you need your brain for a good night prayer?"

His inner laugh almost slipped through his smile. There were times when he needed prayers to find his brain, but never the reverse. "Sometimes a prayer is all I've got left, lamb."

His words grounded him with their deeper truth. Between Sarah walking out, navigating fatherhood solo, and facing Lucy's surgeries alone—at times, prayer had been his only lifeline. And then, with Father's death? And his business falling apart . . . ?

He sighed.

Thank heavens, God understood the pleas of a brainless dad.

He pressed a kiss to her forehead. "But I believe I have just enough brain left for one."

Lucy grinned, pulled her unicorn and dragon up close to her chin, and closed her eyes in preparation.

He took Lucy's free hand. "Thank you for our new home and the kind people we've met this week."

"And for our new sleeping bags."

Finn's lips crooked. "And for our new sleeping bags and for Harry and Margaret's welcome."

"And for cheeseburgers."

Of course.

"And thank you," he added, "for cheeseburgers." And running water. At least they had running water. "Please help us to have sweet dreams tonight."

Lucy wiggled her fingers. "And bring our furniture tomorrow so Daddy can have his special chair."

Finn chuckled, shaking his head. "Amen."

He stood and turned off the lamp, then walked to the barren kitchen, its clean, black-and-white appearance leading into a small breakfast room with a window overlooking the main street of the small town with its distant mountains as a dark silhouette. The apartment fit the two of them well. Renovated but retaining the older woodwork to increase its charm. A set of French doors led from the spacious living room into a smaller room Finn would use as his home office, a central location for access to the door and for keeping his eyes on Lucy.

Harry and Margaret's handiwork was displayed in the subtle wall color after several layers of hideous wallpaper had been removed. And Margaret's careful attention to the updated kitchen made everything easier for Finn's move-in. Yes, this would be a good little home for him and Lucy.

He snatched the new mug and poured himself a cup of warm, welcoming java he'd brought up from the pub's kitchen—his evening comfort along with a few hours of quiet to piece together his thoughts for the next day. He looked over his to-do list in preparation for the upcoming weekend and jotted a few notes on his iPad regarding some final items.

Outside, the town hummed softly—low conversation, the occasional car, the distant glow of streetlights reflecting against the mountains. It was a good place. A safe place.

Lucy started school in a few days, and after a few conversations with the forces that be, Finn felt rather good about the small school.

And who wouldn't love Lucy?

He paused in his notes and glanced out the window. He'd described Lucy's situation to the teacher, but predicting kids' reactions to her scars left a knot in his stomach. Even in this small, Southern town of seemingly kind people, he couldn't protect her in a new environment when she was out of sight. And her scar wasn't horrible. Noticeable but better than he'd expected from the severity of her cleft. The teacher had assured him that she'd keep an eye on the situation.

And Lucy was tougher than the pink fluff and dimpled grin might suggest. A lot tougher.

Finn exhaled and turned back to his coffee. He'd barely lifted the cup when—

"Daddy!"

Lucy's shrill cry shot Finn to his feet. He rushed to the adjoining room to find his daughter sitting up in the sleeping bag.

Twin streams of blood poured from her nose, staining her pillow, her pajamas. Was it even in her hair?

His stomach clenched.

No, no, no—not now.

He snatched her up, scanning the barren room for—anything. No towels. No tissues. Just a useless, blood-stained pillowcase. He marched to the nearest bathroom, trying to keep his voice calm. "Were you picking at your nose again, lamb?"

Lucy pinched her lips into a tiny pucker as he placed her on the sink counter. "Only a little, Daddy, I promise."

"You remember what the doctor said." He kept one end of the

pillow cover on her nose while dipping the other end into cold water, alternating it to wipe at some of the bloodstains on her face.

She nodded, lip trembling. “I’m sorry, Daddy.”

Her big green eyes, filling with unshed tears, gutted him.

After the last series of nosebleeds, the doctor had cauterized the wound on the inside of her nose, just before they'd left England. She must have reopened the wound. There was a chance this one might heal on its own, but he couldn’t know at the moment. He shot a look to his phone. He’d planned to contact their new doctor once they’d gotten settled—thought he’d have more time before another emergency. He wiped at the twin trail still running at such a rate to hint that this pillowcase would not be enough. “It’s an easy thing to do, lamb, but hopefully this will help you remember a bit.”

She nodded behind the cloth. He held in his wince at the state of her face and clothes . . . and he had nothing but paper towels and a soiled pillow cover with which to help her.

He didn’t even have towels for a bath. A washcloth and dishcloth, but no towels. Because everything else was supposed to have arrived with the moving truck. He groaned. Why didn’t he think of such things mere hours ago when they traipsed around the hardware store in search of sleeping bags and a lamp?

He pulled the pillowcase away from her nose. Praise be! Already the blood was slowing a bit. Perhaps he’d be mercifully saved from a trip to the emergency room, but they still needed a place to clean up.

“I’m afraid we must go in search of some help.” From his research, the little town closed by nine. Perhaps the grocery remained open longer?

He gave his head a shake. No, he remembered it closed at eleven, and he looked down at his phone and saw it was just now eleven.

He squeezed his eyes closed, using that last bit of brain power for another prayer. Wait, hadn’t the Realtor mentioned a neighbor?

Finn turned toward the window. A light glowed in the next apartment over Daphne's shop.

Someone was awake. And close. Did Daphne live there? For some reason, he thought she lived with her brother in a house on the outskirts of town, but at least someone would be nearby.

"Looks like we're testing out that famous Southern hospitality, Lucy."

He scooped her off the counter, grabbed his keys, and stepped into the warm night air, taking a set of stairs that led down from his apartment across a small grassy area to another stair leading back up to the next. The evening breeze dampened the summer heat and carried with it the scent of cinnamon. Cinnamon? At eleven o'clock at night? Finn breathed it in, appreciating the memories it unearthed of grandparents and lazy afternoons.

The scent of cinnamon grew stronger as he approached the door, teasing him closer. Oh, he felt fairly certain he knew this neighbor already. There was a real possibility she kept a cinnamon-scented candle burning at all times.

And a little of the tension fell from his shoulders.

She'd help. Maybe not for his sake but for Lucy's.

No doubt.

Finn rapped the red door, same shape and form as his own, only much more colorful. A large wreath of myriad-colored flowers took up nearly the entire top half of the door. The sound of some instrumental montage bled through the wall. He'd heard it before. But where? Intense-sounding. Suspenseful.

He knocked again. This time the music dampened, and a dog barked, followed by a resounding thud. Finn looked down at Lucy, whose eyes widened from behind the pillow cover.

"They have a dog, Daddy."

"Coming," came the singsongy voice of a woman.

A *familiar* voice.

He drew in a breath and pushed on his smile. Well, if he'd been hoping for another chance to apologize, he just might get it sooner than he thought.

• • • • • • • • • • •

Daphne clutched the pillow closer, heart pounding as Ethan Hunt sprinted through shadowed streets, desperate to reach his dying friend. Her chamomile tea sat abandoned, rapidly cooling, while Winston gnawed on a bone at her feet.

A loud knock shattered the moment.

Daphne jolted, flinging the pillow aside and fumbling for the remote. In a perfectly ungraceful sequence, she smacked her beloved teacup, caught it midair with a contortionist's desperation, nearly tripped over her slippers, and managed to set the cup down with only a minor tea casualty—just in time to see Ethan arrive . . . too late.

She exhaled, tension melting. At least the tea was safe.

Another knock jolted her to her feet. She smacked her knee against the coffee table on the way up. "Ow! Good grief." Winston gave a half-hearted bark and trotted toward the door while she limped behind, muttering something unholy as she rubbed her leg.

She squinted at the clock. *11:05 p.m.*

Who on earth—

She cracked the door open just enough to see a pair of very familiar, very infuriating umber-brown eyes staring back from the thin stream of light her door allowed.

Finn Dashwood?

She blinked, hoping he was a figment of too many thoughts on how to beat him at the competition.

Nope. Still there.

He looked decidedly less put together than his usual pub owner persona. Of course, she hadn't seen him since Sunday lunch with Granny

D, but he now wore a rumpled gray T-shirt stretched across his shoulders, paired with khaki shorts, and his hair bore the distinct look of someone who'd run his hands through it multiple times.

Oh, why did rascally have to look so good?

"The sugar-salt stunt wasn't enough?" She scowled. "Come to swap out my tea for coffee?"

"Tempting," he murmured. "But I actually need your help."

That shut her down for a beat. He looked . . . serious. Which was unsettling.

"I'm all out of motor oil at the moment."

One side of his mouth quirked in genuine amusement—none of that practiced charm stuff. "A shame. But I was hoping to borrow a towel." A pause. "Or maybe your bathroom."

She crossed her arms. "That's a new pickup line. 'Can I borrow your towel?'"

A flicker of amusement crossed his face, but the usual playfulness didn't fully surface. Instead, he hesitated—just a beat too long.

And then he shifted to the right, stepping fully into the light.

Daphne's breath caught.

Because in his arms, held against his chest, was his little Lucy. Dark curls, green eyes, and a face smeared in—was that blood?

"Oh my goodness—" Daphne fumbled at the chain lock, wrenching the door open before she could fully process what she was doing. "What happened? Is she okay? How can I help?"

The tenderness in Finn's expression didn't match any version of him she'd seen before. It tugged something deep in her chest—something warm and protective and wholly inconvenient.

She ignored the sudden curiosity. Buried it. Flirts had their place.

But not with her.

Finn shifted his hold on the little girl. "Lucy's had a nosebleed, and we don't have—"

"Come. Come in." She waved them forward, her attention focused on Lucy, though her inner monologue was having a full-blown meltdown. Had she ever had a single man over this late at night? Aside from Jack, of course. Accompanied by Nate, usually.

She glanced up at Mr. Hotface, her mind muddling through a complete scenario of him killing her, stuffing her in a closet, and no one finding her for a week . . . and then what would happen to all her grandmother's teapots?

The logical side of her brain gave the hysterical side a good slap. She knew Finn Dashwood enough to know he wasn't the sort. Especially with a daughter as witness.

"I promise to play *nice*," Finn whispered as he passed her into the room.

Play nice?

Her cheeks flamed in appreciation and the hysterical side tipped a brow.

Very nice. Daphne pinched her eyes shut and mentally replayed their earlier rivalry. He is a smug, tea-insulting, salt-pouring, arrogant Brit. Not a knight in a well-worn T-shirt. And she knew his kind. Here one day, gone the next, leaving a broken heart and the scent of . . . vanilla and cedar behind.

What she needed was boring and faithful.

Because flirty, dangerously handsome, *and* faithful didn't seem to exist in her world.

Daphne ignored the intoxicating draw of a baritone voice and the yummy scent of vanilla and bent down to greet Lucy. Her poor little face had blood smears across her nose and cheeks, but when she pulled the pillowcase away to offer Daphne a smile, the blood appeared to be only tiny traces of its previous . . . mess.

"Is that your dog?"

"It is." Daphne waved toward the sweet, old boy. He'd been Granny's gift to Daphne when Jack moved out six years ago. A guard dog . . . who never really grew into the "guard" part. "His name is Winston."

"As in Churchill?" Finn's brows rose.

"Exactly." Daphne nodded, offering him a warning look. "A solid name for a protector."

Winston, of course, proved utterly useless in discernment, giving one sniff before promptly sitting in full welcome.

"Yes, I see. Top-notch security." Finn's lips tipped up just a little.

"Well," Daphne sighed. "At least he's a good snuggler."

And then she replayed her words and completely avoided eye contact with the man.

Lucy wiggled out of her dad's arms, pillowcase still pressed to her face, and placed one arm around Winston as if they'd been long-lost friends.

At least Lucy didn't seem to be in pain. That was a good sign.

Daphne leaned in Finn's direction, voice low. "What on earth happened?"

"A nosebleed." Finn's voice was steady as he recounted the evening's events. But the flirty pub owner persona had taken a back seat to this other Finn. The protective dad one. "And since our moving truck failed to arrive today, we have no supplies." He exhaled. "It's not dangerous, just messy. And I didn't want to drag her around town this late."

Daphne's gaze caught in his.

"Of course not." She'd seen serious Finn a few times before. Usually when he apologized. And the look beat against the flirt assumptions like an all-out drum solo. This was a tired, caring dad doing his best. Her defenses crumpled slightly.

She pulled her attention from him and crouched to Lucy's level. "Well, Lucy, lucky for you, I'm baking cookies. They should be ready when you're out of the bath."

Lucy perked up. "Chocolate chip?"

"The only kind worth staying up past bedtime for."

"Baking cookies?" Finn arched a brow. "This late?"

Daphne lifted her chin. "It's always a good time for cookies."

She shot Lucy a wink as she stood, then schooled her face before turning back to him.

"Ah, while watching . . ." He gestured with his chin toward her television, where the screen paused quite dramatically on Ethan Hunt running. "Interesting choice for a tea princess."

Daphne opened her mouth. Then closed it. And then, she raised her chin and tightened a smile. "Stereotypes." She batted her lashes and worked up her best English accent. "Nasty little things, aren't they?"

Something flashed in his eyes, warming her cheeks. "It does add a whole new layer to your personality, Miss Austen."

His voice brushed across her skin like velvet. She stepped back automatically, heart thudding far too loud in her ears. Nope. Not going there.

"Come on, Lucy." She waved toward the hallway, refusing to glance at the man behind her. "I'll show you the way."

Finn took Lucy's small hand in his, and that single gesture was almost her undoing. Gentle. Steady. Sweet in a way that felt . . . dangerous.

She closed her fingers into fists at her sides.

Ever since Sunday lunch, when he'd shown up with that crooked smile and his adorable daughter—and then had the nerve to become her business rival—she'd been stuck in a full-on tennis match with her own brain. Admire him? Absolutely not. Crush on him? *Worse.*

And yet, here he was. Being nice. Being grateful. Holding his daughter's hand and trailing behind her like some sort of walking contradiction with an accent.

She flicked on the bathroom light.

And froze.

Oh no, no, no—

Her pink lace bra—her favorite pink lace bra—was hanging in all its humiliating glory from the shower rod.

She made a strangled noise that may or may not have been human and launched toward it, yanking it down and shoving it behind her back.

Silence.

Then a cough. A suspiciously choked one.

Decidedly male.

Her face flared to volcanic temperatures.

"Um . . . towels are in the closet. Shampoo's on the tub." She gestured vaguely with her *empty* hand. "And you should probably turn on the space heater. This apartment stays cold even in summer. It's not been updated like yours."

And hopefully, her heater would last one more winter.

Or two.

Since the plumbing repairs couldn't wait.

Finn was staring at her. Not smirking, not laughing—just looking. Too much. She pulled at her baggy T-shirt. *He's not a nice person. He's a jerk who criticized your precious tea shop and poured salt in your sugar bowls. Right. Exactly.*

Avoid eye contact.

"Well, I'll let you two get cleaned up." Daphne flattened herself against the wall, shimmying past Mr. Hotface with every ounce of dignity she could scrape together.

She was almost clear when—

"Her clothes."

She paused. Turned. Too close. Way too close.

"I forgot to fetch clean ones when we left."

She looked over his wrinkled, blood-specked shirt. Then at Lucy's princess nightgown. And just like that, the tug in her chest resurrected.

"She can stay with me while you run next door."

His gaze snapped to hers. Measured. Intense. Like he was making sure she could be trusted with the most precious thing in his world. And Daphne's heart flipped all over again.

A dad who loved his little girl.

She didn't blink, only held his attention, daring him to doubt her.

Finally, something shifted in his face. That soft look crept a little too close to . . . tender.

No, no. Stop that. He is a rival. An arrogant Brit with an emotional support smirk and an unhealthy aversion to proper tea.

But then he stepped closer. The doorframe was at her back. No escape.

"Thank you."

The air thickened, and Daphne decided to stop breathing because maybe it would help.

Then—because he clearly couldn't help himself—a crooked grin formed on his face, the flirt back in full force. "Be back in a trice."

He disappeared down the hallway, leaving behind the scent of vanilla, cedar, and confusion.

Daphne exhaled. Hard. Whatever *that* was—it needed to stop. Preferably with a bucket of cold water.

She turned back to her neon bathroom with a bloody-nosed little girl staring up at her and tried to sort out what to do next.

"Green is my second favorite color," Lucy announced, matter-of-factly.

"Is it?" Daphne grinned, kneeling to start the bathwater. "I bet I can guess your first favorite."

Lucy's eyes glimmered with a smile mostly hidden behind the pillowcase, granting permission. What had happened to Lucy's mom? Daphne's chest squeezed. She knew the hole left behind from the loss of a mother.

And if Finn was raising Lucy alone?

Well, that implied a lot of possibly painful somethings, didn't it?

"Hmm," Daphne mused aloud, scanning Lucy's bright pink nightgown down to her matching socks. "Blue?"

Lucy shook her dark head, bobbing a few curls. Gosh, she was a cutie.

Daphne grinned and moved to the linen closet, pulling out a fresh towel and washcloth. "Orange?"

Lucy gave a dramatic shudder in full-body disapproval.

"It's a princess color," Lucy prompted.

"Ohhh," Daphne said, drawing out the word, eyes wide with theatrical discovery. "Well, then. In that case . . . pink?"

At that, Lucy lowered the pillowcase, revealing the red-streaked skin beneath her nose and the world's most triumphant nod. "Yes."

"I like pink too." Daphne reached for the washcloth, lowering herself to her knees near the little darling. Her smile came quickly. Her eyes sparkled.

Daphne's assumptions hit a snag. Whatever flirty, smug, infuriating Finn Dashwood was doing, it clearly included being a very good dad.

"Is it your *favorite*?" Lucy exaggerated the word. There was a challenge in her tone—a test of true princess allegiance.

Daphne wrung out the cloth and tilted her head in return. "It's my *second* favorite."

Lucy's eyes widened with the drama such a statement deserved. "Den what's your first favorite?"

"The color of your eyes, Lucy." Daphne leaned close, carefully dabbing a fresh washcloth against the crinkled skin beneath her nose. "I love green best."

....

Finn returned to the sound of Lucy's giggle—and slowed his pace. He'd barely been gone two minutes, still riding the nerves of leaving his daughter alone with a woman he'd known for all of five sideways conversations and one Sunday lunch.

But that laughter? That soft, delighted sound?

It melted the tension from his shoulders faster than butter on a hot griddle.

And replaced the unease with something far less familiar. Something warm and treacherously appealing.

He didn't know what to do with it.

Or, perhaps, somewhere deep inside he knew *exactly* what he wanted to do with it.

So, naturally, he told himself to ignore it.

He eased his way down the hall to the bathroom door and peeked inside.

Daphne knelt beside Lucy, dabbing gently at her face with a washcloth, murmuring something too soft to hear. Her golden hair was pulled into a ponytail, loose strands framing her face, and that absurdly domestic picture hit him straight in the gut.

"Okay, I bet you can't guess this one," she teased, then broke into a softly sung line.

"Dat one's easy," Lucy interrupted, beaming. "*Sleeping Beauty*."

Daphne gasped dramatically. "You are so good at this game."

Her voice held a kind of warmth Finn didn't expect—light, sincere, steady. Like it had been there all along, waiting for someone to need it. For Lucy.

He rubbed absently at his chest, an ache growing in the space beneath his fingers. What was this?

"What's the score?" Daphne asked.

"I have free and you only have one," Lucy declared.

Daphne's shoulders slumped in exaggerated defeat. "Then you should go easy on me next time."

Lucy's giggle sparkled again, and Finn let a grin slip. That laugh had always been his undoing. Since the first time he'd heard it, it had been a kind of magic. His favorite sound.

Lucy launched into the chorus of "Be Our Guest" and Daphne looked skyward, feigning deep thought, though Finn didn't miss the telltale tip of a smile at her lips.

She knew it. Of course she did.

And he . . . could really like her.

Which was precisely the problem.

He wasn't looking for something complicated. With strings. Risky.

He'd done that before. Twice. Once with his heart and once with his business. And each time he'd come out of it with more damage than he knew what to do with. He'd learned the hard way that love came with an expiration date, and he refused to risk Lucy's heart—or his own—again. His job was to protect her, not rewrite some fairy tale for himself.

He knew how these stories ended.

So he shoved the rising knot of hope down deep and leaned into the easier thing: a casual spark. Harmless flirtation. Nothing that threatened to become more.

"*Beauty and the Beast*," Finn said, stepping into the room.

Daphne's gaze shot to his, her smile still warm on her face, and then with a look back at Lucy, she unfolded from her position and stood, handing him the washcloth. "She's very good at this game." She tossed a one-shouldered shrug. "I suppose I need to catch up on my princess songs."

Then with the slightest smile, she slid past him into the hallway, those blue eyes of hers flicking to his as she passed. "I'll be in the kitchen if you need something."

And then she was gone, the faint scent of cinnamon trailing in her wake.

Finn stared after her a moment longer than was strictly necessary.

Cinnamon and sass. Floured fingertips and pink bras on shower rods.

She wasn't what he expected. Not at all.

And that's exactly what made her dangerous. Temptingly dangerous.

"Daddy?"

Finn exhaled, forcing his focus back to Lucy, who was watching him with that small, knowing smile of hers. "Yes, lamb."

"I'm okay if we don't get a puppy right now."

His attention zeroed in on his little pixie, her smile crooked, her eyes dancing. His chest constricted from the effort to withstand the pull of her daydream for a mother. But he'd learned the devastating and hard truth: Love wasn't safe.

And despite his devil-may-care persona, when it came to Lucy's heart, he had to play it safe.

CHAPTER 9

@TeaThymeNC: When life throws you surprise visitors and an unplanned Disney sing-along . . . you do what any self-respecting tea shop owner would: bake cookies.
Do you have a favorite Disney movie and tea pairing? Bonus points if you add a favorite cookie in the mix too. I'm pretty sure my brother's ideal evening is Earl Grey sugar cookies and The Sword in the Stone (very on brand).
PS: I still know every word to "Once upon a Dream."
#PrincessProtocol #EmergencyCookies #BeOurGuestEnergy #LateNightMagic

> **@JackAustenPhotography:** You mean the correct pairing. The Sword in the Stone, sugar cookies, and Earl Grey is canon. Also, explain why a certain British pub owner was seen running out of your apartment like Cinderella past curfew. 👀 Asking for science.
>
> **@GrannyDOfficial:** Lucy told me you sing like a real Disney princess. I expect a performance next Sunday. Bring cookies.
>
> **@MaggiesCottageFlorals:** My vote: Jasmine tea +

Aladdin + shortbread. Because every girl deserves a magic carpet ride and a warm cookie.

@TGDPub: No contest. Tangled and black coffee + classic chocolate chip. #HandsDown #FryingPanProtection

@PastorNateNHC: Robin Hood & sweet tea with mint AND peanut butter oatmeal. Classic combo. And the Tangled movie tracks for @TGDPub aka "Flynn Dashwood." #IfTheBootFits #ItsTheHair

@TGDPub: For the record, the smolder is genetic. And powerful. #ItsTheSmolder

@WisteriaGeneralStore: Just in: Coffee and vanilla-scented candles called The Smolder Blend and a special edition mug that says: "I Got Tangled in Wisteria." Thoughts? Too much? Not enough? Asking for the retail economy. #SmallTownSchemes #MerchIdeasWelcome #WisteriaStrong

"PARDON ME?"

Daphne turned from the oven, Dalmatian-print mitt on her hand, to see Finn standing before her wearing a clean shirt and a somewhat subdued smile. Just the thought of him changing shirts in her apartment had her wondering if she'd left the oven open, because her little kitchen turned sweltering.

Okay, okay, off-limits didn't mean she couldn't admire God's good creation. Her gaze slid down his body and back to his face. Because it was very good. Maybe not as enticing as the car—she emphatically reminded herself—but certainly stare worthy.

He held a sleeping Lucy in his arms, her hair falling over his arm like a sleeping beauty, her breathing quiet and relaxed. Equally as stare worthy.

Daphne's hand went to her chest before she skirted past Finn into the living room. "Why don't you place her here," she whispered, gesturing toward the small love seat. "I'm sure it's way past her bedtime."

Mr. Hotface complied with a raised brow that appeared to be a tattooed feature for most of their conversational exchanges so far. Daphne pulled the quilt off the back of the couch and feathered it over the little girl, sighing down at the sleeping princess.

"I guess she'll have to wait and try one of the cookies tomorrow." Daphne brought her gaze back up, barely keeping her smile in check. "But you're welcome to one, if you'd like."

"A midnight cookie with our beautiful rescuer?" That corner of his mouth tipped as he studied her. "How can I refuse?"

There was a strange sort of undercurrent in his expression she couldn't quite place, a new softness tangled within the resident flirt, and it shifted the air in the room.

It was also nearly midnight and she needed sleep. Which could have had something to do with her bleary-minded thoughts about him.

"Rescuer?" she tossed over her shoulder as she returned to her little kitchen. Well, he'd called her beautiful, but probably hadn't really meant it. Likely just flirt talk. "You'd have done the same for me, right?"

She raised her own brow in challenge, and his grin grew as he searched her face. "I hope so, but I don't sing, so I'd fail miserably at the princess song game."

A soft laugh slipped from her as she offered him a little plate with the cookie she'd specifically kept just for him. "That is a disadvantage when rescuing princesses, I'm afraid."

He suddenly sobered and shifted a step closer to take the plate. "Daphne, thank you." His gaze searched hers in a way far removed from Mr. Flirty Face. "For your help and ready kindness. It truly was a rescue."

Her gaze dropped to his plate, suddenly tempted to take back the cookie. "Um . . . well, it's what neighbors do." She cleared her throat and waved toward him. "Though this is the first time I've had a man in my apartment past 11:00 p.m. in a very long time."

She squeezed her eyes closed as her own words echoed back to her. And that would probably be why it had been so long. Oh, where were her granny's genes when she desperately needed class?

"I'm happy to break your record, for my and Lucy's sakes."

The timer beeped behind her, and she turned to the oven, slipping out another pan of cookies. She placed the pan on the stovetop and turned toward him, mitt still in place. "Well, she's a complete sweetheart."

"Indeed, she is." His smolder turned lethal. "She gets it from her father."

Her pulse responded with an enthusiastic mamba, but she buried it beneath an exaggerated eye roll. "I'm sure she does."

Oh yeah. He could definitely keep the cookie.

He lingered near her, that fresh, appealing scent of vanilla and something clean mixing entirely too well with the lingering aroma of warm chocolate chip cookies. Her brain short-circuited for a second. *Oh mercy. Vanilla and chocolate.* A combination so potent it really ought to be illegal. At least to her.

"Did you say you only had sleeping bags at your apartment?" she asked, grasping onto anything to shift the conversation.

Finn nodded, lifting the cookie to his lips.

And Daphne waited, watching as he took a large bite.

His grin dissolved into something horrified as he chewed. He struggled—valiantly—to maintain composure but failed.

"Oh, sorry." She offered him a sweet smile. "I must have gotten my salt and sugar confused for that one."

His gaze flashed up to her before he coughed—or maybe it was a strangled laugh—and she passed him a bottled water.

"Touché," he rasped, still having a wrestling match between a cough and a smile.

"I would've made you tea to go with it." Daphne plucked the cookie from his fingers and tossed it in the trash. "But since you're a plebeian, I figured you'd refuse."

"I deserved that." His grin made a triumphant return as he took a sip of water, and for some reason, his good-natured reaction only made her like him more.

Drat.

"You sure did." She offered him a fresh cookie from the tray she'd just pulled from the oven. "Try this one. Won't assault your taste buds. Scout's honor."

He took it with exaggerated caution, his gaze never leaving hers as he bit in—and honestly? Why did he have to make eating a cookie look . . . indecent?

That just seemed wrong.

And yet, here she was, rethinking Santa, cookies, and every hallmark of childhood innocence.

Heaven help her if he ever started baking in front of her.

She swallowed as the temperature in the room tipped right back up into feverish. Granny's upbringing had not prepared her for this level of temptation. Like a dark chocolate milkshake with a pump of vanilla and a dash of reckless charm.

At least she had enough country girl stubbornness to keep her cool. Probably.

Still, there was something different about him tonight. The edges of flirtation were still there but softer. Gentled. *Real* in a way that was far more dangerous than smirks and swagger.

Ack! Bring back the flirt!

"Much better," he murmured, finishing the cookie in two sinful bites. "You are an excellent baker."

"Thanks." She leaned against the counter and crossed her arms, needing something to do with them before they betrayed her and started fanning her flushed face. "I do love it. There's something raw and wonderful about taking a mess of ingredients and turning them into something people enjoy, isn't there?"

"Absolutely." His expression became more thoughtful. "I've always found it . . . settling."

Settling! That was how he seemed at this very moment. Settled.

A Finn Dashwood to draw out more from her than a verbal fight. "Right? Like the creativity fuels not only more creativity but a . . . comfort and connection. As if . . ."

She faltered, giving her head a shake. Silly.

But he leaned forward, chin dipped. "As if?"

She waved it off. "As if we were *made* to create."

He crossed his own arms and studied her until her cheeks heated to frying status, but she didn't want to look away. In that moment, she glimpsed a kindred spirit and she didn't quite know what to do with the dichotomy of Mr. Hotface and Mr. Baker Bestie.

"Exactly," he whispered.

The word settled between them and for one ridiculous second, she felt seen by him in a way she hadn't felt seen in a very long time. And the accompanying warmth tremored through her to squeeze at her heart.

"Have you always wanted to be a chef?" She nudged another cookie in his direction across the counter between them.

"Most of my life. Got it from my gran."

That caught her off guard. "Great food and an awesome granny?" She raised her cookie in a mock toast. "A potent combination."

He chuckled—a real one. "She was a force of nature."

"The best grans are, I think." Daphne grinned. "Mine could silence a room with a look and then charm everyone back in the next breath. Slightly terrifying. Utterly iconic."

"Same." Then his grin curled, slow and crooked, like she'd answered a question he hadn't meant to ask out loud.

Daphne quickly busied herself with the tray. Dangerous. He was way too dangerous when he smiled like that. Remember, Daph—he's transient. Said so himself.

But this Finn—the one who talked about his gran and used words like *settling*—had roots. And those roots were looking . . . good. Not that many things could look bad on him. *Sigh.* She inwardly groaned. Yet, this simple tête-à-tête looked a little less like rivalry and a little more like . . . friendship.

He blinked, as if realizing he'd lingered too long in that space—and boom. The flirty persona zipped right back into place.

"Actually," he said, stepping closer, "my gran would've called tonight's kindness scandalously generous. She'd insist I repay you. Possibly with something chocolate or . . ."

Did his attention just drop to her lips? From the sudden explosion in her stomach . . . likely.

She raised a hand to halt his approach, grasping for logic to swoop in and save her from a swoon. "Can you ever have a conversation without turning it into emotional dodgeball?"

He just smiled, that maddening mix of amusement and . . . hunter.

All her defenses entwined with the scent of vanilla, those caramel eyes, and that utterly unfair accent.

She blamed the accent. Fully.

"It's what neighbors do, okay? No repayment necessary."

He paused. Really paused. And something flickered in his eyes again—something not flirty, not snarky. Like he was trying to figure out what made her tick. With a crease of his brow, he stepped back. "It's late." He nodded, as if to himself. "I'd best get Lucy back to the apartment."

Her lodged breath shook free as her thoughts grappled to catch up to the shift. "Is . . . is Lucy likely to have another nosebleed tonight?"

His attention shifted back to her. "Hard to say. I hope not, but with sutures, you never know."

There it was again. That flicker of concern. The kind that didn't fake easily. Maybe even some weariness?

Daphne hesitated. Reason screamed, *Don't do it!* but her mouth didn't get the memo. "It's well past midnight. Seems a shame to move her."

Finn turned slowly, brow raised, and that unguarded look was back on full display. "Pardon?"

She was beginning to really like that look.

"She's sleeping so well." She shrugged as casually as she could manage while her heart climbed up her throat. *Don't offer. Don't offer.* "You . . . you could stay here. In the living room. On . . . on the other couch." She pointed in the direction for emphasis. "That way you'd have running water. Towels. Just in case."

"Stay here?"

"For Lucy." Daphne reiterated with another nod.

The silence that followed was somehow louder than the invitation itself.

Then, softly, "Thank you, Daphne. Truly."

And the way he said her name—gentle, reverent, like he meant it—stilled her breath for an entirely different reason.

She nodded, fighting the flush creeping back. "Happy to help."

And she was. Because this version of Finn—the one who smelled like vanilla, loved his daughter fiercely, talked of his gran, and lit up at the mention of creative recipes—*this* was the one who fit right into cozy movie nights, morning cook-offs, and sweet conversations.

And the flirty one?

He was starting to look like a shield.

....

Sleep came in shallow waves, and each time Finn woke, he found himself on Daphne's couch, with Lucy sleeping peacefully across from him. He lay awake much too long contemplating the events of the night.

Or rather, Daphne Austen herself.

She was a pink-infused anomaly.

He kept trying to place her among the women he'd dated over the past year—sweet, shallow encounters that started with drinks and ended with dessert, never veering beyond. Simple. No complications, no messy emotions.

No one who reached into his world and sparked something hidden—or what he'd believed to be dormant—back to life.

But the way Daphne had knelt by his daughter and made her laugh? Draped a quilt over her with a look of such unabashed tenderness? That wasn't performance. That was *heart.*

And Finn didn't have the emotional real estate for heart.

Or did he? Could he . . . risk more?

More than a single evening of conversation that ended with a good-night kiss and a goodbye.

The past five years had been structured around three priorities: take care of Lucy, run a business, and keep his heart safe. He'd raised Lucy with some help from his dad and sister, juggled life and work with precision, until it fell apart. And he'd gone on the occasional date here or there, of course—casual, uncomplicated, disposable.

But Daphne Austen was none of those things.

She was messy. Surprising. Clever.

And kind in a way she didn't seem to even realize.

Since entering her apartment last night, something unexpected brewed in the air between them, a shift he couldn't quite place. Maybe it was his lack of sleep, or maybe it was just her being . . . her.

Whatever it was had wiggled its way between the cracks of his resolve in a way he wanted to ignore.

Needed to ignore.

His and Lucy's little world worked the way it was.

He didn't have time or interest in . . . more.

With a growl of frustration, he pushed up from the couch, determined to do anything but think. Winston's head popped up, the retriever taking Finn's wakefulness as an automatic invitation for affection.

"Morning, mate." Finn gave the dog a scratch, then padded toward the kitchen, needing something—anything—to occupy his thoughts.

It was still dark outside, but faint light pressed against the edges of the windows. Daphne would be up soon, prepping for whatever cozy chaos she brewed each morning at Tea Thyme. And his movers were due in a few hours.

Hopefully.

His fingers moved without much thought—pulling eggs and bacon from the fridge, setting the kettle on, even locating some coffee grounds in a hidden spot behind copious amounts of tea bag boxes. He hadn't even woken Lucy in the process. Daphne stocked her kitchen intuitively. Exactly as he would have. And he didn't quite know how to process that either.

They weren't alike at all. Opposites. Rivals, even. Yet . . .

A soft hush of movement made him glance toward the doorway.

And there she was.

The most maddening concoction of sexy, humorous, and adorable.

Daphne stood in the doorway, a vision of pajama-clad bewilderment. Hair piled haphazardly on her head like a meringue with ambition. Blue flamingo robe hanging off one shoulder. A pink T-shirt. Flannel pants.

And in her hand?

A curling iron. Held like a weapon.

Something knotted began to uncurl in his chest. He barely bit back a grin.

And surprisingly attractive.

She blinked those large blue eyes at him and examined him from sweatpants to T-shirt before a whimper-like sound bubbled from those pink lips. "You're . . . making breakfast? In *my* kitchen?"

He took his time answering, noting the heightened color in her cheeks and the way her free hand fluttered up to cover her exposed collarbone. She looked much too appealing—especially given the thoughts he'd been trying not to have. It had been a long time since he'd seen a woman in her pajamas, and never one quite like this.

He turned slowly, deliberately, arms folding across his chest. "Good morning?" And then he rested his hip against the counter and nodded toward the curling iron. "If that's meant to tame my morning hair, I won't object. But I'm fairly certain we'll need something more industrial."

Her gaze flicked to the weapon in her hand, and she let out a strangled half laugh before lowering it, her other hand instinctively tugging her robe tighter across her body.

Too cute. Way too cute.

His chest squeezed.

And dangerous.

So, so dangerous.

"Why . . ." She waved the curling iron vaguely in his direction. "Why are you making breakfast?"

He lifted a shoulder, casual—at least on the outside. "Seemed like the least I could do for your kindness to me and Lucy." He gestured toward a few plates on the small table. "After all, you did risk your pristine reputation. Letting the town's new pub owner sleep under your roof?" He gave his brows a shake. "Scandalous."

Her smile went crooked. One brow arched. That chaotic bun wobbled like a bobblehead. His grin slipped wider before he could stop it.

"I don't know how pristine my reputation is." She slid past him and stretched for a mug, even rocked on pink-nailed tiptoe to reach it, and his pulse spiked.

This was too domestic.

Too easy.

Too . . . nice.

"After all, I did foam spray some rather unkind things on your restaurant window after you left last night."

"Did you?" He choked on a laugh, his attention trailing her as she stepped over to the little food-laden table. "Pray tell, what sort of unkind things?"

Without sitting down, she stabbed a cream cheese and strawberry cinnamon toast bite with her fork, clearly wrestling with that grin of hers. "Oh, something like . . . Grumpy Restaurant Owner Seeking Triple-S-G."

He narrowed his eyes. "Triple-S-G?"

She batted those long lashes. "Single. Sweet. Southern. Girl."

"You didn't." He barked out a cough-laugh, half horror, half amusement. "You realize what you've done?"

"If you're going to put salt in my sugar bowls, clearly your subconscious is begging for sweetness." She bit into her toast, her smile almost saccharine.

"I'm going to have to move away now. There will be no peace—"

"Oh my goodness," she interrupted, humming and closing her eyes as she chewed. "This is—" Her eyes flashed wide. "What did you do to this toast? It's . . . wow." She looked down at the rest of the pastry on the table. "You stuffed it with strawberries and cream cheese? Oh . . ." She let out a soft moan, oblivious to the fact that she was unraveling his self-control one sigh at a time. Another bite. "The nutmeg? Perfect." Her moan was practically sinful.

Finn tugged at the collar of his T-shirt, suddenly regretting the extra heat from the stove. "I'm glad you like it," he said, the words barely finding their way around the knot in his throat.

"*Like* feels inadequate," she said around another bite, smiling like he'd hung the moon.

The compliment and the look pressed in on him. He knew he could cook, but for some reason, her appreciation mattered. With a deep breath, he placed a plate of rashers and eggs in front of her, enjoying the way her smile lit her entire face in appreciation.

"No one's made me breakfast since . . ." She trailed off, blinking as if the words had escaped without permission. A small shake of her head. "Well. It's been a while."

The flicker of vulnerability—so fast, so unguarded—landed squarely in his chest.

It mattered to her. *This* mattered to her.

Which only made it harder to pretend it didn't matter to him.

The knowledge shot a direct line to his heart, propelling him to lose all sense and ask, "Would you like some . . . tea?"

She nearly choked down a swallow and turned to take a drink of water before looking back at him, a soft smile playing over her lips. "Do you actually know how to make superior leaf water?"

Her exaggeration pulled another smile from him. Their eyes met. Held.

And stuck.

He cleared his throat, turning back to the stove, grabbing the pot of oatmeal as an excuse to move. What was going on with him?

"Making tea and liking it are two very different things."

"Actually, if you like it, you make it better." She pointed her half-eaten toast at him like a culinary wand. "It's science. Or magic. Or some equally inconvenient truth."

He placed the oatmeal between their plates on the table and remained standing next to Daphne. "You're calling me inconvenient?"

"Oh, definitely." Her grin sharpened, eyes dancing. "And possibly a breakfast saboteur. This is a trap, isn't it? You're trying to sabotage my confidence before the wedding showdown. Undermine my competitive spirit with . . . delicious carbs."

Good, the banter was back. Preferable. More manageable.

"Guilty." He gestured toward the table. "Clearly, I'm superior."

"Hardly." She scoffed and crossed her arms. "This is a one-off miracle. No one should trust the culinary instincts of a man who thinks gas station coffee is a valid life choice."

He chuckled, but it wasn't the charming, calculated kind. It was real.

And it felt good to be . . . real with her. He gave his head a shake.

There she went again.

Slipping beneath his defenses like she'd done last night with that talk of food and grandmothers. Authentic. Unfiltered. And for some reason . . . more dangerous than flirting.

"Food can be terribly persuasive, Ms. Austen." He leaned a little closer. "I might just win you over with it."

She rolled her eyes in a way that should have been ridiculous. It wasn't. It was unfairly charming.

Her grin tugged up at one corner like she enjoyed their back-and-forth just as much as he did.

Too much.

Like a daily dose of something he didn't know he was craving.

Like something he might not want to live without.

He tried to shake it off. Keep things simple. Light. Like the past relationships.

Kiss and leave.

His gaze dipped to her mouth.

Right.

That's all.

"Sweetness can be powerful, Mr. Perfect Teeth," she corrected, lifting an eyebrow. "Doesn't mean the rest of your cooking is."

"Mr. Perfect Teeth?" He blinked. "That's the best you've got?"

"I was taught to *be* nice, not just *play* nice." That soft Southern drawl wrapped around her declaration and tugged at something inside him.

He should've backed off. Thrown a joke in. Flirted just enough to cover the fact that she was getting under his skin in a way no one else had in a long time.

But she was standing so close, and her gaze kept flickering like she didn't want to look—and couldn't quite help herself.

That's when the real trouble began.

"What's wrong with both?" he asked, his voice lower now. "A little fun, a little . . . sweetness, all rolled into one?"

She snorted, even as her gaze drifted slowly down his frame and then locked with his again. And lingered.

His skin prickled with a sudden need.

"Fun, maybe," she said softly. "But *sweet* is not a word I'd use to describe you."

"No?" He stepped in. Just close enough to make her eyes widen slightly. "And how would you describe me?"

She hesitated, her attention snagged at the corner of his mouth—where a little smirk tugged, daring her.

"Dangerous," she whispered.

The way she said it—barely there, barely brave—sucker punched him.

Because it wasn't flirtation. It was a truth she hadn't meant to say out loud.

And suddenly, he wanted to prove her wrong. Show her that there was more to him than cocky grins and casual charm. Once, he'd been the kind of man who knew how to love fully, without hesitation. And look where that had gotten him.

"Dangerous?" His voice dropped, the air between them shrinking by inches. His pulse spiked as his gaze roamed her face, drawn in by those too-perceptive eyes. "I'm not the one who's dangerous, Daphne."

Her brow furrowed. "I don't . . ."

"Genuine kindness," he said, voice rough, "is dangerous too. It makes people hope for things they shouldn't. For things they can't repay."

Like someone staying.

Like love not leaving.

Her gaze softened. "Repayment isn't necessary, Finn."

The way she said his name—soft, warm, wrapped in that Carolina twang—made something ache deep in his chest. Her sweetness. Her sarcasm.

Those lips.

He was unraveling.

Surely, just one taste. One kiss. That would be enough. It would scratch the itch. Get it out of his system. He could kiss her, reset his brain, and walk away like a gentleman.

Like all the other times.

"Perhaps, there *is* a way." The hitch in her breath only fueled his insanity to take another step closer. His gaze dropped to her mouth. "Certainly I could offer you something in return. Something . . . better than stuffed French toast, even?"

"Ah, well . . ." Her voice rasped, attention flickering from his eyes to his lips. "I'm guessing you don't mean something like . . . letting me win the wedding competition?"

He paused his approach to appreciate her humor. He really could like her too much for his own good. "Not exactly."

"Oh . . . hmm . . ." She slipped a step back and raised a finger in mock inspiration. "I know. How about . . . letting me drive your car?"

His car? That actually made him pause. "You want to drive my car?"

She leaned close, giving those golden brows of her a shimmy. "Like I want air to breathe."

He blinked and shifted back a step. "That's a tall order."

"I rescued your sweet daughter and opened my door to strangers. That's gotta earn me something."

His chest squeezed to the needy point, and the feeling shook him. Maybe even scared him. She'd opened the door to more than his daughter. She was opening doors in him he'd sworn to keep locked. Inspiring hope he didn't know what to do with.

And that terrified him more than he'd ever admit.

He liked her. Too much. The way she talked, the way she listened, the way she cared—like it was second nature. Like he and Lucy fit here.

But that kind of believing? That kind of risk?

No.

He couldn't afford it.

So he did what he always did.

Let the charm step forward and take the fall.

"I have another idea in mind." He took a step closer. "Even better than the car."

Her attention dropped to his lips again.

A tell.

An invitation.

Intentional or not, it undid him.

He should stop this. Keep things light. But strawberry cream lingered at the corner of her mouth like an added temptation.

And the last of his restraint shattered.

"How long has it been since you've been properly kissed?"

She cleared her throat, spine straightening like she'd just been called on in class. "I've had my fair share of kisses, thank you."

But the whisper-soft words lacked conviction. Not the kind that said *recently*. Not the kind that said *well*.

"Not from me."

Her breath caught.

And the air shifted.

"Impressive," she murmured, staying close, almost leaning in. "You think that's going to win me over?"

"I don't know." He reached for her, his hand finding the small of her back—and when she didn't pull away, the fragile leash on his control snapped. "Let's find out."

Before he could talk himself out of it, he dipped forward and caught her gasp with his mouth.

The kiss was supposed to be simple. Flirty. A quick indulgence.

The kind of kiss you could chalk up to impulse and walk away from.

But the second their lips touched, a quiet desperation seized him. A longing he hadn't expected. He meant to tease, to dazzle, to leave her dazed.

Instead, he was the one coming undone.

He gentled his caress, urging her to answer his nonverbal request.

And she did, melting into him—warm, yielding, heart rattling—and every careful line he'd drawn around his life blurred. Her sigh sent something through him that felt too much like *belonging*.

He drew her closer, breaking every rule he'd made to keep people out. And when she answered his kiss with a gentle purr of pleasure, he nearly staggered.

He wasn't ready for this.

He wasn't ready for *her*.

And still, he didn't stop.

Instead of shaking up her world a little, she was anchoring him in ways he hadn't anticipated.

This wasn't just a kiss.

This dangled hope.

And he drank it in like a starving man who didn't know how empty he'd been.

He nearly pulled away—nearly did the responsible thing. But then she slid her palms to his cheeks, cradling his face like she didn't just want him—she trusted him. And that wrecked him more than the kiss ever could.

This wasn't supposed to happen. Not with her.

Not with anyone.

Not after someone had promised forever and left him behind with a broken heart and a two-year-old girl asking why her mommy didn't come back.

But Daphne Austen made him want to believe again.

To yield to his heart.

And that terrified him.

Her fingers slipped back to caress his ears, inciting the tiniest moan from him. He nearly brought the kiss to a close on that ground alone.

He never lost control. Not anymore. Not with women. Not when so much was at stake.

And yet . . .

He'd seen something in her eyes. It looked a little too much like faith.

In him.

It slammed into him like a fist to the gut, an unspoken request demanding a reply he couldn't . . . wouldn't give.

He broke the kiss, breathing hard, eyes locked on hers.

She blinked up at him, dazed. Cheeks flushed, lips kiss-swollen, and utterly beautiful.

He almost leaned in again.

She searched his face, and some sort of dawning shifted her expression. She stepped back. Just a small step, but it felt like a chasm.

A sudden sheen glossed her eyes—brief, blinked away—but it stabbed through him.

He'd made a monumental mistake.

He hadn't counted the cost.

"I . . ." Her fingers trembled to her lips as she retreated another step. "I shouldn't have let that happen."

Panic scraped at his ribs. His heart scrambled for cover—for a joke. A deflection. Anything to cover the searing vulnerability. "That bad, was it?"

She let out a shaky half laugh—but the accompanying smile didn't reach her eyes.

"No," she whispered. "It was . . . great."

A beat passed. Then another.

"Too great. For me."

That hit harder than he expected.

Because he didn't want her to think that. Didn't want her to regret this.

"Daphne—"

She held up a hand, halting him. Her eyes met his again, and the heat from before was gone. Replaced with something bruised.

He had the sudden, overwhelming urge to reach for her. To fix it. Comfort her. Undo the damage.

"I . . . I'm not interested, Finn."

"No?" Her words knifed through him, but he tugged the charmer's mask into place. "Not even a little?"

"I don't care in small amounts." The soberness in her tone encouraged more distance than he wanted. Resurrected a wall between them that he, evidently, had forgotten to keep in place.

He should thank her.

"This might be your typical fun, but I'm not a game player. Especially with guys like you."

He flinched.

"Guys like me?" He forced a shrug, clinging to flippancy like a life raft. "You mean tall, dark, and handsome?"

She huffed a laugh, but there was sadness in her eyes now. The kind that lingered and he couldn't—shouldn't—try to reach. "I mean shortsighted and flirt heavy. I'm not into heart games."

"Oh, no worries, luv." He took a step back, the space between them now a canyon. "I only want your time, conversation, and attention. You can keep your heart."

He hated himself the second the words left his mouth.

And judging by the flicker in her eyes, she hated them too. Because for the first time in a long time, he . . . didn't mean them.

"I don't trust myself to keep my heart where you—and your kiss—are concerned." Caution and the tiniest hint of hurt weaved into her expression, dousing his internal temperature. "And I'm not willing to lose it on a bet."

His chest ached.

He hadn't meant to make her feel like a gamble. But maybe that's exactly what he'd done—rolled the dice with something too fragile for casual stakes.

That wasn't who he was.

At least . . . it hadn't been. Before her.

Had she gotten too close? Tempted him to the point of fear? And had he lashed out the only way he knew how?

"Daphne—"

"I'm sure there are plenty of women in Wisteria who'd be happy to play your kind of games," she continued. "But I'm not one of them."

"My kind?" His throat tightened.

"You want the one-night stand." Her eyes didn't leave his. "I want the happily ever after."

And that—*that*—hurt in a place he didn't know still had nerve endings, but he covered the sting with a smirk. "Well, actually, we've already had the one-night stand, and happily ever afters are for fairy tales."

Her eyes dimmed. "Too bad I still believe in them then." She gave him a half smile—wistful, brave, beautiful. The kind he'd remember later. "Silly, I know. But I've never been good with half-hearted or short term."

The need to make things right burst him forward a step. "Daphne, please—"

"Daddy?"

Lucy's sleepy voice drifted from the other room.

They both froze.

Reality snapped back into place.

Daphne took another step back. He let her.

He needed the space. Needed to shove the emotion down.

Lock it up. Bury it where it couldn't hurt either of them.

Keeping her at a distance was safer.

For Lucy.

For him.

For her.

So why did it feel like he'd just blown his one shot at something real?

At something that might have been worth the risk?

CHAPTER 10

@TeaThymeNC: Attention, tea lovers: Did you know that excessive exposure to inferior beverages can dull the senses? Protect yourself. Choose wisely. #KnowYourWorth #BaristasAgainstBeanWater #TeaIsLife

@TGDpub: Funny, I was just about to warn people about beverages that taste like hot perfume. Stay safe out there.

@WisteriaGeneralStore: Okay, I definitely see a T-shirt in the future. Maybe even #TeamTea and #TeamCoffee #OnIt #TeamBrew

@PastorNateNHC: I fear a church divided cannot stand . . . but if there's a bake sale involved, I'm willing to mediate. #BlessedAndCaffeinated

@MapleRidgeFarm: As long as no one slanders hot cocoa, I'll allow this debate to continue. #Switzerland

@MaggiesFlowerCottage: Just here for the inevitable showdown. Also, I volunteer as tribute to taste test both sides. #Peacemaker #PastriesGoWithEverything #SoDoesCaffeine

@TeaThymeNC: @PastorNateNHC I'm happy to provide a proper brew for the mediation. Finn is, of course, welcome to repent.
@TGDpub: @TeaThymeNC Never.
@WisteriaGeneralStore: Merch ideas are now pouring in faster than an over-caffeinated barista on a Monday. #BraceYourselves #TeamBrew #WinBothWays

LINDSAY MONROE HAD CONTACTED Daphne by phone for an immediate taste testing.

And since Flynn . . . er . . . Finn's kiss had done practically nothing else but distract her for an entire day and a half, she welcomed the redirection back to basics. What was reliable. Constant.

And yet . . . ever since he left her apartment with Lucy in tow, her mind had detonated with flavor pairings and pastry combinations like a rogue episode of *The Great British Bake Off* had hijacked her subconscious.

In fact, she'd stayed up all night long creating culinary masterpieces, from familiar favorites to brand-new offerings.

And all of them tasted phenomenal, if she did say so herself.

Rosemary, as her official taste tester, agreed.

"Whatever has inspired this sort of creativity," she'd said, *"I hope it sticks around."*

Daphne refused to confess to Finn as a part of said inspiration. But she couldn't fully deny it.

A very productive, wildly inspired, completely unnecessary inspiration from remembering how his lips had felt on hers. How her knees had gone suspiciously jellylike. How the earth had briefly tilted, and all she could think afterward was, *Oh no.*

No, she'd never been kissed like that.

But it wasn't just the kiss—it was the moment after. The way something had changed in his expression, in his eyes, like he was scared of what had just happened. Like he'd wanted to take it back. Like maybe . . . he hadn't meant it?

Or . . . had meant it and didn't know what to do.

That was the part that wouldn't stop replaying. And the part that led to her unfurling her frustrations into pastries, sautés, and confectionaries.

The very fact she'd managed a semi-cool, semi-sarcastic exit was nothing short of divine intervention. And fear. The kind that came from being left one too many times. Most people hadn't chosen to go—her mom, her granny. But her father had. And her high school boyfriend, once college happened. And a good friend who lowkey disappeared after Daphne had traveled out to Colorado to visit her, following her move.

Her best friend.

Those three had all been similar.

Had the same irresistible, leading-man energy as Mr. Hotlips Dashwood.

Charming. Flirty. The human embodiment of the line "Don't worry, I've got this."

Also? Dangerous.

Because he wanted shallow.

She'd heard him say it himself: *"You can keep your heart."*

And she would. Thank you very much.

But, Lord, have mercy! Her face flushed from the memory—the firm warmth of his mouth, the lazy confidence of his fingers brushing her neck, the way he'd looked at her like she was the only thing in the world worth noticing.

And then, *poof.* Gone. The ghost of his cologne and the confusion his behavior left behind lingering longer than he had.

Her breath shuddered and she shook off the daze, narrowing her eyes at her reflection in the tea shop's display case.

"'Run mad as often as you choose, but do not faint,'" she whispered. *Do not faint.*

Real people disappoint. Real people leave.

A haze of tears rose in her periphery, softening her own face in the glass. So many people had left.

She blinked away the sheen.

Knightley, Darcy, and Thornton—they never left. Fictional men stayed exactly where you needed them: safely pressed between the pages, charming and complicated and loyal. Unlike real men who kissed you like you were air and then walked away like they hadn't just rearranged your internal organs.

Finn Dashwood was further proof that reality ruined more daydreams than fiction ever could.

She took a steadying breath and focused on what mattered. That kiss might've inspired a storm of sugar-fueled ideas, but it didn't change the fact that she had a job to do. This celebrity wedding was her chance to save Tea Thyme, and she wasn't about to let some smirking, broad-shouldered, kiss-like-a-sinner chef derail her goal.

Even if part of her stupid, traitorous heart wished he'd meant it.

Wished he hadn't looked so scared. Or wounded.

Wished he'd stayed.

Daphne set out a delicate porcelain plate on the table she'd meticulously decorated—floral linens, soft gold accents, and a centerpiece of fresh herbs and roses. Everything was curated to perfection. Elegant. Classy. The sort of presentation influencer-slash-model Lindsay Monroe would appreciate, naturally.

Though Daphne had taken a sabbatical from social media over the last year, she'd followed Lindsay faithfully—Wisteria's most glamorous export. The woman had taste. Style. And a fondness for vintage that made Daphne feel like maybe, just maybe, they were kindred spirits across the aesthetic ether. Even if Lindsay had never once glanced her way in high school.

The door jingled, announcing the arrival of the bride-to-be, the woman currently holding Daphne's future in her manicured hands.

Okay, not *Daphne's* future.

But maybe Tea Thyme's.

Lindsay glided inside, somehow glowing under the soft lighting like the entire shop had been staged just for her Instagram. She wore a cozy-chic yellow blouse, distressed jeans, and boots that probably cost more than Daphne's monthly grocery list. But despite the influencer sheen, her smile was warm. Real.

"Oh, this place is adorable!" She took in the room, smile growing. "The photos online just don't do it justice. It feels like I just stepped into a storybook."

Daphne's pride did a little internal curtsy. "That's exactly the idea. Tea should be an experience, not just a drink. A little daily escape."

"That's what I keep telling Travis!" She stopped in front of the food-laden table. "That the food and the setting are part of the whole thing. Our wedding's small on purpose—for the magic, the intimacy."

"And . . ." Daphne arched a brow, gesturing toward a chair in front of the delectable display. "Your fiancé doesn't quite see the vision?"

"Oh, he wants it to be nice. But where food is concerned?" Lindsay sat gracefully, crossing her legs. "He's obsessed with hearty, heavy comfort food. Think steak pies, pasties, full English breakfasts. If it doesn't involve a stick of butter and a food coma, he's skeptical."

Daphne arched a brow. "He sounds like an experience all on his own."

Lindsay laughed. "He's a wonderful man, but when it comes to food, he's almost the equivalent of a walking cookbook from 1974." Her grin softened. "He appreciates refined food of course, but deep down he wants meals that remind him of growing up in Yorkshire."

"That type of food has its place." Daphne filed that away with interest. "But let's see if we can expand his culinary worldview." She laid out the first round of her tasting menu—miniature savory tarts: wild mushroom and Gruyère, caramelized onion and goat cheese, and smoked salmon with crème fraîche and a dill sprig so tiny it looked like it belonged in a dollhouse garden.

After all, her grandmother had been English. And Daphne loved all things British. So surely, with a few tweaks here and there, she could dip further into more extensive savory options.

Think outside the box some more.

She drew in a breath. Not everything had to fit into her self-made boxes, did they? This wedding opportunity certainly didn't. It came out of nowhere. Totally outside her comfort zone.

And she already felt it pushing her in ways she'd been too afraid to try.

But wasn't "necessity the mother of invention"? And maybe even the "mother of creative growing pains" in this case?

Lindsay took a bite of the mushroom tart and groaned softly. "Okay. That's . . . absurdly good. And the crust? Flaky, buttery perfection. Like a hug from Mary Berry herself."

Daphne's heart did a traitorous little skip. Not from the compliment—but because she suddenly realized she wanted this. Not just the job. But the chance to *be* this version of herself in front of more than just her gran or Jack. Confident. Creative. Capable of making a roomful of people melt with food. With joy.

And . . . to afford plumbing repairs was a nice by-product too.

"And that onion tart?" Lindsay was already reaching for the next. "Elegant. Flavorful." She reached into her bag. "Mind if I take some photos? My followers will love this."

Mind? Try *die of internal squealing*. Lindsay Monroe had more than thirty million followers on her lifestyle, travel, and beauty social media pages. And she was posting her dishes! *Hers!*

"Of course." Daphne nodded, her voice breaking into a little squeak at the end.

As Lindsay artfully arranged a few tarts on her plate, Daphne unveiled the sweets: raspberry-rose pavlova with sugared petals, a delicate Earl Grey peach tartlet, and an apple cider tea cake dusted with a whisper of cinnamon sugar.

"Oh wow." Lindsay placed the remaining pavlova in her mouth, angling her phone for the perfect shot. "This isn't just good. It's couture for your mouth." She angled her phone for another shot, this time of the tea cake. "You know what I mean, right?"

"I do," Daphne said with a somewhat-tempered grin. "I like to think of it as emotional support sugar."

"I knew I liked you," Lindsay said, taking a bite of the tartlet and actually moaning. "If your pastries can make me forget that our caterer bailed, I'm calling you a miracle worker."

"Only if miracles include a carb-based coping strategy," Daphne quipped, refilling her tea. "You should see how people melt after a bite of scone and a whiff of bergamot. I'm telling you, baked goods are like therapy."

"Wisteria is like that too." Lindsay sighed as she took another sip of tea. "The entire community has welcomed me like I never left. It's very grounding."

"Well," Daphne said, surprised at the sudden kinship blooming between them, "I think these hills carve out a little spot in everyone's heart who's lived here long enough."

Lindsay nodded, then turned thoughtful. "I never realized how much it would mean to be here again, and now to use a local business for the wedding? It makes it feel more real somehow. Like . . . home."

Daphne froze at the unexpected comradery. Lindsay had been all over the world. Met famous people. Made tons of money. But the fact that Wisteria still meant something to her . . . well, the distance between struggling tea shop owner and world-renowned influencer didn't seem as large as it did a few minutes before. "Home is a special place."

"Exactly." She nodded. "And *special* is exactly what I want people to experience at my wedding," Lindsay continued, her eyes bright. "I don't just want good food—I want food that delights people. The kind of thing where every bite feels like a treat, from first look to last taste. And maybe even helps people experience this"—she waved her hand toward the window—"home of ours. That's why I wanted to meet with you first while Travis is meeting with Finn."

Daphne's heart did a very unhelpful little hiccup at the mention of Finn, but she wasn't sure if it was from professional rivalry . . . or the way he'd kissed her like—her gaze dropped to the peach tartlet—like she tasted good. Heat ticked up her neck and into her cheeks.

Drat that man and his disturbingly nice lips.

"Well," she managed, smoothing the napkins even though they didn't need smoothing, "you'll have plenty to compare notes on later. Just make sure you pick the right person for your big day."

"I plan to." Lindsay snapped another photo, then plucked another tart off the plate. "Travis may fight me on it, but if this is the competition? Finn's in trouble."

Daphne's gaze slid toward the wall separating her shop from Finn's.

He should be in trouble . . .

And preferably avoidable.

After leaving her off-kilter from that kiss, the very least he should do is forfeit this competition, because that kiss probably didn't knock him for as much of a loop as it did her.

"Um . . . so is this kind of a competition between the two of you?"

Lindsay's question pulled Daphne's attention back to the woman's face. "Um . . . well, he is sort of my competition, isn't he?"

One of Lindsay's dark manicured brows rose northward. "I suppose he is." Her gaze moved to the adjoining wall, and then her smile spread wide as she raised a piece of shortbread to her lips. "Mr. Dashwood may very well be in trouble."

Daphne sipped her tea, trying to cool the heat in her cheeks.

Her gaze traveled back to the wall. No, he shouldn't forfeit.

He needed to lose fair and square. Get a good dose of healthy humbling.

Because she was determined to win.

• • • • • • • • • •

Finn had laid out a spread that could've made a lumberjack weep with gratitude—whiskey-glazed pork belly, mini Yorkshire puddings puffed to golden perfection, and a take on bangers and mash that might've brought tears to a stoic Brit's eye. Roasted root vegetables and a display of his favorite desserts rounded everything out.

This was food that stuck to you. Food that made people groan in satisfaction.

Which was exactly what Travis Langford did the moment he took his first bite of the pork. His eyes fluttered shut like he was catching a glimpse of the afterlife. "This. This is a wedding meal."

Finn leaned back against the counter, cool and casual, pulling the towel from his shoulder to wipe his hands. "So I take it you're enjoying yourself?"

"If you don't cater our wedding, I might have to cancel it outright."

Finn barked a laugh. "I'll take that as a compliment, mate—though I feel like your fiancée should weigh in before you make any dramatic life decisions."

"I'm just chuffed we found another option in time. Lindsay was in full-on meltdown mode when the caterer bailed, so Harry's suggestion about you and Daphne came at the perfect time."

"Harry and Maggie are dangerously well connected." Finn gave a mock bow. "And Wisteria hasn't even tasted my best work yet."

"Harry mentioned you're opening this weekend with a limited menu?" Travis speared a roasted carrot. "But if this is your 'limited' menu, I'm almost afraid to see what happens when you offer the full one."

"I hope it brings in a large number of patrons." Finn stood a little taller. Travis's praise was a nice boost to the ego, especially when a bloke was just starting over in a new town with more baggage than a honeymoon suite. Which inspired an idea. "As a matter of fact, Travis, if you are still in town, I'd like to formally invite you and your lovely fiancée to The Green Dragon on Saturday night. Special tasting menu. Drink pairings. I might even shave."

"I'll make certain we are here." Travis nodded. "Because it's going to take all the charm you can muster to win over Lindsay. She's been on this 'curated elegance' kick since January, and of course it fits her entire brand, so why should I be surprised that she's carried it over into the wedding? Says the whole day has to be an *experience*."

"And I'm guessing your version of an experience includes more gravy than glitter?"

"Exactly." Travis scooped up another bite of mash and groaned like the spirit of Yorkshire had descended upon him. "She wants food that looks like it belongs in a bridal magazine. I want food . . . like this."

"And maybe like this too?" He pushed a tray of sweets forward. "Molten chocolate cake, pecan fudge bombs, and"—because he wasn't completely devoid of romantic sensibilities—"a raspberry fool. Light, sweet, deceptively charming."

The words stuck in his throat.

Deceptively charming.

Daphne's face flashed in his mind. The shock in her eyes after their kiss. But worse—the guarded sadness that followed. Like she'd known it would end that way. Like she'd expected him to pull away. And he had.

Because he was an idiot.

A fool indeed.

He should have said something. Anything. But the second her lips left his, it was like a trapdoor had opened beneath him. His pulse had thundered, his chest had seized—and all he could think was, *Not again.*

And yet, he'd wanted to stay. For the first time in a long, long while, he'd wanted to linger. Brew a pot of tea. Sit on her couch. Ask her questions about her ridiculous blend names and that vintage baking tin collection. Maybe even . . . kiss her again. Slower this time.

But instead, like a coward, he'd bundled Lucy up and made his exit.

Because that was safer. And safer was his default now.

Then why did *safe* suddenly feel more like an excuse than a protection?

Travis, mercifully oblivious to Finn's spiraling, looked up like he might propose right then and there. "It's like I've stepped back into my nan's kitchen. If she'd had a Michelin star and a flair for dramatic presentation." His grin grew and he dipped his spoon into the cake first, whimpering with pleasure at the taste.

Finn really couldn't have asked for a better recommendation. He loved this part—watching people light up when they tasted something that hit just right. Food was storytelling. Memory. Sometimes even redemption.

What might work for Daphne? Chocolate?

He stifled a groan. No. Food was much too shallow an apology when the damage was deeper than a burnt caramel or split ganache. And he wanted to apologize. Make things right. Maybe even . . .

What?

Hope again?

Because of her and what those minutes of conversation felt like when all the barriers slipped away? When it was talk of food and family? When it was just him and her without pretense?

Travis pointed his fork toward the spread. "Do you think there's a way to make this look . . . you know, classier?"

It didn't get classier than Yorkshire pudding, but if Finn wanted to be taken seriously by the wedding venue population, maybe he needed to think a little more . . . creatively. Sticky pudding in a dessert glass? Nicer plates? Microgreens?

"I could carve 'happily ever after' into the mashed potatoes," Finn deadpanned. "With a gravy drizzle flourish."

Travis laughed. "As long as the potatoes show up, mate."

Finn chuckled, but his mind wandered—right past the Yorkshire pudding and raspberry fool, to the woman likely serving petit fours and perfumed teas through the adjoining wall.

"Didn't I see you and Lindsay drive in together?" He nodded toward the wall like he could see through it. "I'm guessing Lindsay is with Daphne right now?"

Travis gave a sheepish nod. "She was already planning the Instagram caption in the car."

"Which means Daphne is currently wooing her with bite-size baked goods and frosting." He tried to sound unaffected. Light, even. But a slow ache tugged behind his ribs. "Probably has rose petals scattered on the scones."

Travis paused mid-chew. "I didn't think about that."

"Don't worry," Finn said, injecting false bravado into his voice. "I'll win her over."

He had to. It wasn't just about the gig. Or the timing. Or even the ridiculous joy he got from proving himself.

"You sure?" Travis asked, eyebrows raised, before he delved into the Yorkshire pudding like he hadn't eaten in twelve years. "Because Lindsay has been dreaming about this day since she was five. She's got vision boards. Plural."

"She's romantic. I get it." Finn waved a hand over the food. "But this is a wedding. Not a garden party. People need fuel to dance and flirt and make questionable choices."

Travis grinned. "You're not wrong."

"And look, Daphne's incredible," Finn added before he could stop himself. In fact, the statement slipped right out, complete with a surprising amount of . . . awareness that he believed it. So why would he run away from incredible? He shoved off the thought. "She's got taste. Grace. Probably has her own zip code on Pinterest."

Travis laughed again and then tipped his head, studying Finn. "You know? If Daphne has the look and you have the"—he waved his fork toward the food—"soul. Maybe the dream team is both of you."

Finn's jaw clenched, but he wasn't sure why. Both of them? Sounded like . . . a relationship. "We're not a team."

"Oh?" Travis tilted his head.

"No." He forced up his grin again, attempting to shrug off the way Travis's suggestion twisted uncomfortably into his psyche. "At the moment, we're . . . competitors."

Even if she'd kissed him back.

Finn raised his gaze to the wall, another pang twisting in his chest. He shouldn't have kissed her. He'd known it before he'd leaned in—knew it as surely as he knew how to time a soufflé. Knew she wasn't like the others. And instead of dousing his interest in her, the only thing that kiss had done was make him want more. More of her voice. Her laugh. Her stupid tea metaphors. Her heart.

And that was the part that terrified him most.

Because wanting more meant risking more. And he'd done that once. With someone who had promised forever and left anyway. It had gutted him. Changed him. Made him someone who didn't reach for soft things anymore.

So no—he hadn't kissed Daphne expecting to fall. But it was happening anyway.

And he had no idea how to stop it.

CHAPTER 11

@LindsayMonroeOfficial: Wedding tasting at @TeaThymeNC. Pretty sure I've just stepped into a dream. If this isn't the definition of wedding vibes, I don't know what is. #ElegantEats #SippingPretty #TeaTimeGoals

> **@TravisLangfordConnects:** But I had a food tasting at @TGDpub. If this doesn't end up on the wedding menu, I'm running away with the chef instead. #PubGrubPerfection #SorryLinds
>
> **@LindsayMonroeOfficial:** @TravisLangfordConnects Nothing is that good.
>
> **@CCloves:** You two can't break up because of food. We've been following every step of this story from the beginning to now. We are in it for the wedding.
>
> **@LindsayMonroeOfficial:** @CCloves Our followers are the best, so we won't let you down. We just have a little problem. We now have to pick a culinary winner. How will we choose? Elegance over comfort food? Style over steaks?

"OKAY, WHAT'S GOING ON with you?"

Daphne looked up from her tray of pastries and experimental savory bites to see her brother striding into Tea Thyme, eyes narrowed with the sharp focus of a one-man lie detector.

He was usually a pretty chill guy.

Until he wasn't. And then he made up for lost time.

But surely he couldn't read her mind.

Couldn't see the guilt simmering behind her smile. The flicker of disappointment that hadn't left since . . .

The kiss.

The thoroughly unwise, thoroughly unforgettable kiss.

Which may have sent her into . . . lowkey falling for Finn a little.

Even though she shouldn't.

Her stomach tightened.

Besides, Finn probably hadn't even given it a second thought. Just another kiss in a line of many for him.

She frowned. If only she could forget it so easily!

"What do you mean?" she asked, voice pitched a little too high as she tried not to visibly sweat over a tray of her brand-new creation: Earl Grey and honey macarons.

Jack raised a brow like he could see right through her. "You didn't return my meme jokes last night."

She busied herself with her piping.

"And," he added, thumbing toward the front window, "you've got *three* new menu items on your chalkboard."

She didn't mention the five more she hadn't written up yet.

"I have a wedding competition to win, remember?" She slid a shortbread cookie his way—a buttery little round perfected sometime between 2:00 a.m. insomnia and replaying that kiss on a mental loop. "Besides, since Lindsay's taste testing, she's posted all sorts of great things about Tea Thyme, and it's brought in some extra business."

"Well, that's something." Jack took a bite, chewed thoughtfully, then immediately grabbed a second. "When I was up at the inn shooting engagement photos today, Margaret mentioned Lindsay and Travis are stirring up some sort of social media feud between you and Finn. What's it called—GrubWars?"

"*War* definitely feels accurate," she muttered, glancing toward the wall separating her shop from Finn's, where the faint thrum of rock music vibrated through the drywall.

But . . . at least he didn't turn it on until she closed shop.

That was one nice thing about him.

And the kiss.

Ugh.

And did she even stand a chance against him with his experience and fare? He studied in Paris, for goodness' sake. And Daphne was sure he offered items that appealed to a certain group of people. But, boy oh boy, she wanted this. Needed it.

More than bragging rights or proving she wasn't just the lace-aproned tea girl with pastel signage, this was a chance to save her shop. Fix the leaks. Upgrade the kitchen. Keep Tea Thyme from becoming just another closed-door dream.

When she looked back, Jack was watching her. Too closely.

Heat rushed into her face, and she returned her focus to her piping.

He didn't respond right away, so she spared him a look.

And, drat—now he was staring at the wall!

"The uptick in business is nice," she said, trying to sound breezy, "even if I don't win."

"You have as good a chance as Finn, I'd say." Jack took a bite of another cookie and then pointed with what was left of it. "These are great. Granny would have loved them."

That hit her in the soft spot. "She inspired the tea obsession in the first place."

"I know." He softened. But only for a second. "Still . . . this sudden pastry renaissance wouldn't happen to have anything to do with the coffee slinger next door, would it?"

Daphne froze mid-pipe, then turned to him, face arranged in its most dramatic look of betrayal.

"Why would you say that?" She pointed the icing tip at him. "Your pep talks and meme game are highly powerful . . . especially when I want them to stop."

"Yeah, funny about that. None of my other pep talks ever resulted in you baking like you've joined the Pastry Olympics." He popped the rest of the cookie into his mouth. "But ever since your Good Samaritan rescue of Finn and his daughter, you've been acting like someone spiked your English Breakfast with three shots of espresso."

Before she could respond—or launch a tart in his direction—the front door creaked open, this time with an all-too-familiar and hot-lipped silhouette.

Speak of the Henley-wearing devil.

"I'm closed," Daphne said, turning and pointing directly at Finn. "Especially to you."

Jack's eyebrows launched into his hairline.

But Finn? He sauntered forward like he owned the place—ignoring the sign, the finger, and the very clear no-trespassing glare she was shooting his way.

"You don't get off that easy, Miss Austen." His grin hooked sideways in that maddeningly confident way. "A harmless substitution of salt for sugar does not warrant being hunted by wolves."

Oh, right. She'd almost forgotten her little revenge prank.

"Where's your adorable sidekick?" she asked, hoping to derail him. She'd seen the aftermath earlier—stepping outside after Lindsay left and catching a glimpse of Finn being ambushed by a steady parade of Wisteria's single (and not-so-single) women. Some arrived with casseroles. Others came with mothers. One brought a crocheted scarf.

"She's helping Gavin clean tables because she *loves* cleaning." Finn groaned as he dropped onto the stool beside Jack, then pinned Daphne with a look.

"Gavin?" She gave her head a shake. "You have Gavin York working for you too?"

Of course Finn would convince one of the most well-known grillers in Wisteria to work for him!

Finn shrugged a shoulder like he accepted the power of his own charm. "And don't attempt to divert the conversation from your part of my torture. Because of you, I've been introduced to every eligible woman within a twenty-mile radius. Including two who may have followed me from the farmers market."

Jack turned slowly to his sister. "What did you do?"

Daphne lifted her hands in feigned innocence. "Just tried to help his business. Increased visibility. Good for marketing."

"Help business, my eye," Finn echoed with a glare far too dramatic to be genuine. "I've been drowning in gardenia body spray and casserole-induced trauma. And all because *someone* couldn't keep her foam art off my windows."

She nearly snickered at his turn of phrase. He shouldn't be so fun to irritate. He really shouldn't.

But it was easy. And addicting. And—she blinked—surprisingly safe.

She didn't worry about Finn overreacting. Or becoming angry. Or lashing out. How did she automatically know he could handle it?

"Wait . . ." Jack shifted his attention between them. "Why do I get the feeling my sister has thrown you to the lionesses of Wisteria?"

"She unleashed them." And Finn, complete with a twinkle in his eyes, told Jack about the message she'd left on his restaurant window and the ensuing result.

Jack groaned. "Daph, come on."

But Daphne couldn't quite summon a sincere apology. Not when

Finn was trying so hard not to smile. Why did he have to be such a puzzle? Flirty but sincere? Easygoing but infuriating?

She just couldn't seem to fully make him fit into a box.

"I did, however," Finn said, with a smug little wink, "secure promises from all of them to stop by the pub Saturday night. So . . . business will be booming."

And that, my friend, is how a plan backfires.

Daphne resisted the urge to throw a tart at *his* head and then averted her attention. "So if all you wanted was attention and dinner dates, mission accomplished. No troublesome hearts involved."

The second the words left her mouth, she regretted them.

Finn's gaze snapped to hers—too steady. Too . . . aware.

She shifted a step back from the counter, scrambling for a joke or jab, anything to shove the moment back into safe territory. But her brain short-circuited under his expression.

Then, with a casual lean on the counter, Finn glanced at Jack.

And like there was some kind of invisible bro code, Jack stood and stepped over to the nearby shelf, suddenly finding her turn-of-the-century Dutch Delft Dore teapot very, very interesting.

What was happening?

"About that . . ." Finn cleared his throat, cast another glance at Jack's back, and leaned in just enough to lower his voice to a conspiratorial hush. "That thing. The, um . . . thing that happened. Recently."

Her eyes narrowed for a moment. She wasn't going to let him off the hook that easily for the *thing that happened.*

"You'll have to be more specific," she said, tilting her head and studying him. "What sort of . . . thing?"

Was he . . . blushing? All the way to his ears?

The very idea of this smooth-talking, confidence-wielding, swaggering man blushing over their kiss? It softened something in her. Maybe her gut hadn't been so off the other night after all.

"Right." His eyes narrowed for an instant before he looked away. "Well. There was a moment. A particular moment. Of . . . proximity."

A laugh nudged its way into her throat, but she swallowed it down. "Proximity?"

"Yes. You know." His attention darted to Jack's and back, before he lowered his voice even more. "When two people occupy a shared . . . personal radius. And perhaps make impulsive facial decisions."

Jack flinched.

The desire to laugh grew into a cough. "Impulsive facial decisions?"

Finn's eyes narrowed the slightest bit as he studied her. "I'm apologizing for . . . any and all unplanned proximity that may have resulted in . . ."

Her brows rose in expectation.

All humor slipped from his face, replaced with something low and intense. "Hurting you."

Oh.

Daphne searched his eyes, trying to read what he really meant. This wasn't flippant or coy. It was . . . genuine.

"I was wrong, Daphne," he said quietly. "Forgive me?"

The apology hit her somewhere deep. Her heart gave a traitorous thud.

Wrong? About the kiss?

Her throat tightened.

Or about his interest in her heart?

And then, like the perfect interruption of a Hallmark movie, his phone buzzed.

He held her attention for a breath longer before glancing down at the phone. "It's Gavin."

With another long look at her, he raised the phone to his ear and stepped back toward the front of the shop. And Daphne stood there, staring after him, wondering when exactly her revenge plan had become so . . . complicated.

Jack returned to the counter and then leaned forward. "What is going on between the two of you?"

His whisper breathed harshly across the short space between them.

She dragged her gaze back to her brother. "What do you mean?"

"Unplanned proximity?" Both his brows rose. "Impulsive facial decisions?"

The laugh-cough erupted for a short release. "It's really nothing. A momentary . . . nothing."

"Are you interested in Finn?"

Daphne let out a long breath, trying to exhale the knot in her chest. "He's not my type."

"Not my question." Jack narrowed his eyes.

Heat crept up her neck. She turned back to her piping bag. "I'm not interested in his type."

"Ahhh." Jack stretched out the word. "So much clearer now."

She rolled her eyes for his viewing pleasure.

"He's all the things you've waxed poetic about for years: British, funny, food obsessed." Jack ticked off fingers, then paused, his tone softening. "Is it because he's a dad?"

"No. Actually, being a dad is probably his best feature." Daphne sighed. "And his version of *nice*"—she used air quotes—"is at least fifty percent jerk and ninety percent commitment phobic. He told me so. He's nothing but a flirt."

But even as she said it, the memory of his apology flickered in her chest. Not so flirtatious. Not so light.

"What?" Jack pinched the bridge of his nose and closed his eyes, giving his head a little shake before staring back. "Um . . . being a flirt doesn't always equal shallow or heartless, Daph." Jack shook his head. "No matter what Jane Austen says."

She squinted at him. He grinned. Then sobered.

"A guy doesn't apologize like that if he's indifferent. Whether or not he wants a relationship, he clearly cares about not hurting you. And that's not jerk behavior."

She opened her mouth, ready to object—then closed it. Jack was right.

Again.

Finn wasn't a jerk. He was a good dad. Genuinely decent to people, from everything she'd seen . . . and heard. Polite to Granny D. Friendly with the whole town.

Well—everyone but her.

And still, that kiss had felt . . . different. Like he'd been surprised too.

She nodded, mostly to herself. It didn't matter. Whatever spark existed, it wasn't going anywhere. Not when he made it crystal clear he wasn't looking for anything beyond . . . impulsive facial decisions.

They could just be simple, neighboring competitors till death do they part.

"Who's to say that he's only *really* flirting with you?"

That stopped her mid-thought.

Her bottom lip dropped. "He flirts with everyone."

"Does he?" Jack raised a brow. "Has he flirted with anyone else the way he flirts with you?"

She opened her mouth, ready to list names. Then paused.

Yes, he was friendly. Yes, he was smooth. But . . . was it the same?

And why did that suddenly make her think of all the horrible antics middle school boys engaged in when they were crushing on a girl?

Her face went warm at the memory of his lips on hers. But Finn most definitely wasn't a middle school boy.

Just then Finn returned, phone lowered, looking slightly less amused. "Gavin said we've got a problem at the pub."

Jack stood.

"Oh no." Daphne lowered the pipe. "What is it?"

"Dishwasher." Finn grimaced. "Minor flood."

Her stomach lurched. Was Finn's plumbing connected to hers? Similar to hers, even? Surely her leak and his couldn't be related, could they?

"Gavin is steering suds toward the back door with a pizza peel."

Jack snorted. "Everything falls apart without me, I see."

"Very funny." Finn took a few steps back. "I need to get over there."

"I'll help." Jack followed.

"And, Miss Austen?" Finn turned, those caramel eyes locking with hers. "About the Triple-S-G, don't think I've forgotten we have a score to settle."

Flirting again. But was it different with her?

"We do." She lifted her chin, stepping into it with renewed curiosity. "I believe you're still in my debt, Mr. Dashwood."

Finn narrowed his eyes like a man about to start a war. Or kiss a girl.

She gave him a taunting smile.

Jack rolled his eyes.

Then the door closed behind them, and Daphne stood alone in the quiet bakery, staring after them . . .

. . . wondering which she wanted more.

The war.

Or the kiss.

....

Finn leaned against the prep counter, damp from the mop battle and smelling faintly of citrus cleaner and rosemary chicken. The dishwasher was officially dead, but a replacement had been ordered within the hour, and no one had cried in public. So far, so good.

He'd hired two solid guys as his main managers—Gavin and Jack worked well with him, intuitively.

"Daddy." Lucy pulled her dragon tighter into a hug and smiled up at him. "Mr. Jack put Dragon in one of the bowls and floated it over the floor."

Finn shot Jack a look across the kitchen. Jack just grinned. "When life gives you lemons . . ."

"Or in this case, a minor flood?"

"Make an ark?" Jack shrugged, finishing off the last bit of water pooling near the wall that connected their kitchen to Daphne's.

Finn pulled Lucy up in his arms and placed a kiss on her head. "Jack should stitch that on a pillow, shouldn't he?"

With Jack's laugh echoing behind him, he carried Lucy to the front of the shop and set her down with her late supper. "I'm going to help Mr. Jack finish cleaning up, all right, lamb?" She raised a carrot to her smile and nodded.

Finn returned to the kitchen and reached for a bottled water. "I'm grateful Pete was able to fix the problem so quickly." He tossed a bottle to Jack as the man stood from collecting the last of the dish towels. "Let's hope that's the last of the chaos. I've got too much riding on Saturday night—money, reputation, and possibly a wedding gig that could keep us afloat through the fall." His eyes pressed closed. "And . . . tomorrow is Lucy's first day of school."

"On a Friday?"

"They do this staggered entry thing for kindergarteners. Lucy's turn is tomorrow." Finn gave a helpless shrug. Because of course it would be.

"Well, Gavin and I are here for the full day to help prep. Whatever you need, we're your guys."

Finn nodded, grateful. Jack's help had turned out to be more than just logistical—he'd been a steadying presence in the middle of the bedlam. Between dish disasters, a whirlwind of emotions, and the storm of Finn rebuilding his life, Jack had shown up for Finn like a man on a mission. And had become a friend.

With Harry running the inn, Jack offered a thread of community Finn hadn't realized he'd been craving in the aftermath of a business scandal and the loneliness of single fatherhood.

"By the way . . ." Jack placed the last towels in a bucket by the back door. "I was able to sneak Pete into Daphne's kitchen like you asked."

Finn straightened.

"Said her plumbing's a mess, but he made a temporary fix."

"How temporary?"

Jack shrugged. "He's hoping a few months, but what the shop really needs is a renovation. It's been running on borrowed time—and love—for a while."

Pete Marsh had warned him—the old plumbing that ran between their kitchens was a disaster waiting to happen. His side had been updated in part, but the sections they shared? A cracked pipe away from catastrophe. From what Pete had said, Daphne's side was hanging on by a thread and a prayer.

"How much do I owe you?" Jack reached for his wallet. "For Daphne's part of the repairs."

"Nothing." Finn waved him away. "It needed to be done anyway."

With Wisteria's Womanly Welcome—and Daphne's very public matchmaking stunt—his shop had seen a healthy uptick in interest. Hopefully the costs would even out quickly.

Jack's expression didn't budge. "Finn, the main leak came from her side."

"I know." Finn nodded as warmth flushed through his chest. "But now my side's fixed and hers is patched well enough to get her through a few more months. There's no reason to make more of it than that, Jack. I've got a restaurant to open in two days—and I need a working kitchen to do it."

He could tell that explanation didn't quite convince Jack. He gave Finn a long, assessing look.

"I'm part of this community now," Finn added, keeping his tone even. "And you're the one who said neighbors help each other, remember?" He lifted a brow. "Would you have done the same?"

Jack didn't answer.

But the silence was enough.

"Then let it go." Finn's voice softened. And still, even with the price tag and the lingering doubt, it had been the right call. A good one. One his younger, less-jaded self would have made without question—back before fear of being used or let down had carved him into someone more cautious. "Save your money for when she needs a full replacement. Because she will." He exhaled. "And despite my blunders . . . I do want to be her friend."

Or something more? The question sliced through him with the pain of a knife.

The very fact he was even asking the question said enough.

He was starting to care about Daphne Austen.

And that scared him more than the plumbing bill.

"Friend?" Jack breathed out a sigh and leaned back against the fridge, arms folded. "Look, I don't usually play the protective brother card. But—"

Here we go.

Finn braced.

Jack hesitated, eyes flicking to the sink before meeting Finn's squarely again. "Daphne's known a lot of hurt."

Finn studied Jack, his thoughts spiraling back to the tea shop. No doubt Jack had heard Finn's horrible attempt at a coded apology . . . and had come to his own conclusions.

Finn's defenses twitched. "Do you think I'm the sort who would wish to hurt her?"

Even though he had.

And he hated it.

Jack didn't flinch. "Are you?"

The words hit like a punch to the ribs—sharp and deserved. Similar to the one he'd been giving himself for the past two days.

"I *know* I don't want to hurt her again." He hesitated. "Beyond that? I thought I had a plan. Thought I knew what I was doing. What I wanted." His eyes drifted toward the wall that separated their shops. "But now I'm not so certain."

Something subtle shifted in Jack's stance—like a hinge opening—and he leaned back against the fridge. "Our dad left when Daphne was eight." Jack swallowed. "Couldn't handle our mom's cancer diagnosis."

Finn stilled.

"The three of us moved in with our grandmother—the one who started Tea Thyme. Mom passed not long after we came here. From that point on, it was just Granny. She held us together."

A pause.

"Until last year. Heart attack. No warning. One day we were planning the fall menu, the next"—his gaze came up—"she was gone. We've had a lot of people leave. Most unintentionally."

Finn didn't speak. His chest had gone tight. That kind of loss? That much grief packed into a few short years? It was staggering.

And somehow . . . they still led with kindness.

Still gave.

It humbled him all the more.

"And that's why I'm being up front," Jack said quietly. "Daphne's not wired for flings or games. She latches onto people and loves with her whole heart. She remembers everything about the people she cares about. The way they take their tea"—he waved to Finn—"or coffee, in your case, even if she hates coffee." His grin flashed for a second. "She's the type of person who remembers the names of people's dogs or that offhand comment they made about liking waffles more than pancakes. She files it all away like it means something and then uses it to help them feel special."

Finn's mouth tugged into a small, sad smile, even as something inside him ached.

"Right," he said quietly. "That tracks."

"So if this is just a game for you—don't." Jack leaned in, his tone sharpening just a touch. "I don't care how charming you are. She deserves better than temporary."

Finn rubbed the back of his neck, the weight of Jack's words settling over him. "She does."

Jack watched him for a beat, then gave a slow nod. Like he'd found whatever answer he needed.

Finn sort of wished Jack would let him in on the secret, because currently Finn felt entirely flummoxed from the heart out.

The front door jangled, likely Gavin returning, and Jack pushed away from the fridge. He paused near the counter, expression thoughtful.

"Just remember that, man." His voice was quieter now. "Because she might not say it—she might not even know it yet—but she already cares more than temporary."

Then he stepped away, leaving Finn standing in the wake of that knowledge.

Finn stared at the space Jack had just vacated. A small puddle of water still pooled near the dishwasher, reflecting fractured shapes from the overhead light.

He didn't move.

Because deep down he already knew the truth.

He'd started caring more than temporary too.

And he wasn't sure if he was brave enough for the risk.

CHAPTER 12

@TeaThymeNC: When in doubt, choose elegance. Your wedding day deserves something special. #RefinedTaste #TeaThyme

@TGDpub: Or, you know, food you'll actually remember eating. #NotJustForPhotos #EatLikeYouMeanIt
@LindsayMonroeOfficial: Confession: @TravisLangfordConnects and I love both. How are we supposed to decide? #Help #FoodieDilemma #CantChoose
@WisteriaGeneralStore: You know we're taking bets, right? #TeamTea #TeamPub #WinnerGetsBraggingRights #ItsAllOverTown #GrubWars
@PastorNateNHC: I feel like this requires divine intervention. Or, at least, a very thorough taste test. #ToughJobButSomeonesGottaDoIt
@TeaThymeNC: There's still time to convert to the superior side. Just saying. #LeafOverBean #StyleOverSteak
@TGDpub: Funny, I was about to say the same thing. #LeaveTheLeaf #EatLikeYouMeanIt

SOMETHING WAS DEFINITELY WRONG.

After Lindsay and Travis's joint taste testing of her brand-new wedding items (which she'd secretly named her "punch-throwing menu") of mini steak-and-ale pasties with thyme mustard, smoked salmon tea sandwiches, three-cheese gougères, and the new beer bread with cheddar-chive butter, she thought she'd won Travis over. All right, not completely, because Finn hit all of Travis's nostalgia notes, but enough to impress the guy.

And that should have made her feel excited.

But then, near the end of the testing, Travis mentioned wanting "the best of both worlds" and jested about how this could "only be decided by a cook-off."

The atmosphere in the room instantly changed.

Travis had looked at Lindsay.

Lindsay had looked at Rosemary.

They all had exchanged a look.

A slow, knowing, *scheming* look.

Daphne's stomach dropped like someone had just canceled her access to the whole season of *The Great British Bake Off*.

Which Rosemary only made worse by smiling, waving, and floating out the front door with an ominously chipper, *"I feel really good about this, Daph."*

Daphne groaned.

Why couldn't the choice between caterers just be plain and simple? Her lips twitched. *Her.*

With a sigh and a glance heavenward—inviting an answer from Gran or God, whoever was quicker—she grabbed her watering can and stepped outside. Across the street, bright banners for Wisteria's Harvest Festival fluttered on the breeze: Wednesday through Sunday! The kickoff dinner and dance were less than a week away.

The festival was one of the busiest times of year in Wisteria, great for business and a delightful way to showcase the culture, the mountains, and how much the people of this town loved one another. With a deep breath of the afternoon air, Daphne watered the happy yellow mums she'd placed in her window box in time for the weekend. She loved fall in the Blue Ridge. The mountains wore a quilt of color, and the cooler weather gave her every excuse to pull out her favorite sweaters and fuzzy socks. Mums, crisp breezes, pumpkin spice, corduroy skirts with knee-high socks.

Daphne breathed in the scent of leaves and fresh bread—Finn's, no doubt.

Tomorrow was his grand opening.

She wasn't sure if she was going.

But Jack worked there. And she did believe in supporting local businesses.

And, well . . . her gaze flicked toward Finn's restaurant.

It didn't hurt to keep an eye on the competition.

Warmth skirted up her neck and into her cheeks. It didn't have anything to do with actually being interested in Finn. She was only interested in how her dishes compared to his.

The roar of an engine pulled Daphne's attention away from her mums just as the screech of the school bus's brakes slowed the yellow mass to a stop in front of the shop.

Oh, right. It was Lucy's first day of school!

Daphne took a few steps toward the bus as a dark head emerged from the doors, her little body almost too small for those gigantic steps as she exited.

But instead of the bright smile Daphne expected, the girl's green eyes were wide and tearful.

And then she ran.

Full tilt into Daphne's stomach.

"Oh, honey." Daphne dropped to her knees and wrapped her in a hug. "What happened?"

Sniffles erupted in response, along with something mumbled into Daphne's cardigan.

Daphne looked instinctively toward Finn's shop—no sign of him. He was probably slammed with prep.

"Hey, sugarplum. Let's head inside and text your daddy, okay? Then we'll make the biggest strawberry milkshake this town's ever seen and figure out what's made you so sad. Sound good?"

Lucy sniffled again and nodded, leaning against Daphne as she guided her through the shop door. Daphne had already turned the shop sign to Closed, but she flipped the lock into place to ensure no visitors and then sent Finn a quick text for direction.

After she'd distracted Lucy by asking her for help to make the milkshakes, and after Lucy's sniffles died down a little bit, Daphne directed the little girl up the back stairs to her apartment and into a cozy chair in her living room.

One with pink pillows.

Very important.

Winston seemed to help a little too, his vigorous welcome ushering forth a little giggle. Winston was no stranger to crying princesses.

"It looks like this conversation requires a lot of pink, Lucy." Daphne patted the fluffy shag pillow to her right. "And this is probably the best place for it."

Lucy nodded, her large eyes still rounded and watery. She clutched the milkshake close and nestled in beside Daphne as they both snuggled up into the oversized chair. In pink from head to toe, even her hair bows, Lucy showcased her preference. Daphne sighed. She and Lucy were definitely soulmates.

"Okay, what happened today?"

Lucy's bottom lip quivered, resulting in Daphne kissing her head. "It's okay. We will figure it out, sugarplum. And when your daddy comes, he can help us too."

Another quiver of the lip. A sip of milkshake.

"Was it something that happened at school?"

Lucy shook her head and took a long sip of the milkshake before answering. "On the bus."

Ah, the school bus was a tricky place. Daphne had unhappy memories of some of the antics kids got away with on the school bus.

"Mavis was a second grader."

Hmm . . . big girl picking on little girl scenario? Daphne's internal radar spiked.

"And she said I talk funny." Lucy sniffled. "I said I was from England, and den she said England people talk funny."

"That wasn't very nice at all. Or accurate." Daphne had gotten used to some of Lucy's distorted speech sounds, and they didn't really impact comprehension all that much, except when Lucy spoke fast. "Did you tell her anything else?"

"I said I see a speech teacher for some of my hard sounds."

Kudos to Finn for keeping his little girl informed, but oh my goodness, what a tough introduction to kindergarten. "Great job. I bet there are other kids in your class who see the speech teacher."

Lucy nodded and took another drink of the milkshake. "Den Mavis asked if all English people looked like me."

Looked? Daphne stiffened a little, a cool splash of caution seeping into her skin. "Well, that's a funny question. Of course not all English people look like you, just like all Americans don't look like me."

"She . . ." Lucy's bottom lip trembled anew, those emerald eyes searching Daphne's face. "She asked if we all have broken faces. And . . . and a bigger boy on the school bus . . ." Her little voice increased in urgency. "He said my broken face was ugly."

Oh.

Daphne blinked hard, her vision blurring for a moment.

She pulled Lucy into a hug, fierce and fast. "Oh, Lucy."

If she'd been gifted with heat vision, the side of that school bus would be smoldering right now.

"It hurt my feelings." Lucy's bottom lip trembled again.

"I know it did." Daphne kissed the top of her head. "It hurts because it's not true, and your heart knows it."

What on earth could she possibly offer to a little girl whose heart ached? Who needed some reassurances about truths and lies and all sorts of things in between?

And then—maybe from Gran, maybe from God—a quiet knowing settled in.

Maybe she did have something to offer this little girl who was starting to steal her heart.

••••••••••

Finn took the porch entrance up to Daphne's door, wiping damp palms on his apron. He'd been nearly elbow deep in a batch of beef Wellington, trying to coax the pastry into that golden, flaky perfection that earned Michelin stars—or at least a raised brow from Granny D—and hadn't seen Daphne's text until nearly a half hour after she'd sent it.

Father of the Year, right here.

On Lucy's first day of school too.

He hadn't fully counted the cost of launching his own business and trying to keep tabs on his little girl's every milestone. Nursery school had wiggle room in its pickup time. But a school bus?

He hadn't thought to watch for her.

His shoulders slumped as he crested the stairs and paused in front of Daphne's door, left open just a bit. Like she'd been expecting him.

The wood hung slightly crooked, similar to the back door to her restaurant's kitchen. More was in need of repair than her plumbing. He filed the thought away, his hand brushing the weathered frame as he stepped closer.

Then he heard her voice.

"Well, that's a funny question," she continued, saying something about how English people and Americans didn't all look the same.

Finn tilted his head, squinting through the opening. What was going on?

Then Lucy's soft, shaking voice answered, and heat exploded in his chest. Some boy on the bus had said something cruel.

A growl itched at the back of his throat. He'd had enough practice swatting away people's assumptions about Lucy—her speech, her crooked smile, her absent mother—but those had always come in sideways glances and whispered questions meant for him. Never for her ears. She didn't have the words yet to fight back. She shouldn't have to.

Maybe school had been a mistake. Perhaps he should wait another year.

He took a step forward, ready to storm the room with all the righteous fury of a protective dad. Why had Lucy run to Daphne? Had she seen her first?

"I'm so sorry, Lucy. What those kids said wasn't kind at all," came Daphne's response. He'd missed some of their muffled conversation, but he waited in silence a beat more to calm down before entering the conversation. He shifted another step forward.

Why did kids have to say such horrible things?

Daphne's voice paused his approach. "Words hurt sometimes, don't they?" She remained too calm. Not angry enough. "And those kinds of harsh words hurt even worse if we believe them."

Believe them? He almost rounded into her living room, but Daphne's next question brought him to a complete stop.

"So how do we figure out whether we should believe those words or not?"

Finn braced a hand against the wall. What was she doing?

"I don't know."

"Maybe we have to ask someone who knows better. An expert about the topic."

Finn peered around the corner of the wall to see Daphne curled up with Lucy on a large blue chair, pink pillows around them and Lucy holding a handkerchief in one hand and a . . . milkshake in the other?

Daphne looked around the space and suddenly seemed to find what she was looking for. She picked up Lucy's lunch box that lay beside them on the floor and ran her finger over the pink monogram. "What if Mavis or that little mean boy on the bus"—maybe Daphne wasn't as calm as she seemed—"pointed to this *L* and said that it was an *A*? What would you say?"

"It's not an *A*," Lucy whispered, indignant. "It's an *L*. For *Lucy*."

She still couldn't quite land the *L* sound, but that didn't seem to bother Daphne at all.

"Exactly right. It's an *L* for *Lucy*. But what if Mavis kept saying it was an *A* and didn't believe that it was an *L*? What would you do then?"

"I know how to spell my whole name," Lucy said, a touch of sass sliding into her tone.

Atta girl.

And at least Lucy was distracted. That was much better than the quivering bottom lip and woeful eyes he'd imagined.

"That's because you're very smart." Daphne leaned down and pressed a kiss to Lucy's forehead—and Finn's heart tumbled into a free fall. Just like that. No warning. No parachute. Just plummeting into some terrifying, wonderful void.

"But is there anyone in your class who might be an expert on the letters and writing and . . . teaching?"

Finn's breath squeezed through his throat. Where was this leading?

"Miss Krissy!" Lucy piped up, her previous sadness dissolving.

"Exactly!" Daphne squeezed Lucy's shoulders. "Miss Krissy is the teacher, so she should know a lot about letters, right?"

"Mm-hmm." Lucy took a sip from her frosted glass.

"So you can trust Miss Krissy to be an expert with letters, right?"

Lucy nodded. "And she writes very pretty."

Finn almost grinned.

And from his view of her profile, so did Daphne. "Excellent for a teacher. So, Miss Krissy knows the truth, and she helps you know the truth because she's an expert on letters," Daphne continued, brushing a wild curl off Lucy's forehead with gentle fingers. The feeling in Finn's chest squeezed tighter.

"Well now, if someone says something unkind about *you*, then I suppose we need to ask an expert on you to figure out what's actually true. Right?"

His brain snagged on the question like an epiphany waited just in the shadows of his mind. *An expert?*

"Does anybody know you best of all?" Daphne asked.

Lucy took a proud sip from what was unmistakably a pink strawberry milkshake—because of course it was—and declared, "Daddy."

Finn's eyes burned. He pressed his forehead against the wall, swallowing the knot in his throat.

"That's right. I bet your daddy knows you better than anybody in the whole world."

"Mm-hmm, but God." Her voice grew to show her excitement. "God knows me better than anybody in the whole sky."

He smiled, eyes closed. *That's my girl.*

"Exactly." Daphne chuckled, her voice filled with a tenderness so familiar it settled in around his heart. Daphne cared like she was meant to belong right there with his little girl. "So if we wanted to ask an expert—like, if you're pretty or not—who should we trust? Some boy on the bus? Or Daddy?"

"Daddy." Not even a pause.

Finn's breath shattered. He pressed a fist to his chest, as if that would keep his heart from coming apart entirely.

"And what would Daddy say about you, Lucy?"

"He finks I'm beautiful."

That did it.

His heart cracked, expanded. Wanted to keep whatever beauty made this moment so good and right.

Or rather . . . *who* made this moment so good and right.

"And he thinks you're beautiful all the way through, from the heart out."

Finn opened his eyes and looked at Daphne. The sun caught her hair, casting a warm halo around her as she sat beside his daughter. She was genuine. Compassionate.

Beautiful from the inside out.

Someone to trust with Lucy's heart?

His throat tightened. *Yes.*

"And you know what God says about you?" Daphne asked softly.

"That I'm beautiful?"

Daphne smiled so tenderly it made Finn ache. And when she touched Lucy's cheek, Finn nearly felt the gentleness to his soul. "He does. He also says you're precious to Him. Do you know what *precious* means?"

"Special?"

"That's right. But not just special." Daphne leaned in, like she was sharing the best-kept secret in the world. "A treasure."

"A treasure?" Lucy's eyes widened. "Like pirate's treasure?"

"Bigger than the biggest pirate's treasure." Daphne nodded, their noses nearly touching. "And that's what God and your daddy know about you. That you're wonderful. Precious. Beautiful."

"And a treasure," Lucy added with a giggle.

"Exactly." Daphne tapped Lucy's nose and grinned.

The whole scene blurred in his vision. Something shifted inside him—quiet but seismic. Like the ground beneath him had tilted. Or was that the hesitation inside him unfurling?

"That's exactly right." Daphne wrapped Lucy in a hug.

And just like that, Finn fell.

Hard. Crushing.

Fantastically. No going back.

"Okay, sugarplum," Daphne said, still holding Lucy close. "You remember that the next time someone who doesn't really know you tries to act like they do. If what they say doesn't match the truth, you catch that thought"—she waved her hand above Lucy's head like she was snatching fireflies—"and toss it away." She shook her fingers like she was dusting off crumbs. "Don't hold them in your head for very long."

Lucy nodded and mimicked the movement.

Finn's world tilted upright, like a camera lens coming into focus after far too long of seeing things wrong. For the first time in a long time, emotions he'd buried deep inside his bruised heart expanded through him, filling the broken, hollow places in his chest. Shoring up the weak spots.

And hope rushed in.

Daphne wasn't competition.

She wasn't even a rival.

She was the risk worth taking.

His throat closed. But he'd fumbled things so badly. She didn't trust him. Probably didn't even like him. And as for seeing him as anything close to a suitor? That ship had sailed, sunk, and been picked over by sea creatures.

Still.

"You spying on the competition?" came a voice behind him.

Finn turned to find Jack leaning in the doorway, pizza box in hand and a mischievous tilt to his brow.

"No," Finn whispered. Then sighed. "Well . . . maybe a little. But for good reason." He jerked his chin toward the living room. "Your sister is being her beautiful self and rescuing my daughter's day."

"Her *beautiful* self?" Jack's other brow rose to meet the first, but he didn't question further.

Finn cleared his throat. "Evidently another child said something particularly nasty to Lucy on the bus and Daphne is smoothing things over."

"Sounds like her."

Finn glanced at the pizza box. "Is this why you're never available Thursday evenings? Pizza night?"

"It's tradition," Jack said, grinning. "Thursday night engagement and wedding photo shoots, followed by Austen Gang Game Night. It's sacred."

Austen Gang? Game night? The two of them? Finn might as well have walked into a cozy sit-com. And he kept liking it more than was good for his mental health.

Or . . . perhaps it was exactly what his mental health needed?

"Can I have another cookie?" Lucy's voice brought his attention back to the little scene in front of him, a new lightness in his chest.

"Just one more, but don't tell your daddy. It'll ruin your supper, and he'll get fussy with me."

Finn shot Jack a grin and stepped into view. "Fussy with you, my dear Miss Austen? You wound me."

"Daddy!" Lucy launched at him, and he caught her with ease, swinging her onto his hip and kissing her cheek.

"Hello, lamb. Have you had a proper chin-wag with Miss Daphne?"

Jack rounded the corner into the room next and set the pizza on the table as Daphne rolled her eyes and stood, hand on her hip, holding a cookie like a gavel. "Jack brought you to game night? Desperate times—he must need help reevaluating his tragic Uno strategy."

"You wish," Jack shot back.

Finn stepped closer to Daphne, lowering his voice. "I was only just able to get away. Thank you."

She looked at him longer than she needed to, something searching in her eyes. Maybe she noticed the red-rimmed edges of his. Maybe she saw more.

"So," she said finally, "how long were you eavesdropping?"

"Long enough to know you're a wonder."

Then she shrugged and winked. "Only when it comes to little girls and baked goods."

She winked. His grin bloomed into something ridiculous. She was beautiful, tenderhearted, authentic, *and* fun? How had he dismissed all of those qualities before when all he could see was his own fear?

He shifted Lucy to the floor, and she skipped over to Jack. Which meant—blessedly—Finn could take one step closer.

"It seems we owe Miss Austen another debt," he said, meeting Daphne's gaze. "That's, what, rescue number three? Should I just go ahead and relinquish my car keys in gratitude?"

"Your car?" Her whole face perked up like a kid who'd been promised a pony. Then she caught herself, reined it in with a casual shrug. "Sure. That sounds . . . great."

He couldn't stop staring. Seeing her in new ways. Trying to regain some semblance of balance. "What if we check both our schedules and make a . . . date of it?"

Her smile faltered. Her posture shifted. And the wariness returned like a curtain being drawn across a window. Argh. He hated he'd left that impression on her heart.

"I'm all for gratitude," she said slowly. "But what's the catch?"

"No catch." He held her gaze. "And maybe a realization that I've been blind to the value of some of the people in my life."

She tilted her head, studying him. Her chest rose and fell a little faster.

Did she hear it? The truth tucked between the lines?

"Okay, you two are getting a little too gross for me to enjoy my pizza." Jack plopped a slice onto a plate and handed it to Lucy with a grin—no need to ask Finn's permission anymore. Over the past week of working together at the restaurant, Jack and Lucy had become a bit of a dynamic duo. She adored him. He made her feel important. Gave her little jobs, lavished her with dramatic praise.

Finn glanced at Daphne.

Whoever raised these two—Gran, most likely—had left behind a legacy of generosity. Of quiet, resilient kindness.

"You don't have to repay me, Finn," Daphne said softly. "Sometimes people just do the right thing because it is the right thing. Like caring about Lucy. It's easy."

"I don't mean it as a repayment, but more of a thank-you." He searched her face. How had she grown even more beautiful in the past half hour? He prayed he hadn't blundered things beyond repair.

She stared back, a little of the wariness waning. Still around the edges but not quite as sharp.

"Not everyone adjusts so easily to Lucy's . . . speech differences or to strangers the way the two of you have done."

"Gran always welcomed strangers." Jack chuckled. "She and Granny D were a wild duo when it came to generosity. Took in every stray soul who wandered through town. Half of Wisteria probably owes them a casserole."

"And Lucy's speech isn't that bad," Daphne said, moving to grab a bag of chips. "Nothing that should scare people off. Besides, anyone who can't see how special she is? That's their loss."

"People don't always like differences or . . . the unexpected. It makes them uncomfortable." He studied her and then looked back at Jack. "But you two seem to take it in stride."

"In stride?" Daphne stilled, shot a look at Jack, and said, "Funny you should put it that way."

"Don't—" Jack groaned, but Daphne only shrugged.

"Jack, take your legs off."

Finn blinked. "I'm sorry—what?"

Lucy looked up from slipping crust to Winston. Even the dog paused.

Jack let out a sigh that suggested he was all too familiar with this bit. "He would have figured it out eventually anyway."

"Not with you wearing black jeans and white button-downs all the time for your work uniform." Daphne waved him away and turned back to Finn. "We understand about the struggle with differences because Jack was born with phocomelia. Congenital limb malformation."

Finn's head whipped toward Jack.

Jack stood there like any other man. Confident. Capable. Solid. "Congenital limb malformation?"

"Without legs." Jack shook his head and shot Daphne a weak glare. "Or in my case, part of my legs were missing." And with another exaggerated sigh, he sat down on the nearby chair and raised one of the trouser legs to reveal the gleam of a metal prosthetic. "Left leg's gone from the thigh down. Right from just under the knee."

Finn stepped closer, staring. "But . . . I've seen you run. Climb ladders."

Jack tapped the leg with a knuckle. "Been using these since I was a toddler."

Daphne gestured toward her brother with a smile full of both pride and affection. "An entire life of questions, stares, low expectations . . . all of which Jack's blown to smithereens."

"Now you're just trying to make up for outing my prosthetics like they're a party trick," Jack grumbled, though his tone held no sting. "It's not a big deal anymore. I don't lead with it because most people don't know how to react. They can't handle"—he glanced at Lucy—"differences or the unexpected, like you said."

The implication landed heavy in Finn's chest. Could that have been another reason their father left? Because he couldn't accept a child who didn't fit the world's expectations? The thought raked over Finn with extra pain. A man who left his family when they needed him. Who saw his children as less than or not enough? The ache in Finn's chest spread as he looked at Lucy—bright, funny, brave Lucy—and imagined the shadow of that kind of rejection. Then his attention flicked to Daphne. What scars would that have left behind? He looked to Jack. What wounds?

"Just don't challenge him to a trampoline contest," Daphne said, pouring a glass of iced tea and handing it to her brother with a grin. "Still a bit tricky."

"They're tricky for me, and I have nothing like your excuse." Finn shook his head and chuckled. "You both are remarkable people."

"One of us is," Jack said, taking a sip of tea and throwing a look at Daphne. "The other is a nuisance."

"Thank you." Daphne dropped into a small, theatrical curtsy. "I do try."

Finn's smile lingered, but something deeper stirred beneath the amusement.

This—the teasing, the ease, the warmth—this felt like family. Like belonging.

He hadn't realized just how much he'd missed it.

His dad used to be the gravitational pull that made Finn feel at home, but after the funeral Finn had drifted, trying to find where home was next. Without Dad.

And maybe he hadn't fought the drift. Maybe he hadn't had the strength.

But maybe now, maybe *this*—Daphne, Lucy, even Jack—was his second chance.

"I know you're busy with prep for opening Saturday." Jack tossed a slice of pizza on a plate and walked over to Finn. "But since I work with you, I also know you're ready." He offered the plate. "You and Lucy want to join us for a short game night?"

"I'm not certain." He rubbed the back of his neck. He really should go back over everything, but the cozy idea of staying just a little longer in this welcome environment tugged at him. "I probably should double-check the back-order list and—"

"It would be good for Lucy," Daphne threw out there.

"And good for you, mate," Jack said in the worst fake British accent Finn had ever heard.

Daphne shot him a frown. "Never do that again. Gran would be horrified." She shook her head and turned back to Finn, the light in her eyes a sudden warning. "I think Finn is just scared that I'll not only beat him at securing the wedding job but at Uno too."

That smile—with that teasing curve that made his chest feel too tight—was pure trouble.

Beautiful trouble.

Finn held her gaze a moment longer, testing the air between them. Trying to see if there was room—space—for more than rivalry. Could she still believe something good about him?

Was it possible to prove to her that he could be the guy worthy of a future with her?

"We can stay for an hour," he said more to Daphne than Jack. "See how I fare for a game or two?"

The catering competition might still be on. And Daphne still proved his competitor.

But maybe—just maybe—it wasn't the wedding he wanted to win anymore.

He was out for a much more precious prize.

An unexpected treasure.

Daphne Austen's heart.

CHAPTER 13

@TGDPub: You ever notice how coffee drinkers just . . . drink their coffee? Meanwhile, tea drinkers need an entire personality quiz, a three-act play, and the alignment of the planets before they can take a sip? #JustAnObservation #DrinkAndGo #TeaPeopleExplain

> **@TeaThymeNC:** @TGDPub Oh, I'm sorry, do you need me to apologize for having standards? The beauty of tea is in its subtlety. A gentle balance of flavors. An experience meant to be savored. Not burned to a crisp and buried under gravy. Some of us prefer elegance over culinary aggression. #TeaCulture #DelicacyMatters
>
> **@TGDPub:** @TeaThymeNC The beauty of a real meal is flavor. Something tea culture wouldn't know about since you people think "notes of chamomile" count as excitement. Try a full English sometime and then tell me a lavender biscuit changed your life. #FlavorOverFrills #JustEatTheChicken
>
> **@TeaThymeNC:** @TGDPub I have tried your full English. My palate hasn't recovered. You seasoned the potatoes like you were mad at them. Also, for the record, a good

lavender cookie (we are in the US after all) can change your life. Especially when not served next to something that looks like it survived a pub brawl. #RespectTheTea

@WisteriaGeneralStore: We've got #TeamTea and #TeamCoffee mugs in stock. Also a tote that says, "Don't talk to me until the leaves have steeped." #WisteriaWares #ShopLocal #GrubWars

@SheriffGrady: Are they flirting or fighting? Because I truly cannot tell. #SmallTownDrama

@PastorNateNHC: As long as they bring snacks to the next potluck, I don't care what they're drinking. (Though I'd like to remind everyone that coffee is mentioned in the Bible. Hebrews. Just saying.)

@TeaThymeNC: @TGDPub and @PastorNateNHC And lo, the prophet Isaiah said, "In quietness and trust is your strength." Which sounds an awful lot like steeping to me. #SteepAndKnow #BlessedAreTheBrewmakers

@OldManRutherforton: Back in my day, a fella with this many opinions on a lady's breakfast would've just bought her a meal and called it courting.

@TeaThymeNC: Not helpful, Mr. Rutherforton, but I'll happily serve you breakfast.

THE AFTERNOON WITH LUCY had rattled Daphne more than she wanted to admit.

Not because she didn't love comforting that sweet little girl.

And not because she didn't believe every word she'd said about truth—words her granny had once tucked into her heart, now passed along to another.

But because of Lucy's complete confidence in her dad. In Finn's sweet adoration of his "lamb." The way she'd curled into his arms like it was the safest place in the world. The way he had looked at her like she was the moon and stars and all the best parts of the sky.

Daphne had no memory of a father's love like that. No real idea of how it anchored a heart. But she recognized the certainty—the rootedness—of being loved by a father. She'd seen it in Lucy. In Rosemary. In dozens of people she'd grown up around.

They understood a security Daphne recognized in theory, and in her faith. And she got a little taste of it with Jack. She almost smiled at her reflection in the mirror. She knew she could count on him. There had been times in their lives when they only had each other.

And he'd always been there.

But her heart ached for something different. Security from the man who would hold her heart someday.

And then, the way Finn and Lucy had joined into game night like they just . . . belonged there? It was unnerving and sweet.

When Rosemary and Nate had shown up an hour later, Finn had stayed. Long after the polite escape window had closed. His charm and humor had blended right into the cozy chaos of their "gang" . . . and added just enough spice to keep her toes curled.

That accent.

That hair.

That smile that made her feel like she'd swallowed warm cider and maybe a few fireworks.

The secret ingredient to her downfall.

It wasn't fair.

And then he'd had the audacity to dangle his car as a date option.

A date.

Which could mean anything.

And probably did.

His definition of *date* and hers were likely worlds apart.

She'd always seen dates as the possible first step toward forever.

So, yeah.

There was pressure. But she couldn't seem to think smaller.

Building emotional connections in a disposable way felt . . . heartbreaking.

And she'd had enough heartbreak to last a lifetime.

She smoothed her hair before sliding on a pair of silver earrings, delicate with a little sapphire bead that caught the light. They matched the flirty dress she'd chosen—a deep blue that hugged her curves and suggested more poise than she felt. The entire ensemble boasted a simple, classic look. And the shade matched her eyes.

If she was going to walk into her competition's grand opening, she might as well look like a woman in control.

The pub had only been open an hour and already had the low, golden hum of success. Candles flickered in mismatched brass holders. The stone fireplace cast a low, cozy heat. Laughter lilted through the air like music.

And Finn—blast him—was behind the counter in rolled-up sleeves, shaking hands, laughing easily, and passing out plates like he had the corner on happiness.

Just Finn Dashwood doing what Finn Dashwood did best: charm an entire room with that smug, stupidly attractive smile and ridiculously enjoyable humor.

Daphne's grin wavered.

Charming could be dangerous.

Her mother had said the same about Daphne's father. And he'd vanished the moment life turned demanding.

But Finn? Whatever happened with Lucy's mom meant he'd taken on a responsibility alone. A tough choice, regardless of whatever circumstances surrounded Lucy's mom. Could someone look like a Frank Churchill and at heart be a George Knightley?

Was that possible?

"Glad you finally decided to show up," a familiar voice said behind her.

She turned to find Jack, balancing a food tray with the ease of someone who'd spent years in their granny's kitchen. "Didn't take you for a coward."

She offered him a tight smile. "Funny."

His eyes skimmed her dress, brows lifting. "You do know this is a pub, not The Marches?"

Her smile dipped into a frown at his mention of one of the oldest inns in Wisteria that also had a high-end restaurant attached. "Class doesn't need a boundary line, Jack." She tossed out his name like an insult. "Didn't Granny teach you anything?"

"Oh, I'm so innately classy, all I need is my smile." He waggled his brows and gestured with his chin toward a booth nearby. "Granny D's already here, holding court with Travis, Lindsay, and Rosemary."

She followed his gaze to a back booth.

"If you're looking for some table company, that would be the place to go."

"Oh dear," Daphne murmured.

"Yep." Jack grinned. "She's already told them the story of when she and her husband"—he looked skyward—"number two?—saw Bigfoot, so it can only get more entertaining from there."

A laugh slipped from her lips just as a blur of pink and sequins came flying at her.

"Miss Daphne!"

Lucy hurled herself into Daphne's legs in a hug, her shirt blinking Princesses Have the Best Smiles in LED confidence.

"Well, hey there, sugarplum." Daphne bent to return the squeeze—just as Finn rounded the bar, clearly in motion toward them.

Her gaze snagged his over Lucy's shoulder, and just like that, every coherent thought left the building.

"Miss Daphne." He dipped his head, and the way his voice swooped to say her name took a little of her breath along with it.

His gaze dropped to her dress—*lingered*—and suddenly she felt far too aware of the neckline, the fit, and that flirty little ruffle at the hem.

That smile of his should've come with its own LED warning.

Her knees wobbled.

She was officially ridiculous.

But she couldn't seem to stop the fluttering in her chest. And the worst part?

She wasn't sure she wanted to.

"Hey," she managed, instantly annoyed at the way her voice came out breathy. She cleared her throat. "Looks like a solid turnout."

"It is." His gaze didn't leave hers. "Better now that you're here."

There it was. The flirt. Exhibit A.

She raised a brow. "Do you say that to all your guests?"

"Only the ones who make me regret not wearing cologne."

She rolled her eyes for his benefit, but the grin tugging at her lips was harder to fight. He turned toward the bar, grabbed a drink, and returned with a tall glass of iced sweet tea.

Her favorite.

"Ice over steeped leaf water and a scandalous amount of sugar," he said, offering it with a wink. "Just how you like it."

Exhibit B. Still unfairly charming.

"Thank you." She accepted the glass, willing her knees to obey reason.

"I'm drinking tea too," Lucy announced proudly, lifting her own glass like a toast. "And Daddy's letting me give out menus!"

To which Lucy turned and plucked a menu from a nearby pocket attached to the side of the bar, sweetly offering it to Daphne. "Is he?"

Finn nodded solemnly. "She's been promoted to menu delivery assistant."

That earned a slip of a laugh from her—*blast it again*—and she turned her attention back to Lucy. "Well, I can't imagine a better one. You'd brighten anyone's day, sugarplum."

Lucy's grin tilted in that lopsided way Daphne was growing dangerously fond of.

"And I see your dad is pulling out all the stops to win this competition." She narrowed her eyes. "Adorable helpers? Very strategic."

When her gaze came back up to Finn, something in his expression caught her full attention. It looked the same as the one she'd seen when he came to pick up Lucy in her apartment yesterday. Gentle and intense at the same time. Stalling her breath all over again.

"Just proves how hard I have to work to compete with you."

Her smile flared before she could stop it. Competition had never looked so appealing. *Doggone it.* Time to rein in her face.

"Forty or so people here," she said, glancing around. "All looking very charmed into loving you and your food, I see."

"Not everyone." Finn lifted a brow. "Still working on one."

Her cheeks heated instantly, so she ducked her gaze to the menu. "I guess, then, I should try some of the food to see for myself." She zeroed in on the first meaty item—anything to escape his stare. "The ribs?"

Safe choice. She could hide in a napkin if needed.

"Bold move in such a dress, Miss Austen." His grin tipped as he skimmed over her with another toe-curling look. "But a smart one." He offered a little bow. "Take a seat." He gave his dark brows a playful wiggle. "I'll bring you the order personally."

She gave him a very deliberate eye roll and turned on her heel toward the booth where Lindsay, Travis, Rosemary, and Granny D sat. Granny was just finishing a story about her great-grandfather Bum Jacobs and a moonshine run gone wrong.

Appalachian names had their own . . . something. She wasn't sure what. But they had it.

"Oh, Daphne, you're in for a treat." Lindsay waved her forward, and Daphne slid in next to Granny D. "Finn has these beer-battered onion rings that are change-your-life delicious."

"I think they could be at the wedding," Travis added, his eyes sparkling with a hidden laugh. "But Lindsay doesn't agree."

"We are *not* having onion rings at our wedding." Lindsay shook her head. "No matter how good they are."

"Okay, but what about the smoked Gouda mac?" Travis all but pleaded, waving toward his plate. "I'm serious, Linds. Everyone in my family and yours would love it. I'd throw elbows for this stuff."

Despite herself, Daphne laughed. "It's that good?"

"I imagine he'll bring some with the ribs." Lindsay pointed her fork toward Granny D. "It's what *she* ordered and"—her smile turned apologetic—"it would be delicious at the rehearsal dinner."

The words slipped through Daphne like a pin to a balloon. Her smile faltered.

Finn was going to win.

Three weeks in Wisteria and he was already stealing this opportunity with that charming grin and culinary wizardry.

She took a long sip of her tea to keep from pouting. Her gaze drifted back to the bar.

Finn stood behind the bar again, regaling a pair sitting on the stools near him. The way his hands gestured as he talked. The quick flash of his grin. The attentive way he listened to every customer as if they were the most interesting person he'd ever met.

After everything she'd lived through—after all the heartbreak and caution she'd built like armor—she should be smart. She should fit him into a neat category and be done with it.

But Finn Dashwood didn't fit into boxes.

At least not the ones she expected him to.

"But ribs?" Lindsay sighed. "How do I justify ribs when I'll be wearing white?" She looked at Daphne. "That's one reason I love your options. Neat. Classy. Tasty but . . . delicate."

"With less need for twenty napkins," Daphne added, nodding

toward Granny D, who'd built a pile of used napkins that rivaled her tea glass in height.

"That just means I'm enjoying myself," Granny D declared, brandishing another rib. "Gracious sakes, honey, I ain't never tasted meat this good in all my days."

"Is that so?" Daphne chuckled out her question, curbing the tiny twinge of concern. She should be happy for Finn's successful opening. Any new restaurant deserved a strong launch. And if he hadn't been competing with her for a job she really needed, she'd have been even happier for him.

"I'm tellin' you true, girl." Granny D nodded, taking up another rib. "If I were forty years younger, I'd marry the man who made these."

"Granny!" Daphne groaned. No ribs were good enough to usher up a proposal.

"I'd be jealous," Rosemary said slyly, "but I think he's already found his main dish."

Daphne shot Rosemary a look.

Cue Finn, arriving like a perfectly timed line in a rom-com, platter in hand, setting down a dish of ribs, mac and Gouda, and gently steamed veggies in front of Daphne—and offering Granny D a wink. "Guess I owe you a proposal then."

"Shucks, boy." Granny D grinned, sending Daphne the world's least subtle side-eye. "I've got excellent taste in men. But you're a might bit young for me. I'll leave you to Daphne."

A thoroughly unladylike laugh barked from Daphne's lips. "Oh goodness. I'm way too straitlaced, fancy food, and boring for the likes of Mr. Dashwood," she said quickly, trying to steer the conversation far from Finn and Daphne sitting in a tree k-i-s . . . er . . . Well, they'd already done that part.

No reminders needed.

"Straitlaced is growing on me." Finn's eyes locked with hers. "And you're anything but boring." His grin deepened. "Not too sure about the food, though."

"Speaking of food . . ." Daphne looked down at the plate, the smell of those ribs causing her mouth to water in a rabid way. "Are you going to keep distracting me or let me see if you've earned your bragging rights?"

"By all means." He stepped back, one hand over his heart. "But I warn you: These have been known to inspire spontaneous declarations of love."

She shot him a challenging look, nonverbally assuring him she would do no such thing. Granny D may think they're the first step to matrimony, but not Daphne.

No way.

Then she picked up a rib—and took one bite.

Her eyes widened.

Heaven. Help. Her.

The sauce was smoky-sweet perfection. The meat practically melted. Her eyes fluttered shut, and a soft, traitorous sound escaped her lips—a cross between a sigh and a moan. What on earth had he done to this cow?

When she opened her eyes, Finn was staring at her.

Not the casual kind of stare. Not playful or teasing.

No, this one was locked, loaded, and full of heat. Like his thoughts had gone right back to the kiss in her kitchen.

Her breath lodged in her throat.

"Um . . ." She lowered the rib, grasping for dignity. "Nice. It's . . . nice."

"Nice?" He tilted his head, studying her with an intensity that made her skin tingle. Then he promptly slid down in the seat across from her. "Your response would suggest a little better than nice."

She looked away, only to find all four other people at the table staring at her with varying degrees of amusement. She returned her attention to the half-eaten rib and decided to focus on taking another bite. The flavors exploded again—rich, bold, decadent, teasing every one of her tastebuds.

Something about the flavor sparked a memory . . . or idea . . . or . . . "You know, this would be a perfect pairing for my rosemary sea salt focaccia."

When she opened her eyes, Finn had leaned closer. "Say that again?"

"Your short ribs. They need something earthy. That sauce wants to soak into something hearty and crusty. I have a bread that—" She caught herself and sat back, cheeks flushing. "Sorry. I didn't mean to—"

"Don't stop." His voice was low. Earnest. Inviting. "Keep going."

"Law, girl," Granny D added. "If there's something that makes these ribs even better, you'd better spill it."

She hesitated for a beat, searching Finn's face. But really, if she had the rare opportunity to food nerd with someone who actually *got it*, why hold back?

"Okay. So. The sauce is sweet, rich, has depth—molasses?" she guessed, narrowing her eyes at him.

"Brown sugar and sorghum," he answered, grinning.

"Aha." She pointed her rib at him. "That's the bass note. You need something with bite and body to hold that kind of richness. A thick crumb. Crusty enough to scrape your palate clean between bites but not so dense it kills the balance."

"And that's your rosemary focaccia bread?"

The rest of the table faded away. The clatter, the conversations, even the competition—all of it blurred beneath the strange, electric thread running between them.

Two food nerds. One language.

And for once, it wasn't about being on the defensive or guarding her heart.

It was just . . . connection.

And she wasn't sure she'd ever tasted anything quite like it.

"Yes, but with a cracked pepper crust and caramelized onion folded in. The salt brings out the herbs, the onion gives it umami, and the rosemary plays off the brown sugar and sorghum." She glanced down at the ribs, then back up at him, heart picking up speed. "It'd be rude not to let them meet, don't you think?"

His mouth curved in that slow, appreciative way that made her stomach do backflips.

"I think I'm in love."

Her whole face froze.

Someone—Lindsay?—snorted.

"Um . . . with the bread or the ribs?" Daphne asked, trying to sound dry and unaffected.

"Obviously the pairing," he deadpanned. "I'd never want to separate a perfect match."

She wrestled with her smile, forcing it down but failing completely. She wasn't a natural flirt. In fact, half the time she wasn't even sure if she was flirting. But the way Finn was watching her now—amused, intrigued, maybe even a little captivated—gave her the kind of boldness she usually lacked.

And he was listening. Not just politely. Fully present. Like she mattered.

That? That was more disarming than any flirty line.

"Well," she said lightly, tapping her finger against the rim of her plate. "I suppose if you believe in soulmates, it's only fair they find each other . . . even if one of them is bread."

His smile deepened, just a hint of his dimple now, and warmth rose into her face that had nothing to do with the spices on the meat.

"I do believe in soulmates," he said, tone low and playful. "Especially when they're handmade and seasoned just right."

She rolled her eyes, but it was more to keep herself from grinning like an idiot. "Careful, Dashwood. That sounds suspiciously like a compliment."

He leaned in, elbows on the table, eyes still locked on hers. "I wouldn't dare compliment a woman who uses words like 'umami' with a straight face."

Her laugh slipped out—quick, surprised, and far more honest than she meant it to be.

He looked so pleased by the sound that something inside her uncoiled.

She caught Lindsay looking at her with some sort of glint in her eyes, and Daphne quickly looked away.

"Um . . . well, if you'd like to test the theory." Daphne sat back, shrugging a shoulder to try to displace whatever grins lit Lindsay's, Granny D's, and even Travis's face. "I could bring you a loaf. Of the focaccia."

No big deal. Just two people sharing . . . food together.

"Perfect," he said slowly. "We'll let them meet properly. No pressure. Just two chefs. One table. Some objectively brilliant food."

"Exactly." She slid a glance to Lindsay and back to Finn. "Just because we're competitors doesn't mean we can't appreciate each other's . . . unique tastes."

"Not at all," he added, never looking away.

She swallowed down another drink of tea, drew in a deep breath, and refused to make eye contact with anyone else at the table.

Because just like that, the line between competition and something else entirely had gotten perilously blurry.

• • • • • • • • • • •

Finn wiped down the bar counter as the last stragglers ambled toward the door. The evening had gone far better than he'd imagined. Not just in money earned but in the response of the community.

Only a few weeks in Wisteria, and he already felt . . . embraced. It didn't make sense.

And he didn't need it to.

After losing his wife, his dad, then his business, followed by half a year of trying to claw his life back together, he'd landed in the most unlikely of places. And somehow, it fit.

Game night yesterday. A packed house tonight. Maybe it didn't take years to find home.

Maybe it only took the right people.

Daphne's face flashed to mind . . . a particular scene.

Her sitting across the table in a dress that highlighted her petite frame. One elegant hand lifting a rib. Just one bite.

And Finn felt it in his chest like a meteor strike all over again.

Daphne, who usually had the poise of a royal portrait, made a sound that definitely did not fit Miss Tea Shop. Her eyes fluttered closed. Her head tilted back just slightly. And then she muttered something under her breath that sounded suspiciously like, *"Heaven help me."*

And he forgot how to breathe.

She moaned. Over *his* ribs.

And then her appreciation turned into another conversation between them that he wanted on repeat forever. The flirting gave way to something deeper. Her caution melted into this connection he'd never known before.

She wasn't trying to impress him or compete with him. She was just being *her*—smart, creative, passionate. Animated in that way that made him want to lean in and never miss a single word.

As she talked—caramelized onions, cracked pepper crust, earthy flavor balance—he found himself nodding, absorbing, resisting the very real urge to clear the table and kiss her senseless.

Because sure, the ribs were good. And yeah, his sauce deserved to be soaked into something spectacular.

But watching her light up, talk like they were coconspirators of some culinary masterpieces—that was the real magic.

And, heaven help *him*, he was absolutely, irreversibly . . . toast.

"I'd call this night a definite success." Harry walked back from locking the front door, apron still tied. "Everyone—and I do mean *everyone*—in Wisteria popped in."

Finn sighed, a slow grin spreading. "Not complaining."

Harry edged onto one of the barstools across from Finn.

"Told you this place was worthy of your dreams. These people too."

Finn fixed two glasses—one for Harry, one for himself—using the familiar motions to buy time. The word *success* felt too small. It wasn't just a good night.

It felt like something had clicked into place. A lock turned.

A sense of . . . *belonging*.

In each pat on the back, friendly hello, and even begrudged smile.

"It doesn't make sense," he said, leaning forward on his elbows, gaze drifting toward the darkened windows. Only the streetlamps down Main Street glowed. "But they do make you feel a part rather quickly."

Harry gave a knowing chuckle. "They make the *right* people feel a part quickly. That's Appalachian clannishness for you. If you fit, you're in. If not"—he shrugged—"might take a while."

Finn nodded, taking a drink. "It was like that for you?"

"Absolutely. I came in skeptical. But somehow I ended up in a small Southern town with people who treat me like kin." His grin softened. "For better or worse. And I know you needed that too."

So that's why Harry pushed for Finn to make the move.

He knew what Finn had needed even more than he'd known himself.

Finn studied the older man. "What else are you trying to say, Harry?"

Harry's grin returned and he leaned back a little on the stool. "Do you remember the time you were invited to be a guest chef on the telly?" He snapped his fingers in thought. "What was the show?"

"*Well Done*?" Finn groaned, heat climbing the back of his neck. He'd hated watching himself on-screen. It had been a huge opportunity—and it led to Sarah. Better chef. Big name. Glossy ambition. And he'd gone starry-eyed and pudding-brained over her. Never paused to figure out if they *fit*.

Idiot.

"I remember the moment you got the call. You, me, and your dad were sitting around that table."

"He'd just gotten back from hospital." The first of a long trail of visits.

"Right." Harry nodded. "And the pride on his face . . . I don't think I've ever seen a man beam like that. He knew how hard you'd worked."

Finn took another drink just to have something to do. His eyes burned. "I remember." His father had always been the best cheerleader. The loudest. It was like he was making up for two parents.

"And the look on your face, well, it said it all. A dream had come true. You'd found your place."

Finn's attention shifted back to Harry, eyes narrowing. "I feel as though you're trying to make a point."

"Tonight, I saw that same look." Harry leaned in. "That light. Joy, even. The sense you were exactly where you were supposed to be."

"Like we said, this town really showed up—"

"It wasn't from the opening, Finn." Harry shook his head, expression gentling. "It was when Daphne walked in. When you sparred over ribs. When she spoke to Lucy." Harry leaned closer. "You're friendly with everyone, but anyone who knows you could have read you like a book."

"She's great, isn't she?" Finn tried for a smirk, but it landed somewhere in lovesick-puppy territory. "Smart, creative, beautiful. Too good for me."

"So that's the problem?"

"I'm the problem, Harry." Finn's shoulders caved beneath the truth. "She thinks I'm a player," he muttered, rubbing the back of his neck. "And I don't blame her. When we first met, I was . . . careless. Flirty. I didn't know what this was going to become. I didn't expect—" His voice cracked. "I didn't expect her."

Harry's eyes softened.

Finn stared down into his glass. "I've never felt this way. Not even with Sarah. It's like—being near Daphne is . . . oxygen. I'm better around her. I want to make her laugh. I want to listen to her talk about scones or tea pairings or obscure Austen quotes and just . . . never stop listening." He shook his head, almost in disbelief, the realization settling deeper. "With Sarah, it felt like I had to work for those perfect moments. But with Daphne? Even when we're bickering, it feels . . . easy. Right."

"You've grown since Sarah." Harry gave a slow nod. "You know the difference between something that looks right and something that *is* right."

"Yeah." Finn huffed a humorless laugh. "Grown—and still managed to act like a complete idiot."

"You're not an idiot. You did what a lot of hurting people do." Harry gestured with his glass. "You built a wall. A pretty one. Made of charm and banter and friendliness. But a wall all the same."

"For Lucy," Finn murmured. "And me."

"But here's the thing—walls don't just keep pain out. They keep *possibility* out too."

Finn winced. Daphne's face flashed in his mind again. Those wounded eyes. Her voice like flint: *"No troublesome hearts involved."*

"I want to change how she sees me," he said softly. "But I don't know how."

"You change it by being honest."

Finn looked at him sideways. "I'm a lot of things, Harry, but sentimental confessions aren't exactly in my toolbox."

"You're a chef, Finn. You know presentation matters—but it's the flavor that makes someone stay."

Finn leveled his friend with a long look. "Are you really going to use cooking metaphors?"

He shrugged his answer. "Stop feeding her surface-level charm. Give her the deep stuff. The real you." Harry's smile crooked. "Still be your usual gregarious self, but this time lead with your heart. She's smart. She'll see the difference."

Finn was quiet for a long moment. "I . . . was hopeful she already had, at least a little."

Harry chuckled. "Nobody argues that passionately about ribs and focaccia unless there's something sweeter simmering under the surface."

Finn's lips quirked. "Simmering?"

"What?" Harry raised a brow. "Roll with it."

Finn chuckled and then looked down at his glass. "I just hope it's not too late."

Harry gave his shoulder a solid clap. "For real love? The kind that surprises you, makes your daughter smile like that, bowls you over?" He leaned in, eyes alight with humor. "It's never too late. Just don't wait until the teapot boils over."

CHAPTER 14

<u>**@TGDPub:**</u> What would you rather have for lunch?

1. Pasties
2. A cookie on a fancy plate

Vote wisely. #TeamPub #FoodWars #TeamCoffee #BeanWaterIsLife
PS: Thanks for making opening night for #RealFood an amazing success, Wisteria!

> <u>**@TeaThymeNC:**</u> Wow. I see we're asking the hard-hitting questions. Careful, Finn. The internet might just prefer sophistication over beer snacks. #TeamTeaRoom #TeamTea #SteepedLeaf4Life
> <u>**@TGDPub:**</u> Pasties are sophisticated. They've got layers. Also, wasn't it you who nearly proposed to a short rib last night? #TeamPub #SmokedMeatIsLove #SheMoaned #Receipts
> <u>**@TeaThymeNC:**</u> A moment of weakness. Clearly. And it was a private moment between a woman and a very good

rib. Lord, help me! You just told the whole town! And I did not moan. #FakeNews #RibsRNotWorthThis

@JackAustenPhotography: [blurry zoomed-in photo of Daphne's face mid-bite] I believe the technical term is food euphoria. Evidence submitted to the court. #SorryNotSorry #BigBrotherDuties #ReceiptsCaptured

@TeaThymeNC: DELETE THAT IMMEDIATELY. #Betrayed #NoMoreFreePhotography #TimeForANewWillAgain

@TGDPub: I'd like to order a framed print, please. For the pub wall. For . . . customer testimonial purposes. #HighestPriority #WillPayPremium

@TeaThymeNC: [photo of perfectly plated rosemary sea salt focaccia next to a teacup] Don't you dare. Or you'll never seen how well this pairs with your ribs. #NotAboveBlackmail #BreadSwoon

@PastorNateNHC: Remember, friends: "Pride goes before destruction, a haughty spirit before a fall." Proverbs 16:18. That said, my vote's for the collaboration. #JustSaying #BringingPeopleTogetherSince2019 #AlsoThoseRibsAndFocacciaSoundAmazing

@TGDPub: Listen to the preacher, Daphne. You bring the focaccia. I'll bring the ribs. Let's see what happens. #CollabOrFlirt #ISayBoth

@TeaThymeNC: Fine. But only if you try some of my best tea too . . . with photo evidence. Also, I demand another piece of that sticky toffee pudding. #TermsAndConditions #BreadBeforeDudes #StillNotFlirting

@WisteriaWeekly: A surprise collaboration (#TeamFocacciaRibs) Vote now! Results in next week's issue! #WisteriaFoodWars #BettingPoolInProgress #GrubWars

@NCFoodies: Thanks so much for alerting us to the #FoodieWar happening over in #Wisteria @LindsayMonroeOfficial They're all over social media. #WeWantIn

@WisteriaWeekly: You two are causing more commotion than the upcoming Harvest Festival. Just imagine if you had your own booths. Now that would draw a sizable crowd at this point.

@SheriffGrady: It would. More people. More revenue for our dear town.

@TGDPub: Did the sheriff just comment on my social media page?

@TeaThymeNC: It's about revenue. Of course he did.

@JackAustenPhotography: And to get his name on the same page as Lindsay and Travis. #PlayingWithTheBigBoys

@SheriffGrady: I've been playing the game longer than y'all have been alive.

@LindsayMonroeOffical: I love helping my hometown. And maybe that means the folks of Wisteria can help us decide about our caterer. Especially with a real cook-off? What do you say, folks? Send help. Or votes. #WeddingWars #HowDoWeChoose

@TravisLangfordConnects: @LindsayMonroeOfficial Great idea. The whole town is following the plans online anyway. Might as well let them join in.

A QUIET KNOCK STIRRED Daphne from the kind of slumber that only happened by accident—and only when you were so cozy that your body gave in before your mind did.

Lucy lay curled on the couch beneath a fuzzy blanket, her long, dark hair fanned across a floral pillow. A sprinkle of freckles peeked over the bridge of her nose, and one arm had flopped dramatically over the side like a princess who had fainted mid-ball. Daphne blinked fully awake, gently closed *The Lion, the Witch, and the Wardrobe*, and stretched to stand, careful not to wake the sleeping beauty in her living room.

About an hour after arriving at Finn's pub, Lucy had started to yawn. Another half hour in, she'd wilted just a little more—still smiling, still game to pass out menus and wave like a celebrity, but the sparkle had dimmed behind her eyes. So Daphne had offered to take her back to the apartment, let her rest if she wanted.

Finn thanked her, told her he'd expected Margaret Coleman from the inn to take Lucy for the night, but the woman had come down with a stomach virus that morning, so she was out of commission.

What followed had felt like a balm to Daphne's slightly weathered soul.

A cup of tea for both of them—in real china, thank you very much—and a round of princess braids while Lucy made up a bedtime story involving a sword-wielding duchess and a dragon who liked sparkly accessories. It had made something warm bloom in Daphne's chest. Not quite grief, not quite nostalgia. Just . . . a sweet ache. The kind that whispered of things you hadn't realized you missed . . . or wanted.

Another knock. This one gently insistent.

Daphne padded barefoot to the door and opened it to find Finn on the other side, looking like a well-worn dream. His shirt was open at the collar, sleeves still rolled up at the elbows, and his hair was doing that tousled thing that looked expensive and intentional but Daphne suspected came from running his hands through it five hundred times. He offered a tired smile, and she nearly melted to the wood floor.

He looked unfairly good at midnight after a long day of work. Which was rude.

And weird things happened at midnight.

Or so the stories said.

He held up a small container like a peace offering. "You didn't get a chance to try this before leaving, so I saved you a piece."

"You mean a bribe," she teased, stepping aside to let him in. "You're bribing me with food."

"Or thanking you." He passed the container into her hands. "And in my defense, you already liked my ribs, so I supposed you'd like a bit of molten bourbon chocolate cake too."

She wiped a hand across her mouth just to be sure she wasn't drooling.

Either from the cake or the man . . . or the unjust combination of the two.

"Well, you do owe me after sharing with the entire cyberworld about my uncommonly public weakness for excellent food." She took the offering. "That was a low blow, Dashwood."

His eyes lit, and for some reason it made her want to keep up the banter.

"I regret nothing. The internet loved it. And how could I let the opportunity pass?" He leaned back against the doorframe, his grin flicking crooked. "There's nothing quite as rewarding to any chef as having another worthy competitor value their work."

She studied him a moment, her ire reducing to a slight simmer at the truth. It did matter. That shared recognition of something good. In fact, the little tête-à-tête about bread and ribs and spices she'd had with him earlier in the evening still hummed a welcome theme through her mind. Still seemed to tether her to him in some way . . . like a lingering aroma.

"Well, I'd love to garner the same response, but it seems you're allergic to trying my food." She turned toward the kitchen.

"I've had your scones," his low voice permeated the space behind her as he followed. "They were delicious, but it does smell like you've been working on something else."

"A peach cobbler tartlet recipe for the wedding, but something's missing." She placed the container on the counter and turned back toward him. "However, what you probably smell are the cookies Lucy and I made." She waved toward the stovetop where a plate of cookies in various shapes, from hearts to flowers, were piled in a mound of sugar and sprinkles. "Not to worry." Daphne raised a finger. "I only allowed her to eat one."

"I appreciate that." He glanced at her, still smiling in a . . . new way? The same as at the restaurant. What was that about? "So. Our rivalry's officially trending."

"I saw that! A woman today said she only came in because she 'needed to witness the tension for herself.'" Daphne made air quotes with her fingers.

"I had ten people visit tonight because they'd seen the rivalry online."

A laugh escaped her as she leaned back against the counter. "Right? I've had a consistent uptick in numbers, which can't be a coincidence."

Finn chuckled. "Glad we're amusing the masses."

"It's good for business," she said lightly.

"And fun," he added, grinning as he leaned one hip against the counter. "Especially the part where I get to flirt shamelessly with you and call it marketing."

"Flirt?" Her stomach did an unhelpful somersault. She forced herself to scoff. "With me? Please. You flirt with everything that breathes."

"Untrue." He tilted his head, a playful glint in his eye—though something quieter, more sincere stirred beneath it. "I'm friendly."

"Friendly, is it?" She handed him a water bottle and leaned back against the island, doing her best to appear unimpressed. "So you don't *mean* to flirt?"

He took the bottle from her, letting his fingers graze hers in a way that absolutely wasn't accidental. "Not like I'm trying to seduce the entire town, no. I like people. I like talking. Banter. Light engagement with men and women alike." He took a long drink, then set the bottle down with a soft *thunk*. "But when I *mean* it . . . I'm apparently terrible at hiding it. Or so Harry says."

Daphne's throat tightened. What did *meaning it* look like, then? Because online flirting felt safe. Manageable. But in person, with Finn—his voice, his scent, his infuriatingly kind eyes—it felt anything but safe.

"Daphne?"

His sudden seriousness seized her breath. His expression. The sincerity. She wasn't quite sure what to do with it. Maybe it was just part of that midnight magic in the storybooks. "Yes?"

"We may be rivals online for marketing, but I hope we can manage to be friends in real life." His smile softened. "You've proven to be fairly wonderful to me and Lucy."

The compliment sent lovely warmth through her.

"Friends?" She narrowed her eyes at him. Could he be a friend? But the last few days made her wonder. Game night. The nerd-out over ribs. "Don't those involve long-term plans and . . . hearts?"

He breathed out a long stream of air before looking back at her. "I have every intention of a long-term commitment to Wisteria and the people who live here." He shifted a step closer. "As far as hearts are concerned, I hope to treat the ones in my life with much better clarity than I may have in the past."

She held his gaze, heat soaring up her neck into her cheeks. Which version of Finn Dashwood could she trust? The one who kissed and dashed away or the one who gave off these tender vibes and brought dessert? Perhaps friendship was a good place to start . . . to see if the facade wore off.

She tried to recover with a shrug. "Can you do the whole 'just friends' thing without trying to steal kisses or recipes?"

"Depends." His mouth curved. "Do you plan to keep moaning over my food?"

"I . . ." She faltered, then huffed. "That was one time."

"A memorable one time." He moved to lean against the counter across from her, arms crossed, gaze lazy and amused—and far too attentive. "But if you are willing, Daphne Austen, I'd truly like to start with friendship."

Start? Daphne studied him, the casual posture at odds with the weight behind his words. "Well," she said slowly, "I don't have the best track record with flirts, but . . ." She trailed off and handed him a sprinkle-covered cookie, a peace offering disguised in sugar. "I'm willing to"—her breath squeezed out the word—"to give friendship a try." She arched a brow. "If you *mean* it."

One of his brows arched into a fallen strand of hair. His gaze dropped briefly to her lips, and her breath stopped for a whole different reason.

A beat passed.

Then, he straightened, his eyes meeting hers again. "Friends it is, then." His tone was quieter now.

He looked past the cookie toward the stove, his attention landing on the tray of tartlets. "May I?"

Her stomach still clenched like a constant Pilate's hold, but she nodded, watching him with way too much interest.

He took a bite, paused, then popped the rest in his mouth, his brow furrowing thoughtfully. "Delicious."

"But you didn't moan," she teased. Oh heavens! Why did she go and say that? *Who was the flirt now?*

His eyes narrowed for the briefest moment. "You shouldn't say things like that, Miss Austen, if you're hoping to keep my mind in a 'just friends' direction."

Don't ask. Don't ask. "Why is that?"

He looked at her again, his gaze tracing the curve of her mouth before he released a long breath and stepped back. "Because if I'm going to maintain my intention of friendship with you, the memory of you moaning over my ribs might tempt me more than I can afford."

The words hit differently than she expected. Less about heat. More about restraint. Heart. Like maybe the man who stole a kiss last week had been the one letting his guard down, not playing a game.

And that knowledge nestled in against her fear. Wedging a space for hope to slip in a little.

He drew his attention back to the tartlet and took another thoughtful bite. "I think these tartlets are only missing one thing." His brows did the shimmy. "Cardamom whipped cream."

Her gaze shot to the half-eaten tartlet in his hand, and without thinking, she took it from his fingers and popped it in her mouth, envisioning his suggestion. "That . . . that's a great idea."

"And," he said, looking a little too pleased with himself, "you already have the ingredients. Which you could use. Tonight. If you wanted."

Her hands went to her hips. "How do you know what I have in my kitchen?"

"I've cooked in it before, remember?"

The warm tone, the slight dip in his voice—oh, she remembered. Branded-in-her-brain remembered. And the fact that he wasn't even trying to flirt at the moment made it somehow worse.

"Right," she murmured, suddenly needing to look anywhere but at him, yet he held her attention. *Friends?* How in the world was that going to work?

His gaze roamed over her face for a moment, and then he took another step back. "I should get Lucy back to her own bed."

She hated how a sudden tug of disappointment tightened behind her ribs.

"Thanks again for taking such good care of her," he added, his tone softer.

Daphne followed him to the threshold of the room, drawn in by whatever change made him even more appealing than before. "She's easy. Such a sweetheart."

"Indeed, much better than I deserve."

Those words hit something in her chest. "You two seem close."

"We make a good team, don't you think?" He winked. "Perhaps she softens all of my rough edges."

Her grin tugged upward. Maybe the flirty side of Finn wasn't so bad. "She does bring out the sweetness in you." And then, on impulse, wanting to prolong the conversation, she asked, "How long has it been just the two of you?"

He hesitated. She braced for a joke, a dodge. But instead—"Lucy's mother left when Lucy was about eighteen months old."

Daphne's bottom lip dropped open and a painful squeak released from the sudden pang in her chest. She looked toward the living room where Lucy lay asleep. "How . . . how could she possibly leave you?"

Finn stared at her with that puzzling expression again—like he was searching—and then his expression gentled into a tender smile she felt all the way to her heart.

What would something like that do to a man? How would it change him?

He gestured toward the living room with his chin. "Lucy was born with a bilateral cleft lip and palate," he said, voice quiet. "A fairly severe case."

Bilateral cleft? Her confusion must have shown because his frown softened. "Bilateral means that both sides of her upper lip, beneath both nostrils"—he pointed to his mouth to give a visual—"were open from the lips back through the bony part of the roof of her mouth, the hard palate."

Daphne's tongue followed the direction he'd described, her imagination trying to make sense of it. "Oh."

So that was why Lucy had the little scar above her lips. Was that the reason for some of her speech sounds too?

"By the time Lucy was eighteen months old, she'd had several surgeries to help correct it, along with some medical difficulties that come along with a cleft. For example, ear infections, feeding complications, and speech impediments."

Daphne's stomach hollowed. "And . . . her mother couldn't . . . ?"

He studied her again in that strange sort of way and then cleared his throat. "She didn't want kids. Or marriage. I was young. I thought love would be enough to change her mind." He shrugged one shoulder. "Turns out I was more naive than charming. A little arrogant too." His smile turned wry. "Imagine that."

Something cracked open inside Daphne. A tiny fissure where assumptions had lived. She saw him even more differently now—clearer—less like a flirt, more like a man who'd been burned and learned to armor himself in charisma.

"I think we've all been there at some point." The words emerged softly. "Naive. Hopeful. A little blind trust? It's what makes the best heartbreak stories."

His gaze sharpened on hers. "Sounds like you've got a few chapters of your own."

"Enough to know how the plot goes." She sighed. "But nothing like yours. I'm so sorry, Finn." Her words rasped for a totally different reason, the raw awareness of being left behind by someone who should have loved you more than the circumstances . . .

Yes, she understood that.

Viscerally.

"You've done a great job with Lucy. She's wonderful."

His lips crooked, a fresh glow lighting his eyes, softening his smile.

And she *felt* his love for his little girl.

"Despite my best attempts at getting her to listen to rock music and despise all things princess."

Daphne fought against a renewed rush of warmth in her eyes. Her past flashed to the surface. "Well, there's nothing wrong with those fairy tales. Sometimes children need them in order to believe that all of the hard things won't last forever. They're predictable, and no matter how many times we watch them or read about them, the ending is always good. The men don't leave their true loves behind. The dark stuff goes away." He blurred in her vision. "And we're *promised* a happily ever after."

His gaze searched hers. Held. Studied.

The gravitational pull toward him renewed with a fervor. It would only take one step and she'd be in his arms . . . and what would that feel like? To have a man who'd wrap her in a hug and help her believe that fairy tales could rise out of their bindings and into the real world. To have someone stay even when life was hard or dragons reared their ugly heads. To hold her hand when the world shifted.

Could flirty Finn Dashwood be that sort of man? For her?

Finn stepped closer—close enough she could feel his warmth again.

And for a suspended moment, it felt like a fairy tale. Or the edge of one.

His hand lifted slowly, brushing a strand of hair from her cheek. His gaze never left hers. "There's a quote I read once by"—he looked toward the ceiling in thought—"Ernest Hemingway, I think." His attention came back to hers. "'The world breaks everyone, and afterward, many are strong at the broken places.'" His fingers hovered on her skin, gaze fastened with hers. "You deserve a happily ever after, Daphne."

Could he see her scars? Read the wounds left behind her eyes? The way he looked at—*saw*—her made her wonder.

Her breaths shallowed, the warmth in his look pulling her a half step closer.

His attention dropped to her lips again, and he drew in a deep breath, stepping back.

"I'd best get back to my place."

And within a minute, with a sweet bundle in his arms and a final look and "good night," he left her alone.

Painfully aware of how much she wished for another five minutes with an English flirt.

....

Text from Travis and Lindsay to Finn and Daphne:

> Can you two meet at Tea Thyme at four today? We've made our decision.

The chime above the door sounded as Finn stepped into Tea Thyme, the familiar scent of baked goods and steeped tea perfectly capturing the essence of the owner. The shop always smelled like her—refined, warm, with a hint of something unexpected. A little citrus?

A lot of sass, as the locals said.

He almost chuckled at the very thought. He was beginning to think like these people!

And there she was, behind the counter—floral dress cinched at her waist, golden hair in a long ponytail.

Finn had stopped trying to keep his emotional distance from her, but that didn't mean he'd plunge forward with any heartfelt declarations. Not with that look he'd caught in her eyes more than once—that guarded flicker, like she'd been left behind one too many times and expected him to do the same.

But he wouldn't. Not now that he saw her for who she was.

Her humor. Her wit. Her kindness.

What would it feel like to earn such a love?

His broken perspective provided little comparison. And with his mother's early death, he had very little to go on with his parents. Harry and Margaret offered a glimpse of a well-suited, healthy relationship—one for which to aspire.

But last night, when Daphne had stood so near—her large beautiful eyes searching his—well, he'd realized a deep truth. His honesty might open a door to, perhaps, win her trust.

And her heart.

Her gaze flicked to the door as he stepped in, her smile hesitant, but there.

That was something.

"So I guess this is it?" Her voice was light, but her hands were fussing with a dish towel that didn't need fussing.

Hmm . . .

He stepped forward, taking a stool at the counter opposite her. "I hope you win, Daphne. You deserve it."

She rolled her eyes. "Don't start acting noble on me now." And she pushed a plate across the counter between them. "But since you're early, try this."

He looked down. Focaccia?

He raised a brow. "Is this the famed bread you've been taunting me with?"

A smile teased the corners of her mouth as she tipped her head. Her ponytail swished, and Finn had the ridiculous urge to tug it, just to see her reaction.

"Seemed only fair. You needed to know how good it would taste with your ribs."

That glint in her eye pulled him closer, the line between teasing and flirting growing delightfully thin.

He tore off a piece of the bread, never looking away. The crust was golden and crisp, the inside warm and airy, with olive oil and rosemary clinging to his fingers. He took a bite—and blinked.

Rich. Herby. With just the right kick of sea salt and lemon zest. "You're right," he said slowly, holding her gaze. "A perfect match."

The combination fit in ways he hadn't imagined. His grin almost tipped. And maybe it wasn't such a stretch to think the two people involved in this little meal creation might combine just as well?

Color rose into her cheeks, a pink that crept so slowly, she likely hoped he wouldn't notice. But he had. Oh, he had. A lovely rose to match the color of those lips.

"You're just being nice," she said, trying to tuck her expression back to neutral, but the light in her eyes defied that forced frown.

He took another bite, savoring it. "No, sincerely. It's incredible."

"Careful," she warned, eyes dancing. "I might start believing you actually like my cooking."

"I've liked it from the start, if you recall." He shrugged one shoulder. "It's the tea I took issue with."

She gave a mock gasp, one hand over her heart. "Blasphemy."

His chest burst with the desire to cross the counter and seize her lips. "Coffee is still better."

She promptly ignored that comment. "Well, I'm also experimenting with a new shortbread recipe to tempt you because you said shortbread is bland."

Her brain worked like his. He could practically see it. Inventorying ingredients, substituting spices, piecing things together in a new way. He leaned in, forearms braced on the counter. "Are you trying to seduce me through baked goods, Miss Austen?"

"What?" Her mouth parted. "No . . . absolutely not."

"Because it's working."

Daphne blinked rapidly, then turned her attention to the bread like it had suddenly grown much more interesting. "You're impossible."

"But charming."

"Debatable."

"That wasn't a no."

Her lips twitched, her pleasure in the moment almost palpable. He loved her smile . . . and her fight against it. "You're very annoying, you know that?"

"I've heard rumors," he murmured, watching with quiet fascination as another blush crept up her neck and into her cheeks. A few golden wisps fell from her ponytail, framing her face—soft, teasing things.

"I just think an Englishman really ought to like shortbread."

"There you go again with those assumptions." He studied her. "Besides,

I thought you were determined to keep all your recipes as they've always been. No changes, no compromises. And now here you are"—he lifted another piece of bread—"wooing me with carbs and rosemary."

Another startled laugh slipped free from her smile, and she brushed a floury hand over her apron. "Well, maybe I . . . I needed the challenge more than I realized." Her gaze came back to his. "A nudge"—she waved toward him—"or *shove* outside of my comfort zone."

"I'll take that as a compliment." His grin slipped wide. "That focaccia is dangerously good."

"I didn't realize how much I wanted to create until it happened," she said, almost to herself. "And . . . now I can't seem to stop."

The words hit him square in the heart. Straightened his spine. Whether for good or ill, his special brand of nudging had helped stretch her beyond her fear—and that mattered. More than he could say. The idea of being even a small catalyst toward her awareness not only humbled him but deepened whatever connection grew between them. For his part, anyway. "Daphne." He paused, then pushed the words out. "I want you to get this catering job."

Her eyes narrowed and head tilted to the side. "So you said . . ."

"I'm backing out."

"No you're not." Her eyes sharpened now, finger jabbing at his chest. "You're staying in this, Dashwood. All the way."

He raised a brow.

"I don't want a pity win, Finn." She leaned forward slightly, her voice fierce. "If I win or lose, I want it to be fair and square. That I *was* better."

He searched her face—flushed cheeks, fire in her eyes, fingers curled against the counter. She looked absolutely stunning!

"You are," he said softly. "Better, I mean."

The words hung in the space between them. Her expression faltered for half a breath before she looked away, busying herself with stacking napkins that didn't need stacking.

"I meant what I said," she added. "Your savory dishes are phenomenal."

"But not very pretty."

She chuckled, the tension in her shoulders easing. "That's an easy fix, and you know it."

His heart tugged.

There it was again—that ache to cross the distance between them and taste that smile. To see if the spark still hummed between them like it had the first time . . . only deeper now. Sharper. His heart had finally gotten the memo, and it was all pointing in one direction.

Straight toward her.

But he didn't move.

Because attraction was easy. But wooing her heart? Much more difficult, especially after his beginning. But he wouldn't give up. This was much more than attraction. He liked her. Admired her. And the combination held an allure he hadn't realized he'd been missing with his ex-wife.

It scared the daylights out of him.

Because he wasn't sure how to do this right. Not when he knew her heart had been broken by the one man who should have kept her heart the safest. Not when Finn had been so careless and scared himself that he'd blundered things.

A chime above the door rang, signaling Lindsay and Travis's arrival, both looking much too pleased with themselves to offer any bad tidings.

"Thanks so much for meeting with us today," Travis said, gesturing for Lindsay to sit before claiming the spot beside her.

"We really need to make a decision," Lindsay added, her gaze bouncing between Finn and Daphne with barely contained excitement. "The wedding's in a little over two weeks."

"Of course." Daphne nodded, her smile tight.

"You must decide," Finn echoed, leaning on the counter beside her.

"Exactly." Travis dipped his chin toward Lindsay, as if to cue her. "And we have an idea."

Lindsay sat straighter, clearly delighted to be the one with the reveal. "I'd forgotten how much I love Wisteria. The charm. The community." She shook her head as if in wonder. "So many of the people here hold a special place in my heart, and watching the two of you compete for this wedding gave me . . ." She looked to Travis. "Gave *us* an idea not only to get a caterer but to celebrate Wisteria."

A knot twisted low in Finn's stomach.

"You know, with the whole town taking sides," she went on, "#TeamTea vs. #TeamPub is becoming a full-on local obsession. And . . . we think it's time to make it official."

Finn exchanged a wary glance with Daphne, who looked like she was preparing to bolt through the kitchen.

He turned to Travis. "What do you mean by 'official'?"

A hint of mischief lit Travis's eyes. "A cook-off. A town-wide tasting event during the Harvest Festival. People vote on their favorite dishes—savory and sweet. Settle it once and for all."

Finn blinked. "A live showdown?"

"It fits with Lindsay's whole 'celebrating community through food and story' thing," Travis added, shrugging like it was no big deal.

Daphne looked from Linday to Travis, eyes wide. "You're really suggesting a cooking contest between me and Finn? With the whole town participating?"

"Exactly." Travis's grin spread to massive proportions. "Think of it as the ultimate showdown, but with a mutual prize. Both of you will get visibility, regardless of who wins."

"Wednesday night is the festival's kick-off dinner," Lindsay continued, clearly already picturing it all. "There'll be dancing after. It's a perfect moment to showcase what you both do best."

The vision took root and grew in Finn's mind. Yes, he was new to Wisteria and he didn't even know what the festival was, let alone how many people would be there. But the idea of going head-to-head with Daphne? Publicly? Somehow it didn't feel like a threat.

It felt like an opportunity.

"That's two days away," Daphne squeaked.

She needed the visibility. The chance to be brave. "Daph," he said gently, waiting until her eyes flicked up to his. "You said business was up. That the online attention was helping. This—this is a good idea. Strange, perhaps. But good. For everyone."

She stared at him like he'd grown two heads.

Lindsay jumped in. "The people are already getting into your rivalry, and it's making news outside of Wisteria. Extra tourists will come. More business. It will benefit the entire community, Daphne, which I know you love." She took Daphne's hand across the counter. "We can't invite them all to the wedding, but this is a wonderful way for them to play a part and for us to show our appreciation for them too."

"And support two caterers whose work we've come to admire," Travis added.

Daphne kept blinking and shifting her attention to each face in the room like a trapped rabbit. Poor hen.

Time to rescue her—or push her buttons. Maybe both.

"Daphne?" He let his smile stretch slow and lazy. "If you're afraid I'll best you in front of the whole town, maybe we should decline. Wouldn't want to embarrass you on your home turf."

Her blinking stopped cold.

She turned her head with exaggerated calm and pinned him with a stare hot enough to scald.

"Best me?" she repeated, folding her arms like she was preparing for war.

"You do seem incredibly reluctant," he said mildly, though the wink that followed likely ruined any attempt at innocence.

Her glare was pure fire. Well, not completely fire, because her lips twitched—just slightly. She was definitely enjoying the challenge as much as him.

"I'm not afraid, Mr. Dashwood." She turned to Lindsay and Travis, her posture suddenly regal. "Sounds like an excellent plan." Then she looked back at him, golden brow bowed in challenge. "And may the best chef win."

Finn swallowed the grin that threatened to take over his face.

Oh, it was on.

And creating the recipe to win Daphne's heart had just begun.

CHAPTER 15

@LindsayMonroeOfficial: Just had the most charming meeting with the culinary rivals of Wisteria. Sparks flew. So did passive-aggressive compliments. Can't wait for the cook-off at the Harvest Festival! #TeamPub vs. #TeamTea #WisteriaWeddings #FoodieDramaIsMyLoveLanguage

> **@TravisLangston:** Big news coming to the Harvest Festival: a cook-off for the ages. One pub. One tea shop. One couple—ahem, pair—of caterers who definitely don't have unresolved feelings simmering under every dish. #WisteriaFoodWars #WeddingSeasonShowdown
>
> **@WisteriaWeekly:** Breaking: Tea Thyme's Daphne Austen and our newest restaurateur, The Green Dragon's Finn Dashwood, to face off in a culinary duel at this year's Harvest Festival. Citizens are advised to take sides responsibly. #TeamTea #TeamPub #PrayForTheJudges
>
> **@SheriffGrady:** For the record, I'm not choosing sides. Unless one of them bribes me with lemon bars or beef Wellington. Then it's every man for himself. #LawAndOrderAndSnacks

@PastorNateNHC: Some things are meant to go together. Peanut butter & jelly. Loaves & fish. And two certain business owners who seem a little too obsessed with each other's opinions. #JustSaying #LetHeWhoHasEarsHear
@JackAustenPhotography: Listen, I work with Finn and I'm related to Daphne. Neither of them is emotionally prepared for this conversation.
@RosemaryatThyme: Preach.
@WisteriaGeneralStore: Coming soon: "Emotionally Unprepared" hoodies. Available in Team Tea Pink and Pub Gold. You're welcome.
@MayorWilsonOfficial: As mayor, I must remain neutral in the great Wisteria Food Wars. That said, my calendar shows lunch at @TeaThymeNC tomorrow and dinner at @TGDPub. For civic duty research. #ToughJobButSomebodyHasToDoIt #PublicService
@HarryColeman: Is this what the kids call flirting these days? 🤔
@MargaretColeman: Darling, don't meddle. (But yes, it absolutely is.)

THE SCENT OF ROAST chicken, yeast rolls, and Granny D's famous sweet potato casserole wrapped around Daphne like a carb-heavy hug. Sure, she could make all those things on her own, but her attempts always lacked that special Granny D-ness she somehow infused into every dish—equal parts wisdom, stubbornness, and sass, baked until golden.

What Daphne didn't like, however, was the current dinner table commentary.

Her brother and Pastor Nate, usually content to bicker about fantasy football or who deserved the last piece of pie, had turned their full attention to her.

Even Granny D had veered off her usual path of widow tales and questionable home remedies, steering them all straight into the land of—ugh—Finn speculation.

Only, they weren't calling it speculation. Oh no. They kept using words like *flirting*, *chemistry*, *relationship*.

Daphne narrowed her eyes at her brother across the table while she passed the butter to Granny D. She still hadn't forgiven him for the rib-photo betrayal. That thing had more likes than her Earl Grey–glazed scone reel—and way too much visibility for her peace of mind.

Brothers.

Her phone lit up beside her plate. Another notification on her morning post. The numbers? Phenomenal. The comments? Unhinged. Way too suggestive of anything between her and Finn—but also . . . fun.

Especially the ones from Finn.

Let's just say, flirty-emoji use was its own dialect.

Aimed at her? Surely not. He meant it for everyone . . . right? For mere marketing purposes?

She hesitated. Could Jack be right? Did Finn flirt with her differently?

She'd seen him at the early service—Lucy's little hand tucked in his. And the way he looked down at her when she whispered something during the children's sermon? It had bloomed a powerful tender feeling in Daphne's chest. Something that ached suspiciously like longing. Something only her dog and God heard her cry about.

And then there was Saturday night's big reveal about Finn's ex-wife and Finn being the one who wanted the family, who tried to make the relationship work.

The man who made eyes at her across the counter and winked like he was auditioning for a rom-com? He also apparently stuck through hard things. Loved his little girl with gentle fierceness. And had been willing to walk away from the competition—for her.

That didn't line up with the charming-but-commitment-phobic file she'd mentally stuffed him in.

But maybe . . . maybe it wasn't him who didn't fit. Maybe she'd just been too scared to really look.

"You're smiling at that phone like it's a love letter." Jack met her eyes over his glass of iced tea.

"It's called engagement," she shot back, raising a forkful of casserole with the kind of tight smile that promised violence.

"Engaged, huh?" Jack grinned. "Is that what we're calling it now?"

"It's for the wedding." Daphne tried for breezy but sounded more like "*Drop it, bro.*" "Finn and I are just . . ."

She paused. What were they? Rivals, sure. But they were also . . . more. Acquaintances didn't sleep over at your house. Or see you in your flamingo pajamas. Heat soared into her face. Both of those internal statements did not help her argument against whatever Jack was implying. But . . . they had agreed to start a friendship, right?

Jack's grin spread like he could read her mind. "Hey, I'm just saying, if it walks like a flirt and winks like a flirt—"

"It's probably . . . engagement?" Pastor Nate interjected, grinning around his biscuit. "Definitions are relative when it comes to you and Finn at this point."

Daphne raised a roll like a fastball.

Nate just lifted his glass in a conceited salute. Preachers could be jerks too. Especially ones who acted like her brother!

"Lord, have mercy." Granny D fanned herself with her napkin. "That man's got a voice as attractive as his roast beef."

Jack shot her a look. Nate choked on his tea. Daphne considered moving to Alaska.

"His accent has a certain . . . appeal, there's no denying that. But we're just competitors," she said, trying to convince herself as much as anyone else.

"With chemistry," Jack added.

She kicked at his shin, but he dodged like a practiced older sibling.

"Whatever you are, y'all are putting this little town on the map," Nate said, pointing his half-eaten biscuit at her like he didn't even notice her death glare. "I heard Mrs. Applebaum say she checks both your Instagram accounts every night before bed."

"And Mrs. Meadows down at the library has seen a run on cookbooks," Granny D added, plopping another helping of potatoes on her plate. "Ain't nothing wrong with inspiring a little culinary curiosity."

Daphne blinked. That . . . was actually kind of sweet.

"Half the town's wearing your merch," Jack added, eyes twinkling. "And one of the elementary classes turned it into a science lesson." He turned to Nate. "Didn't we see a T-shirt that said something about baking and romance?"

Daphne groaned. "Don't even—"

"Oh, right!" Nate said with a snap. "Was it Whisks, Winks, and Wedding Rings?"

"No, I think it was You Bake Me Crazy," Jack added helpfully.

"I hate you both." Daphne rolled her eyes, cheeks heating to a broil.

"No, no . . ." Nate shook his head, sending a peripheral look to Daphne. "Hot Buns and Hotter Feelings?"

Jack's laugh erupted. "Wait, what about Whisked Off Her Feet?"

"You are both fired!" Daphne half shouted.

"I don't even work for you," Nate said, laughing.

"I do," Rosemary called as she strolled in with a pan of apple crumble in her hands and a smug grin on her face. "But I'm not fired until after dessert."

"Just in time," Jack said with a flourish. "We're conducting a relationship intervention."

"Which is so unnecessary," Daphne mumbled.

"Absolutely necessary." Rosemary plopped into the empty chair beside her and grabbed a roll. "It's either this or we make you write your feelings in icing."

Daphne gave her the driest look she could muster. "Traitor."

"I've seen the way you look at him."

"Like a warning label?" Daphne tried.

"Like a woman who's thinking romantic thoughts during scone prep." Rosemary grinned and elbowed her. "And I'm pretty sure he's thinking the same from the way he looks at you."

"I think he looks at everyone like that," she said softly. Then more loudly added, "It's just who he is."

"No, it's not," Nate said, shifting into his pastoral discernment face. "He saves the 'heart-eyes emoji in real life' look for you."

"Heart-eyes emoji—"

"It's totally different with you." Jack nodded. "It's like his flirt filter malfunctions when you're around."

That image was almost enough to make her smile.

Finn Dashwood: glitchy flirt, steady father, surprising friend?

Then her thoughts paused. What if . . . what if *he* wasn't the one running. Maybe *she* was.

Her brain hitched on that idea.

Her tremulous heart began to shiver with a very real possibility that not every flirt, not every charming man, was her dad in the making. That perhaps Finn was exactly who her heart had been waiting for all along and she'd been so lost in her own assumptions, she'd failed to see the truth.

"Looks like those thoughts are settling in." Granny D pushed a steaming mug toward her with a knowing glint in her eye. "I think a cup of tea is exactly what you need."

Daphne reached for the cup . . . and stopped.

Across the front, in bright green letters, it read: "The tea is hot and so is the chef."

"Just in case you need an extra nudge, sugar," Granny D said, all innocence and no shame.

Daphne sighed.

Surrounded by traitors.

And amateur matchmakers.

And she still had a competition to win.

....

Finn couldn't help it. He had to wear the shirt to the cook-off.

From the front, it looked like a nice button-down, crisp and blue with a tasteful #TeamPub embossed over the left side of the chest. Classy. Showed loyalty. Clear and concise.

But on the back?

His grin twitched.

"Warning: Contents may cause swooning."

Thanks, Wisteria General Store.

He couldn't wait to see Daphne's reaction.

Walking through town in all its festival glory only deepened his sense of belonging. Autumn bunting crisscrossed the street above him. Booths spilled down the sidewalks. The scent of cinnamon kettle corn mingled with crisp air and roasting pecans.

And apples. The scent of apples flooded almost every intake of breath, and in various forms of deliciousness. Ah yes. He needed to use those in a recipe very soon.

People waved, raved about his food, asked how Lucy was doing, joked with him like they'd known him all his life.

He'd not even been open a week, and already he had regulars—people who stayed to chat over coffee, who updated him on town gossip whether he asked or not, who already knew how he organized his bar. But mostly, he'd felt the community embrace him.

They'd folded him into the story of Wisteria with an ease that caught him off guard and completely transformed his definition of *home.*

And of course the town had gone all in for the cook-off.

Banners stretched over shop windows. All sorts wore T-shirts declaring loyalty to either #TeamPub or #TeamTea. The local embroidery shop had added oven mitts and aprons to the mix. Some voters were loud about their allegiance. Others whispered it with shifty eyes like it was classified intel.

And still, the energy perked with pure fun. Friendly. No fights.

Yet.

Finn kept looking up the hill toward the pinnacle of the street where the focus of the festivities came to their crowded and most colorful culmination. One of the beauties of the town was how it rose from the bottom of Main Street at the Ashbourne River to the top in a slow incline until it crested at the point of the town hall, First Baptist Church, The Marches, and Wisteria Public Park . . . which happened to house an amphitheater with musicians ready to play.

Live music echoed faintly, weaving between tents and booths. Streamers wrapped around lampposts. Balloons bobbed overhead.

And the center gazebo had been turned into the town's culinary battlefield. Two booths stood side by side, one trimmed in pale pink ribbon with "Team Tea" written in delicate script, and the other bold and bright with gold streamers spelling out "Team Pub."

He scanned the booths and spotted her. His lovely opponent.

She stood behind her counter, pink shirt tucked into jean shorts that did a criminal sort of justice to her legs. A matching ribbon held her ponytail back. She leaned over a tray of delicate tea cakes, laughing with a little girl holding a glitter-covered notebook.

His grin took a slow journey from one corner of his mouth to the other. Oh, he *liked* her.

Her humor. Her grit. Her intelligence and kindness.

He liked the way she didn't let him off easy. But he also—if he were being honest—liked the way she looked with the sun painting her cheekbones and that wild sparkle in her eyes when she laughed.

She was sunlight and spice and *everything* nice, and she tangled herself around his heart in a way that felt part fairy tale, part rom-com, and all permanent.

They hadn't talked much in the few days since he'd carried Lucy from her apartment. Business had been good—which meant hectic—but he'd caught glimpses. Short ones. Teasing exchanges in the café. Brief hellos when Lucy stopped by Tea Thyme right after school on Monday for, heaven help him, *tea* and—evidently—some princess talk.

But none of those had been enough to gauge where Daphne stood. Not enough to ask the important questions: Did she feel it too? And how about a more-than-friendship option?

"Ah, finally," Daphne said, placing a hand on her hip as he approached. "I was beginning to think you'd chickened out."

Heaven and earth! Once she'd given way to the banter, she'd gone all in.

And he was happily here for it.

"Not a chance. I've got a town to win over, a reputation to defend, and"—his gaze slid slowly over her ensemble—"a rival to distract."

"You wish." Her eyes narrowed, but her smile gave her away. "I've got the town's sweet tooth in my back pocket."

"Maybe." He leaned a little closer, catching a whiff of cinnamon. "But I've got short rib sliders on cheddar brioche, espresso salted caramel brownie sundaes, and a T-shirt that's already trending on social."

"Salted caramel brownie sundaes?" she squeaked, her bottom lip dropping into a fetching look of surprise.

"Swoon-inducing, even." He searched those eyes, allowing the heat between them to kick up a few degrees.

She blinked and stepped back, shrugging as if he hadn't caught the slight hitch in her breath at his nearness. Ah, perhaps he did have a chance. "Where is your much more adorable sidekick this evening?"

If she'd hoped to deter the attraction, her wit only enhanced it more. "Margaret took her to the pony rides, and how could I ever compare to ponies?"

She fought her grin for a moment, her cheeks still a lovely shade of rose, and then tilted her head as if trying to see the back of his shirt. "So, what does *your* shirt say?"

With a wiggle of his brows, he turned slowly, just enough for her to read it.

Her laughter burst out. "Oh wow. Jodie at the general store sure clocked you, didn't she?"

He whipped back around to see her grin, and then his gaze fell to the logo on her shirt. #TeamTea? Ah, one of Jodie's creations too.

"Your go. Turn around."

Her golden brows arched in challenge, and she mimicked his slow rotation. His laugh erupted as he read: "No coffee necessary to roast the competition."

And in that very moment, his heart gave way to the pull completely and entirely. He was in love with Daphne Austen, and there was no going back.

"Touché," he said, watching her continue to battle with her smile. "But actions speak louder than T-shirt quotes, so we'll just have to see what the town has to say."

"Good luck then." She offered her hand, and as soon as his fingers wrapped around hers, she gave his hand a squeeze and said, "You're gonna need it."

CHAPTER 16

<u>**@WisteriaWeekly:**</u> It's happening, folks. The cook-off begins TONIGHT. Get your taste buds ready and your vote tickets in hand. #TeamTea #TeamPub #HarvestFestivalThrowdown

<u>**@LindsayMonroeOfficial:**</u> Mood: sitting front row with a fork in one hand and popcorn in the other. May the best chef (and best slow-burn love story) win. #TeamSwoon #MatchmakersUnite

<u>**@RosemaryatThyme:**</u> Just saw Daphne calmly adjust a garnish while Finn blatantly checked her out. This isn't a cook-off. It's a culinary rom-com. @LindsayMonroeOfficial #IYKYK #MatchBaker

<u>**@LindsayMonroeOfficial:**</u> Right? @RosemaryatThyme. What are we really voting on? #FoodOrRomance #SugarOrSpiceButAllOfItsNice

<u>**@TeaThymeNC:**</u> @TGDPub doesn't deserve to win. He just tried to sabotage my careful food placing by winking at me. If my soufflé falls, he's to blame. #CheatersNeverProsper #FlirtFail

<u>**@TGDPub:**</u> #Unashamed

@JackAustenPhotography: Guys. You're standing three feet apart. We can see the heart eyes.

@PastorNateNHC: The Lord moves in mysterious ways. Sometimes through miracles . . . sometimes through muffins. Let's all remember to support one another in love, patience, and pastry-based outreach. #GraceAndGlaze #PrayForTheScones

@GrannyDOfficial: Her granny raised her better than to let a man's wink ruin her soufflé. But then again, that man can cook and he's mighty handsome. Let her have a moment, Pastor. She's only human.

@TGDPub: @GrannyDOfficial You do know you're my favorite, right?

@MayorWilsonOfficial: Let the record show I voted once. (With my stomach.) And I'm abstaining from further comment. #JustBusiness #Mostly

@RosemaryatThyme: Weaponized flirting. Delicious. I'll take two.

@WisteriaWeekly: New headline: "Local baker victim of baked-good sabotage via perfectly placed smolder."

@OldManRutherforton: Back in my day, we settled rivalries with an arm wrestle, not a tart-off. That said, #TeamTea. I know good structure when I see it.

@SheriffGrady: Bribery by baked goods: a proud Wisteria tradition.

@WisteriaGeneralStore: We're printing "Weaponized Flirting" aprons and "Will Stop for Swoons" tea towels as we speak. Available by end of day. Limited edition.

@QuiltedandCozy: I don't even cook and I need that apron. Do they come in "blush" or just "full-blown fluster"?

@ClemAtTheGym: Is there a matching oven mitt that says, "Flirting is my love language"? Asking for inventory purposes.

@CoraReadsRomance: If someone doesn't write a romantic suspense novel titled *Weaponized Flirting*, I swear I'll do it myself.

@TeaThymeNC: I feel attacked. But also . . . can I preorder a pink one? Asking for a friend.

@TGDPub: Make mine black. Embroidered. Extra smolder.

DAPHNE ADJUSTED A LINEN napkin on her display and tried to ignore the sound of Finn whistling "Rule, Britannia!" from his booth next door.

Loudly. Proudly. And entirely off-key.

They'd been bantering for over an hour, volleying jokes and playful digs back and forth like it was a two-person comedy show. The crowd had eaten it up—both figuratively and literally. News crews had come by, a few from as far as across state lines. Food bloggers with cameras and sleek leather boots. Tourists who'd clearly never heard of Wisteria before this week. It was exhilarating. And mildly terrifying.

All there to take part in the great Wisteria Cook-Off.

Lindsay and Travis had passed by several times, between confirming their florist and meeting with Jack for photography. Each time they walked by, their eyes glimmered with the matchmaking mischief.

This town had too many matchmakers in its ranks!

And the crowd that had settled between the booths only grew as the hours went by.

Finn hit a particularly painful note, and Daphne angled her head toward him, arms crossing. "Really? Feeling patriotic, are we?"

Finn grinned without missing a beat. "Just channeling a little British pride. You know, in case my actual food overshadows your delicate nibbles."

A few dramatic gasps and chuckles floated from the nearby crowd.

"Delicate nibbles?" Daphne's voice rose a full octave, her hand finding her hip. "That's rich coming from a man who considers smoked paprika and bravado their own food groups."

A nearby customer snorted into her lavender lemonade.

Finn lifted his hands in mock innocence. "Bravado pairs beautifully with a hint of Southern cinnamon class, don't you think?"

His gaze trailed down her, leaving a wave of heat in its wake that had nothing to do with the temperature in the air. In fact, heat rose into her face so fast it could have steeped tea.

It wasn't fair that his smolder held such power. It really wasn't.

Well, she wasn't about to let "Flynn" Dashwood know it mattered to her in the least.

"That smolder might melt your sliders, but I prefer a more authentic and classic approach." She waved toward her display, causing a few more chuckles in the crowd. "Refined flavors and excellent presentation create the best combination for a couple's *wedding* day." She gestured toward his booth. "Now, if we're trying to have a barbecue . . ." She let the comment linger.

"You sound as though you're trying to convince *me*." Those caramel-colored eyes of his lit, and he edged nearer.

"Oh, I am determined to woo you to the light, Mr. Dashwood."

She should have chosen different wording, because the way Finn's gaze darkened nearly sent her pulse boiling over.

"Team Tea for the win," someone called from the crowd, egging Daphne on.

"Which is why"—Daphne turned back to her table with flair and retrieved a small, heart-shaped plate—"I made this."

She placed the plate dead center on Finn's booth table, right in front of his amused face.

He eyed the trio of perfectly browned shortbread rounds, each topped with a delicate lemon glaze.

"Shortbread?" His brows lifted in mock horror. "You wish to woo me with shortbread?"

The crowd exploded with encouragement, so she played along, although the heat in her face intensified. "Whatever it takes."

"Daphne?" He stepped closer, voice low enough that the crowd probably missed it. "You don't have to stoop to manipulating flour and sugar to woo me."

"Marry him now!" came a call from the watchers—the voice sounding mysteriously like Rosemary's—clearly proving his voice wasn't quite low enough.

Finn didn't look away from her. "Just say the word," he whispered with a wink.

She cleared her throat and shoved the plate closer anyway, hanging on to her composure by a thread. "This is not just any shortbread," she said with a tilt of her chin, ignoring his comment and the flames of volcanic proportion likely emanating from her face. "Spiced brown butter lemon shortbread. Made specifically with doubters in mind."

He picked up one of the shortbread rounds and held it like it was sacred, giving it a theatrical once-over. "You know how to flatter a man."

"I know how to surprise one," she said, and crossed her arms again. "Or are you too chicken to taste something that isn't slathered in aioli?"

Finn chuckled—low, warm, devastating—and took a bite.

Then froze.

Daphne leaned in, waiting.

He chewed again.

Swallowed.

And then let out a low, defeated sigh. "I hate how good this is."

A few people nearby laughed, and her smile bloomed. But it wasn't just because of the compliment—it was the way he'd made sure people heard it. Like her work, her talent, she herself was worth celebrating out loud.

She held his gaze, and his expression shifted back into the man she'd spoken to at midnight a few nights ago. The tenderness. The *seeing*. It pulled again at a thread buried way too deep in her chest.

And she realized . . . she wanted this.

Her breath caught.

Him.

He pointed his half-eaten cookie at her. "You laced this with something illegal, didn't you?"

She hesitated, trying to climb out of the internal realization with some pride intact. "Brown butter and a dash of cardamom." She gave him a mock bow. "Goes straight to the soul."

"Indeed it does." Finn popped the rest of it into his mouth, chewing as he circled the booth to stand near her. "Do you recall the old adage . . ." He looked up as if thinking, his voice low as he turned away from the crowd. "What is it? The way to a man's heart . . ." Slowly, deliberately, he lifted another cookie from the plate, holding it between two fingers like a proposition.

Her heart hiccupped.

Was he joking again?

She didn't move. Just stared at him, wondering how in the world one man could be so disarmingly charming and steady at the same time.

And then—

"I'm ready to place my vote, Finn."

A sultry voice snapped the tension. Daphne turned toward the source and nearly groaned.

Jayla March. Draped in designer linen, glowing like she owned the sun, and flanked by two equally glamorous friends.

Finn turned toward her, smile easy, open. "Well, I do hope I can impress you enough for a vote, Miss March."

The raven-haired beauty breached the distance, her hand sliding onto Finn's forearm like it was a familiar path. "My daddy's particularly interested in trying those sliders we keep hearing about."

With practiced ease, Finn shifted behind his booth, voice lifting to match the crowd's energy. He laughed. They flirted. And Jayla's friends, now crowding in, leaned into the performance like it was a Broadway show.

And something twisted in Daphne's stomach.

Of course he was charming. That was just . . . who he was. Friendly. Approachable. Dangerously charismatic. Like that with *everyone.*

His gaze slid back to her a few times, hesitating, warming, before Jayla pulled him back into conversation by the Designer Trio.

"Cast your final ballots for Wisteria's Cook-Off, folks!" Mayor Wilson's voice rang out from the amphitheater stage.

Daphne turned mechanically toward the sound.

Lindsay and Travis stood next to him onstage, both looking like they just stepped out of their own designer magazines.

"We're closing up votes in five minutes, so if you're going to get yours in, better hustle over to Daphne's and Finn's booths while you can!"

"And while there's still food left," Lindsay added with a wink, earning a ripple of laughter.

"Ms. Monroe and Mr. Langston have volunteered to count the votes to see who their wedding caterer will be, so stay tuned for the announcement," the mayor continued.

"And in the meantime"—Travis gestured toward the stage—"let's get the dancing started!"

More giggles erupted from Finn's booth. Jayla leaned in closer. Finn said something that made her throw her head back and laugh like she was out for his heart.

And maybe she was.

And maybe—maybe it didn't matter. Because if that kind of charm was just part of the Finn Dashwood experience, then none of it was real. Not with her. Not with anyone.

Daphne blinked hard and turned away, the cookie still untouched in her hand.

But . . . but she couldn't shake the memory of him with her having conversations about grannies and cooking and heartbreak. Something deeper and sweeter than superficial.

As soon as the mayor wrapped up his announcement, she slipped from her booth, weaving through the crowd with a forced smile. The music floated behind her.

Her mind buzzed. Tried to reason. Tried to sift through memories for truth.

She didn't stop walking until she reached the edge of the square, near the rose garden. The booths and music fell away, and she finally exhaled.

Why did it matter? Why did *he* matter?

He flirted with everyone. It was safe for him. Natural.

But it was dangerous for her. Because she didn't just want fun. Or flattery. And definitely not the kind of attention that flickered on and off like a stage light.

She wanted something real and . . . forever. The perfect ingredient for the recipe of her life.

And what scared her most—what made her stomach twist and her chest ache—was the terrible, impossible suspicion that maybe, *just maybe*, Finn Dashwood could be exactly that.

And if she let herself believe it and was wrong?

She wouldn't just risk losing the competition.

She'd lose her heart.

CHAPTER 17

@WisteriaWeekly: From shortbread debates to swaying under the stars. Wisteria, are we witnessing the rivals-to-romance arc of the century? #FromFeudToFlirt #LanternLitLove #FestivalEnemiesTo...

> **@RosemaryatThyme:** I saw the look. The "I'd bake you a thousand scones" look. Also, I have cinnamon rolls left if anyone's stress-eating their feelings. #SconeGoals #WisteriaWatchesEverything #HeLookedAtHerLikeSheWasPie
>
> **@WisteriaGeneralStore:** To whoever carved a heart into the cider tasting table and labeled it "D + F": We're not mad. We're monogramming mugs. Also, we've created paired oven mitts that read: The Couple Who Bakes Together Stays Together #BlessThisMessyRomance #JustFriendsMyFoot
>
> **@JackAustenPhotography:** If this turns into a kissing book, I want veto power. And fair warning. Just saying. #Gross #Inconceivable
>
> **@PastorNateNHC:** "Love your enemies," they said. Pretty sure Luke 6:27 didn't have

dancing and heart eyes in mind, but here we are. #EnemiesToLovers #BlessedAndBothered #OfficialWisteriaWatchCommitteeMember

@WisteriaGeneralStore: New item: T-shirts that read: Official Member of the Wisteria Romance Watch Committee. Also, aprons that read: Flirt First, Bake Later. #JustKeepinItReal

@GrannyDOfficial: I taught her everything she knows. And if she doesn't make him work for it, she's getting a lecture with extra lemon bars. #RaisedRight #BakeItTillYouMakeIt

@SavorTheSouthEats: Um, hi, just casually witnessing the cutest culinary rivals-to-lovers story of the year? Wisteria, NC—you're officially on our must-visit list. #FoodieRomance #SavorTheDrama #DaphneAndFinnForever

@LocalHistorian82: I haven't seen this kind of romantic speculation since the '78 Founders Day Pie Incident. This is better. Keep going. #HistoricalSwoonData #DocumentingTheDashwoodEffect

@WisteriaGeneralStore: "The Dashwood Effect" mugs will be up for purchase within the week.

DAPHNE HAD WANDERED PAST the amphitheater and into the quieter stretch of park behind it, craving space. Distance. Air not saturated with Finn Dashwood and all the maddening emotions that came with him.

Why couldn't this be simple?

She cared for him. He cared for her. *Ka-ching*, happily ever after, right?

Ha!

She followed the sound of children's laughter until it led her to the petting zoo and pony rides.

And there, right by the split-rail fence, stood Margaret Coleman—lemonade in hand, posture impeccable, and looking more composed than Daphne had felt in weeks. She wore a sun hat the size of a dinner plate, but instead of looking ridiculous, she somehow made it seem like the height of class. All *Southern Living* and elegance.

Margaret spotted her and offered her signature smile in welcome. "Is the cook-off finished already?"

"Just," Daphne said, brushing wind-tossed hair out of her face and trying not to sound as emotionally scrambled as she felt. "Voting closed a few minutes ago."

"It's all so exciting," Margaret said, eyes following the ponies as they clip-clopped by. "Fantastic visibility for both of you."

"Truly." Daphne nodded, eyes locked on a little girl trying valiantly to get her pony to trot. "A once-in-a-lifetime opportunity."

"You're adored in Wisteria, dear," Margaret continued, her tone like chamomile tea with just enough honey. "But it's nice to see others finally noticing what we've always known. All that hard work. And that divine food."

"Thanks." Daphne turned toward her. "I've . . . actually loved the push of all this. I think I've been stuck for a while and didn't even realize I had so many ideas in me until Finn showed up."

Margaret's brow lifted slightly—the kind of lift that said, *interesting*, while her lips remained diplomatically silent.

Daphne flushed and quickly amended, "I just mean, competition gets the creativity flowing."

"Mmm." Margaret sipped her lemonade, her smile unconvinced. "He's got the sort of presence that stirs things up, doesn't he? But he has a good heart too. And Wisteria suits him. Don't you think?"

He *did* seem to have a good heart, but was it a faithful one? "He fits better than I expected," Daphne admitted, watching another pony circle. "And the town has basically adopted him."

"Well, of course. Did you expect anything less from Wisteria?"

"No." A reluctant smile tugged at Daphne's mouth. "Once you're in, we keep you."

"Harry never even mentions going back to England, and he's not half as outgoing and charming as Finn." She paused, lips twitching. "Charming, but not like *that*."

A soft neigh drew Daphne's attention back to the ponies. Lucy, perched atop a little white one with a pink ribbon in its mane, caught sight of her and lit up like a sparkler. She waved both hands, nearly toppling sideways in her saddle from the enthusiasm.

Daphne's heart went completely and irrevocably squishy.

"She's smitten with you," Margaret said fondly. "And Finn talks about you like you're family. Your ideas, your likes and interests. You've made quite the impression on him."

Daphne's cheeks flamed. "He's just . . . friendly. With everyone."

"He is friendly. One of his many charms." Margaret tilted her head, amusement flickering in her eyes. "Has been as long as I've known him, and that's at least ten years."

"And such a flirt."

That eyebrow lifted again. "And that bothers you?"

Daphne hesitated, trying to untangle her own heart. She looked back at the ponies, waved again to Lucy. "It's just . . . when do you know if it's more than flirting? If it's real? Or just . . . fun for him?"

"Do you want it to be real?"

Yes? The answer flew to her mind too quickly, but she paused. "I . . . I don't know. Maybe."

Margaret turned, leaning her back against the fence and studying Daphne. "So you want him to stop with the flirting? The teasing?"

"No." It slipped out too fast, too honest. "I just—I don't want to be the only one who thinks it means . . . something."

Her voice sounded small. A little scared. Which was inconvenient, considering she hadn't meant to be either of those things today.

"What makes you think he doesn't mean it?"

Daphne looked away.

Margaret sighed. "Sweetheart, flirting's easy. Light. But he knows you. Makes room for you—in his day, with his ideas, in his conversations. Your thoughts matter to him. Flirting may be the icing, but it's held up by sturdier stuff beneath."

Daphne chuckled despite herself. "So, he's cake?"

Margaret's smile gentled with her expression. "You're scared he'll be like your daddy?"

Daphne flinched and then . . . the picture began to clear in her mind. No. Finn wasn't like her dad. If she looked at the evidence, the only comparison was his ready wit. But he'd weathered hard decisions and made the right choices. Offered his little girl a steady, secure love.

Stayed . . . for Lucy.

"Maybe it's time to look at him with fresh eyes, Daphne." Margaret's answer came softly. "Without fear clouding your vision. He's not perfect. And he can teeter toward arrogant, but he's got a track record of caring well. And the way he looks at you?" She leaned in just slightly. "That's not a look you can fake. Not from the good ones anyway."

They stood in silence a moment longer, the breeze rustling through the trees, Lucy's laughter floating on the air.

Margaret straightened and waved her hand back toward the crowd. "Now go show that man how a Wisteria woman handles healthy attention."

Daphne arched a brow. "With quiet dignity and measured responses?"

Margaret's grin turned deliciously sly. "I was thinking more along the lines of looking fabulous and making him sweat a little."

Daphne laughed. Maybe she didn't know exactly where this was headed. Maybe her heart was still a little afraid. But she wanted to get to the truth. Finn Dashwood might be a flirt.

But he was much more.

And it was time to find out if that "more" included her and her future in the mix.

....

The stars had only just begun to prick the velvet sky, but the lanterns—dozens of them—already glowed golden around the amphitheater, their light dancing over the lawn like fireflies in formation. The grassy space in front of the stage was already crowded with people swaying and stomping to the jubilant cry of a bluegrass fiddle.

Daphne hovered at the edge of the clearing, cradling a warm mason jar of cinnamon cider like it might deflect incoming emotion. Or at least Finn-shaped confusion.

The scent of woodsmoke curled through the crisp air, mingling with roasted peanuts, caramel apples, and someone's cologne that was two cloves past subtle. String lights stretched from the gazebo to the oaks like low-hanging constellations.

It was all so perfect.

Like something from a Hallmark movie.

Like . . . home.

And then she saw him.

Finn.

Still looking unfairly good even after a long workday, then a few hours at the food booths. His dark hair was mussed in that way that made her fingers twitch. And his smile—ugh. That infuriating, crinkly-eyed, lopsided smile.

He was dancing an upbeat song with Rosemary, and it appeared she was teaching him the steps. His attention fixed on Rosemary's upturned face, complete with that "no one else in the room" look.

But of course he'd be focused if he was trying to learn a dance.

His laugh burst out as he took a wrong turn.

And that reaction warmed her heart.

Her father—when he'd messed up—had scowled. Blamed someone. So had her ex-boyfriend. But Finn? He laughed at himself. Took it in stride.

So what else had she been misreading?

He kept his distance respectable, his grin at the ready, his expression friendly, but—her hand squeezed the cider jar—it wasn't the same. Not like he looked at her. Not the splitting of distances she'd noticed between them.

Carrie Long asked him for a dance next. And with an exaggerated bow, he took her hand, his dark hair dipping over his forehead as he attempted to repeat the dance with a new partner. Daphne's grin itched to react.

It was the same as with Rosemary. His touch was that of a gentleman. Nothing more.

And if she'd been willing to see it earlier—without the fog of past hurts—she might've realized he'd been like this all along. Welcoming. Kind. But careful.

A flutter of uncertainty stirred in her chest.

And then . . . he looked up.

Caught her watching.

And he didn't look away.

Daphne's stomach tensed . . . and then flipped.

Could he tell? That she was seeing him more clearly now? Did he really want more than friendship with her? Hearts even?

"What are you doing hiding all the way over here in the shadows?" came Lindsay's voice from behind her.

"What are you doing attending Wisteria's Harvest Festival when you have a ten-day countdown until your wedding?" Daphne shot back, maybe a little too comfortable with a veritable celebrity.

Lindsay grinned, all glossy hair and relaxed elegance. "I grew up here, remember?" She gestured toward the crowd. "Besides, I needed a little grounding before the glam whirlwind. And these folks are good for that."

Daphne turned toward her fully, giving her brows a little wiggle. "You mean . . . like a palate cleanser before the chaos?"

"Nice reference." Lindsay chuckled and then sighed, her attention drawn back to the dancers. "It's easy to forget who you are when the world keeps asking you to prove yourself with filters and follower counts. I needed the reminder that I matter because I'm *me*. Not because of a dress size or trending recipe."

Daphne nodded, something inside her easing at the truth in those words.

"And Travis?" Daphne asked. "He's not overwhelmed by the Wisteria way?"

"Oh, he's head over heels." Lindsay's eyes twinkled. "With the town *and* with me. And I think maybe I forgot how much this place shaped me. I wanted to get married here for a reason, you know?"

"I get it. Wisteria might be simple," Daphne said, smiling. "But not less."

"No ma'am." Lindsay met her eyes. "Definitely not less."

The music dipped into a sweet, fiddle-led waltz as children's laughter echoed across the field and the familiar turn of Finn's accent blended with the crowd. These people had held her up through grief, celebrated her courage when she took over the bakery, and today? They'd shown up—for her. For Finn. For the whole messy, beautiful journey.

Yes—home *sweet* home.

Her eyes drifted back to him. Finn. Laughing as Carrie Long spun away and ended the dance. His gaze cut through the crowd like a compass—and landed straight on her again.

The flutter returned, stronger now.

Lindsay's fingers looped through Daphne's arm. "Come on. You deserve a little celebration."

"What are we celebrating?" Daphne asked as Lindsay tugged her forward.

"A day of great food. Good people." Lindsay marched impressively fast for someone in heels. "And . . ."

"And?"

"And an excellent pairing."

"An excellent—"

Before Daphne could finish, Lindsay executed a devious little pivot and spun her directly onto the edge of the dance floor—right into the path of Finn Dashwood.

He blinked at her.

She blinked back.

Excellent pairing indeed.

"Hi," he said, as if she hadn't just crash-landed into his personal space.

"I was pushed," Daphne said flatly.

The soft strains of the fiddle swelled into a waltz, almost like a melodic nudge to draw closer to Finn.

"Well, then," he said, voice warm as cider as he stretched his hand out toward her. "I'd be a fool not to take advantage of someone's excellent timing."

Daphne stared at his hand, her words failing to emerge at first.

"Now, Daphne. I know you can dance. I've seen it on display with my daughter." His grin hitched up—*that* grin—and her pulse promptly tripped over itself. His gaze dipped, just briefly, then bounced back up to meet hers. "And I couldn't help but notice—your very nice legs seemed to be working quite well all day."

Both her brows rose.

And suddenly, a vulnerability stole into his expression. He searched her face before he stepped closer, hand still outstretched. "Dance with me?"

The question came out quiet. No smugness. No games. Just him. Waiting. Earnest.

The entreaty in his voice pulled her forward. She slid her hand into his, and his warm palm smoothed around her waist to settle at her back, tugging her close, anchoring her near him. Her breathing remained stalled for a few more seconds, attempting to adjust to his touch.

Um . . . so . . . this was certainly not how he'd danced with Rosemary.

A few beats of silence passed, the world narrowing to the feel of his arms around her. His scent—something warm and clean and faintly spicy—enveloped her. He smelled as good as he looked, which was saying something.

He brought her closer, their bodies brushing, their feet moving in an unhurried sway while the music melted into the background. With another little tug, he lowered his head, cheek pressing lightly against her temple. "You smell like cinnamon and sugar," he murmured near her ear.

The words sank straight into her skin, sending a delicious ripple down her neck.

She tilted her head up, their faces close. "Not salty enough for you?"

His smile curved—slow, tender, achingly sweet—and it took everything in her not to miss a step. "Perfect, actually." He leaned in, breath feathering over her temple. "Daphne Austen: sugar and spice and everything nice."

She absolutely, positively refused to allow him to see her entire body swoon . . . or her entire nervous system short-circuit.

"Lathering on the charm a little thick, aren't we?" she teased, trying—futilely—to inject some playful distance.

"Just telling the truth." His voice stayed low. "You are—and have been—lovely."

Her throat tightened, her heart vaulting like it was just waiting to jump directly into whatever those eyes offered.

His sincerity hit too . . . much. It was too poignant. Too real. "Another sweet comment?" she managed, narrowing her eyes. "You must be pretty confident you're going to win this competition."

He chuckled, the sound a rumble that she felt in her chest.

"Actually . . ." He dipped his head slightly, hand on her back, not rushing, not pulling—just holding her there like he had all the time in the world. Or . . . like he knew *she* needed the time? "The prize I'm after has changed. Significantly."

"Is that so?"

"Mm-hmm," he hummed. His hand pressed more firmly against her spine as if to punctuate his admittance, the heat of his touch chasing straight through her. In truth, it was a little knee-weakening.

Her gaze dropped to his lips.

Okay, *a lot* knee-weakening.

"But," he added, eyes locked on hers. "I'm afraid I might need to work a bit harder to convince her I'm serious." His expression turned sheepish. "And I must admit to hoping for more than friendship." He swallowed hard, jaw tightening. "But if friendship is all she can offer, I'll take it."

The air in her chest stalled.

Oh.

Well, she'd wanted honesty . . .

"So . . . what caused the change of mind?"

He tipped closer, those caramel eyes searching hers, his vanilla-spice scent enveloping her.

"More of a change of *heart*," he said, his voice a husky murmur. "I started seeing you more clearly and"—his lips quirked—"to be perfectly honest, I've been smitten ever since."

Smitten.

That did not sound temporary.

"But," he continued, "I've blundered rather fantastically. So I understand if you have doubts."

She hadn't expected this. Not the repentant pull in his voice. That earnest, almost boyish regret flashing across his usually confident face. All of it pounding against her fear.

So in a trembling leap of faith—with hope that whatever this was between them might just lean toward the *forever* side of happily ever after—she swallowed through the knot in her throat. "I . . . I don't think you've blundered beyond repair."

His jaw slackened, surprise flickering across his face, followed by a soft, almost reverent smile. "I'll take that."

She exhaled, a slow unspooling breath, something uncoiling in her chest. Something that might have been trust. Or maybe just the first fragile whisper of it.

And a little hope? It snuck in through all the little cracks she'd tried to patch over with suspicion and self-protection.

Warmth pricked her eyes, right before the music came to an abrupt, screeching halt.

A collective murmur spread through the crowd, followed by the unmistakable squeal of a microphone.

"Sorry to interrupt all the boot scootin' and sweet talkin'," Mayor Wilson's voice boomed, "but we've got a very special announcement we know y'all've been waiting for!"

Daphne's stomach dropped.

Oh dear . . .

How many emotional roller coasters could one woman survive in a single evening?

The crowd whooped and clapped. Daphne's cheeks caught fire.

This shouldn't be a big deal. It was just a friendly competition.

Except . . . in this moment, with Finn's hand warm against her back and the weight of his words still stirring in her chest—it didn't *feel* friendly anymore.

It felt personal.

Too much like a popularity contest.

Her gaze snagged on Finn again.

He was so much more charismatic than she was. And his food was delicious. And he even had a cute daughter as a trump card in this game.

How was she supposed to compete with that?

Finn stood beside her, all strong and present. She nearly leaned into him. Absorb some of that steady confidence. Breathe in another hit of his intoxicating scent.

But no.

For this announcement, she needed to stand on her own.

Because if he won—no matter how much she liked him—she'd have to carry that disappointment solo.

Mayor Wilson handed the microphone to Travis, whose grin practically crackled with mischief.

His eyes found Finn and Daphne in the crowd.

"Come join us onstage," he called, waving them forward.

And then—oh no—he handed the mic off to Lindsay.

Who turned toward the videographer.

Videographer.

Oh good heavens.

Stage.

Public humiliation.

Possibly live-streamed.

Could this night get any worse?

Daphne forced up a good-natured smile—at least, she hoped it looked good-natured—and made her way to the stage with Finn's hand steady at her back.

"When Travis and I lost our caterer three weeks before the wedding, we never imagined becoming a part of such a rivalry as #TeamTea and #TeamPub."

Cheers erupted from the crowd.

Someone shouted, "I love you, Finn!"

Daphne's eyes pinched closed.

Finn chuckled and leaned her way. "It was the ribs."

And she giggled, despite the boiling temperature in her face and the very real chance she was about to lose this competition in front of the entire town like some low-budget reality show contestant.

"Surprisingly," Lindsay continued, "this rivalry has helped quiet some of the chaos leading up to our wedding—and reminded me just how much this community means to me. How much it's *shaped* me."

"And that's why we want to invite everyone to the reception," Travis said, nodding toward the crowd. "Hosted by the Wisteria Inn and Lindsay's team at Lindsay Monroe Official."

"And sponsored by Travis's company," Lindsay added, giving his hand a squeeze.

The crowd erupted in cheers.

Daphne blinked. *They were inviting the whole town?*

What on earth was happening?

This was not a wedding. This was an *event.*

"We also didn't plan to struggle so much choosing between two incredible culinary artists," Travis said, gesturing to Daphne and Finn.

"And the outpouring of support, fun, and social media chaos has been absolutely fantastic," Lindsay added. "Honestly? I think we're all winners tonight—because we've proved just how special Wisteria really is."

Another rousing response.

Daphne couldn't help the smile that tugged free. Eccentric? Yes. Chaotic? Often. But this town had wrapped around her and Jack in the hardest moments of their lives. And today they'd shown up again—for her and Finn.

"For decades Daphne's lovely presentation and mouthwatering recipes have been a staple in Wisteria," Lindsay said warmly. "Handed down by her beloved grandmother."

The mention of Granny in such a moment brought another rush of warmth to Daphne's eyes.

"And though Finn is new to Wisteria," Travis continued, "his savory dishes have already made a lasting impression."

"And drool-worthy reactions," Lindsay teased, prompting chuckles as way too many eyes turned toward Daphne.

She groaned.

Finn grinned down at her, and the look he gave—sweet and gentle—was somehow more devastating than any flirty line he'd ever delivered. But then his mouth crooked, adding just enough mischief to remind her the flirt was definitely still in there.

"We're so glad this competition gave both of them the spotlight their food—and their personalities—deserve," Lindsay continued. "Which is why we're thrilled to announce the result of your votes."

A dramatic pause.

Daphne, despite herself, reached out and clutched Finn's arm. She caught herself a second too late, but he only sent her a wink—an infuriatingly adorable one—and she rolled her gaze heavenward. She was ridiculous.

So was he.

And, as if heaven heard her internal monologue, Lindsay and Travis announced at the same time, "It's a tie!"

Cheers exploded across the lawn.

Daphne blinked. "A *what*?"

Lindsay clapped her hands like a fairy godmother two glasses into the punch. "A perfect, glorious, destiny-kissed tie! Which means . . ." She turned to Finn and Daphne with the full force of a woman practically sparkling with matchmaking glee. "You'll both be catering our wedding!"

Daphne gaped at them. Work with Finn? *Closely?* For ten days?

Panic and something suspiciously close to giddy excitement battled for dominance in her chest.

Her brain stumbled, and as the shock began to dissipate—despite the heat climbing up her neck at the idea of such close daily proximity to Finn—the reality of the situation hit her.

They had less than two weeks.

She wouldn't have been able to do this alone.

But together?

Lindsay gave her an entirely unapologetic smile. "Why choose when you can have two people—or food styles—that pair so well together?"

Finn leaned in, his voice just for her. "Two's usually better than one anyway, don't you think?"

She shot him a sideways glance. "Depends on the two."

His smile turned slow and lethal. "Well, lucky me—looks like the real challenge has just begun."

And despite herself—despite the spotlight and the looming chaos of this next week—Daphne smiled back.

One week. One wedding. One chance to figure out if Finn Dashwood's charm was surface level . . .

Or if the man she was starting to believe in was the real deal.

Close proximity. Flirty distractions. Late-night planning sessions.

Heaven help her.

This was either the best idea she'd ever agreed to . . . or the most dangerous.

But ready or not—her heart needed to know the answer.

CHAPTER 18

@TeaThymyNC: Just because we have to work together to cater a wedding doesn't mean our tastes are the same. The battle of Team Tea vs. Team Pub is still very much on. It's a simple choice: elegance, refinement, and a proper afternoon tea experience . . . or, well, whatever @TGDpub serves.
How to Join #TeamTea:

1. Order a classic Afternoon Tea at Tea Thyme
2. Dress with dignity (bonus points for hats)
3. Recite a Jane Austen quote at checkout for a very small but very dignified discount

Join us and prove that culture still exists in this town.
#TeaOverGrease #ChooseWisely
#GotToSupportWisteriaGeneralStore

....

@TGDpub: Oh, it's on. Since @TeaThymeNC insists that dainty sandwiches and lukewarm tea count as a meal, allow me to present an alternative: #Team Pub. Do you want tiny snacks or a real meal? Do you want food you barely nibble at or food you remember with tears in your eyes and sauce on your chin? Exactly.

How to Join #TeamPub:

1. Order a burger, wings, or anything that requires two hands to eat
2. Toast to the supremacy of hearty food
3. Bonus points, and a possible discount if you roast a tea drinker in the process #EatLikeYouMeanIt #BurgersBeforeBiscuits #NoTinyForksNeeded

@TeaThymeNC: Elegance over indigestion. Choose wisely. ✨ #RefinedTaste #TeaTimeMagic

@TGDpub: Real food. Real full. Real happy. #NotJustForPhotos #NoPinkiesUp

@LindsayMonroeOfficial: I love both! And, just maybe, both are better together??? #FoodieDilemma #CantPick #UnashamedMatchmaking

@SecondHandTreasures: I've moved beyond food bets. I'm taking wagers on when Finn and Daphne finally kiss. Proceeds go to the town charity! #WisteriaRomanceWatch

@OldManRutherforton: Reminds me of when my wife and I nearly called off the wedding over the thermostat. True love finds a way. (And eventually lands on 72 degrees.)

@LindsayMonroeOfficial: I think @OldManRutherforton just agreed with "both" too. #TrueLoveFindsAWay

@GrannyDOfficial: If they don't kiss by the rehearsal dinner, I'm bringing my cane and locking them in the bakery's pantry myself. #ElderPrivileges #WisteriaLoveLockdown

@WisteriaWeekly: Breaking: Sources confirm that the true winner of Team Tea vs. Team Pub will be . . . LOVE (and possibly a very messy kitchen). #OperationGetThemTogether #OurFavoriteSportIsMatchmaking

@PastorNateNHC: Love is patient. Love is kind. Love is also stubborn and in deep denial. #DontMessWithGrannyD

STEPPING INTO ANOTHER CHEF'S kitchen to share cooking space was an intimate thing. Finn knew it well. It was where magic happened. Where failure happened. Where frustrations boiled over into mortifying reactions—and sometimes where something extraordinary was born.

Daphne had agreed to meet for a planning and cooking session Friday morning while Lucy was in school and before his shop opened. In her kitchen, in case she was needed at Tea Thyme.

He tapped at the back door, balancing a tray loaded with ingredients and a few early-morning preparations. No answer. He knocked again, then cautiously nudged the door open.

The instant he stepped inside, the scent wrapped around him—freshly baked sweet breads, steeping tea, and . . . apples? His smile spread. Perfect. She was already doing what he'd decided on after the Harvest Festival night before last: Use what's in season.

And apples were everywhere.

He stepped farther inside and his grin grew. He'd been inside it once before, when offering the sticky toffee pudding, but he'd been more focused on Daphne than her surroundings.

The space fit her perfectly. Light. Airy. Tidy to the point of perfection. White shelves neatly stacked. Canisters symmetrically lined up like little soldiers. Bowls organized in a patchwork of muted tones, the utensils hung near the stove in a fashionable arrangement of smallest to largest. Even the dish towels matched. The entire room looked like something out of a magazine. It was incredibly impressive, a little unnerving, and tempted Finn to go through it and rearrange a few things . . . just for fun.

He refrained.

Above the oven, a little plaque caught his eye: "When in doubt, say a prayer—and add butter."

His grin unfurled fully. Butter and prayer—could there be a more fitting motto for Wisteria?

He edged farther inside, sunlight spilling through lace curtains, catching motes of flour dusting the air like fairy magic. His chest tightened unexpectedly.

The night before last Daphne had given him a flicker of hope. That maybe their wildly different personalities could not only amicably coexist but blend like sugar and spice.

Because every additional moment he spent with her only made him want another. He could almost see a life together—a life of life and food and laughter and banter—a life he *wanted* to build.

And then, like she'd been conjured by his very thoughts, Daphne pushed through the swinging door, arms laden with a crate of apples. Wisps of hair had escaped her ponytail, curling around her flushed cheeks. She wore jeans, a flour-dusted apron, and a soft-blue blouse that matched the sparkle of her eyes. Her apron read: Whisk Me Away.

Finn's heart responded with, *Pick me,* in Morse code.

"Is that an invitation?" he asked, pointing at her apron.

"What?" She glanced down and immediately blushed, the color blooming high in her cheeks. Her eyes narrowed even as she brushed a strand of hair from her forehead. "We're here to work, Mr. Dashwood. Not flirt."

"You say that like the two are mutually exclusive." He edged a step closer. "I'm rather sure they mix beautifully. I always cook better when I'm inspired."

Something flickered in her eyes—a battle she was clearly fighting. Her mouth quirked. "Well," she said, gesturing toward the crate on the island, "I hope apples inspire you. We've got plenty. Lindsay specifically requested apple dishes for her autumn wedding."

"No problem there. I have some great ideas for apple dishes." His grin sharpened. "Very inspiring ones."

She shook her head and then nodded toward the island in the center of the room. "I thought we could plan first? Talk about menus?"

A notepad and pens waited neatly. Of course she would have thought of that.

He slid onto a stool, and after a fractional hesitation, she sat beside him, her spine ruler straight.

Their dance at the Harvest Festival hovered between them, and he wasn't certain how to navigate his steps into more, because in all honesty, he just wanted to slice the tension with a kiss.

Daphne's gaze flitted to his. She shifted the notebook on the counter and then cleared her throat.

Nervous seemed to be the order of the day.

Well, that wasn't the best recipe for them, especially if they were to brainstorm a wedding menu or tip this simmering romance into a boil. Oh no.

Time to stir things up.

"Your kitchen is very . . . tidy."

Her fidgeting immediately stopped, and she slowly turned her head in his direction. "And that's bad?"

"Of course not." He raised a brow. "Merely an observation."

She turned fully toward him now. He had to press his lips together to keep from laughing.

"I suppose yours isn't tidy?" she challenged, lifting both brows. "More like a culinary explosion?"

He shrugged. "An explosion—with style."

Her grin bloomed, and she let out a breath. "Then maybe we should cook here," she said. "Since I'd like to avoid any . . . surprises."

"But"—he leaned in conspiratorially—"surprises sometimes make the very best dishes."

"Not for a celebrity wedding we're catering in a week." She pointed her pen at him like a weapon. "Surprises are not good for that."

"You're confusing surprises with accidents." He waggled his brows just to see that pretty flush race up her neck again. "Surprises should be nice. Pleasant things. Like . . ." He waved a hand lazily in her direction. "Like you've been for me."

Her gaze caught in his, searching like they did on Wednesday night at the festival. As if she were trying so very hard to place him in a category she wanted him to be.

And, from the look in those searching eyes, he wanted to be that man too.

She pulled her attention from his and tapped the little notebook on the kitchen island. Perhaps he was slowly breaking through whatever assumptions she'd held about him and, admittedly, he'd encouraged in the beginning. And winning such a beautiful heart?

He could only hope.

"From what Lindsay said, Harry and Margaret are covering the welcome grazing board at the inn, so we won't have to worry about that." She tucked a strand of hair behind her ear, her ponytail clearly losing its grip.

It was her preferred hairstyle, he was beginning to notice. And, at this point, beautifully distracting.

"But we're covering lunches, right?" he asked, nudging the conversation—and the warmth between them—forward.

Some of the tension in her shoulders eased.

She nodded and tapped her elegant script in the notebook. "A bridal luncheon and a groom's lunch."

"Which should be pretty straightforward on who covers which," he teased, angling for another smile.

Sure enough, one corner of those pink lips crooked ever so slightly. "Unless you need help with the *classy* side of things, of course."

Ah, there it was.

The jab he'd been waiting for.

"Men don't need pretty. Just tasty." He added a wink for good measure. "But if *you* need advice on how to feed the ladies more than toast, jam, and cucumbers, I'm available for consultations."

"Funny." She narrowed her eyes in a mock glare, but the soft laugh behind it made his heart kick against his ribs. She tapped her pen against her lips, and—he wasn't proud of this, or perhaps he was—he promptly forgot every coherent thought he had for a solid three seconds.

"But that leads us to the rehearsal dinner." She pulled a clipboard from beneath the notebook, the page so covered in notes that Finn wasn't sure there was any white left.

He leaned closer, pretending to read it, mostly just enjoying being near enough to catch the scent of apples and something softer, sweeter—her.

"I know you're excellent at savory dishes and I've reviewed your current menu at The Green Dragon, but I think we need at least one refined dish." She looked up at him. "And something vegan. For both the rehearsal dinner and the wedding meal."

"With apples." He gestured toward the crate.

"Yes." The way her whole face brightened in response nearly knocked him flat. "With apples."

He paused, running through the options he'd been tossing around most of the night. "If you want something more . . . refined"—he tilted his head, catching the way she gave an exaggerated sigh, as if already bracing herself—"I make an excellent apple walnut stuffed pork loin. It's seasonal but still elevated enough for a wedding. You could pretty it up however you like."

She blinked a few times, and then her nod grew more vigorous. "That's—" She flipped to a fresh page and scribbled something down. "That's a great option." She paused her scribbles. "And what about a popover as a side?" she added, twirling the pen between her fingers like a magic wand. "Maybe a rosemary-parmesan one. The rosemary's earthy flavor would match the autumn vibe."

"And the pastry would soak up the pork juices." He caught on to her excitement.

"Exactly." She leaned in, eyes alive with creativity. "And there's this risotto recipe I've been dying to make. Apple Cider Risotto. Not too apple-y—just the right hint of flavor. It would offer a creamy side option, and the Parmesan would complement the pork really well." Her pen did another spin. "Tie it all together."

Like the knot growing in his chest. He had no idea how he was supposed to concentrate when she looked at him like that, like they were creating something extraordinary together.

Honestly, if she kept talking in this manner, he was going to end up proposing by lunchtime or, at the very least, kissing her after every delectable sentence. But then they really wouldn't get much cooking done. Well, or they'd get the wrong kind of cooking done, so to speak. But he certainly wouldn't complain.

"You should definitely make it." His voice came out lower than intended, rough with the effort of keeping himself in check. "And for a side vegetable—what about simple sautéed green beans with lemon and almonds?"

Her smile stretched so wide it crinkled her eyes. "Let's try it!"

His head came up. "Now?"

"Yes, if you can. Granny D and Rosemary are covering the shop today."

He stared at her for a beat too long, his brain short-circuiting somewhere between *now* and *alone in her kitchen.*

"Let me ring your brother and a few other staff to make sure we have the pub covered." His grin tugged at his mouth, completely unstoppable. "Because, for the record, Daphne Austen"—he leaned in just enough for her to catch it, just enough to make her breath hitch—"I'm looking forward to cooking up one unforgettable wedding with you."

....

Two hours later—after a quick grocery run and even more teasing—they'd taken their positions. And to the dignified refrains of—God help him—Beethoven, they began their work.

Like her apartment kitchen, Daphne's setup was intuitive.

Finn somehow knew where to find ingredients, even without looking at her alphabetized labels. They slipped around each other easily, he offering a wink or comment now and then, she rolling her eyes—sometimes laughing—in response.

It was a different kind of rhythm than he was used to. He thrived in the louder chaos of the pub kitchen: clashing pots, shouted orders, the clang of metal and noise. But here, her movements were quieter, more deliberate.

Like a dance.

And he paused to admire it a few times.

All right, maybe more than a few times.

"Do you have coarser salt?" he asked, peering into a dainty porcelain jar on the counter.

"That's flake sea salt." She frowned slightly. "It's the best for finishing."

"I meant for crusting the pork." He shook the jar gently. "We'll need something heavier to stand up to roasting."

"Oh!" She blinked. "I don't usually use a ton of salt."

He tsked, slowly shaking his head at her. "But aren't you Southern?"

She cast him a mock glare.

"I suppose it's because you make such sweet things, luv," he teased. "Salt's the knight in shining armor of savory cooking. Can't joust without it."

"Then sugar must be the princess," she shot back, skimming by him so closely her cinnamon scent wafted around him. "Which is why I don't need as much since I'm already so sweet."

His internal predator gave a low, approving growl of the tilt in those flirty lips of hers. He might have even shifted a little closer just to stay in her orbit. Enough to watch her swallow hard and reach into the nearby cabinet.

She brought out a container of kosher salt to wedge between them.

"Excellent," he murmured, brushing her fingers on purpose as he took it.

And the look she gave him flickered with enough curiosity to have him humming back to his spot at the counter.

They worked side by side, the chime of a nearby clock ringing out the hour.

The kitchen smelled fantastic—savory, sweet, buttery, spiced—like all the best parts of belonging blended together. As if *they* belonged.

But Daphne's jokes grew fewer. Her first batch of popovers fell flat, literally, and she'd forgotten the shallots for the risotto. Finn offered a substitution—yellow onions and a kiss of garlic—and she accepted but rolled out her tart dough with unnecessary aggression.

Was she concerned about what he thought of her?

Had he wrecked her kitchen vibe somehow?

Scanning his workspace, he winced. Maybe a little.

But it wasn't just the mess. She'd gone too quiet, too stiff—nothing like the lively, sharp Daphne from an hour ago.

Her forehead wrinkled, and she kept checking the clock like it was ticking down a bomb.

"As cute as you are when you're worried," he said, edging closer,

"I'd rather you tell me what's going on in that pretty head so we can work through it."

Her gaze snapped to his. "I'm just . . . working. This is a big deal." She cleared her throat. "And I'm not exactly used to having . . . *you* in my kitchen."

So.

He *was* the problem.

But from the flush blooming in her cheeks, the problem wasn't entirely negative.

"I can work up in my apartment if that would help."

"No!" She said it so fast she startled herself. "It's not that I don't want you here. It's just—" Her shoulders dropped. "There's so much to do. And I need this catering job to work. I have to build more business so I can make some desperately needed updates."

"Then perhaps," he said carefully, "we *need* to take a break."

Her eyes shot wide. "How can you say that? We barely have a week to prepare as it is! We can't make great food if we don't have time to practice what we're making."

He stepped closer and wrapped his fingers gently around the rolling pin clenched in her hand. "We also don't make great food while clenching the utensils like weapons," he said, voice low. "Or rolling dough like it insulted Granny D."

She scowled, pulling her hand free and pointing the rolling pin at his chest. "Some of us don't operate on island time, Finn. Some of us respect deadlines."

"Daphne . . ." he murmured, even softer now. "Put down the rolling pin."

She hesitated. Frowned deeper.

"We don't have time for—"

Her words came to a grinding halt as he reached around her and, with one hand, took the rolling pin while the other untied the apron with a little tug.

The soft slide of the fabric untying seemed to suck the air straight out of the kitchen.

Heaven help him, she was so deliciously close, her breath brushing his jaw.

"We have time." He stepped back before he forgot every good intention he had.

"I'm not leaving." But her whispered response held very little conviction.

"You are." He grinned. "Because you need to. And because"—he leaned closer, lowering his voice—"I'm bribing you."

She narrowed her eyes, wary. "Bribing me with what?"

"With a drive." Finn jerked his chin toward the back door. "A much overdue ride in the Cabriolet."

Her breath actually caught. That lovely mouth dropping open.

"The . . . the Cabriolet?"

"I owe you."

She swallowed and gave her head a little shake. "That's totally unfair."

"Maybe," he said, chuckling. "But it's a very good idea for a very good reason."

She glared at him for a full three seconds.

"Come on, Daphne." He reached for her hand and gently rubbed her fingers. "Sometimes you have to breathe a little before you bake a lot."

Her eyes shuttered and she gave her head a slight shake. But the small tilt of her lips betrayed her. "Did you get that from a fortune cookie?"

"A Southern cooking magazine." He winked.

And she—thank heavens—laughed.

"Of course," she muttered, finally waving toward the door. "Fine. One drive. A short one."

"Of course," he echoed, and pulled his keys from his pocket. "But once you start driving *Ladybird*, you may change your mind."

She caught sight of the keys and froze. "Wait . . . you named your car *Ladybird*? Isn't that like a ladybug in England?"

"And," he said, handing her the keys, "a term of endearment. Like darling. Or sweetheart."

"Oh." Her gaze tangled with his—softer now, sweeter.

He pressed the keys into her palm.

Her fingers curled around his—and didn't let go.

The kitchen, the food, the clock—they all faded.

It was just him, her, and the simple, stunning truth of her hand in his.

Almost as if she were answering a question he hadn't even dared to ask yet.

"Okay," she whispered.

....

Finn Dashwood cooked like he was auditioning for a Food Network disaster special.

And somehow he still looked infuriatingly good doing it—leaning against her counter with a dusting of flour on his T-shirt, a few wild hairs sticking up like he'd wrestled a mixer, and still managing to look like he belonged on the cover of a lifestyle magazine.

He was everything she wasn't.

And yet, Daphne was starting to wonder if maybe—*maybe*—he was exactly what she'd been looking for all along.

Cooking with him had been like a dream . . . at first. They'd worked together easily, trading advice here, swapping stories there.

And then she'd overcooked the popovers. Right in front of him.

And her brain had spiraled into a full-on anxiety tornado of all the other ways she could fail this once-in-a-lifetime opportunity.

Naturally, her entire body had joined the revolt.

To such a degree that Finn—not exactly the poster child for subtlety—had noticed.

Which had only humiliated her further . . . until she realized he wasn't laughing at her.

He wasn't patronizing her.

He was *worried* about her. Showing he cared.

Not so much for the wedding.

For *her*.

And then he'd offered his car.

It was unfair. Dirty pool, really. And yet—brilliant.

Because somehow he'd shifted her spiraling panic into something else.

From failing everyone to relaxing.

To freedom.

Then he'd called the car *Ladybird*, like it was the most natural thing in the world.

The man was such an exasperatingly attractive cocktail of unexpected things—sharp wit, soft heart, and maddeningly good hair—that it should be illegal.

Or at the very least, off the menu.

But no. Now, here she was—speeding up the Blue Ridge Parkway with the top down, her dream car wrapped around her and a dashing Englishman in the passenger seat.

A man who'd once annoyed her right down to her carefully organized socks.

But now . . .

Now?

The open air blew his spice-and-vanilla scent toward her.

And somewhere between mile markers, she realized with a start—*he mattered.*

More than competing neighbors. More than friends.

"The brown signs point to the parkway." Daphne gestured forward as they turned up the entrance to the parkway, casting Finn a grin. "You'll want to know, because one visit will ruin you for life."

His chuckle enveloped her like a favorite sweater as another easy silence settled between them. The kind of silence that only came when you didn't have to force anything.

When it felt . . . safe.

Daphne's brain flinched at the awareness. How had that happened?

"So . . ." His gaze stayed forward, but his lips crooked in profile, readying her for a flirty comment, no doubt. "This infatuation with my car—should I be concerned?"

Her shoulders squeezed at the memory. "I really was fawning all over it that first day, wasn't I?"

"I've not seen a woman look at anything like that outside of a shoe store."

Her laugh burst out. "Oh, I've been that woman too. But this"—she smoothed her hand over the dashboard almost reverently—"this is a much more thoughtful obsession than Steve Madden, Vince, or Paul Green could ever inspire."

Finn's eyes narrowed. "Are those rugby players? Because they cannot possibly be shoes."

Another laugh slipped from her.

He kept doing that—catching her off guard, surprising her into laughter when she least expected it.

"And . . ." His rich voice curled like red-velvet icing. "I hope you don't think that answer satisfies my curiosity."

She flicked a glance at him, noticing the wind tossing his hair into a riot. Oh, she was in so much trouble. "Granny came to the States for school, met my grandpa, and stayed. She used to tell me stories about her childhood—open fields, picnics, afternoon teas, and the tiniest, most perfect cars buzzing along country lanes."

"Thus your love for Britain?"

"Granny was amazing, so everything she loved, I ended up falling in love with too." The admission pricked with bittersweet memories. So many. Crowding in as they often did in unexpected ways. "Her favorite car was a 1965 blue Cabriolet," she said. "Grandpa bought it for her when they were newly married. They couldn't afford fancy trips, so they'd fill up the tank and drive until they ran out of daylight—camp under the stars, dream together, plan their family together. All in that little blue car."

She sighed, the familiar road and the company somehow unwinding all her tense muscles.

How had he known she'd needed this?

"And your mother was one of those dreams?" he asked gently.

Mom. The familiar ache twisted tighter. "Grandpa died in a car accident when Mom was just a few years old." She tried for a light shrug, but the grief still clung to her like a shadow. "I'm sure they would've had more kids if they'd had more time. Granny loved children."

The road curved sharply, and ahead a tunnel yawned open from the mountainside.

"Oh, tunnel ahead." Gratefully seizing the excuse to shift gears, she glanced over at Finn, mischief sparking. "My mom always warned me about tunnels. I like to be prepared."

His deadpan response came without missing a beat. "Shocking revelation, Miss Austen."

She snorted, and the tension in her chest cracked open a little more.

"Is sarcasm a permanent character trait for you?" she asked as the tunnel swallowed them in darkness.

Beside her, his voice dropped, low and wicked in the dark. "Some people inspire it more than others."

Oh wow.

That voice . . . in the dark.

Her pulse floundered. "I'm flattered," she said, aiming for breezy but hearing the breathlessness underneath.

"You should be."

The tunnel spat them out into blinding sunlight, but the moment between them clung to the air.

She tossed the hair off her face and glanced briefly over at Finn. "I think one of my more prominent character traits is that I love giving other people surprises."

She threw him a wink and caught the flash of something dangerous in his eyes before she turned her attention back to the road.

Whew.

"Good surprises? If not, that seems highly unfair of you." His voice was rougher than before.

"I see it as generosity," she tossed back. "Giving rather than receiving."

He chuckled. "Ah, so not only are you magnanimous with the pressure of your foot on the gas pedal, but also with your surprises?"

She started to laugh—then caught the sly jab—and instinctively eased off the accelerator. "Sorry." She shot him an unrepentant grin. "I forget the first time on this road can feel a little . . . death-defying."

"I've only seen my life flash before my eyes twice in the last half hour." He gestured to the stunning vista unfurling around them. "But if I had to go, this view"—his eyes caught hers, lingered, softened—"would certainly make for a memorable send-off."

Volcanic heat infused her middle and into her face to the teary-eyed spot. Heaven and earth! She tried to redirect the reaction to something she could handle while driving. "I can do better than just a drive-by view." She nodded ahead. "There's an overlook with a short hike for an even better view."

She veered into a small, paved turnout and flung open her door. "Come on," she called over the roof of the car, willing her pulse to behave. "You're going to love it."

Or at least she hoped he would.

Finn rounded the hood to meet her, and without thinking she grabbed his hand and tugged him toward the trailhead.

He didn't just let her; he laced his fingers through hers like he'd been waiting for the invitation. And her heart settled into the touch, even as it lit a thousand nerve endings through her she didn't even know she had.

They crested the overlook together, the view exploding open before them—layers upon layers of blue mountains rolling toward the horizon, the trees already whispering hints of gold and crimson at their edges.

The sky stretched endlessly overhead, clear and impossibly blue, and her smile stretched with it. This was home. She breathed it in.

Finn stopped beside her, his hand still linked in hers.

Silent.

Awed.

"It's . . . magnificent." His whisper surfaced with reverence, his attention fully fastened ahead.

Then—without looking her way—he shifted his grip, threading his fingers tighter through hers, grounding her like an anchor against the breathtaking view.

Her heart stumbled. His hand felt so steady. So certain.

And the realization of him knowing her, caring for her enough to come here with her . . . well, it pierced deep and then branched out through her chest.

They stood there, suspended in a moment too perfect to rush.

Then Finn squeezed her hand. "And what about this footpath you promised?"

With a grin, she tugged him toward the worn trail leading into the trees. The birdsong and gentle rush of the breeze from up the valley brought all sorts of wonderful autumn scents—goldenrod's honeyed sweetness, pine's sharp snap, the distant smoke of someone's woodstove curling into the sky.

Home. Comfort. Her gaze trailed to Finn. And him?

"Jack told me a little about your mum and granny," Finn said quietly, matching her slower pace. "I'm sorry, Daphne."

The tenderness in his voice nearly undid her. Unwrapping wounds that were still finding a way to move from fresh to scarred. Some days, it seemed they didn't hurt as much, but then, out of the blue, they'd nearly debilitate her with the gaping holes of those missing lives.

"They were the best women," Daphne said, slowing her pace even more and sending Finn a small smile. "Granny would have really liked you."

"Oh?" His smile tugged at one side of his mouth. "She had a thing for tall, dark, and devastatingly handsome?"

"She did." Daphne chuckled, grateful for the levity. "But even more for quick wit and a good heart."

At that, Finn stopped walking. Gently, he tugged on their joined hands until she turned to face him.

"A good heart, huh?" His gaze searched hers, something more serious flickering behind the teasing. "Is that a windup, or do you mean it?"

She shrugged and started walking again. "I'll let you figure it out."

They kept to the path in silence until the trees gave way to reveal an even more panoramic display than before—the layers of mountains now almost a painting of blues and golds.

Finn inhaled sharply, expression rapt—and she liked him even more for it.

"This," he said, voice rough with wonder. "This feels like home."

She tucked a hair behind her ear, easing close enough to him for their arms to touch. "Granny always said it looked a little like England."

"Not England." Finn shook his head slowly, his gaze still on the horizon. "This moment. This view. And . . . you." His gaze swung to her, crooked grin intact, like he hadn't just left her swooning from the kneecaps upward. "All we're missing is Lucy to make it perfect."

And that—*that*—was what finally unraveled her last threads of resistance. Adding Lucy only solidified the fact that he wasn't trying to "chat her up" as Granny would say. This was authentically Finn. The flirt, the dad, and the tenderhearted romantic all rolled up into one.

Something in Daphne's heart roused as if from a long slumber, slowly walking into the light. And the thread of fear that had been coiling inside her for so long began to unwind with each recognition of who Finn really was. One smile, one act of care, one teasing remark at a time.

"I . . ." The words tumbled out before she could second-guess them. "I know you care about me."

He turned fully toward her, brow creased, as if bracing for the other shoe to drop.

She squeezed his hand, reassuring him. "And . . . I don't know how to do this." She cleared her throat. "I've been scared of a relationship for so long that . . . if I seem cautious, it's because I am."

She swallowed through her tightening throat, attempting to find the words. "My dad left when I was little. Then a boyfriend ghosted me after high school. And then . . . Mom. Granny."

Finn caught her other hand, cradling both of hers in his and pulling them to his chest. "There's no rush, Daphne. If you need time, take it." His grin flashed, boyish and sweet and completely sincere. "I'm not going anywhere."

Her heart squeezed so tight it hurt.

She pushed up a wobbly smile, and then with a shivering breath, she stepped into him.

And Finn gathered her close without hesitation, folding her into his chest like she belonged there. He smelled like soap and spice and autumn air, filling her lungs, her heart. And the waiting tears slipped onto her cheeks, warming her face, blending in with the heat from Finn's body.

But they weren't painful. They were soft. Healing.

She burrowed deeper, pressing her face into his shoulder, letting the warmth and strength of him fill all the hollow spaces she hadn't realized were there.

The wind sighed around them, and Finn drew her closer into his embrace, his chin resting lightly on her hair.

And somewhere, in the deepest, quietest part of her, the fear finally began to evaporate and give way to something much more promising.

Hope.

CHAPTER 19

@TeaThymeNC: Popovers: 0. Panic: 1.
Fortunately, the charming chaos in my kitchen had a name . . . and a ridiculously good head of hair. Still not convinced he should be allowed near a mixer, though. But his car is nice! Makes me think of blueberries. Anyone interested in a lemon-blueberry tart to help stave off the gloominess of all this rain? #TeamTea #DisasterChef #MoodBaking #RainyDayTreats

> **@TGDPub:** You say chaos, I say culinary creativity. And I have a great many ideas of how to stave off gloominess. #JustAsk #TeamPub #CinnamonSpiceAndSideEye #ChefInTheRain
>
> **@GrannyDOfficial:** Culinary creativity? What's really cookin' in that kitchen? #SugarAndSpice
>
> **@WisteriaPublicLibrary:** I second the lemon-blueberry tart! And third the flirting. Books go well with tarts and staying in. #ReadAGoodBook #RainyDaysRMade4Reading
>
> **@PastorNateNHC:** As it is written in Second

Barista-lonians: "Let the rain fall and the pastries rise." #HeBrewsAndBakes #PastryProverbs

@OldManRutherforton: I once proposed over a lemon tart. Still married. Coincidence? I think not. #WhenLifeGivesYouLemons #OldManAdvice

@WisteriaGeneralStore: New umbrella design incoming with the phrase "Let it rain. There's tart to share." Or "Wisteria Forecast: 100% chance of love and baked goods." #PastriesAndPrecipitation #UmbrellaOfLove #SoggyButSweet

@LindsayMonroeOfficial: Can the tarts get the rain to stop before the weekend? No bride needs poodle hair. #SomeCurlsAreGood #TheseAreNotThose

@WisteriaBookClub: This rain is clearly symbolic. Cleansing. Foreshadowing. Someone better kiss in it.

@TeaThymeNC: @WisteriaBookClub If you're trying to manifest something, could you also include "clear skies by Saturday"? I know @LindsayMonroeOfficial would appreciate it.

A KNOCK AT THE door pulled Finn from the last sips of his coffee before bed. He glanced at the clock. Midnight? On a Sunday night? Who on earth?

He'd just gotten home from closing the restaurant—another good day, made even better by a surprise visit from Daphne. She'd walked in wearing a little red dress and her hair down around her shoulders, looking better than anything he'd ever plated. His fingers had itched to touch those golden strands. Did they smell like cinnamon too? Or distraction, because for the entire time she remained in the pub, he certainly couldn't think straight.

When they'd first met, he'd have called her pretty. Smart. Sweet. The kind of woman who made lists and smiled at children and never forgot birthdays.

Not the kind of woman who made a man think about pinning her against a wall.

And yet, the more he'd gotten to know her, the more the wall-pinning sounded like the best idea of his life . . . all while murmuring his thoughts about her beauty against her neck.

Heat skimmed to his hairline and his pulse took an uptick. He lowered his cup and glanced toward the door, his grin tipping. But she fit the cuddle-on-the-sofa image too. Bantering in the kitchen. Going for long walks with Lucy betwixt them.

His grin stretched. Or doing just about anything else, as long as she was near.

Daphne fit into their life. Into his life.

She'd snuck past every defense without even trying. Not only her kindness and sass—though, heaven help him, he loved that sass—but the way she looked at Lucy alone had him falling all the way.

Irretrievably.

They'd spent the weekend either texting or calling each other about food options while they created their own "assigned" items separately in order to bring them together on Monday afternoon for a taste testing and pairing.

And in between batter discussions and spice pairings, they'd somehow become . . . more.

He missed her. Actually *missed* her. And how had she worked her way into his expectations so quickly? He couldn't wait for the next conversation, the next shared look, the next time he pulled that glowing smile from her.

He was completely barmy—and it was the best he'd felt in years.

Another knock—this one louder—jolted him from his thoughts.

Rain lashed the window in steady waves, increasing with each passing hour since early evening. So whoever was out there at midnight in a thunder-soaked storm either really needed him . . . or had terrible timing.

He moved to the door, peered through the peephole—and blinked.

Plaits? Golden ones?

He unbolted the lock and pulled open the door to find Daphne standing on his porch, hair in two braids, holding a covered dish and wearing pajamas dotted with . . . Were those Highland cows?

The woman looked decidedly huggable.

Perhaps he was living a fever dream from some soft-focus rom-com—and he didn't know whether to laugh, kiss her, or drag her inside. Perhaps all three?

She smiled so brightly, his grin answered on instinct.

"I saw your light through the window and figured you were still up." She winced. "I mean, I wasn't *watching* you through the window like a weirdo. I just . . . noticed."

His laugh burst free. He *almost* tugged her into his arms on the spot. She could do with a good kiss. From him. For a very long time.

"I was going to say I hoped you liked what you saw." He tsked. "But then you went and ruined the moment."

She rolled her eyes, but the corners of her mouth twitched. "You're impossible."

"And you're wasting perfectly good flirtation standing in the rain." He stepped back and glanced toward the downpour. "Come in."

She shook her head, pushing the dish into his hands. "I don't want to wake Lucy. I'm dry under the porch, and I just finished making these. I couldn't wait for you to try one."

Warmth unfurled through his chest. She'd made something and brought it *here*—to *him*. At midnight. In cow pajamas.

The kiss-her-senseless fantasy returned with even more clarity.

After the car ride and the hug, their relationship had shifted into more intimate territory, but this? This was a special kind of trust. She wanted his opinion. Trusted her idea with his care.

He took the dish and lifted the lid.

Mini cheesecakes.

"If you don't mind?" She whipped out a fork like a magician pulling a rabbit from a hat. "I want to get your reaction."

"No pressure." He raised a brow. "And these look like finger foods, right?"

She lowered the fork, nodded—eyes still locked on his.

"You're not going to tell me what's in them?"

"That would ruin the surprise." She shrugged innocently, like she wasn't trying to inadvertently seduce him with dessert at midnight in the rain wearing hairy-cow pajamas.

Certainly not a combination he'd considered sexy before tonight. But here she was.

He narrowed his eyes, selected a cheesecake, and—never breaking eye contact—raised it to his lips. The scent of pumpkin reached his nose just before the taste hit his tongue. The velvety blend of pumpkin, cream cheese, sugar, and spices hit with a toasty crunch of the crust. Was that . . . molasses?

He paused mid-chew. "Is that a gingersnap crust?"

Her teeth skimmed over her bottom lip with her smile in answer.

"It's excellent, Daphne." He took another bite, the flavors deepening. "The blend, the texture. Are you thinking for the wedding day meal?"

"If we go with your beef tenderloin and the herb-crusted chicken, I thought these might be the perfect finish." Her gaze searched his. "But I'm not sure. The whipped cream on top feels like it's missing something."

That small question—that invitation—meant more than she probably realized.

He polished off the last bite and allowed the flavors another rumination before looking back at her. "Do you trust me?"

Her smile faltered a little. "Yes?"

"That sounded like a question."

"No." A breath. Then a firmer nod. "Yes. I trust you."

Her answer knocked the grin right back into place. "How about a burnt sugar caramel drizzle? Served warm. Just enough bite to contrast the sweetness."

She studied him, and he could practically see her analyzing flavor balance in real time.

"Slow-cook the sugar until it flirts with bitterness," he continued, watching her closely, "so it deepens the whole flavor profile. Think dark honey, a touch of toffee—cuts through the richness like a well-timed wink."

He winked to demonstrate.

Her smile bloomed—full, amused, and just this side of playful. She folded her arms. "Are we still talking about the cheesecake," she asked, "or . . . something else?"

Oh, she was flirting back. And his wall-pinning thoughts rushed to the front of his mind. He stepped closer. "*I* was talking about dessert, Miss Austen. What exactly were *you* talking about?"

Color rose in her cheeks. She gestured vaguely toward the container. "The dessert. Obviously." Her gaze lingered on his mouth. "Of course."

"You know," he murmured, gaze dropping to her mouth for half a heartbeat, then he gestured inside. Just a few more minutes with her. Or an hour? Or . . . maybe forever? "It's raining. You're here. *And* you brought cheesecake."

"Ooh . . ." The word shivered out of her and her attention gave his lips a once-over before she glanced behind her as if someone might be watching. "It's late. I'd better get back to my apartment."

"Probably smart." He nodded, drawing in a calming breath. "Or I'm going to kiss you right here on the porch and scandalize the neighborhood."

Her bottom lip dropped and a tiny squeak emerged. He almost carried through on his threat. She took a step back, despite the way her attention kept shifting to his lips.

The woman was going to drive him mad.

"Are you still fine with watching Lucy tomorrow after school? I know the timing is all wrong, but I need to meet with the food inspect—"

"You know I never mind spending time with Lucy." Her grin spread. "She can help me taste test a few items for the bridal breakfast."

"Thank you." He shifted a step closer, almost close enough to slip his palm right around the waist of those ridiculous pajama bottoms.

She half turned, hesitating like part of her didn't want to go. "Of course." Her voice went breathless again. "I'd better . . . you know." She pointed toward her apartment. "Go."

Finn watched her dash back into the rain, take the steps up to her apartment, and with a lingering look at him from across the distance—and a smile—she closed her door.

....

Having the apartment above the pub made single-dad life workable. Finn usually met Lucy when she got off the bus—unless she detoured to Daphne's first, which was happening more often lately. She'd hang out at the pub for an hour until Daphne arrived, stay with her through the early evening, and then Finn took over again—long enough for stories and silly dances and tucking her in. Then, with a monitor at his side and regular upstairs checks, he returned to pub life.

It had worked well.

But adding Daphne into the mix?

It worked *better*. For him and for Lucy.

Maybe especially for him.

He jogged up Daphne's porch steps two at a time, a container balanced in one hand. It was his turn to share a culinary creation, and this one might just tempt her out of her comfort zone—and maybe, if he played it right, just a little farther into his arms.

Lucy had been with Daphne for four hours. One more than planned, thanks to a waiter calling out. But Daphne had texted that Lucy was no trouble and could stay as long as needed.

He'd believed her. Exhaled. Trusted.

Sheltering under the eaves from yet another downpour, he knocked on the door. The latest bout of rain was, according to pub gossip, thanks to a tropical storm stirring somewhere south. Apparently western North Carolina had a habit of soaking up extra weather in advance, but other than finding shelter and watching for flooding basements, no one appeared concerned. Which was good for Finn to hear, since he was very little accustomed to such weather. And since, as the natives said, the winds would turn to the west and all should pass before the wedding next week, Finn didn't give it too much thought.

Except to wear a mackintosh while outside.

No one responded to his first knock, so he repeated the action.

Silence. Well, not complete silence. He could hear muffled music coming from behind the door.

He pushed it open.

Then came the scent.

Baked sugar. Chocolate. Cinnamon.

Daphne's unofficial love language.

He stepped inside, finding the living room empty. "Daphne?"

A giggle floated down the hall.

He grinned, set the container on the counter, and moved toward the sound. "Daphne?"

"No, no!" came a muffled call from behind a door at the end of the hall. "You have to wait out there. Lucy has a surprise for you."

A rush of warmth poured over him. He rolled his eyes at the ceiling but couldn't stop the smile tugging at his lips. "Girls," he muttered with no heat.

Is this what his little girl had been missing all these years? Another woman's presence like this? And Daphne embraced Lucy as if she'd always cared about her.

He edged nearer the door, Lucy's little voice giving some animated directions about a color and maybe—glitter? With a sigh, he tucked his hands in his pockets and let the moment settle over him until the music from behind the door began to bleed into recognition.

"Classical again?" he called. "Are you trying to corrupt my daughter?"

"*Enhance her life*, I believe, is the phrase you're looking for," Daphne replied through the door. "Classical music is good for brain development, remember? I'm actually *helping* your beautiful daughter."

Beautiful daughter.

He grinned. And no doubt, Daphne was helping her feel even more beautiful.

"It's *Sleeping Beauty*, Daddy," came Lucy's voice. "Like de movie."

Finn stopped and listened with more intention. Tchaikovsky.

He let the music fill the silence and examined the photos on the wall nearby. A little girl, who looked like a younger version of his favorite tea princess, stood between two women who resembled each other—one much older than the other. Daphne's grandmother and mother, perhaps?

She looked to be about seven or eight, maybe. And she'd grown into a woman who wasn't just charming and pretty. She was something *rare.*

Generous. Funny. Effortlessly kind.

And he wasn't about to be careless with her again.

A soft nudge at his hand pulled his attention down to Winston, the Lab seeking affection.

"You understand, don't you, mate?"

Winston sat, leaned into Finn's hand, and exhaled like he agreed.

Daphne was no longer a crush or a rival or a neighbor with wicked scone skills. She was the woman who held his heart. And he hoped he could prove worthy of hers.

"Are you ready?" Daphne's singsongy voice pulled him from the room and back into the hallway.

The door creaked opened and Daphne emerged first, face beaming like she'd just personally orchestrated Christmas morning.

And then—Lucy.

His little girl stepped into the light with a grin so wide it nearly swallowed her cheeks. Her hair had been swept back into a stunning series of braids that twisted elegantly to one side, forming what looked unmistakably like a rose. A shimmering pink ribbon had been threaded through like a fairy-tale flourish.

Finn dropped to his knees, utterly undone. "You look beautiful, lamb."

Lucy responded with a triumphant spin, arms flared. "It's like Rapunzel!"

"Yes, it is." He chuckled and pulled her into a careful hug, avoiding the braid. "Very much like Rapunzel."

With another giggle, Lucy danced down the hallway to the music, Winston in joyful pursuit.

He raised his gaze to Daphne, who stood quite proud with her arms crossed. "She likes Tchaikovsky."

"She likes *you*." He cleared his throat and tried for a casual smile as he stood. "And anything you like is basically gospel at this point."

Daphne shrugged, clearly pleased. "Well, I only like excellent things. So she's in good hands. Also—her hair is perfect for braids. Thick, coarse, holds like a dream. My fingers were tingling with excitement."

"She's certainly going to be spoiled to it now. Your results are much better than my attempt at plaits."

"Oh well, it's not so hard." Daphne reached for her ponytail. "It's a French braid with a little twist for the rose." She tugged her band loose and her hair tumbled down like a thick blanket of gold around her shoulders, framing her face and capturing his senses with the tantalizing combination of cinnamon and vanilla wafting in his direction.

Finn forgot how to swallow.

Her fingers moved through it casually, like she had no idea what kind of personal crisis she was inciting.

"I'll show you," she said. She separated a section and began to braid slowly, narrating like she was on a cooking show. "You just add a small piece to each section as you go—like this . . ."

Finn stared at her hands. At her hair. At the curve of her smile. At everything.

Her expectant gaze found his as she unthreaded the braid. "Now you try."

"What?" His voice cracked. He sounded thirteen. *Brilliant!*

"Since you figured out regular braids, you should be able to learn this one really quickly." She gave her hair a playful toss, then waved it at him like a golden challenge. "Go ahead. I can teach you."

Dream. Come. True.

"Here, let's go to the couch. It'll be easier for you to reach." She caught his hand, and like the complete goner he was, he followed without hesitation.

She sat down wonderfully close, and he tried not to visibly combust. Lucy sat cross-legged on the floor across the room, putting ribbons in Winston's fur, humming to herself like a tiny stylist in training.

"Clearly, it's a braiding party, Mr. Dashwood." Daphne smiled over at him. "You're honor-bound to participate."

"No argument from me, Miss Austen." His voice came out lower than he expected. Rougher.

And her gaze caught in his, softening. Heating? Practically begging for a kiss.

Which he would have done if Lucy weren't directly within his frame of vision.

Because a first kiss—technically second, but first with actual meaning—needed privacy. Reverence. Maybe a moonlit sky and a decent cologne. But definitely privacy.

Not a backdrop of dog-hair barrettes.

He sank his fingers into her hair. Silky. Soft. He attempted to usher up a teasing comment, but the intimacy of the act closed off any verbal response. He wasn't even sure he could remember how his fingers worked.

"Take small pieces," she murmured, shifting slightly so their shoulders brushed. Her hand found his, guiding. Their eyes locked—again. And stayed.

She wasn't just pretty.

She was *breathtaking.*

"A . . . um . . . French braid means . . . little pieces," she rasped.

He forced his hands into motion, enfolding one strand with another. Out of his depth? Understatement of the century. This was the intimacy Olympics, and he had shown up with two left hands and no emotional armor.

Say something clever, mate. Anything.

He managed a few lopsided loops. "I . . . suppose you've earned another drive in my car."

Her lips tipped slightly from her profile, the line from her chin following beautifully to her perfect ears.

Heat shot up his neck. *Perfect ears?*

"Careful, Dashwood. That's starting to sound like a reward system."

He was about to retort when his clumsy fingers tugged too hard. "Ouch."

"Sorry," he murmured with a grin.

He finished the lopsided braid with a few extra prompts from Daphne, and when she finally pulled back, his fingers flexed, still holding the ghost of her softness.

"Thanks again for watching Lucy," he said, throat scraped raw.

"You know I never mind." Her gaze slid back to Lucy, who had now adorned Winston's tail with a scrunchie. "We've had very important conversations. Princess rankings. Proper tea ceremony etiquette. Heroic dogs."

"Clearly essential topics." A strand he'd missed slipped down over her cheek. Without thinking, he reached up and tucked it behind her ear. "And an excuse to see you, you know."

One of her gold brows curved northward. "So the whole wedding challenge was just an elaborate excuse to spend more time with me?"

"Go big or go home."

Her laugh came soft. "Or criticize my tidy kitchen and mock my beverage selection?"

At the moment, he was heroically trying to determine if her eyes were periwinkle or gray-blue and failing spectacularly.

"I've since repented," he said solemnly.

"Oh no." Her brows lifted. "You're going soft on me."

"Terrifying, isn't it?"

At this range, with her braid still warm between his fingers, she was much too close not to kiss. And if Lucy wasn't directly in his peripheral vision, he absolutely would have.

This amount of willpower ought to win him an award. Maybe ten.

"Actually, my thoughts were much more amicably directed." He stood, because if he didn't find some privacy right now, he *would* kiss her, right here, in front of his kid and a beribboned dog. "I actually came bearing gifts." He offered her his hand. "In the kitchen?"

Her fingers slid into his. "Lead the way."

....

Daphne had never related more to tea in her life.

Or maybe—to the kettle.

Because this attraction to Finn? It had simmered for weeks, but now that she'd finally accepted her feelings—and trusted his—it was a rolling boil. And she was absolutely about to bubble over. And kiss him.

She looked down at the hand he offered. With a smile, she slid her fingers into his. If touches were preludes to the next act of her story, then the way his warm fingers curved around hers promised a heart-thudding performance.

"We'll be in the kitchen, lamb," Finn called over his shoulder to Lucy, not breaking eye contact with Daphne as they rounded the corner into the smaller room. He scooped up a little container as they crossed the threshold and, without asking, went straight to the drawer where she kept her silverware.

Releasing her hand—unfortunately—he plucked out a spoon and offered it, along with the container.

"Your turn to try a new creation of mine."

Okay, she *had* hoped that gleam in his eyes meant he wanted to kiss her again.

She lifted the lid.

Ooh—chocolate. Mousse, by the looks of it.

Not kiss-you-again-until-your-toes-curl good.

But still—solid.

"What is it?" she asked.

He tilted his head and gave her a look that read, *Turnabout is fair play.*

"Fine, I'll figure it out myself," she said, wrestling down her grin as she sniffed the contents. Hazelnut and . . . was that coffee? She almost narrowed her eyes at him but instead dipped the spoon in and brought it to her lips—her attention fixed squarely on Finn.

And his shift in expression.

Predatory.

Which she *would* have appreciated more if the mousse hadn't just hijacked her undivided attention. Dark chocolate melted over her tongue, silky and rich, with that whisper of coffee deepening the flavor. Her eyes fluttered shut as she chased every last note, the texture, the nuance—heaven on a spoon.

"Oh my goodness," she murmured, licking the last bit off her lips. "I love you."

Her eyes snapped open. Finn had gone still. Staring at her lips like he envied the mousse. Heavens!

"I . . . I mean . . ." She squeaked, her breaths pulsing, his spicy scent melding with the chocolate to make a rather tantalizing combination. "I love that you get inspired by the same things I do and can do something about it. Like this."

His gaze finally rose to meet hers, dark and dangerous. "Is the way to a woman's heart through her stomach? Because I really want your heart, Daphne."

Her name on his lips vibrated straight through her. She reached out for balance and—naturally—latched onto his shirt. "Mousse is a great starter."

"And what would you suggest as—"

He hadn't even finished the sentence before her fingers curled into his shirt and tugged him the final few inches forward.

She'd kissed Finn before. Or rather, he'd kissed her, but nothing prepared her for the instant connection of their lips meeting. Everything was different this time around. It wasn't just chemistry and sparks. It was so much more. Intentional. Full.

Sure, the chemistry was still there. And the way his palm smoothed up across her cheek to delve into her hair had sparks flying inside her chest, but she knew him better now. Saw him. The flirt, yes—but also the soft heart behind the teasing. The man who showed up, who protected, who loved quietly and fiercely. A man who didn't just flirt—he stayed.

Her palms slid up to crest his shoulders, linking at the base of his neck, her fingers threading into his glorious hair. A rumble rose from his chest, reverberating into hers. Her entire body weakened as his mouth took more control and she shifted back against the wall; his body followed, warm and solid, holding her up, pressing her back.

He cocooned her. His scent and strength surrounding her.

And she'd never felt so safe. Or . . . so on fire.

When he finally pulled back—one arm braced above her head, the other snug around her waist—he looked down at her with a grin so soft, so reverent, she forgot how to inhale.

Safe . . . and loved?

"You know," he rasped, "the mousse has coffee in it."

She pulled her brain from the intoxicating post-kiss mental fog and blinked up at him. "What?"

"Do you feel like a traitor?"

Her hand slid from the back of his neck to press lightly against his chest, her thoughts clearing just enough for her to muster a teasing brow lift. At least she hoped her look conveyed more sass than dazed wonder. But with a kiss like that . . .

"I guess it's not so bad if you add just the right amount of chocolate and sugar."

He leaned forward, his nose skimming over her cheek before he placed a gentle kiss there. "With that kind of answer, I may reward you by drinking some of your strongest tea. Fair?"

"Mm-hmm." Her lips curled as he brushed another kiss to the corner of her mouth. And then—an idea. Almond lace cookies. One stuck into the mousse glass like a fancy garnish. Perfection. "You know what would go *really* well with that mousse?"

He raised his head from placing another kiss to the other side of her smile, gaze locked with hers and the tiniest tip to his grin. "Seconds?"

And he kissed her all over again. Much more than seconds.

So she decided the cookie suggestion could wait.

CHAPTER 20

@TGDpub: [Photo: a swirl of hazelnut coffee mousse in a glass dish, topped with a delicate almond lace cookie. In the background, a smudge of chocolate on Daphne's cheek . . . and Finn definitely looking at her instead of the mousse.] Test kitchen got a little out of hand today. But the mousse? Worth it. #HazelnutHeaven #DefinitelyDidntLickTheSpoon #WorthItInMoreWaysThanOne

> **@JackAustenPhotography:** Oh no! They're posting photos together now. What's next? A puppy? A couples' cooking class? Matching aprons?? #HelpABrotherOut #Gross
>
> **@PastorNateNHC:** Temptation comes in many forms. Apparently, one of them is hazelnut. #LeadUsNot #ButDeliverUsDessert
>
> **@SecondHandTreasures:** @PastorNateNHC I don't think the hazelnut is what's leading Finn into temptation #ChocolateSmudge #DirectEyeContact
>
> **@TeaThymeNC:** Do none of you follow the romance code of minding your own business?!

@JackAustenPhotography: Those codes are more like guidelines really. #SmallTownProblems #BlurredButBelievable
@WisteriaToyBox: Siri, how do I explain "smolder" to my toddler? Asking for a friend. And by "friend," I mean myself.
@OldManRutherforton: My wife and I got together over a dropped piecrust and a broken measuring cup. Don't fight fate. #ThePowerOfChocolate #OldManWisdom
@ClemAtTheGym: My man Finn out here using ganache as a love language. Respect. #WhatRutherfortonSaid
@MayorWilsonOfficial: This town is one cheesecake away from live-streaming a proposal. Pace yourselves, people.
@TGDPub: Did Daphne just type "romance" in reference to a certain dashing Brit? #GrinningLikeAFool #TeamRomance #WhoIsWithMe
@RosemaryatThyme: You know, @TGDpub @TeaThymeNC . . . I really think you two should start a YouTube channel or something. People would devour the content. Sugar and spice, baby.
@TeaThymeNC: @TGDPub Did I mention romance? I thought we were discussing chocolate. #DrawYourOwnConclusions #IHaveAJobToDo
@WisteriaGeneralStore: New apron drop: "Sugar. Spice. And One Very Distracted Brit." Design includes a teacup and coffee mug in close proximity followed by a trail of chocolate kisses. #Unashamed #Here4TheTension
@WisteriaBookClub: We're officially taking bets.

A) Kiss happens before the wedding
B) OR during the next dessert test

#ResearchInTheNameOfRomance

@SecondHandTreasures: I'll bring the mistletoe. Doesn't matter that it's September. #TrueLoveHasNoDeadline #TheChocolateSpeaks

THE KITCHEN TABLE LOOKED like a battlefield of mismatched plates—torn bread crusts, half-full soup bowls, slivers of pie, and the aftermath of three different entrées—all in various stages of taste testing.

But menu planning had never been this fun.

At least not for Daphne.

Now that she wasn't trying to dissect Finn's every intention or shield her heart from possible catastrophe, their banter had only gotten more enjoyable . . . with a few bonus hugs and kisses sprinkled in like cinnamon on top. Warm, sweet, a little addictive.

"Okay, so here's the test." Daphne tore off a piece of honey oat bread and dipped it into Finn's beef bourguignon. The rich sauce hit her tongue like a velvety bomb of flavor.

"Oh . . ." She closed her eyes and chewed. "That's . . . annoyingly good."

"Annoyingly?" Finn smirked. "Then it's definitely mine."

She handed him a piece of the bread. "Try it."

He did as she instructed, his eyes widening as the flavors melded. "All right, that's not bad at all."

"Not bad?" She lifted her half-eaten bread toward him in a toast. "My bread just made your dish exceptional."

"I'll admit," he said, reaching around her for another dip, "it's a game changer." His gaze lingered on her face with that slow-burn look that made her forget all about bourguignon. "But maybe it's my stew making *your* bread exceptional."

His voice dropped just enough to trigger a flutter under her ribs. Mercy! How was she supposed to stay objective when he sounded like her favorite audiobook narrator and looked like a kitchen ad in a European magazine?

"Fine," she conceded with a grin. Either way she won. "We'll call it a tie."

He held her gaze for a second longer, heat lingering like a slow simmer, then stepped back with a mischievous glint. "Now for a test of my smoky tomato bisque as a starter for the wedding meal." Finn waggled his brows and held out a spoonful of his newest creation. "I'm ninety-nine percent sure it'll change your life."

That playfulness. It was starting to grow on her in ways she hadn't anticipated—stretching her humor, inspiring her creativity, gently untangling all her old defenses and offering this sense of sweetness in their relationship.

And the way he looked at her? Like she was still the loveliest woman in the world, even with flour in her eyebrows and a lopsided knot of hair on her head? It was a miracle she wanted to accept as a daily perk.

Oh, so sweet!

Her gaze trailed to his, those creamy brown eyes lit, his lips crooked in adorable challenge, all while a stray lock of hair dripped over his forehead like a tease.

Okay, sweetness with a whole lot of spice wrapped in one frustratingly irresistible package. But didn't the best things in life require a healthy balance?

"That one percent is concerning." She eyed the spoon. "What's the risk?"

"It might ruin all future soups for you. Forever."

She leveled him with a look despite her smile's desperate escape plan, and opened her mouth. He brought the spoon to her lips with slow, deliberate care in a wonderfully intimate move. It made her chest ache in the best way.

The moment the bisque hit her tongue, her body relaxed. It was smooth with layers of depth—perfectly seasoned and utterly decadent.

"Oh, that's good."

"Yeah?" He leaned over and kissed her. "A reward for your *excellent* taste."

Her grin burst free. "Whose reward are we talking about here?"

He looked mildly offended and then leaned in again. "Both. We deserve it."

And he kissed her again, longer this time. Okay, so *maybe* she'd held him in place a little too. But if he was handing out rewards, he needed to commit to the full prize package.

Gracious! Cooking with her boyfriend really was one of the hottest things she'd ever done. Or dreamed of. Or even dared to wish for—and she wasn't even halfway through her streusel bars yet.

They were working out of his kitchen this afternoon, since Margaret was coming by soon to whisk Lucy off to the children's museum. The rain hadn't let up, but Lucy was still all smiles, building a throne for Winston out of soup cans and napkin rings.

Surprisingly, Finn's kitchen was in good order. Not label-perfect like hers, but intuitive. Thoughtful. Clean in the way a space is when someone actually cares about what they're creating.

"You know my cheddar chive scones?" she asked as she sprinkled brown sugar over the apple streusel topping.

He nodded instantly. "That would make a perfect pairing. Do you think you could make a batch this morning for us to try out?"

"Sure." She reached for a clean bowl. "Just let me finish this first."

He scribbled the addition onto their nearly finalized menu. "I've got a few folks lined up to help prep and serve, so we should be covered on numbers."

"Great." She let out a breath she hadn't realized she was holding. She'd forgotten about needing extra hands for something like this.

Her eyes caught Finn sneaking another forkful of her lavender and lemon chess pie—his fourth . . . no, fifth bite?

"What are you doing?"

He froze mid-bite. "Quality control," he said solemnly, licking a bit of cream from his thumb. "It's called professionalism, Daphne."

"It's called sugar rush, Finn." She lunged for the dish, but he caught her and kissed her cheek.

She sighed into him, resting her palms against his arms. "You think we can really do this?"

His brow creased and he searched her face. "I *know* we can."

The certainty of his voice steadied her.

She nodded. "Right. We can."

A gust of wind rattled the windowpane, the kind that made trees sway and made you second-guess your outdoor plans. They both turned toward it.

"Still coming down out there?" She looked over at him. "I heard about a few flash flood warnings south of here overnight. The Ashbourne River and Penner's Creek are rising fast."

Finn raised a brow. "Is that unusual?"

Oh, right. He didn't know Wisteria weather patterns yet. "That creek barely trickles most of the year. But the ground's already soaked. If the wind keeps picking up . . ."

He winced. "Wet ground and high winds. That's . . . not ideal."

"But we've still got three days," she said brightly, injecting as much optimism into her tone as she could. "The storm could pass. Things might clear up by Friday. Maybe soggy—but doable. If the roads don't close."

He nudged her hip with his. "Let's not cast worry for future problems." His arm slipped around her. "Right now, our job is to make this the best wedding menu anyone's ever tasted. The kind of thing that goes viral, makes us famous, and lands us interviews with food bloggers who wear bow ties and know obscure cheeses."

"Famous, huh?"

"All right, maybe not *famous* famous." He dipped his fork back into the chess pie. "But a steady stream of customers wouldn't hurt."

He popped another bite into his mouth just as a wall of rain slammed against the window. His arm tightened around her instinctively.

"So . . ." She tried for casual. "If the roads *do* wash out—what's plan B?"

"We improvise." He leaned back against the counter again, drawing her toward him. "We're smart and capable people. Between the two of us, we could probably cater a wedding from a canoe."

She snorted. "Only if you bring your secret espresso bean stash to keep up your paddling stamina."

"Oh, luv." He gave her a look of mock insult. "You think I don't already have a waterproof tin labeled Caffeine Apocalypse?"

She rolled her eyes and threw a wadded paper towel at him. He caught it with ease—and she leaned in, pressing a quick kiss to his mouth as his reward.

Because honestly?

If this was what weathering a storm looked like with him, she was all in.

....

__@TeaThymeNC:__ [Photo: a cozy sitting nook with a mug and a teacup on the table and Lucy in the background looking at a picture book with Winston napping at her feet. The storm is visible through the window.] Storm's brewing, Wisteria. Time to put the kettle on and settle in with something warm, comforting, and definitely not created with bean water.
Best storm beverage: a proper cup of tea.
Best storm activity: reading, baking, or hypothetically cuddling with someone who understands the importance of a cozy blanket and interesting conversation. What's your cozy comfort? #StormyTeaTime #CuddleUpWisteria #TeaIsLove

@TGDpub: Tea won't keep you warm like a double chili burger and someone who knows how to build a fire. Both kinds. Just saying. #TeamPubSnuggles #ForksOptional #FireStarterFlirting

@SecondHandTreasures: Two cups. One apartment. One shared domestic aesthetic? #Sus #StormWatchButMakeItRomantic #WisteriaShippingSquad #BeveragesInCloseProximity

@JackAustenPhotography: Did no one else notice the reflection in the mirror? Zoom. Enhance. That's a man's elbow in a plaid shirt. Daphne, we know Finn owns exactly one flannel. Plus, we can see both of your faces. Not just the cups are in close proximity. #Gross #CSIWisteria #YourSecretsAreNotSafe #SubtleSisterFail

@PastorNateNHC: "Two are better than one, because they have a good return for their labor." Ecclesiastes 4:9. Also, is that lipstick on his mug? Or his cheek? #NotJudgingJustBlessing #LookAway

@OldManRutherforton: Storms always did bring people together. Back in '78, we had thunder, lightning, and four engagements by sunrise. #BarometricPressureEqualsRomance #HistoryRepeats

@GrannyDOfficial: I've got tea steeping, soup simmering, and binoculars pointed directly at the pub. This better end in a kiss or a pie. #GrannyDSeesEverything

@MrsWinslow: Daphne posted "cuddle" and thinks we won't assume it's about Finn? Girl, please. Besides, if you read what's on his mug through the reflection in the mirror (thanks @JackAustenPhotography), does that say, "Coffee First, Kisses After"? #MugMathChecksOut #WelcomeToTheWatchlist

@LindsayMonroeOfficial: It's giving Hallmark Original meets British Bake Off afterparty. That mug. That lighting. That child. You're toast. And I love it. #HotDadsDrinkTeaToo #DaphneBlushingSomewhere #MatchmakingPerfection

@WisteriaGeneralStore: Just confirming the "Coffee First, Kisses After" mug is ours. Available in store or online. Monogrammed versions coming soon. #BrandingWithFeeling #WisteriaSellsRomanceNow

@SheriffGrady: Official town ruling: Two mugs, one storm, lipstick smudge = probable cause for investigation. Sherlock Holmes could retire. #NotOurFirstRodeo #StormSnuggleSurveillance #EyesOnTheMugs

@MrsWinslow: You can delete the caption all you want, sweetheart. The mugs told us everything. #OfficiallyInItNow #KnewBeforeYouDid

@WisteriaGeneralStore: New stock alert: "Official Wisteria Cuddle Committee" blankets. #YouAskedWeDelivered

"Nice job, Lucy. Those raspberries are perfect."

Daphne smiled down at the little girl beside her, who beamed with sticky pride as she arranged a final swirl of fruit on the mini tarts—raspberries, blueberries, kiwi—bright against the creamy custard. Two days until the wedding and the pressure was on.

Not to mention some high concern about the weather. Overnight it had shifted from dreary to downright ominous.

Lucy's school had been canceled—something about "erring on the side of caution." So Daphne had volunteered to keep the little cherub while Finn met with Harry up at the inn to finalize the groom's breakfast setup. But that shouldn't take too long, hopefully.

And then he'd be back with them. Safely nearby.

According to the news stream on her iPad, tropical storm Danielle had veered wildly off course and was barreling straight toward western North Carolina. Thunder grumbled low in the distance, a quiet warning. The wind had been picking up all day, and customers were already trading stories about downed trees and closed bridges. All the usual ones, sure—but still. Days of rain plus high winds? A recipe for disaster.

With wedding guests arriving in a couple of days, maybe they *should* invest in a canoe.

The lights flickered in the shop, and Daphne flipped her attention to Lucy, who kept happily humming as she decorated the tarts with fruit. At least she wasn't afraid. One less thing to distract Daphne.

A breaking news alert interrupted the quiet lull of the kitchen.

"Folks within the path of Buckwater Dam are advised to find higher ground as our station has just been notified that a lightning strike has hit the dam's control center."

Daphne wiped her hands on her apron and reached for the volume button. The image cut to a field reporter standing beside a grim-faced engineer. "We are with Dr. Jacob Davies, one of the engineers who helped design Buckwater Dam back in the 1970s. Dr. Davies, based on your knowledge of the dam, what is the main concern here that our viewers should be aware of?"

"Well, the dam's control station automatically opens the spillway gates to allow any excess water to release to keep pressure down behind the dam, but if the control station has been damaged, then that's not happening."

"But isn't there a manual control for it if the power goes out?" the reporter followed up.

"And backup generators." Mr. Davies nodded. "But those generators can't handle the pressure coming in for too long." He paused to look down at his phone, his frown deepening. "And I just got word from the manager of the dam that the access road to the dam is flooded. Emergency crews are having to go *around* the mountain—forty-five minutes on a good day."

Daphne's face went cold. She turned to the window, but the rain was coming so fast and heavy, she couldn't see past the glass.

"And why is that a concern?"

He shifted his gaze away, hesitating, and then looked back at the reporter. "I warned the town council a few months back of a hairline crack in one of the critical concrete abutments of the structure. With the amount of water pressure coming in and now a control station failure, I just don't know . . ."

The reporter stared at the man a moment, coming to the same conclusion as Daphne. "Are you saying the dam could break?"

"There's a real possibility," Mr. Davies replied, his voice grim. "Especially with the circumstances being what they are."

Daphne's chest hollowed. *What did that mean?*

As if reading her mind, the reporter leaned in. "And what . . . what would that mean for our local viewers?"

Davies drew in a deep breath. "Buckwater isn't a large dam, and it was well-placed when it was built, but . . . it means anyone along Gulf Hollow or Laurel's Rest needs to get out now. Until the storm passes. Because—God forbid—if the dam breaks, the excess water won't just rush down the mountain. It'll fill existing bodies of water and cause additional flooding. So . . . the higher you are, the better."

Daphne's gaze shifted to the window. The Ashbourne River curled around one side of Wisteria. Penner's Creek bordered the south. With waterways already swollen, how far could a break reach?

And who did she know in its path?

Her fingers flew across her phone, group-texting Jack, Nate, Granny D, Rosemary—anyone she could think of—urging them to pass it on.

"I only ate four more blueberries," Lucy confessed solemnly from the counter.

The words pierced through Daphne's spiraling panic like a warm light.

She turned, managing a smile. "Only four? I'd call that admirable restraint. Blueberries are my favorite too. And we certainly wouldn't want any of them to go to waste." She winked at the little girl, who promptly snagged another one with a delighted grin.

"I'm going to peek at the weather outside for a sec, okay, sugarplum?"

Lucy nodded, now rearranging the last two tarts like a fruit-focused architect.

Daphne slipped her phone into her pocket and cracked open the front door.

Wind whipped water into her face and bent nearby trees low. The row of shops on her side of town backed up to the park, which led into small neighborhoods and pastureland beyond. It wasn't the lowest part of town—but even here large pools of water dotted the park, much bigger than anything she'd seen before.

Her eyes narrowed toward the road leading to the Laurel's Rest neighborhood. A manmade pond bordered the entrance. It had breached its banks, spilling across the road. A passing car sent water splashing high onto its roof.

Oh Lord, protect us.

Main Street sat on a gradual knoll, with the north end higher than the south. Tea Thyme was closer to the lower half. Finn's pub sat even lower still. The water rushing down the street likely fed straight into the river below, raising its already dangerous level.

How high was the Ashbourne now?

The TV's volume spiked behind her, drawing her back inside.

"It seems that Tropical Storm Danielle has stalled over the region," the announcer said, "dropping continued rainfall on already saturated ground. Flooding is imminent. Move to higher ground immediately."

Daphne shut the door with trembling fingers and grabbed her

iPad. "I think we should take these tarts up to my apartment," she said, keeping her voice chipper as she reached for a tray. "Want to help?"

It was just rain. They'd had floods in the area before.

Lucy perked up. "Ooh! Can I see Winston?" She crawled down from the stool and started for the stairway.

"Of course. He's probably napping on his bed, dreaming about you." Daphne swooped the tray of tarts and fruit into her arms. "And maybe we can put on a movie while we wait for your dad to get back from the manor, but I'm going to grab a few things from the shop first."

Lucy nodded and followed Daphne into the shop where Daphne took her two favorite teapots from the special shelf and set them on the tray . . . just in case. "All right, Lucy, let's get upstairs and text your dad."

They'd just turned toward the stairs when the front door burst open, jangling the welcome bell. Wind swept in—and so did Finn, soaked and hauling five sandbags.

He met Daphne's gaze. His was grim.

"You heard?"

She nodded.

He dropped the bags by the door with a heavy *thump* and shook back his hood. "I'm stacking these around your door. There's at least four inches of water rushing down Main Street, and the river's made it to Joe's filling station."

She blinked. That was only five buildings away.

"I'm taking Lucy up to the apartment," she said evenly, hoping calm counted for something. "Higher ground."

"And we're gonna watch a movie!" Lucy added cheerfully. "A princess one. You fink?"

Finn smiled, the edges of the worry on his face softening. He knelt and kissed her forehead. "Perfect."

Thunder rumbled in the distance.

"We'll make it a loud one," Daphne added with a small grin. "With singing. The obnoxious kind."

Finn didn't respond to her humor but instead stepped closer, lowering his voice. "Jack just got back from the inn. Back bridge is out. And two of the main roads into town have partially collapsed."

Daphne's breath stalled. "Which means it's probably not the best idea to try and leave?"

He held her gaze. "Probably not."

Her phone buzzed at her hip. Granny D's name flashed on the screen.

Daphne's stomach dropped. "Granny D?" she answered on speaker. "Please tell me you're not at home right now."

"I'm here," came the clipped reply. Tense. Unusual for her. "Car's nearly been washed away. Chicken coop definitely has."

Which meant the water was already way too close to the house.

And Granny D lived at the very edge of Gulf Hollow. Too close to any trajectory of water from the dam break.

Finn was already yanking up his hood. "I'm on my way, Granny D," he said, searching Daphne's face and backing toward the door he'd just entered. "Get Lucy upstairs. I'll be back as soon as I can."

She grabbed the truck keys from the counter and tossed them to him. "Take mine. It's bigger."

At least bigger than a Cabriolet.

Their eyes locked. His grin crooked—just for a second.

"Be careful," she whispered, her arms tightening around the tray.

He held her gaze for a breath longer. Then with a glance at little Lucy, who had no idea what any of this meant, he turned and bolted into the storm.

CHAPTER 21

@WisteriaGeneralStore: Rain, rain, go away . . . but while it's here, we've stocked up on batteries, lanterns, and granola bars (and a few lemon tarts for morale). Stay safe, neighbors. We're open till 4:00—unless the creek claims our front stoop. #WisteriaStrong #StormSnacks #PrepareWithPastry

> **@PastorNateNHC:** Yea, though I walk through the valley of overflowing gutters, I shall fear no rain . . . for the Lord invented galoshes. We're checking on elderly neighbors—text if you know someone who needs help. #LightInTheFlood #FaithAndRubberBoots #LoveThyNeighbor
>
> **@TGDPub:** Closed early due to flash flood risk. But if the pub floats down Main Street, I expect it to land upright and still serve stew. Stay safe, Wisteria. #ClosedButStillCooking #PubOnTheMove #StewAndSafetyFirst
>
> **@MargaretColeman:** All events at the Wisteria Manor are postponed until further notice. Also, all pony rides are off—our ponies are not fans of thunder. Stay warm.

Stay dry. And check on your people. #HistoryOnHold #PonyStrikesAgain #WisteriaWeatherWatch

@GrannyDOfficial: Storm's loud enough to drown out the Hallmark Channel. I'm not sayin' it's serious . . . but I just made a triple batch of biscuits just in case. #GrannyDPrepares #StormComforts #ButterAndPrayer

@MayorWilsonOfficial: ROAD UPDATE:

Backbridge Road closed
Laurel's Rest Road partially washed away
Avoid driving unless you're rescuing someone—or you're a duck.

We're patrolling through town. Text your neighbors, check on the elderly, and stay high and dry. #SheriffSaysStayPut #NotASwimmingRoad #WisteriaWatch

....

Jack: Did you leave the apartment?

Daphne: No, Lucy and I are still here.

Jack: Okay, stay there for now. The river's rising, and with the current and some floating debris, I don't want you risking getting out in this.

Daphne: What if the dam breaks?

Jack: Just stay where you are. The inn is sheltering folks from lower-lying areas. Worse-case scenario, I'll come and get you to bring you here.

Nate: The church is being used as a shelter too. We have hot food. And Mr. Rutherforton's left the hardware store open for anyone who needs supplies. Spread the word if you can. And pray. It's worse than you think.

Jack: Headed out to help with some rescue efforts.

Finn: Trees are down everywhere. I had to go a back way around Route 122 because it was impassable.

Daphne: Be safe, y'all.

Nate: I'll join you, Jack.

•••••••••••

Thank the good Lord for happily distracted little girls.

Daphne moved through the apartment, stuffing clothes, her laptop, chargers, a flashlight, and a handful of emergency snacks into two tote bags. If she'd had access to Finn's apartment, she would've packed for him and Lucy too. As it was, she'd settled for keeping his daughter safe—and that felt like the weightiest job of all.

Her mind ping-ponged between two options: trying to get to the top of Main Street during a storm with a little girl and a dog or hunkering down where they were. Upstairs in her apartment wasn't ideal, but it was solid, dry, and elevated. For now.

And as evening approached, a better option.

At least they had electricity, height, and phone service.

The lights flickered again, the ceiling fan slowing to a crawl before swirling back to life.

Okay, electricity *for now.*

Daphne's phone, which had been buzzing nonstop for the last hour, lay face up on the counter nearby, awaiting news from anyone, everyone.

She drew in a deep breath. However, there was no need to panic. No major issues had been reported so far, just the awareness that catastrophe *could* happen. Her shoulders slumped. Like a dam breaking. Or another bridge going out. Or a mudslide.

She pressed her eyes closed a moment, collecting herself.

Granny D had checked in five minutes ago, still waiting for Finn, but there was no knowing what the roads were like for him to get there. One bridge nearest her house, in particular, may prove the trouble . . . if it was even still intact at all.

Daphne moved to one of the front windows and stared out across Main Street, water creeping up the street, forming a river over the pavement. There had to be a least a foot or two gathering near the bottom of the street, not to mention what was rushing down from the top of the hill.

Her phone flicked to life.

> **Finn:** River is cresting Granny D's bridge. Just made it over and parked, but her house is already about two-feet deep in water. I'm grabbing her as fast as I can and we're heading back. Don't leave unless you must. It's not safe out here.
>
> **Daphne:** Okay. Be careful.

She stared at the message longer than necessary, her thumb hovering like she wanted to say more. *Come back to us* felt too . . . intimate? But *us* was exactly what it felt like now. Her, Lucy, Finn.

And if anything happened to him . . .

Another person . . . gone?

She forced a breath and sent a quiet prayer heavenward, then flipped through a few news reports on her phone. Widespread flooding, downed trees, power outages, water rescues.

This was like something from a movie.

Her attention traveled the length of the room to land on Lucy, who sat cross-legged on the rug watching *Tangled* with Winston beside her. Lucy's favorite. It had definitely moved up Daphne's favorite's list because . . . well, Flynn Rider. And smolders.

Daphne nodded and braced herself. Finn had trusted Daphne with the most important person in his world. So no matter how hard her heart pounded or how tight her throat felt, she would keep it together. For Lucy. For Finn. For whatever came next.

But surely they'd be all right in an upstairs apartment on Main Street! The water, even if the dam broke, wouldn't reach that far, would it?

A sharp crack of thunder sent Winston to his feet and to her side, and Lucy's eyes grew wide. "That was a big noise."

Daphne reached down to rub a hand over the dog's head and shot Lucy a smile. "I think we may hear a few big noises with all this rain right now."

The answer seemed to suffice for the little girl at the moment and she turned back to the movie. But the two had already talked about how the rain makes very big mud puddles and if the puddles got too big, well, they'd need to find a place farther away from those puddles to wait for Daddy.

Another bolt of lightning sliced through the sky, lighting up the hill behind the east side of Main Street.

And then—something else. Her stomach seized.

Not lightning. A flash of unnatural orange, almost like—

No. She shifted closer to the window, drawn to the sight as if in a trance. *Was that one of the towers on the hill? Had it been struck?*

And then a strange sort of movement sliced through the rain. Otherworldly.

She gripped the window frame, staring out, as the top of the ridge gave way, just like icing melting off a hot cake. Earth, trees, rock—an entire section of hillside collapsed, taking with it trees and mud, crashing down behind the toy store two buildings over, sweeping through the backyard fences and uprooting a power pole.

And she kept staring, her stomach knotting tighter the longer she watched. Like she couldn't process what she was seeing. That one whole side of that massive hill just . . . fell.

Oh Lord, please keep people safe! From her limited view, the collapse didn't appear to have taken buildings, but she couldn't see everything clearly.

Another unnatural flash of light sparked in the distance to her left, almost like the world was setting off some strange domino light effect all around her. The *boom* popped in her ears.

Then the light shut off, the TV screen went black. The fan stilled. Every appliance stopped humming in the sudden hush.

And the late-afternoon light cast a gray hue across the room.

It wasn't temporary this time. The power was gone.

Lucy looked up at Daphne in expectation.

"I think the storm might have caused the power to go out for a while," Daphne said gently, crossing over to her and kneeling down. Her insides trembled. But she stroked Lucy's hair, working up her voice. "No big deal. We can read a book instead, can't we?"

Lucy didn't seem to notice the tremor in Daphne's voice, for the little girl simply nodded.

"I brought my Rapunzel book with me in my backpack."

"What a great idea. Why don't you bring it to the couch and we can pick up where the movie went off."

Lucy stood and dashed over to her bag, Winston at her side like the guard dog he was not, and Daphne stepped back to her phone on the counter to see if she could find out any more news. But there was nothing. No signal. No bars. Just a spinning wheel where the service should be.

"Okay," she whispered. "Okay. That's fine. We're fine."

Her gaze raised back to the window. The street had taken on a strange sort of stillness. No shop lights, no car headlights. Not even people. Just the eerie glow of storm clouds and the distant flicker of fire dancing along the broken edge of the hill.

And at the moment, all Daphne could do was wait . . . and pray.

• • • • • • • • • • •

@WisteriaEmergencyServices: East Side Communication Update: Cell service and internet are currently down across much of the listening area due to damaged tower. For updates and emergency alerts, please tune into 1040 AM–WNCWisteria Radio. We'll be broadcasting hourly with evacuation info, road closures, and shelter updates. Stay safe and stay informed. #WisteriaStrong #EmergencyUpdate

Finn had never seen anything like this in his life.

The river had swollen to three or four times its size. He'd even witnessed a storage building floating down it like a boat. He blinked at the memory. He'd really seen that—and it was only one of the many surreal things he'd passed on his drive from town to Granny D's.

He couldn't even count the number of trees in the road he'd dodged, a few times even driving off the edge to get around them.

A trip that should have taken fifteen minutes had stretched to nearly forty-five. By the time he reached the old bridge crossing to her house, he'd nearly turned back twice, but there was no call for it. Someone had to help the woman! And if he was capable, he'd certainly try.

Besides, Daphne was with Lucy. And he had full confidence in Daphne's heart to care for and protect his little girl. The revelation settled over him with a little surprise blended in. Love did that, didn't it? Wove its way into the cracked places of a heart and shored it up to hope and trust again.

He loved Daphne Austen.

And once he got back to her and Lucy, he planned on telling her outright.

With a deep breath, he crept the truck across the flooded structure, river water already lapping over the concrete to slap against the tires. How long the bridge would last was anyone's guess.

He'd already passed a few that had collapsed inward, swallowed by water and soft earth. Hopefully, this one wouldn't be next.

He'd barely crossed the bridge when he brought the truck to a stop.

From his elevated perch on the old gravel ridge, Finn could take in the valley below—and the sight gutted him.

Granny D's house sat low, tucked near the bend in the creek like it always had, but now that creek looked more like a bayou. And her two-story white farmhouse looked like an island rising from a pond of murky, brown water. The yard was gone and water rose to the windowsills and lapped against the porch steps. Her old Buick under the carport was nearly submerged, just the roof and antenna poking out like a periscope.

He surveyed his options.

No way he could risk taking the truck down into that. One wrong turn and they'd never make it back to the road.

He threw it into Park and yanked the keys, shoving the door open and stepping into the thick, squelching earth. Mud sucked at his boots with every step as he half ran, half waded toward the house.

Where was Granny D? Surely she would've gone upstairs by now.

He sloshed forward, the water creeping higher with every step. Debris floated past—a flower pot, a bucket, a birdhouse spinning slowly like a lost top.

He reached the porch steps just as another wave sloshed against them, soaking his jeans to mid-thigh. "Granny D!" he shouted, slapping the side of the doorframe.

No answer.

Dear Lord, help me find her.

He shouldered the door open and stepped inside. The water spilled in behind him, dragging mud and twigs and heaven knew what else. The pieces of furniture had already begun to float, knocking lazily against each other like bumper cars.

He turned toward the stairs, and there she was, standing at the top, a basket perched in her arms—and, sweet mercy, was that her cat inside it?

Rembrandt's orange fur was plastered against the sides, eyes narrowed with full feline judgment, as if this flood were somehow Finn's fault.

Typical cat behavior.

His attention moved back to Granny D, who seemed perfectly fine. In fact, was she smiling?

"I knew you were a hero from the first time I saw you, sugar," she said, starting down the stairs with the poise of someone hosting a dinner party rather than surviving a natural disaster. "You had the hair for it."

He nearly laughed, despite the water now reaching the base of the banister. "That theory might be tested today, Granny D. We're in quite a fix."

Her expression sobered. "I didn't mean to put you in such a bind, handsome. Harry Coleman called not an hour ago and told me to come up to the inn for the night. Just to be safe. But by the time I packed a bag and wrangled Rembrandt, the porch was nearly underwater and the car was covered up to the windows." She shook her head, the weight of the situation finally showing. "It came on fast. Faster than anything I've ever seen."

He offered her a grin to try and douse the worry lines around her eyes. "At least you saved the most important thing, of course." He gently nudged the basket free from her arms.

"Ain't that the truth. They say if you leave a faithful cat behind, they come back to haunt you. And I reckon nothing haunts quite like an angry cat."

He volunteered his free arm to her, and she took a strong hold as he helped her the rest of the way down the stairs. The water inside reached his calves—her thighs. And it was rising.

Fast indeed.

"Oh gracious." Her voice pitched higher, probably from the chill. A set of bowls floated by. "My second husband got those for me. Never did like 'em all that much."

Finn shook his head. Humor in disaster. He could respect it. It was his leaning too.

He tugged her through the narrow entry and shoved open the front screen door with his shoulder, bracing against the weight of water. This was mad! All of it.

It didn't make sense, the speed of it all. His gaze rose to the mountains surrounding them. Unless . . . the water pooled, didn't it? Rushing down from those heights to the lower levels. Causing it all to converge in the lower streams and rivers that were already swollen from days of rain.

He focused back on the task. Getting Granny D to the truck.

But how on earth was he going to get her through even deeper water in the front yard to make it back to the truck?

"Well, handsome, I thought my swimming days was over a few decades ago, but looks like I'll be giving it another try, don't it?"

Heaven help him. He had no idea how to make it through the hip-deep water with a hobbit-sized woman and an irritable cat.

Then something caught his eye.

Across the flooded yard, tethered to a post at the edge of what used to be the creek but now looked more like a canal, was a boat.

From Granny D's third husband, wasn't it? The fisherman.

A small skiff. Rusted. Paint peeling.

But an option.

"Granny, wait here with Rembrandt." He pressed the basket back into her arms. "I think we've got a way out, and you won't even have to take a swim."

She followed his gaze. "*Old Rusty*?" Her face lit up. "It's a good thing you're as smart as you are handsome."

He almost smiled, eyes flicking toward the hill where the truck waited. If he could get her in the boat and navigate the calmer stretch of yard, they could reach the truck. Then drive out.

Within a few minutes, he'd sloshed through the water, dragged the boat to the porch, and tied it to the railing to keep it steady.

And that's when he heard it.

Felt it.

A low, distant roar—not thunder. Deeper. Guttural. Unnatural.

He froze.

His head whipped toward the hills just as a plume of mist and tree branches exploded from the distant tree line. A chill swept down his spine.

The dam.

"Granny D—" He grabbed her by the waist, her eyes wide now. "We need to go. Now."

Without waiting, he lifted her and the cat into the boat and scrambled in after her.

"Whew!" she huffed. "I ain't had a man touch my waist in twenty years."

He might've laughed if his adrenaline wasn't spiking. The first surge of water hit just then—a wall of runoff crashing through the creek bed and slamming into the yard.

"Hold on to Rembrandt—and the boat," he said, shoving *Old Rusty* free just as the next wave struck. "It's going to get rough."

They weren't in the direct path of the breach—thank God—but they still got the brunt of the runoff. The water slapped the hull, spinning them halfway around before Finn dug an oar into the current and fought to stabilize them.

Old Rusty, despite its name and peeling paint, was a sturdy, flat-bottomed thing. Built for this kind of shallow water. But even it groaned under the strain.

"Ever been on the back of a bull, handsome?"

He glanced at her. Laughed despite himself. "Granny, you're a legend."

The current surged again, pulling them hard toward the bend in the creek. Debris whipped past—broken limbs, a section of someone's fence, and what once might have been a lawn gnome. Finn rowed hard, teeth gritted, shoulders screaming.

Granny D let out a low whistle. "You row like a man who's done this before."

"Rowing team at school," Finn muttered.

"Did they teach you how to dodge tree trunks too?"

A log barreled past. He grunted, pivoting them with a sharp sweep of the oar.

They reached the wider stretch of the creek—a natural runoff. The turbulence ebbed slightly, and Finn took the moment to breathe and reassess.

They weren't out of it yet.

The house behind them was half submerged now. Water gushed through the windows like the whole thing had sprung a leak. The Buick under the carport was gone, vanished beneath the surface.

They passed a pickup truck caught sideways against a tree, half submerged. Finn used it to push off, guiding them onto a safer path, he hoped.

But what was happening on Main Street? How had the dam break impacted them?

He had to get back to Lucy and Daphne, but how? There was no going back to the truck now.

The only option was forward—following the current and praying it led to higher ground.

CHAPTER 22

DAPHNE HAD NEVER IN her life known a feeling of isolation like this.

No phone. No internet.

In a world where connectivity seemed just a touch away, suddenly the silence had grown expansive. Especially now, when she had no way to reach Finn or Jack.

And the water kept rising.

She'd heard a few crashes downstairs, and after getting Lucy settled with a snack, she walked down the stairs to peer into her shop kitchen with her flashlight, only to find at least a foot of muddy standing water. She'd doubled over on the stairs, drawing in her breath, attempting to control her rising emotions as her brain tallied the damage.

Would insurance even cover something like this? A flood in the middle of the mountains? She lowered her head into her hands. She didn't have flood insurance, and most likely eighty percent of the town didn't either.

She stilled her emotions and swallowed hard. There was nothing she could do about it now. She needed to get her and Lucy to safety, and that meant trying to make it to the top of the hill.

And she'd probably have to carry Lucy.

But they desperately needed to get where other people were. This was not a time to be alone. It was going to take an entire community to get through this.

Daphne flicked off the flashlight and stuffed it into her back pocket, her fingers trembling. The apartment had grown colder in the last hour, the damp creeping into her bones. Every creak in the walls made her skin stand on edge as if . . . How sturdy was this building?

She entered the living room, and saw Lucy sitting by the window where Daphne had placed her with a little plate of cheddar scones, apple slices, and ham rosettes, lantern light pooling over her.

Even though the rain had started to slow, darkness was creeping into what little light the cloudy sky provided. That meant getting to safety would only prove more difficult.

Daphne stepped toward the little girl. "Lucy, finish up that snack, and we're going to try and walk up to the town hall, okay?"

Her big eyes rounded even more. "But . . . Daddy's not back yet."

"I know." Daphne sat next to her in the window seat. "But he wanted us to be safe first of all, and I'm not sure how safe we are here right now. There's a lot of water in the tea shop." Which meant even more was in Finn's pub since it was slightly downhill from her. Daphne tucked a curl behind Lucy's ear. "He'll know where to find us. I'll leave him a note."

Lucy's lip wobbled. "Will he be okay?"

"He's very smart and strong." Daphne swallowed, tugging the little girl into a hug. "I'm sure he'll find us really soon."

Lucy nuzzled in close, and Daphne held her for a few beats longer and then pulled back. "You ready, sugarplum?"

Lucy nodded.

"All right, then get your boots and raincoat on, and make sure you've packed all the things you want into your backpack, okay?"

In about ten minutes, after a mad search for Lucy's stuffed dragon,

Daphne tugged on her jacket and grabbed the duffel she'd packed, then scrawled a note on a piece of printer paper.

> Finn—Water is rising. We're headed to the town hall or the inn. Stay safe.
>
> Love, D.

Taping it up with about a dozen pieces of tape to her apartment door, she turned and grabbed Lucy's hand and Winston's leash, then began the slow descent down the stairs into the shop kitchen. It was slow work with a duffel, a little girl, and an anxious dog, especially when they reached the last few steps and the water-covered floor came into Lucy's view.

"Dere's water in your kitchen, Miss Daphne," Lucy said, peering down at it like it was exactly the anomaly it was.

"I know, sugarplum." Daphne stepped down into the water, knee-deep now.

Don't think about what's in this water, Daphne. Or what's been destroyed. Just do the next thing.

"And you're going to ride on my back so I can keep you as dry as possible." Daphne turned around and edged back to the stairs.

After a slight hesitation, Lucy's arms came up around Daphne's neck, and the little girl crawled into place. Then Daphne nudged Winston to follow.

The dog stared down into the water, unmoving, and then looked back up at her as if she were crazy. Poor guy. He'd been taught to stay nice and clean for so long; this broke all the rules.

"It's okay, buddy." She tugged on the leash. "Splash to your heart's content."

With a lift of his ears and a double check to Daphne, Winston almost seemed jubilant as he jumped into the water. Lucy gave a little giggle as the waves he made brushed up against her boots.

"Winston likes de water."

Daphne held the sounds of Lucy's little giggle and Winston's happy swimming close. Because everything else was topsy-turvy terrifying.

She waded down the hallway to the front of the shop, Winston at her side and Lucy on her back.

As she turned into the room, her gaze moved to her teapot shelf and the origin of the crash came into full focus. The shelf had collapsed, and shattered porcelain floated in various parts throughout the water, but most likely lay beneath the murky mess. One pot, a blue-and-cream one with tiny bluebells, was still intact, wedged against the partially collapsed shelf. One of her granny's.

She'd rescued two of them. They were safe upstairs in her apartment.

But . . .

She stared at the teapot a moment, gauging whether she had time to grab it. And then she shook the thought away. No, there was no time, nor did she have a hand free to hold it.

Just then—*thud*. Something slammed against the shop's front window with a deep, hollow knock, like a fist from the storm itself. Lucy whimpered at her ear.

"It's all right. It's probably just something floating outside."

But whatever that something was . . .

They made it to the front door, and Daphne shoved against it, water both inside and out, holding the door in place. The pressure was too strong.

"Come on," she whispered, leaning with her shoulder, gritting her teeth.

Then, with a sucking sound, it gave way.

A rush of water poured in, nearly knocking her backward. She grabbed the frame to keep her balance.

Okay, step one complete.

But the sight that met her nearly distracted her from step two.

Outside, Main Street was a river. To her left, the Ashbourne River had taken over the lower street, up to the windows of Joe's Filling Station, and there was no road leading into town. It was only . . . river.

The town looked like a ghost of itself—street signs half drowned, porch swings floating like driftwood, flowerpots bobbing like buoys.

She turned away from the sight and stepped onto what used to be a sidewalk, but with the mixture of mud and water, she couldn't see it beneath her feet. She could only go by instinct. The pavement leading upward toward the church and the town hall was slick beneath her feet, completely obscured, but she could see pavement ahead where the rising water hadn't fully reached yet.

She climbed a few slow steps against the rush of current. Winston paddled beside her, Lucy held tight to her neck, all of them quiet. Focused.

And then she heard her name from up ahead.

She looked up again, nearly losing her footing, her ankle twisting and pitching her forward.

"I've got you!"

A strong arm caught her. Jack.

Drenched, panting, mud up to his knees and hair spiraled into ringlets, he gripped her with one hand and Lucy with the other, anchoring them against him.

"Jack—" she gasped.

"Mr. Jack." Lucy grasped onto him, relieving the weight from Daphne.

"Hey, bug." He jostled her against his side, his grin not reflected in his eyes. "Waterlogged yet?"

Lucy's grin flashed, brightening the moment a little. "I have on my jacket and hood."

Then his grin grew. "Smart girl. Let's get you outta here." He gestured up the hill, gaze focusing on Daphne. "Truck's at the top. I came to get you as soon as I could make it out of the inn safely. Trees are blocking roads everywhere, and I've been cutting through with my chainsaw for an hour."

"I was just trying . . . to get—"

"I know." He steadied her and nodded forward. "We've got to go. The main road's washed out. Completely. No way in or out from that direction, and last I heard from the local police, most other roads into Wisteria are blocked too."

The words hit like another wave. So they were landlocked . . . in a very unconventional way. For how long? Her knees wobbled, but she kept moving, following Jack's lead.

"Have you seen Finn?" she rasped as they kept fighting against the water's pull.

He turned toward her. "He's not back."

Her stomach lurched as she shook her head.

Jack pushed forward, bringing her along. "Let's get you two safe, and then I'll go find him."

Her gaze trailed back behind her, the water surging, a chair floating past.

Oh God, please let him be safe.

....

Finn had floated with Granny D for a half hour, the current leading them nearer town, from what Granny D said. They'd even picked up a few stragglers along the way sitting on top of their front porch. A mother, her son, and their dog—the latter Rembrandt did not appreciate in the least.

Once the boat reached a safe spot along the creek's overrun banks, Finn helped the little collection of people onto the soggy earth, and they walked about half an hour before being picked up by a passing fire truck.

Which seemed to be an experience on Granny D's bucket list.

Either that, or being rescued by a burly and handsome firefighter.

Finn wasn't sure which one.

Night had started falling by the time they were dropped off at New Hope Church, where Pastor Nate and the ladies from the quilting circle were already setting up cots and passing out dry socks. When Finn had attempted to take Granny D's arm to help her to a nearby chair, she'd waved him off with "Don't be an idiot, handsome, I survived the storm of 1962," which he'd taken as both a blessing and benediction.

At least fifty displaced natives waited inside the church, all waiting for the wind and rain to die down enough to assess the damage.

Because there would be much more to uncover in the light of day.

But hopefully, replaceable things were the only things lost. Not the irreplaceable.

Without phone access, Finn had no way of knowing if Daphne and Lucy were safe and still in Daphne's apartment. Nate hadn't heard either. With a flashlight and a backpack of emergency supplies he hoped he wouldn't need, he jogged down Main Street until he hit water, slowing his pace.

His breath came hard and fast, every window he passed dark, the rising current tugging at his legs like it wanted to pull him under.

The water splashed thigh-high by the time he reached Daphne's shop—its cheery painted trim now dulled and streaked with grime. Finn's pub was just downhill from it, built into the same long brick building, connected by a shared wall but cursed with two fewer steps of elevation.

He didn't want to even consider what waited inside for him. All that money. All that planning for a new business. This place had been his fresh start. His leap of faith. And now . . .

He shook away the thoughts and made it to Daphne's door, and with an effort, pushed it open. His flashlight shone into the dingy space. Chairs tipped. Wallpaper curled. The shelf that had once held her prized teapot collection now lay face down in the water.

His chest clenched.

"Daphne!" he shouted, voice hoarse. "Lucy!"

No answer.

He pushed through the water, making it to the stairs up to the apartment. A flicker of white on the door at the top of the stairs drew him the rest of the way. A note was taped to the door. Smudged but legible:

Finn—Water is rising. We're headed to the town hall or the inn. Stay safe.

Love, D.

He let out a shaky breath and rested his forehead against the note like it might vanish. Safe. They were safe. He closed his eyes and let the words sink in—*headed to the town hall or the inn.*

With a push back from the door, he raced down the stairs and back into the shop, his flashlight's glow skimming ahead to light the way. Then he saw it—just above the waterline against the wall.

A teapot.

The blue-and-cream one with little flowers. The one Daphne said reminded her of Scotland, for some reason.

He reached for it gently, fingers brushing mud from the porcelain.

The shelf had gone down. Dozens of teapots ruined. But this one had wedged against the wall. Whole.

He tucked it under his arm and sloshed toward the front door, just as some lights beamed from outside.

Out in the street, two small boats drifted by in the murky current—Pastor Nate in one, Jack in the other.

"Finn!" Jack called, paddling toward him. "They made it. I got them to the inn hours ago."

Finn gripped the doorframe, torn between the instinct to run to them and the deeper pull of everything that still needed to be done.

"You sure?" he called back.

Jack nodded. "They're helping those in need."

Finn exhaled, chest aching with something too big for breath alone.

"And what are you doing?" he rasped out the question.

"Searching for anyone who still needs help," Jack called back, and gestured toward the side of town where the river had taken over.

If Daphne and Lucy were safe, that's all he needed to know. "Then let's go."

"Thought you might say that." Jack's grin was grim but approving; he offered a hand and pulled Finn up into the boat.

The boat turned away from the higher ground and toward the deeper floodwaters, toward those still waiting for a lifeline. And as Finn paddled into the current, one thought stayed close, offering a hint of warmth against the internal chill of the devastation around him.

Daphne and Lucy are safe.

And Daphne had signed the note, *Love, D.*

CHAPTER 23

DAPHNE AND LUCY HAD barely entered Wisteria Inn before Daphne was pulled straight into action. There wasn't time to do anything else—not with the entire building humming with need, service, confusion, and fear.

Just on the drive from Main Street to the inn, she'd seen some of the devastation. Downed trees, submerged houses, rivers overtaking fields and barns. And people, all sorts, walking through sludge to find a dry place of shelter as night grew closer with each minute.

Harry and Margaret Coleman, generous beyond a doubt, had flung open the doors of the forty-five-room estate to anyone needing refuge.

And the people had come.

Even with the town hall, a half dozen churches, and the middle school gym offering shelter, the inn was packed—families huddled on cots, elderly folks wrapped in blankets, toddlers clinging to soaked teddy bears. Daphne hadn't expected this many. No one had. But Margaret, on the brink of panic, had found her and handed her the reins with a breathless, "Please—help me organize this."

Daphne had barely nodded before diving in. Organizing was what she did. It helped her make sense of her world, gave her some semblance of order. And it kept her mind off the fact that she was very much out of control and had no idea where Finn was.

Or Granny D.

Or about two dozen other people from town.

And without any means of communication to find out, everyone . . . waited.

And prayed.

Because even if she didn't know, she trusted God did.

And He was taking care of them.

Her throat tightened. Whatever that meant in His economy.

After helping convert the front parlor into a children's playroom, Daphne left Lucy and Winston in the arms of a small army of grandmothers equipped with games, crayons, and unconditional love. Just being around people—instead of alone in her apartment—lifted her spirits. And the inn, thanks to its backup generator and water system, had power, plumbing, and plenty of room, which made a world of difference in comfort, even if it meant a little crowded comfort.

She was surrounded by people she knew, and those she didn't know all seemed to be working toward the same goal: service.

In as many varied ways as the imagination could conjure up.

The place buzzed with activity. The butler's pantry was now a first-aid station. The solarium held rows of cots. The long buffet table in the dining hall overflowed with bottled water, granola bars, and donations that came out of nowhere—and everywhere. Work boots from the hardware store. Dry socks and thermal blankets from Packed-Up's camping shop. She'd even heard of local farmers using their tractors, backhoes, trucks, and wagons for rescue efforts or to build makeshift roads over washed-out places in order to get people out.

It was chaos. Beautiful, hopeful, sometimes heart-wrenching chaos.

And the whole town showed up for the assignment.

Someone from the Wisteria Fire Department had parked their truck out front and was helping triage the elderly as they came in.

A man she recognized from the vet clinic came in with a load of pet carriers and started helping get animals into one corner. "Figured folks wouldn't leave without their critters," he said. "Heard you had room."

"We'll make it work," Daphne said, setting up another folding table.

Volunteers poured in—shop owners, high school students, church members, even teenagers from the hiking club. People showing up not because someone told them to but because it's what one did in their town.

They lent a hand. Or a coat. Or a shovel.

Whatever they could to help a fellow Wisterian.

Case in point, Daphne walked by a storage closet that had been turned into a make-shift communication center where Milo Jenkins—fifteen, homeschooled, and fiercely proud of his FCC license—had dragged his ham radio up from his basement the minute the cell towers went down and looked for a place to be useful. With a thermos of lukewarm cocoa and his granddad's World War II headset clamped over his ears, he was patching through updates from emergency services, giving local volunteer updates—especially related to the dozen churches that had not only opened their doors but were offering hot meals from their grills and gas stoves, recounting calls for extra hands with four-wheel drives, and passing them across Wisteria. He and old Wallace Granger—army signal corps veteran and local lawn-chair philosopher—had been taking turns at the helm of the "radio club" for the past few hours.

No cell towers. No internet.

But plenty of connection. In the face-to-face, arms-wide kind of way.

And stories. So many stories.

People walked in soaked to the bone and carrying hope like it weighed nothing.

For the past three hours, Daphne had been in full work mode as daylight faded into dusk. But there was an overwhelming amount to do, and at the moment not only was she busy, but she began to realize more and more that she'd been one of the more fortunate ones.

The water levels had stopped rising. The rain had ceased. So, even if her shop was destroyed, she still had all the things in her apartment to salvage. From the stories coming in, so many people had lost homes. Some—her chest squeezed—had lost much, much more.

Reuniting loved ones had become her favorite pastime of the last few hours.

She'd even helped a man find his missing dog.

Daphne directed teens from the hiking club to organize shoes by size. She sent two shopkeepers to assist in the kitchen, organizing meals over propane burners. She labeled donated clothes with a Sharpie and helped translate for an elderly couple who'd lost their hearing aids in the storm.

Each task gave her purpose. But none distracted her for long.

Because every time that front door creaked open, her heart jolted. *Please be him.*

And every time it wasn't, she buried the fear deeper and kept moving.

Then finally—the front door opened and . . .

"Granny D!" Daphne dropped her clipboard on the nearby table.

Granny D, wrapped in a blanket like a warrior-queen returning from battle, was flanked on one side by a young woman trying to give her directions and a man who looked as if Granny D had already given him a piece of her mind . . . because he walked a few steps behind.

"Oh, I'm so glad to see you." Daphne rushed across the foyer. "Are you okay?"

"Fit as a fiddle, darlin'. Though I'm so damp I'm either going to mildew or sprout something green."

Daphne choked out a laugh and wrapped the older woman in a hug. "And Finn?"

"He's fitter than me, and that's a fact, though he's likely even soggier." She huffed out her laugh as Daphne adjusted the blanket around the woman's shoulders and focused on her every word. "We got a ride in the fire truck, and let me tell you, them boys were something special. I've always wanted to be carried around like a prize, and they were just the ones to do it."

Daphne's whole body sagged with a sudden wave of relief. "So . . . he's okay?"

"Half mad but alive. Last I heard, him and Jack were floating around on a boat looking for stragglers. That man can paddle like an Olympic rower. I saw it with my own eyes." And her grin crooked enough to let Daphne know that Granny D was mighty impressed with what she saw.

Another much-needed laugh shook from Daphne's chest. "Good. Great." Daphne breathed out the words and guided Granny D to a room nearby lit by a warm fire and even warmer company.

"Did you say you was lookin' for Finn Dashwood?" A woman, clothes damp and wrinkled, stepped forward as Daphne returned to the entry hall.

"Yes, I am."

The woman's bottom lip quivered, her dark, damp hair plastered to her forehead. "He got me and my boy off the roof of our house. I heard he joined up with Jack Austen."

A man nearby enough to overhear joined the conversation. "And Pastor Nate's out there with a few of his elders doin' the same. They cut through the woods out on Possum Run and brought my mama to the church."

And as more folks poured in—soaked, stunned, thankful—the stories kept coming.

"Finn and Jack just got Mrs. Jessup off her porch roof!" someone said.

"Pastor Armbrister brought the Stanley twins in a kayak—they were clingin' to their swing set."

"Jack dove right into that water and rescued a cat that didn't want to be rescued, given the scratches he left on Jack's cheek."

On it went. Story after story. Hands offered. Lives saved. Each person carrying a bit of someone else who'd helped them along, tying everyone closer together in the middle of such enormous tragedy. Unexpected loss.

Hope among the devastation.

This is what it looked like.

And then, Mr. Clark, who'd been rescued from his antique shop that stood right next to Finn's pub, brought a painful truth to light.

"I don't know how we're gonna recover," he muttered. "Forty years in business, and now it's gone. Finn just got that pub up and running. Brand-new. I don't know if he'll want to rebuild. If he even *can* rebuild."

Daphne froze.

He'd invested so much into The Green Dragon. Would the loss push him to leave?

After all, he'd only been here a couple of months.

What if, once this was all over, he looked at the wreckage of his pub—his dream—and decided it wasn't worth salvaging? What if the people of Wisteria—*she*—were not enough to get him to stay?

Imagining what tomorrow might look like for anyone who'd lost part of their lives nearly sent her into hysterics. But she had a community here. A life here. It was home.

What choice would Finn make after the waters cleared and the devastation shone in the light of day?

She told herself not to panic. Told herself to trust.

But her fingers curled tighter around her clipboard.

Because how could she expect Finn to stay when he lost everything that brought him to Wisteria in the first place?

....

The boat skimmed past a mailbox, its red flag barely visible above the rushing brown water.

Finn turned the steering wheel hard to avoid a floating trash can, then angled around a submerged sedan—the back window smashed in.

He prayed that meant the occupants got out.

Jack, hunched in the bow, shielded his eyes and scanned the water. "That's the Cottrell house—two kids, I think. Second floor."

Finn didn't answer. Just gunned the throttle and turned toward it.

Dusk was falling fast, and the spotlight mounted to the front of the boat barely cut through the haze. What they couldn't see, they had to trust they'd feel—or miss by inches.

The damage was biblical. Trees tangled into snarled heaps. Unnatural empty patches of forests. Hillsides slumped into the roads like melted clay. What had once been driveways were now rivers. And yards—yards that had smelled of honeysuckle and barbecue just days ago—were overcome by silt and gasoline.

The loss glared back at them in painful clarity.

There weren't words for what they'd seen. The heartbreak. The things they couldn't unsee.

And yet, somehow they kept finding people. That was the only thing that kept the grief from overtaking him. That—and the quiet strength of the man beside him.

"There!" Jack pointed.

A man was waist-deep on a porch, struggling to hold up a woman and two kids. Finn swung the boat around, slicing through the current.

"We're coming!" he shouted.

And the rush of relief and gratitude doused the pain a little. A few more found.

A few more safe.

The man didn't hesitate—just lifted one child, then another, and passed them over the porch railing into Jack's arms. Finn steadied the boat as the woman climbed in, crying softly. The man hesitated, staring at the house as if trying to memorize it.

"My mother," he said hoarsely. "We couldn't get her downstairs. And . . . and her medication . . ."

Finn's jaw clenched. He reached across the gap and gripped the man's wrist. "We'll send someone back. Right now, we need to get you to safety."

The man nodded once—numb—and climbed in beside his family, wrapping his arms around his kids like they were the only thing tethering him to earth.

"I'll call it in." Jack reached for the radio mic. "This is Jack Austen out at the Cottrell house on Woodbridge. Elderly woman upstairs—likely in need of medical assistance."

Static cracked. Then a calm voice came through: "Copy that, Jack. Dawson Craig's on the west loop with the medic boat. I'll patch him in."

Finn stared at the house, his hands curled around the steering wheel. Could Dawson reach her in time?

He didn't get to decide. Jack leaned close and murmured, "Next house. Second floor. I saw a light."

Right. Next one. That's how they kept going. What they'd been doing for hours. And they'd helped dozens.

He could feel the pull in his shoulders, the ache in his spine, the water soaking him to the bone. But none of that mattered. Not when people were still waiting.

He steered the boat and headed for the yellow house on the corner.

They passed a watering can bobbing near the peak of a flooded shed. A skeleton of a swing set jutted out of the water. The air smelled like rot and gasoline.

Water lapped over most of the first story of the house, but as they drew closer, he spotted a young woman holding a baby and waving frantically from the second-floor window.

Jack took over the steering and radioed a message while Finn stood, anchoring his legs as he reached for the porch post and used it to swing the boat close to the side of the house.

"Can you make it down on the porch roof?" Finn called.

The woman looked down, shaking her head.

Finn shot Jack a look, steadied himself on the edge, then vaulted from the boat onto the porch roof—wet, steep, slick. His boots slid, but he caught himself on the window frame and eased the woman out slowly as she clutched her baby against her chest.

Mr. Cottrell stood, offering his assistance, and within a few seconds, mom and baby settled into the boat with the rest of them, and Finn dropped in beside them.

Boat full. Time to get them to safety.

They pushed off.

The baby let out a small, indignant wail. Finn looked down, breath catching.

It was one of the most hopeful sounds Finn had heard all day.

Even surrounded by devastation, life cried out.

Jack was shining the spotlight ahead, sweeping past another house, when a shout broke the quiet.

"Hey, pub guy!"

Finn squinted. A man on a nearby roof waved both arms like he was hailing a taxi. Was that—?

"Tad Akers," Jack said, confirming it.

Finn grinned. He'd been called "pub guy" more than once today.

It always pulled a laugh from someone. A dozen people had promised to stop by The Green Dragon once it reopened. A few had asked if Lucy was okay.

They'd *known* to ask.

"One more?" Finn looked to Jack, even as Jack steered in the man's direction.

Tad climbed in, soaked and grinning like he'd just won a raffle. "I owe you a pint when this is over, Dashwood." He nodded to Jack. "You too, Austen. I might even throw in a steak or two."

And it hit him—the warmth that swelled in his chest wasn't just from being useful. It was from being known.

These people had started to know him. They saw him. He mattered here.

Not just in the storm, but even before.

He hadn't just opened a pub. He'd started putting down roots.

Little Laney Parks had cried on his shoulder a couple of weeks ago when her dog had run away. Mr. Clark's grandson had asked him to taste test his baking project. Old Mr. Harper had fixed his front step and refused to charge. The entire town had shown up to vote on whether he or Daphne would win a contest over a wedding. *A wedding!*

He almost laughed.

And the realization took hold. This wasn't just where he worked.

It was where he belonged.

Not just for Lucy. Not just because of Daphne—though, heaven help him, she was stitched into his thoughts like she belonged there.

No matter what the morning revealed about this town or his pub, this was where he *wanted* to stay.

Because somehow, without him realizing, Wisteria had become home.

And now, he was going to fight for it.

•••••••••••

Poor little Lucy missed her dad.

And she wasn't the only one.

As the clock ticked past 10:00 p.m. and Finn still hadn't shown up, Daphne had set aside the clipboard she'd been using to coordinate cots and casseroles and spent a little cuddle time on the velvet love seat near the front desk, Lucy curled beside her. She'd read *Tangled* to Lucy—again—and sometime between Rapunzel healing Flynn's hand and the part with the floating lights, the little girl had fallen fast asleep with her head on Daphne's lap.

Daphne's fingers moved absently through Lucy's curls. The weight of the child, the warmth of her small hand curled against Daphne's thigh, calmed her. The comfort went both ways.

It was sweet. Tender.

Some of the emergency workers had been going since first thing that morning—hauling people out of flooded homes, navigating washed-out roads, digging through debris. Heroes in volunteer T-shirts and turnout gear. How they kept going, she didn't know.

She closed her eyes and whispered a prayer for them, for the ones still missing, for the ones who'd already lost too much.

So many prayers.

The lobby had quieted. Kids curled in donated quilts, the elderly dozed on borrowed cots, and the scent of peanut butter sandwiches and rain lingered in the air. Even the volunteers were running on fumes now, slumping against counters and folding chairs with the slow-moving weariness of people who'd given everything they could today.

A light rain still dripped from the eaves outside, but the worst of the weather had passed.

She rubbed a hand over her bleary eyes as the front door creaked open across the foyer. Another found person? Another family member searching for a loved one? Another emergency worker in need of food or rest?

She straightened, readying to help—and her breath left her.

Finn stood in the entryway, soaked through, mud on his jeans, a line of exhaustion etched deep in his brow. He looked heavier somehow—like the weight of everything he'd seen was still clinging to his shoulders.

But his eyes—those warm, tea-colored eyes—landed on her, and the weight shifted.

Something in her melted.

He let out a breath she felt across the room.

With a shift of her body to lower Lucy's head onto the couch, Daphne stood, her legs shaky, and then she moved.

Didn't run, didn't cry—just walked straight into his arms.

The heaviness of the past few hours crashed over her as she pressed in as close to him as their bodies allowed. Pulling from his strength. Giving of her own. Sharing the unspoken burden.

They stood in the middle of the foyer, and neither of them said anything. Just held each other, his head resting on hers, her palms pressing in on the back of his wet jacket. He clung to her like he never wanted to let go.

Daphne exhaled against his neck. The scent of rain and woodsmoke and something uniquely *him* tucked between them, relaxing her coiled muscles.

He was safe.

"I had to help—" His voice cracked, low and hoarse.

"I know."

"So many people needed us . . ."

"Here too," she whispered, pulling back just enough to look at him. His eyes were rimmed in red, his lips pressed tight. She reached up to touch his jaw, mud-splattered and rough. "You did the right thing."

He swallowed hard, his gaze flicking around the room—checking on Lucy, the crowd—before coming back to her. He lifted a hand and tucked a strand of hair behind her ear, his fingers grazing her cheek.

"You smell like baby powder and peanut butter," he said, the corner of his mouth twitching. "It's a new scent for you. But . . . oddly, not terrible."

She huffed a tired laugh, blinking fresh tears.

"There was a minor explosion while I was hunting down baby powder. For about twenty minutes, I looked like a cupcake."

"Sounds like I missed the best part of the day."

"You didn't." Her voice dropped as she searched his face. "You showed up just in time for it. And I'm so glad—"

He covered her lips with his. Not a long kiss, but a sweet one. Grateful. Somehow communicating strains of how much he cared about her in mere seconds, rewiring the emotional architecture of a moment.

"Called it!" a voice shouted from behind them.

They broke apart to see Mr. Rutherforton hobbling into the lobby from the makeshift clothes closet, his cane clicking on the tile.

"I pegged the two of you from the start. Two people can't prank each other as much as y'all and not end in either romance or jail. I bet on the former."

"I voted for both at the festival." Jodie from the general store approached, wiping her hands on a towel. "Either way, I won. The two of them have increased my sales exponentially with all their flirting."

"Flirting?" Daphne said, attempting to object to the notion.

Finn's grin only broadened as he tucked an arm around her waist, keeping her close.

She nestled right in.

"I mean . . . you did call me *infuriatingly attractive* that one time." He looked down at her, his brows raised. "In front of two small children and a minister."

"I said *infuriating and attractive*," she muttered.

"Semantics," he said, and winked.

"Thou shalt not lie, Daphne Austen." Nate strolled into the room, looking as soaked and harried as Finn, with Jack on his heels.

"We already knew how this would end, Nate." Jack waved a dismissive hand toward them. "It's way too predictable . . . and gross." His nose wrinkled with his frown, and he reminded Daphne of his ten-year-old self. "Anyway, that hot soup we heard about in the doorway sounds loads better."

"Follow me, fellas." Jodie gestured with her chin. "We got plenty. But, Jack, I may make you a mug that reads: 'Cupid, keep walkin'. I'm just here for the pie.'"

"Honestly," Rosemary said, appearing in the playroom doorway with a sleepy toddler on her hip, "if you two don't keep collaborating on menus, I'm starting a petition. The short ribs and lavender biscuits from the cook-off still haunt my dreams."

"I want to be a taste tester!" Clem from the gym called as he ducked inside and away from the rain.

"Me too!" Cora from the Wisteria Book Club chimed in from the water bottle table. "I volunteer as tribute!"

Daphne looked up at Finn, searching his face. "Assuming you're rebuilding?"

She needed to know his answer. And, at the same time, feared what he might say.

His expression gentled. "How else is Wisteria going to get a savory counterbalance to your dainty confections?"

She laughed—and then cried a little—and nearly launched herself back into his arms. But a soft voice broke through the chorus of teasing.

"Daddy?"

Lucy blinked awake from her place on the little couch, her expression moving from drowsy to delighted in a heartbeat. She pushed back the donated blanket, slid off the couch, and ran to her dad.

Finn caught her up and kissed the top of her head. "There's my girl." His words rasped out, his gaze trailing back to Daphne. And with a look to the crowd and a flick of his grin, he added. "Both my girls?"

The charmer emerged in that moment, and Daphne embraced him—crooked grin, kissable lips, flirtiness, and all.

Daphne stepped to his other side, pressing a kiss to his smile.

"Oh yeah. Your girl . . . *and* the better cook."

The crowd laughed, and for a moment, the heaviness of the day eased.

Yes, there were going to be many hard moments in the weeks and months to come, much grief to bear and many struggles to work through. But Finn's answer promised that he wasn't going anywhere.

This—this moment of connection, of healing, of joy in the midst of ruin—was proof of something enduring.

Something that tasted a lot like hope.

Whatever was unfolding between her and Finn—sweet, spicy, decadent, and slightly chaotic—felt like the beginning of something worth holding on to.

Something lasting.

And she'd welcome that in her kitchen and her heart every day.

•••••••••••

The loss was devastating.

Even though Daphne had heard story after story from folks pouring into the inn over the last forty-eight hours—had seen the photos, the shaky videos—nothing prepared her for the sight in person.

Words didn't cover it.

Mud. So much of it. Everywhere. It coated the streets, clung to the sidewalks, piled inside buildings like someone had shoveled a few feet of it in each one.

And now, as the sun began drying everything out, the muck turned into a fine, gritty dust that hung in the air. Cloaking the town in the scent of mold, waste, and . . . brokenness.

Her beautiful world—her wonderful town—looked like the ruins you'd see in a postapocalyptic movie. A ghost town.

She walked down Main Street with Jack on one side and Finn on the other, each step bracing her for what she already knew she'd see. The upper third of the street gave the impression of business as usual—power still out, sure, but flower boxes on the antique shop's windows still stood at attention, as if trying to pretend the world hadn't crumbled beneath them.

But the farther downhill they walked, the more the damage came into focus. Boarded-up windows. Others gaping dark and empty. Sludge-caked entryways littered with soggy chairs, splintered shelving, a teddy bear lying face down in a puddle. An overturned car rusting into the sidewalk. A streetlamp folded in half. A once-cozy park bench pretzeled into a tree.

And an alarming lack of green. Something she'd never imagined before. Dirt covered much of what had once been grass, and many of the trees lay splintered, wind stripped, or dust covered, their natural beauty failing to patch into the dull hues of their surroundings.

All around her, Daphne walked the street in slow, quiet steps. Faces stunned. Moving with an eerie silence of unutterable loss. Grief and numbness layered over everything like the film of dust still drifting through the air.

And when Tea Thyme came into view, her chest pulled tight.

She'd expected it. Jack had sent her a photo to prepare her. But still, seeing it in person, sunlight almost too bright and raw against the dim, mud-smudged windows, sliced pain through her middle.

The chalkboard lay in two pieces across the door's threshold. Her café tables were sludge-smeared or missing entirely. One of the chairs had somehow ended up two buildings down, propped like it had simply wandered off.

Finn veered away, dodging a flowerpot that had once stood across the street, to make it to the door of The Green Dragon, its windows as dark and lifeless as her own.

"It's going to be tough, Daph," Jack whispered, searching her face and handing her a mask to help protect from the mold infecting the air inside.

"I know." She took his offering with a nod and slipped it onto her face.

He nodded and, with a careful step forward, pushed open the front door and flipped on his flashlight. A gust of damp, basement-scented air drifted out—mold, oil, and something else she didn't want to define.

She followed Jack, the large boots he'd brought for her to wear squishing into the mud as she crossed the threshold of her dear shop.

She couldn't see the floor. At least a foot of mud covered the dining room. Tables and chairs had toppled in chaotic disarray, some jammed into the far corner where she'd once hung a painting of Haddon Hall—her granny's favorite English estate. The painting now lay face down in the sludge.

The force of the water must have undercut some of the shelving, because several of the counters slanted, leaving appliances stuck in the mud. Her teapots—Granny's, hers, the ones with the sweet hand-painted flowers—lay scattered in glinting shards beneath the muck.

"We need to get as much out of your apartment as we can," Jack said, moving carefully toward the back, "and transfer it to my house. I think I can get the truck behind the shop. There's a semi-clear path."

She nodded numbly, her gaze still locked on the ruined room.

She and Winston had been staying at Jack's place—his cabin perched on the ridge above town. He'd gotten by with only a damaged garage and flooded driveway.

Last night they'd sat on Jack's couch in silence for a few hours.

No words. Just grief shared side by side. Until he'd gone back out to continue with rescues.

Another grief.

Another loss.

Her attention pulled back to Jack as he made slow progress forward in the room. He looked exhausted. Pale.

But whole.

And alive.

At least she still had him.

Some dear people in Wisteria couldn't say that. Some had lost much more than their shops or homes or cars. They'd lost their pets. Even their people.

She swallowed through the lump in her throat as tears trailed down her cheeks.

Rosemary's grandpa had been swept away in the current. Found two miles from his home.

Jodie—sweet and sassy Jodie from Wisteria General Store—had lost her brother, a first responder. He'd saved a little girl but hadn't made it out of the floodwaters himself.

And there were dozens of similar stories of loss.

Too many. And more to come, she suspected.

The comparison didn't lessen the pain of looking over her devastated shop.

Or make the gaping hole of loss any less.

But it did bring things into perspective.

"I've got the whole upstairs of the cabin where we can keep your things until we can repair the shop," Jack said, leading the way to the kitchen.

Until we can repair the shop? Was that even possible?

She swallowed the growing lump in her throat and followed him. It was too much to think about. Right now, all she could do was put one foot in front of the other.

The kitchen looked similar to the front of the restaurant. Mud everywhere. Broken items in various places around the floor. Wallpaper peeling like shedding skin. Several of the lower cabinets stood open, revealing mud-covered pots and pans.

Among the brown and gray mess, her attention caught on the sight of some red tape wrapped around a pipe beneath her larger sink that abutted the wall connecting Finn's restaurant to hers. She moved closer, bending to get a better look.

Was that new piping too?

She blinked. But she hadn't asked Mr. Lawson to fix those pipes yet.

"Finn paid for it to be temporarily repaired until you could get to it," Jack said, bringing some of the untouched cookware from the top shelves and placing it in a box he'd carried in with him. "He didn't want me to tell you. Just wanted to help you get by."

Tears blurred her vision as the words settled in.

Finn.

His pub was closer to the river than hers, even if just a little. He had to have lost more. His brand-new kitchen. Refinished floors. Custom tables. All of it.

And still . . .

He'd paid for *her* plumbing?

Before they were even together?

She looked around at the peeling wallpaper, the shattered teapots, the life she'd built—now swimming in sludge.

And then—from somewhere outside the back door—came a sound.

Laughter.

High-pitched. Surprising. Pure.

Daphne turned toward it.

Across the river, two little girls raced beside the florist's shop, a floppy-eared puppy barreling after them through the mud. Their giggles echoed over the quiet ruins. Someone had set out a few pots of vibrant flowers—bright yellows and reds against the gray-brown wreckage, like a declaration: *We're still here.*

Life and hope still remained.

Rising from the remnants. From the hearts.

Her breath came out in a long, shaky exhale. Her gaze lifted to her brother—and then toward the adjoining wall.

The damage and loss were real. But the most important things?

They were still here.

So she stepped forward into that hope.

"Let's go see what Finn needs," she said softly. "Then we can start loading up the truck."

She turned and slogged back to the front door, stepping over Finn's broken sign to enter his restaurant. The scene was similar to her own shop. Mud. Shattered glass. The stillness of a place still sitting in shock.

He stood in the middle of the room, his back to her, hands at his sides and shoulders hunched. As they neared, he turned. Eyes red-rimmed. Jaw tight.

His body straightened. "How's Tea Thyme?"

"The same," she said gently. "Hard."

He nodded once. "It is."

"Nate's truck is out back, Finn." Jack's voice broke into the silence as he looked up from his phone. "Said you're welcome to use it—to salvage anything from the pub or the apartment."

The offering reminded Daphne that the Cabriolet sat somewhere beneath the river's slowly decreasing waters.

Finn swallowed, his Adam's apple moving slow and heavy. "Tell him . . . thanks."

Jack dipped his head and moved back through the restaurant toward the kitchen, likely making a similar assessment as he'd done in Daphne's shop.

Or giving Daphne and Finn some privacy.

Seeing the struggle on Finn's face spread the growing ache through

Daphne all over again. That quiet grief that came when one wasn't sure whether to cry or rage or just sit down in the middle of the mess in shock.

This kind of loss hit people differently. Some crumbled. Some rebuilt. And others . . . left.

When it came down to it, would Finn really stay?

He didn't have roots here. And she wouldn't blame him if the cost to rebuild was too high.

But suddenly, losing Tea Thyme didn't feel like the biggest risk.

Losing him and Lucy did.

"It's going to take a lot to rebuild." Finn breathed out the words, almost as if he'd been reading her mind.

Her body tensed as he stepped away and picked up a bag from a nearby table. "But maybe this will help."

She studied him and took the bag, its contents surprisingly heavy. With a little pause, she opened the bag and a whimper curled from her throat. Inside, all cleaned up, cream with blue flowers, was her Scottish teapot. The one her granny had ordered from a special shop in Inverness called Hopewell.

Hope. There was no escaping it.

Even in the wreckage, *hope* found a way.

Her voice broke. "How . . . ?"

His eyes softened as he watched her, likely accompanying a smile behind his own mask. "When I came looking for you and Lucy, I found it. I'm sorry, it's the only one that—"

"It's perfect, Finn." Her voice cracked as she pressed a masked kiss to his cheek.

His eyes creased, soft with warmth.

And then Daphne's gaze landed on an item across the room. A framed piece of Mrs. Morgan's wallpaper. The only remnant of the wallpaper that was left. She almost grinned. Finn had kept a part of it. How had she missed seeing it before?

Even back then—she'd mattered?

She looked at him again, at the weariness on his brow, the heartbreak behind his eyes, and realized just how much she'd come to love him. And Lucy. And this stitched-together, snarky, gentle, sweet, full-hearted version of a life they'd started building—without even meaning to.

And right now, he needed her.

Just like she needed him.

No matter what came next. She could love him now. However many *nows* God gave her with him, because if she'd learned nothing else in her life so far, life was unpredictable.

She crossed the room, lifted the frame from the wall, and held it up. "I see you have something to start over with too?"

His eyes lit. And he laughed.

A quiet laugh, but one nonetheless. "It'll be the first thing I hang in my new pub," he said, voice still rough but lighter now. "A tribute to Wisterian history—and God's sense of humor."

"I think that's an excellent plan."

She stepped closer—and before she even reached him, he caught her free hand in his.

"I want to rebuild here," he said, voice steady now. "This exact spot. If I can."

"Do you?" She grinned up at him, some of the pain dimming in the glow of his tender look.

He nodded. "Because it's right next to you. And that's where I want to be. Even if it means I occasionally drink tea or eat"—he shuddered and topped it off with a wink—"pretty little snacks masquerading as meals."

She laughed. "Well, at least you'll be surviving with class."

And then, with another chuckle, this one with a bit more volume, he slipped his mask down, tugged at hers, and pressed a quick kiss to her lips. "Sounds like an excellent beginning to me."

EPILOGUE

Five months later

@WisteriaWeekly: Make sure you show up early in Wisteria this weekend, folks. Travis Langston and our very own Lindsay Monroe-Langston may have tied the knot in a private ceremony back in October when their initial plans had to be redirected due to the storm, but as so many of you know, they've been raising money for the people of Wisteria over the past months. And Friday night they're hosting a benefit concert with renowned country music star Beau James. The Rustwood Ramblers are opening for him with some of their bluegrass classics. Our local favorites Finn Dashwood and Daphne Austen are teaming up at Tea & Tap for a preconcert barbecue. Donations accepted. All proceeds go to Wisteria Town Council for #FloodRelief #FromFloodTotheFuture #TeaAndTap #WisteriaStrong

@WisteriaGeneralStore: Tea & Tap T-shirts are already on sale in the shop. Ignore the mess. We're still rebuilding, but while you're shopping, don't forget

your #WisteriaStrong hoodies too. #SupportLocal #WisteriaStrong
@OldManRutherforton: Told y'all they were cooking up more than cobbler. Somebody save me an XL tee—I'm officially Team Tea & Tap. #MatchmakerHardwareMan #TeaAndTap
@CoraReadsRomance: I came for the romance, stayed for the pulled pork, cried during the testimonials. Don't skip the book table—every sale helps restock the Wisteria Public Library. #ReadersRebuild #BarbecueAndBooks
@JackAustenPhotography: Snapped a moment between @LindsayMonroeOfficial and a kid whose home they helped rebuild. It's blurry because I was crying. #BehindTheLens #WisteriaStrong #MoreThanALoveStory
@GrannyDOfficial: If love was a pie, we'd all be having seconds tonight. I brought four cobblers and a pound cake to the benefit. All gone. Just like Finn's single status. #TeamTeaAndTap #GrannyApproved #WisteriaStrong
@LindsayMonroeOfficial: Public Service Announcement: I'm challenging Jodie to make the perfect T-shirts for our newest darling duo @WisteriaGeneralStore. #ProudMatchmaker #ToldYouSo
@WisteriaGeneralStore: Challenge accepted.
@PastorNateNHC: Today felt like resurrection in small-town form. Hope, barbecue, banter, and the kind of music that makes your soul remember joy. May we all rebuild with love like this. #GraceInTheGravel #WisteriaStrong
@ClemAtTheGym: Finn grilled enough meat to feed the entire county. I volunteered as taste tester. For the good of the town. #WisteriaGains #BarbellAndBrisket
@TeaAndTapNC: Thank you, Wisteria, for showing up hungry—for food, for hope, and for each other.

> We're proud to be part of a town that knows how to rebuild—with flavor. Same team. Same table. See you soon. #TeamTeaAndTap #FromFloodToTheFuture #WisteriaStrong #LoveServedHot

AS THE SUN DIPPED behind the hills, fairy lights flickered to life from the town hall to Wisteria Public Park and all the way down Main Street. Even over the dozen shops near the river that still sat in various stages of restoration and recovery.

The town had changed. The river, swollen and rerouted, had demanded a new bridge—now strung with fairy lights of its own, a glowing promise arching into the evening.

Because tonight Daphne's beloved town was celebrating.

Life. Community. Grit.

And hope.

Hope blooming from the town just like the first blooms of spring on this chilly March evening. Because the town hadn't wanted to wait one more day to prove it was still alive.

Still healing? Absolutely.

But still here.

Travis and Lindsay had invited a small group of locals from Wisteria (of which Finn and Daphne had been a part) to their intimate New York wedding back in October, where they'd announced a major donation to food relief. Now, with Wisteria's roads repaired, a new hotel opening soon, and local businesses reopening, the newlyweds wanted to do even more.

And what better way than with music and food?

Because here in these mountains, those two things went hand in hand.

Locals gathered on the park lawn, plates piled high with maple-bourbon ribs, Earl Grey baked beans, and Daphne's lemon-lavender shortbread—which had already disappeared twice over. The scent of Finn's smoked brisket and Daphne's sweet tea peach cobbler mingled in the air, much like their reputations—blending a little unexpectedly but undeniably well.

Locals had affectionately started calling them "Tea and Tap" and so . . .

In the middle of all the chaos of flood recovery and renovating their own shops, they'd joined forces—and funds—and opened a restaurant together.

Tea & Tap.

Finn had grinned when the sign went up. "Not really a merger," he'd said. "More like . . . a truce?"

And then he'd kissed her like the word *truce* meant *forever.*

And the combination had worked.

Two opposites. Two creators. One shared space. Antique teapots lined the left window; a rotating tap list chalked up on the right. He handled the savory. She handled the sweet. And in the middle? Magic.

Finn had even given the teapot he'd rescued from the storm its own shelf with a plaque beneath it that read: Still Steeping. Still Standing.

As the Rustwood Ramblers tuned up their banjos for the opening set, kids ran barefoot between picnic blankets, and the smell of herbed barbecue chicken mingled with lavender in the breeze. Beau James himself was spotted near the food table—probably after a second helping of pulled chicken on a cheddar-chive biscuit. And through it all, the donations poured in, every bite and banjo twang bringing Wisteria one step closer to continued rebuilding.

Sure, some lives in Wisteria would never be the same.

Changed forever.

But maybe that wasn't the goal.

Maybe the goal was something stronger. Deeper.

New blooms dotted the thinned woods and offered an added

sense of new beginnings. Daphne smiled as she slipped from Wisteria General Store wearing a long-sleeved T-shirt specifically designed for her.

She couldn't wait for Finn to see it.

The past five months had only drawn them closer—through drywall dust and late-night taste testing, through laughter and tears and Lucy's endless giggle sessions. Finn and Lucy weren't just part of Daphne's life now. They'd become her future.

Both in business and in heart. And, somehow, not only had they made their differences in personalities work together, but they'd made their foods meld too.

No, Finn hadn't converted her to coffee.

And she'd not gotten him to love tea . . . yet.

But together they'd crafted something new: a hybrid menu full of charm and flavor, which still held true to classic favorites. Some with a Southern flair, like taking Victoria sponge and turning it into blackberry and Earl Grey sponge cake, or bangers and mash . . . with cheese, or smoked pork belly Scotch eggs. And then, of course, corn bread and honey scones, sweet potato biscuits with maple butter, and crispy hushpuppies with Guinness cheddar dip . . . and so much more.

The ideas never stopped. But that's what happened when you loved what you did and who you worked with.

She weaved through the crowd back toward the large booth some local carpenters had built for Tea & Tap to house their food, with a straight shot down Main Street to the restaurant in case they needed something.

Daphne slipped back behind the booth, resuming her role at keeping things organized as Finn charmed everyone waiting in line. Lucy perched proudly on a stepstool beside him, handing out napkins and declaring her dad's food "very yummy but not as pretty as Daphne's."

From the corner of her eye, Daphne caught sight of Jack taking photos of the whole thing for the shop owners' social media feed, while Rosemary coordinated the scone tower and Granny D walked around with a tray of strawberry iced tea samples like a small-town sommelier.

Finn appeared beside Daphne, brushing a crumb from her collarbone with far more attention than necessary. "Your lemon tart is about to outsell my mini sliders," he murmured near her ear, sending delightful tingles down her neck. "You know what that does to my ego."

She turned toward him. "I'm in your life to keep you humble."

His grin lit his eyes. "Which takes a feat of great strength and perseverance, I am sure." And then he looked around. "Where did you go off to anyway?"

"Jodie at the general store told me to pick up a T-shirt she specifically made for me." Daphne waved toward her shirt.

Tea & Tap was written on the top left corner of the shirt with a teacup and mug poised together beneath, a heart between them.

"Nice," Finn said, and then with a grin, Daphne turned around so he could read the back: "Contents may be too hot for the chef."

She looked over her shoulder to catch his slack-jawed expression. "You're walking around in that shirt on purpose."

"What do you mean?"

"And you know it." His eyes narrowed and he leaned in. "With a message that is turning my internal temperature into a possible health code violation."

"I think you can handle the pressure."

His gaze dipped to her lips. "I think your increased flirting abilities may cause me to internally combust." He drew in a deep breath and shook his head. "Mercy!"

"She made you one too." She reached over behind the counter and tossed it to him. Tea & Tap was on the front, like hers, and on the back it read: "I came for the brisket. Stayed for the baker."

A laugh shot from him. He wrapped an arm around her waist, tugging her closer. "I only get distracted by the best."

From the other side of the counter, Lucy piped up, "Are you guys flirting again?"

"Obviously," Finn said, scooping her up. "The couple that flirts together stays together." He shot Daphne a wink.

"I fink *forever* is a very good word," Lucy said, kissing Finn's cheek, then reaching to do the same to Daphne.

"It sure is, sugarplum." Daphne's gaze flitted over to Finn, whose quirked grin only broadened.

Just then, the music faded and Mayor Wilson's voice boomed over the speakers.

"Welcome, everyone. This is our first official town-wide celebration since the flood swept through Wisteria five months ago. We've grown stronger—together. The heart of this town hasn't just survived . . . I'd argue we're better than ever."

Cheers erupted.

So many people. Some from Wisteria. Some from out of town. All for the same reason.

"And now, let's welcome the hosts of tonight's benefit concert—Travis and Lindsay Langston!"

Applause swelled as the couple stepped onstage. Lindsay smiled, glowing with hometown pride. Very classy, high-end hometown pride.

"Thank you for being here tonight and for giving to the restoration of this lovely town and these wonderful people," Lindsay said. "This is my hometown. I fell in love with Nancy Drew books at the downtown library."

Someone whooped in agreement.

"And learned how to make the perfect milkshake while working at Iced-Up at the corner of Maple and Carter Streets."

Another affirmation from some in the crowd.

And I got my first kiss behind the football bleachers—thanks, Davis Kent."

The crowd laughed and a few whistled.

Travis took the microphone from her, sending her a playful look. "I'd better take this before I find out too many other childhood secrets I'm not prepared for."

More laughter.

"I didn't grow up in this town. However, the warmth and welcome I received here quickly made an impression on me. And when Wisteria experienced an enormous amount of devastation, we immediately wanted to find ways to help. As of yesterday, our combined efforts and the generosity of hundreds of people have allowed us to raise over one million dollars."

Gasps rippled through the crowd. He handed the microphone back to Lindsay.

Lindsay jumped in. "And that money has already helped restock the library, rebuild homes, repair dozens of private and backroads, and bring businesses back."

More applause.

"And tonight," Travis added, "we hope to raise even more to continue the restoration process."

"Let's celebrate Wisteria tonight!" Lindsay said, raising a triumphant arm in the air.

As applause rippled through the crowd and the band launched into another song, Daphne leaned into Finn as Lucy wedged between them. She looked out at the crowd—families dancing, neighbors hugging, volunteers laughing in the glow of lantern light. Her eyes burned, heart swelling with more gratitude than she thought her chest could hold.

They were rebuilding. Together.

Lucy wriggled down and ran to join a cluster of kids dancing in the grass, her giggles lifting into the night air and wrapping around Daphne's heart.

"You know, I never imagined moving to this little town would give me so much more than a pub," he murmured, voice low and intimate, his arm slipping around her waist. His lips warmed her cheek. "I want to do this"—he waved his hand as if encompassing the booth, the people, and all of Wisteria—"this life. With you. Every day."

She leaned into his warmth. "You already have it."

"And I plan to keep it up for as long as you'll have me." His voice dropped, intimate and steady. "In a *till death do us part* kind of way."

They'd talked about the future—marriage, a family, forever. But this felt different. Imminent. "I'm game for that sort of long-term competition."

"Competition?" His brows raised as she looked up at him, their faces so close. "Oh good, because I have a very specific question to ask you later this evening." He gave his brows a shake. "I've already hired Lucy to look adorable, so you can't say no."

Despite herself, she grinned. "What if I already say yes—with no bribery required?"

His brow creased in a mock frown. "Where's the fun in that?"

Her laughter caught in her throat as he breached the distance between them to claim her lips.

And as she returned her head to his shoulder and listened to the music, she closed her eyes and embraced the joy, which shone a whole lot brighter because of all the hurts.

The gratitude, which penetrated so much deeper because of the loss.

The hope, which promised sweeter things ahead, even if they had to work through the hard things to get there.

And in a town still stitching itself back together, *that* was the real beginning.

AUTHOR'S NOTE

THIS STORY DIDN'T START with a hurricane in mind. It started with the idea of two opposites pranking and arguing their way into romance. But when Hurricane Helene hit Asheville, North Carolina—my city—right before I started writing this book, I knew I wanted to give a glimpse of the resilience and community I witnessed throughout our town and mountains.

Though my characters in *A Brewed Awakening* aren't experiencing a hurricane directly, they are feeling the effects of hurricane-like conditions and flooding. Some things words can't fully capture—and that's what those weeks felt like for us. But the experience also revealed something beautiful: people from all different backgrounds, political affiliations, faith systems, and socioeconomic situations joining together to help each other not only survive, but thrive. I hope you will feel that connection and hope as you read this story.

As a speech-language pathologist, I sometimes take the opportunity to raise awareness about speech differences through fiction. Lucy is one example in *A Brewed Awakening*, but I have to tell you . . . I found it nearly impossible to accurately represent some of the speech sound differences caused by a repaired cleft lip and palate. Nasal air emissions and hypernasality are tough to translate into written form, so I did my best to give readers an idea of her sound quality through description. For those of you who know what it's like to talk to a child with a fistula, you'll understand! For others, I hope you at least get the basic idea. 😊 Since she's missing some of her front teeth, you'll notice that her /th/ sounds are replaced with the "d" or "f."

Last but certainly not least, my little cousin Cade (whom we affectionately call Super Cade) was born with the same physical condition as Daphne's brother, Jack. It's not commonly known, and I knew very little about it before Cade came into our family. His parents—my cousin Ashley and her husband Zack—have been fantastic examples of supporting Cade in such a way that he doesn't see his differences as disabling, but as opportunities to overcome and adapt to meet his goals. Their faith that God made all of us for His glory shines through in how they parent and encourage both their kids, and it was a delight to learn more about all of this to incorporate into the story. (They also each have a fantastic sense of humor that Cade has definitely inherited.)

I hope you'll see and appreciate the vast array of characters that make up the community of Wisteria, North Carolina . . . grumpy, swoony, funny, sweet, charming . . . and all.

ACKNOWLEDGMENTS

THIS BOOK WAS A challenge to write for several reasons. One, it's an enemies-to-lovers, which isn't my preferred trope to write (I'm Southern—I just want folks to be nice to each other). But it was also challenging because of the ending. Bringing in the storm created new obstacles, and I'm so glad I was willing to incorporate it into this story because I think it really showcased the sense of community this book celebrates throughout.

With that in mind, it really does take a community of amazing people to write a book. I am always incredibly grateful for the many people who spend their time encouraging, celebrating, reading, and influencing my stories.

As usual, I have to give a shout-out to my street team, The Pepper Shakers, and my awesome early readers, Beth Erin, Joy Tiffany, Laura Wiersma, Tiffany Wade, Deena Peterson, and Lisa Kelly!

I will never cease to be in awe of getting to work with my amazing team at Thomas Nelson. Colleen, Taylor, Kerri, Savannah, y'all make this experience all the better with your kindness, wit, and willingness to encourage me along. And to my editor, Becky: I know I say this a lot, but I am so grateful to get to work with you. I cannot imagine having a better editor helping celebrate these stories with me!

Some people are cheerleaders, and then there are megawatt encouragers! That is my agent, Rachel McMillan. From checking in on me to making sure I get paid to giving faithful encouragement that "yes, you will finish this book and write again," I am continually grateful for her role in this bookish journey of mine.

To my cousin Ashley and her husband Zack, as well as their son, Cade! Thank you so much for letting me ask you questions and pick your brain. And thank you for being so encouraging to me! Love y'all!

As ever, my family is such an amazing support system for me, and though this past year has been a tough one for us, with people dispersing in different directions, I will never cease to be in awe and tremendously grateful that God allowed me to be a part of this intimate community of some of the best people I know. Also, a few of them are happy benefactors of me trying out some of the recipes I wrote about in this book.

And lastly, to the Author of creation and of my imagination, my Savior Jesus. He wrote the ultimate *enemy*-to-more book (me as the enemy, Him as the MUCH more) in my life when He changed my hateful heart to love Him. I am forever transformed and eternally grateful.

DISCUSSION QUESTIONS

1. Have you ever been to (or do you live in) a small town? Did any of the characteristics of small-town life ring true for you?
2. What were two of your favorite scenes and why?
3. Have you ever had a tangible dream, like Daphne's desire to own the Cabriolet, that was based on a memory or sentimentality? Did you achieve that dream, or did it change into something else?
4. How does belonging show up in this story? What happens to help Finn begin to trust in the relationships developing around him and build community?
5. Did you have a favorite quote that ended up on merchandise in this story—a T-shirt, mug, or apron? Why was it one of your favorites?
6. This book has a LOT of food in it! What were some of your favorite recipes you read about? What is a favorite recipe you enjoy making (or eating)?
7. How does grief show up in different ways in this story—whether from death or from other kinds of losses (such as the loss of a marriage, a job, etc.)? And how do the characters deal with that grief in healthy and unhealthy ways?

8. Though Daphne and Finn were different in a lot of ways, in what ways were they the same, and how did that help to connect them?
9. First impressions (as well as prejudices or preconceptions) can really impact building relationships with people. How do you think we can maintain caution with new people while also extending grace?
10. A tragedy happens near the end of the book that leads to a community response. Have you ever been part of a community coming together, whether over something large or small? What was it, and how did people "show up" to support each other?

ABOUT THE AUTHOR

Michael Kaal @ Michael Kaal Photography

PEPPER BASHAM is an award-winning author who writes romance "peppered" with grace and humor. Writing both historical and contemporary novels, she loves to incorporate her native Appalachian culture and/or her unabashed adoration of the UK into her stories. She currently resides in the lovely mountains of Asheville, North Carolina, where she is the wife of a fantastic pastor, mom of five great kids, a speech-language pathologist, and a lover of chocolate, jazz, hats, and Jesus.

....

You can learn more about Pepper and her books on
her website at www.pepperdbasham.com.
Facebook: @pepperbasham
Instagram: @pepperbasham
X: @pepperbasham
BookBub: @pepperbasham